"I know which the young woman interrupted. "That's why I sought you out. I have a proposition for you. So to speak," she added, her cheeks pinkening.

Max blinked at her, sure he could not have heard her properly. "A *proposition?*" he repeated.

"Yes. I'm Caroline Denby, by the way. My father was the late Sir Martin Denby of Denby Stables."

Thinking this bizarre meeting was getting even more bizarre, Max bowed. "Miss Denby. Yes, I've heard of your father's excellent horses. My condolences on your loss. However, whatever it is you wish to say, perhaps Mrs. Ransleigh could arrange a meeting later. Truly, it's most imperative that you quit my presence immediately, lest you put your reputation at risk."

"But that's exactly what I wish to do. Not just risk it, but ruin it. Irretrievably."

* * *

The Rake to Ruin Her
Harlequin® Historical #1129—March 2013

JULIA JUSTISS

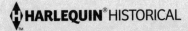

HARLEQUIN® HISTORICAL

Recycling programs
for this product may
not exist in your area.

ISBN-13: 978-0-373-29729-0

THE RAKE TO RUIN HER

Copyright © 2013 by Janet Justiss

Printed in U.S.A.

www.Harlequin.com

Did you know that these novels are also
available as ebooks? Visit www.Harlequin.com.

Author Note

The 2012 London summer games are unfolding as I write this note, and as the athletes tell their stories I'm repeatedly reminded of how many years of hard work and single-minded dedication are necessary to earn them a place among the best of the best. Yet sometimes, after devoting all one's energies to achieving an aim, some totally unexpected catastrophe destroys in an instant the possibility of reaching that goal. Standing shocked and disbelieving amid the wreckage of that dream, the survivor is forced to find a different path.

Such is the case with "Magnificent Max" Ransleigh, earl's son and charismatic leader of a group of cousins known as the *Ransleigh Rogues*. With his father a force in the House of Lords, Max has prepared all his life for a high diplomatic position, and seems well on his way when he's chosen as one of the Duke of Wellington's aides at the Congress of Vienna. But when an assassination attempt on the duke is perpetrated by relatives of a Frenchwoman Max has befriended, even his valor at Waterloo can't resurrect the tatters of his career.

Returning after the battle, with none of his former associates—including his father—willing to see him, he turns to the Rogues. He stops at Alastair's country home, unaware that his aunt, Alastair's mother, is hostessing a house party to acquaint her youngest daughter, soon to make her London debut, with other young ladies of the Ton.

While Max mourns the loss of a conventional future, Caroline Denby schemes to destroy her own. Sole heiress of a wealthy baron, she has good reasons for avoiding wedlock, and is actively resisting her stepmother's attempts to marry her off so she may return to Kent and run the horse-breeding farm she established with her father.

When Caro discovers the infamous Max Ransleigh has dropped in on her hostess's house party, she decides he is just the rogue to ruin her. With her reputation in tatters, her suitors will depart, her stepmother will refocus her matrimonial schemes on her own daughter, and Caro will be left in peace to tend her horses.

But sometimes the goal we yearn for turns out *not* to be the path for which we're destined. And a love we never expected to find becomes the most precious blessing of our life.

I hope you'll enjoy Max and Caro's journey.

Soon to follow in 2013 and 2014 will be the stories of the other rogues: "Wagering Will," illegitimate son of the earl's brother, who never met a game of chance he couldn't win; "Ingenious Alastair," philosopher and poet who thinks to best Byron until a humiliating betrayal turns him into the worst rake in England; and "Dandy Dominic," handsomest man in the Regiment, who returns from Waterloo maimed, scarred and searching for meaning in the ruins of his life.

I love to hear from readers! Find me at my website, www.juliajustiss.com, for excerpts, updates and background bits about my books, on Facebook at www.facebook.com/juliajustiss and on Twitter @juliajustiss.

Prologue

Vienna—January 1815

The distant sound of waltz music and a murmur of voices met his ear as Max Ransleigh exited the anteroom. Quickly he paced toward the dark-haired woman standing in the shadowy alcove at the far end of the hallway.

Hoping he wouldn't find on her more marks of her cousin's abuse, he said, 'What is it? He hasn't struck you again, has he? I fear I cannot stay; Lord Wellington should arrive in the Green Salon at any moment and he despises tardiness. I would not have come at all, had your note not sounded most urgent.'

'Yes, you'd told me you were to rendezvous there; that's how I knew where to find you,' she replied. The soft, slightly French lilt of her words was charming, as always. Lovely dark eyes, whose hint of sadness had aroused his protective instincts from the first, searched his face.

'You've been so kind. I appreciate it more than I can say. It's just that Thierry told me to obtain new clasps for his uniform coat for the reception tomorrow and I haven't any idea where to find them. And if I fail to satisfy my cousin's demands…' Her voice trailed off and she shivered. 'Forgive me for disturbing you with my little problem.'

Disgust and a cold anger coiled within him at the idea of a man—nay, a *diplomat*—who would vent his pique on the slight, gentle woman beside him. He must find some excuse to challenge Thierry St Arnaud to a boxing match and show him what it was like to be pummelled.

Glancing over his shoulder toward the door of the Green Salon, the urgent need to leave an itch in his shoulder blades, he tried not to let impatience creep into his voice. 'You mustn't worry. I won't be able to escort you until morning, but there's a suitable shop not far. Now, I regret to be so un-chivalrous, but I must get back.'

As he bowed and turned away, she caught at his sleeve. 'Please, just a moment longer! Simply being near you makes me feel braver.'

Max felt a swell of satisfaction at her confidence, along with the pity that always rose in him at her predicament. All his life, as the privileged younger son of an earl, others had begged favours of him; this poor widow asked for so little.

He bent to kiss her hand. 'I'm only glad to help. But Wellington will have my hide if I keep him waiting, especially with the meeting of plenipotentiary officials about to convene.'

'No, it wouldn't do for an aspiring diplomat to fall afoul of the great Wellington.' She opened her lips as if to add something else, then closed them. Tears welled in her eyes. 'I'm so sorry.'

Puzzled, he was about to ask her why when a pistol blast shattered the quiet.

Thrusting her behind him, Max pivoted toward the sound. His soldier's ear told him it had come from within the Green Salon.

Where Wellington should now be.

Assassins?

'Stay here in the shadows until I return!' he ordered over his shoulder as he set off at a run, dread chilling his heart.

Within the Green Salon, he found chairs overturned, a case of papers scattered about and the room overhung by the smell of black powder and a haze of smoke.

'Wellington! Where is he?' he barked at a corporal, who with two other soldiers was attempting to right the disorder.

'Whisked out of the back door by an aide,' the soldier answered.

'Is he unharmed?'

'Yes, I think so. Old Hookey was by the fireplace, snapping at the staff about where you'd got to. If he had not looked up when the door was flung open, expecting you, and dodged left, the ball would have caught him in the chest.'

I knew where to find you...

Those French-accented words, the tears, her apologetic sadness slammed into Max's gut. Surely the two events couldn't be related?

But when he ran back into hallway, the dark-haired lady had disappeared.

Chapter One

Devon—Autumn 1815

'Why don't we just leave?' Max Ransleigh suggested to his cousin Alastair as the two stood on the balcony overlooking the grand marble entry of Barton Abbey.

'Dammit, we only just arrived,' Alastair replied, exasperation in his tones. 'Poor bastards.' He waved towards the servants below them, who were struggling to heft in the baggage of several arriving guests. 'Trunks are probably stuffed to the lids with gowns, shoes, bonnets and other fripperies, the better for the wearers to parade themselves before the prospective bidders. Makes me thirsty for a deep glass of brandy.'

'If you'd bothered to write that you were coming home, we might have altered the date of the house party,' a feminine voice behind them said reproachfully.

Max turned to find Mrs Grace Ransleigh, mistress of Barton Abbey and Alastair's mother, standing behind them. 'Sorry, Mama,' Alastair said, leaning down to give the petite, dark-haired lady a hug. When he straightened, a flush coloured his handsome face; probably chagrin, Max thought, that Mrs Ransleigh had overhead his uncharitable remark. 'You know I'm a terrible correspondent.'

'A fact I find astonishing,' his mother replied, retaining Alastair's hands in a light grip, 'when I recall that as a boy, you were seldom without a pen, jotting down some observation or other.'

A flash of something that looked like pain passed across his cousin's face, so quickly Max wasn't sure he'd actually seen it. 'That was a long time ago, Mama.'

Sorrow softened her features. 'Perhaps. But a mother never forgets. In any event, after all those years in the army, always throwing yourself into the most dangerous part of the action, I'm too delighted to have you safely home to quibble about the lack of notice—though I fear you will have to suffer through the house party. With the guests already arriving, I can hardly call it off now.'

Releasing her son's hands with obvious reluctance, she turned to Max. 'It's good to see you, too, my dear Max.'

'If I'd known you were entertaining innocents, Aunt Grace, I wouldn't have agreed to meet Alastair here,' Max assured her as he leaned down to kiss her cheek.

'Nonsense,' she said stoutly. 'All you Ransleigh lads have run wild at Barton Abbey since you were scrubby schoolboys. You'll always be welcome in my home, Max, no matter how…circumstances change.'

'Then you are kinder than Papa,' Max replied, trying for a light tone while his chest tightened with the familiar wash of anger, resentment and regret. Still, the cousins' unexpected appearance must have been an unpleasant shock to a hostess about to convene a gathering of eligible young maidens and their prospective suitors—an event of which they'd been unaware until the butler warned them about it upon their arrival half an hour ago.

As he'd just assured his aunt, had Max known Barton Abbey would be sheltering unmarried young ladies on the prowl for husbands, he would have taken care to stay far away.

He'd best talk with his cousin and decide what to do. 'Alastair, shall we get that glass of wine?'

'There's a full decanter in the library,' Mrs Ransleigh said. 'I'll send Wendell up with some cold ham, cheese and biscuits. One thing that never changes—I'm sure you boys are famished.'

'Bless you, Mama,' Alastair told her with a grin, while Max added his thanks. As they bowed and turned to go, Mrs Ransleigh said hesitantly, 'I don't suppose you care to dine with the party?'

'Amongst that virginal lot? Most assuredly not!' Alastair retorted. 'Even if we'd suddenly developed a taste for petticoat affairs, my respectable married sister would probably poison our wine were we to intrude our scandalous presence in the midst of her aspiring innocents. Come along, Max, before the smell of perfumed garments from those damned chests overcomes us.'

Thumping Max on the shoulder to set him in motion, Alastair paused to kiss his mother's hand. 'Tell the girls to visit us later, once their virginal guests are safely abed behind locked doors.'

Max followed his cousin down the hallway and into a large library comfortably furnished with well-worn leather chairs and a massive desk. 'Are you sure you don't want to leave?' he asked again as he drew out a decanter and filled two glasses.

'Devil's teeth,' Alastair growled, 'this is *my* house. I'll come and go when I wish, and my friends, too. Besides, you'll enjoy seeing Mama and Jane and Felicity—for whom the ever-managing Jane arranged this gathering, Wendell told me. Jane thinks Lissa should have some experience with eligible men before she's cast into the Marriage Mart next spring. Though she's not angling to get Lissa riveted now, some of the attendees did bring offspring they're trying to marry off, bless Wendell for warning us!'

Sighing, Alastair accepted a brimming glass. 'You'd think my highly-publicized liaisons with actresses and dancers, combined with an utter lack of interest in respectable virgins, would be enough to put off matchmaking mamas. But as you well know, wealth and ancient lineage appear to trump notoriety and lack of inclination. However, with my equally notorious cousin to entertain,' he inclined his head toward Max, 'I have a perfect excuse to avoid the ladies. So, let's drink to you,' Alastair hoisted his glass, 'for rescuing me not only from boredom, but from having to play the host at Jane's hen party.'

'To evading your duty as host,' Max replied, raising his own glass. 'Nice to know my ruined career is good for *something*,' he added, bitterness in his tone.

'A temporary setback only,' Alastair said. 'Sooner or later, the Foreign Office will sort out that business in Vienna.'

'Maybe,' Max said dubiously. He, too, had thought the matter might be resolved quickly…until he spoke with Papa. 'There's still the threat of a court-martial.'

'After Hougoumont?' Alastair snorted derisively. 'Maybe if you'd defied orders and *abandoned* your unit before Waterloo, but no military jury is going to convict you for throwing yourself *into* the battle, instead of sitting back in England as instructed. Some of the Foot Guards who survived the fighting owe their lives to you and headquarters knows it. No,' he concluded, 'even Horse Guards, who are often ridiculously stiff-rumped about disciplinary affairs, know better than to bring such a case to trial.'

'I hope you're right. As my father noted on the one occasion he deigned to speak with me, I've already sufficiently tarnished the family name.'

It wasn't the worst of what the earl had said, Max thought, the memory of that recent interview still raw and stinging. He saw himself again, standing silent, offering no defence as the earl railed at him for embarrassing the family and complicating his job in the Lords, where he was struggling to sustain a coalition. Pronouncing Max a sore disappointment and a political liability, he'd banished him for the indefinite future from Ransleigh House in London and the family seat in Hampshire.

Max had left without even seeing his mother.

'The earl still hasn't come round?' Alastair's soft-voiced question brought him back to the present. After a glance at Max's face, he sighed. 'Almost as stubborn and rule-bound as Horse Guards, is my dear uncle. Are you positive you won't allow me to speak to him on your behalf?'

'You know arguing with Papa only hardens his views— and might induce him to extend his banishment to you, which would grieve both our mothers. No, it wouldn't serve…though I appreciate your loyalty more than I can say—' Max broke off and swallowed hard.

'No need to say anything,' Alastair replied, briskly refilling their glasses. '"Ransleigh Rogues together, for ever,"' he quoted, holding his glass aloft.

'"Ransleigh Rogues,"' Max returned the salute, his heart lightening as he tried to recall exactly when Alastair had coined that motto. Probably over an illicit glass of smuggled brandy some time in their second Eton term after a disapproving master, having caned all four cousins for some now-forgotten infraction, first denounced them as the 'Ransleigh Rogues.'

The name, quickly whispered around the college, had stuck to them, and they to each other, Max thought, smiling faintly. Through the fagging at Eton, the hazing at Oxford, then into the army to watch over Alastair when, after the girl he loved terminated their engagement in the most public and humiliating fashion imaginable, he'd joined the first cavalry unit that would take him, vowing to die gloriously in battle.

They'd stood by Max, too, after the failed assassination attempt at the Congress of Vienna. When he returned to London in disgrace, he'd found that, of all the government set that since his youth had encouraged and flattered the handsome, charming younger son of an earl, only his fellow Rogues still welcomed his company.

His life had turned literally overnight from the hectic busyness of an embassy post to a purposeless void, with only a succession of idle amusements to occupy his days. With the glorious diplomatic career he'd planned in ruins and his future uncertain, he didn't want to think what rash acts he might have committed, had he not had the support of Alastair, Dom and Will.

'I'm sure Aunt Grace would never say so, but having us turn up now must be rather awkward. Since we're not in the market to buy the wares on display, why not go elsewhere? Your hunting box, perhaps?'

After taking another deep sip, Alastair shook his head. 'Too early for that; ground's not frozen yet. And I'd bet Mama's more worried about the morals of her darlings than embarrassed by our presence. Turned out of your government post or not, you're still an earl's son—'

'—currently exiled by his family—'

'—who possesses enough charm to lure any one of Jane's innocents out of her virtue, should you choose to.'

'Why would I? I'd thought Lady Mary would make me a fine diplomat's wife, but without a career, *she* no longer has any interest in me and *I* no longer have any interest in marriage.' Max tried for a light tone, not wanting Alastair to guess how much the august Lady Mary's defection, coming on the heels of his father's dismissal, had wounded him.

'I wish I could think of another place to go, at least until this damned house party concludes.' With a frustrated jab, Alastair stoppered the brandy. 'But I need to take care of some estate business and I don't want to nip back to London just now, with the autumn theatre season in full swing. I wouldn't put it past Desirée to track me down and create another scene, which would be entirely too much of a bore.'

'Not satisfied with the emeralds you brought when you gave her her *congé*?'

Alastair sighed. 'Perhaps it wasn't wise to recommend that she save her histrionics for the stage. In any event, the longer I knew her, the more obvious her true, grasping nature became. She was good enough in the bedchamber and possessed of a mildly amusing wit, but, ultimately, she grew as tiresome as all the others.'

Alastair paused, his eyes losing focus as a hard expression settled over his face. Max knew that look; he'd seen it on Alastair's countenance whenever women were mentioned ever since the end of his ill-fated engagement. Silently damning once again the woman who'd caused his cousin such pain, Max knew better than to try to take him to task for his contemptuous dismissal of women.

He felt a wave of bitterness himself, recalling how easily *he*'d been lured in by a sad story convincingly recited by a pretty face.

If only he'd been content to save his heroics for the battlefield, instead of attempting to play knight errant! Max reflected with a wry grimace. Indeed, given what had transpired in Vienna, he was more than half-inclined to agree with his cousin that no woman, other than one who offered her talents for temporary purchase, was worth the trouble she inevitably caused.

'I've no desire to return to London either,' he said. 'I'd have to avoid Papa and the government set, which means most of my former friends. Having spent a good deal of time and tact disentangling myself from the beauteous Mrs Harris, I'd prefer not to return to town until she's entangled with someone else.'

'Why don't we hop over to Belgium and see how Dom's progressing? Last I heard, Will was still there, looking after him.' Alastair laughed. 'Leave it to Will to find a way to stay on the Continent after the rest of us were shipped home! Though he claimed he only loitered in Brussels for the fat pickings to be made among all the diplomats and army men with more money than gaming sense.'

'I don't know that Dom would appreciate a visit. He was still pretty groggy with laudanum and pain from the amputation when I saw him last. After he came round enough to abuse me for fussing over him like a hen with one chick, he ordered me home to placate my father and the army board.'

'Yes, he tried to send me away too, though I wasn't about to budge until I was sure he wasn't going to stick his spoon in the wall.' Setting his jaw, Alastair looked away. 'I was the one who dragged the rest of you into the army. I don't think I could have borne it if you hadn't all made it through.'

'You hardly "dragged" us,' Max objected. 'Just about all our friends from Oxford ended up in the war, in one capacity or another.'

'Still, I won't feel completely at ease until Dom makes it home and…adjusts to life again.' With one arm missing and half his face ruined by a sabre slash, both knew the cousin who'd always been known as 'Dandy Dominick', the handsomest man in the regiment, would face a daunting recovery. 'We could go and cheer him up.'

'To be frank, I think it would be best to leave him alone for a while. When life as you've always known it shatters before your eyes, it requires some contemplation to figure out how to rearrange the shards.' Max gave a short laugh. 'Though *I*'ve had months and am still at loose ends. You have your land to manage, but for me—' Max waved his hand in a gesture of frustration. 'The delightful Mrs Harris was charming enough, but I wish I might find some new career that didn't depend on my father's good will. Unfortunately, all I ever aspired to was the diplomatic corps, a field now closed to me. I rather doubt, with my sullied reputation, they'd have me in the church, even if I claimed to have received a sudden calling.'

'Father Max, the darling of every actress from Drury Lane to the Theatre Royal?' Alastair grinned and shook his head. 'No, I can't see that!'

'Perhaps I'll join John Company and set out for India to make my fortune. Become a clerk. Get eaten by tigers.'

'I'd feel sorry for any tiger who attempted it,' Alastair retorted. 'If the Far East don't appeal, why not stay with the army—and thumb your nose at your father?'

'A satisfying notion, that,' Max replied drily, 'though the plan has a few flaws. Such as the fact that, despite my service at Waterloo, Lord Wellington hasn't forgotten he was waiting for *me* when he was almost shot in Vienna.' The continuing coldness of the man he'd once served and still revered cut even deeper than his father's disapproval.

'Well, you're a natural leader and the smartest of the Rogues; something will come to you,' Alastair said. 'In the interim, while we remain at Barton Abbey, best watch your step. Mrs Harris was one thing, but you don't want to get *entangled* with any of Jane's eligible virgins.'

'Certainly not! The one benefit of the débâcle in Vienna is that, with my brother to carry on the family name, I'm not compelled to marry. Heaven forbid I should get cornered by some devious matchmaker.' And trapped into a marriage as cold as his parents' arranged union, he thought with an inward shudder.

Picking up the decanter, Alastair poured them each another glass. 'Here's to confounding Uncle and living independently!'

'As long as living independently doesn't involve wedlock, I can drink to that,' Max said and raised his glass.

Chapter Two

'No, no, you foolish creature, shake out the folds before you hang it!'

Caroline Denby looked up from her comfortable seat on the sofa in one of Barton Abbey's elegant guest bedchambers to see her stepmother snatch a spangled evening gown from the hapless maid and give it a practised shake.

'Like this,' Lady Denby said, handing the garment back before turning to her stepdaughter. 'Caroline, dear, won't you put that book away and supervise Dulcie with that trunk while I make sure this girl doesn't get our evening dresses hopelessly wrinkled?'

'Yes, ma'am,' Caroline replied, setting down her book with regret. Already she was counting the hours until the end of this dreary house party so she might return to Denby Lodge and her horses. She hated to lose almost ten days' training with the winter sales approaching. The Denby line her father had bred had earned a peerless reputation among the racing and army set, and she wasn't about to let her stepmama's single-minded efforts to marry her off get in the way of maintaining her father's high standards.

Besides, while working in the fields and stables in a daily regimen as comfortable and familiar as her father's old riding boots, she could still feel the late Sir Martin's kindly presence, watching over her and the horses that had been his life. How she still missed him!

Sighing, she closed her book and dutifully cast her gaze over at Dulcie, who was currently lifting a layer of chemises, stays and stockings out of a silken rustle of tissue paper. She should be thankful she'd been delegated to supervise the undergarments and leave the gowns to her stepmother. At least she wouldn't have to cast her eyes on them again until she was forced to wear one.

Better to appear in some hideously over-trimmed confection of unflattering colour, she reminded herself, than to end up engaged.

'I'll help with the unpacking, but afterwards, I intend to ride Sultan before the light fades.' As her stepmother opened her lips, probably to argue, Caroline added, 'Remember, you agreed that if I consented to come to Mrs Ransleigh's cattle auction, I'd be allowed to ride every day.'

'Caroline, please!' Lady Denby protested, her face flushing. Leaning closer and lowering her voice, she said, 'You mustn't refer to the gathering in such terms! Especially…' She angled her head toward the maids.

Caroline shrugged. 'But that's what it is. A few gentlemen in search of rich wives gathering to look over the candidates, evaluate their appearance and pedigree, and try to strike a bargain. Just as they do at cattle fairs, or when they come to buy Papa's horses, though I suppose the females here will be spared an inspection of their teeth and limbs.'

'Really, Caroline,' her stepmother said reprovingly, 'I must deplore your using such a vulgar analogy. Just as the ladies wish to ascertain the character of prospective suitors, gentlemen want to assure themselves that any lady to whom they offer matrimony possesses suitable background and breeding.'

'And dowry,' Caroline added.

Ignoring that comment, Lady Denby said, 'Couldn't you, for once, allow yourself to enjoy the attentions of some handsome young men? I know you don't want to spend another Season in London!'

'You also know I'm not interested in getting married,' Caroline said with the weariness of long repetition. 'Why don't you forget about trying to lure me into wedlock and concentrate on making a match for Eugenia? My stepsister is beautiful and wealthy enough to snare any suitor she fancies, and she's eager enough for both of us. Only think how much blunt you'd save, if you didn't have to take her to town in the spring!'

'Unlike you, Eugenia is eagerly anticipating *her* London Season. Besides which, though I don't wish to be indelicate, you are…getting on in years. If you don't marry soon, you will be considered quite on the shelf.'

'Which would be quite all right with me,' Caroline retorted. 'Harry won't care a fig for that, when he comes back.'

'But, Caroline, India is such an unhealthy, heathenish place! Marauding maharajas and fevers and all manner of dangers. Difficult as it is to consider, you must acknowledge the possibility that Lieutenant Tremaine might not return.' Lady Denby's eyes widened, as if the notion had only just occurred to her. 'Surely he wasn't so heedless of propriety as to ask you to wait for him!'

'No,' Caroline admitted. 'We have no formal understanding.'

'I should think not! It would have been most improper, with him leaving for Calcutta while everything was still in such an uproar after your papa's…demise. Now, I understand you've known Harry Tremaine for ever and are comfortable with him, but if you would but give the notion a chance, I'm sure you could find some other gentleman equally…accommodating.'

Of her odd preferences for horses and hounds rather than gowns and needlework, Caroline silently filled in the unstated words. With Harry she'd had no need to conceal her unconventional and mannish interests, nor did she have to pretend a maidenly deference to his masculine opinions and decisions.

For her dearest childhood friend she might consider marrying and braving the Curse—though just thinking about the prospect sent an involuntary shudder through her. But she certainly wasn't willing to risk her life for some lisping dandy who had his eyes on her dowry…or the Denby stud.

Unfortunately, she was wealthy enough that, despite her unconventional ways, there'd been no lack of aspirants to her hand during her aborted Season, before news of her father's sudden illness had called them home. Caroline remained sceptical of how 'accommodating' any prospective husband might be, however, once he gained legal control over her person, property—and beloved horses. With the example of her now much-wiser and much-poorer widowed cousin Elizabeth to caution her, she had no intention of letting herself become dazzled by some rogue with designs on her wealth and property.

If she must marry, she'd wait to wed Harry, who knew her down to the ground and for whom she felt the same sort of deep, companionable love she'd felt for her father. Another pang of loss reverberated through her.

Gritting her teeth against it, she said, 'In the five years since Harry joined the army, I've not found anyone I like as well.'

'Well, you certainly can't claim to have seriously looked! Not when you managed to talk your dear father, God rest his soul, out of taking you to London, or even attending the local assemblies, until I managed to convince him of the necessity last year. It's just not…natural for a young lady to have no interest in marriage!' Lady Denby burst out, not for the first time.

Before Caro could argue that point, her stepmother's expression turned cajoling. 'Come now, my dear, why not allow Mrs Ransleigh's guests to become acquainted with you? It's always possible you might meet a gentleman you could like well enough to marry. You know I have only your best interests at heart!'

The devil of it was Caroline knew the tender-hearted Lady Denby did want only the best for her, though what her stepmother considered 'best' bore little resemblance to what Caroline wanted for herself.

Her resolve weakening in the face of that lady's genuine concern, Caroline gave her a hug. 'I know you want me to be happy. But can you truly see me mistress of some *ton* gentleman's town house or nursery? Striding about in breeches and boots rather than gowns and dancing slippers, stable straw in my braids and barn muck on my shoes? Nor do I possess your sweetness of character, which allows you to listen with every appearance of interest even to the most idiotic of gentlemen. I'm more likely to pronounce him a lackwit to his face, right in the middle of the drawing room.'

'Fiddle,' her stepmother replied, returning the hug. 'You're often a trifle…impatient with those who don't possess your quickness of wit, but you've a kind heart for all that and would never be so rag-mannered. Besides, it was your papa's dying wish that I see you married.'

When Caroline raised her eyebrows sceptically, Lady Denby said, 'Truly, it was! Though I suppose it's only natural of you to doubt it, since he made so little effort to push you towards matrimony while he was still with us. But I promise you, as he breathed his last, he urged me to help you find a good man who'd make you happy.'

Caroline smiled at her stepmother. 'You brightened what turned out to be his last two years. Knowing how much you did, I suppose I shouldn't be surprised that, at the end, he urged you to cajole me into wedlock.'

Lady Denby sighed. 'We were very happy. I've always appreciated, by the way, how unselfish you were in not resenting me for marrying him, after it had been just the two of you for so long.'

Caroline laughed. 'Oh, I resented you fiercely! I *wished* to be sullen and distant and spiteful, but your sweet nature and obvious concern for us both quite overwhelmed my ill humour.'

'You're not still concerned about that silly notion you call 'the Curse'?' Lady Denby enquired. 'I grant you, childbirth poses a danger to every woman. But when one holds one's first child in one's arms, one knows the risk was well worth it! I want you to experience that joy, Caroline.'

'I appreciate that,' Caro said, refraining from pointing out again just how many of her female relations, including her own mama, had died trying to taste that bliss. Her stepmother, ever optimistic, chose to see their deaths as unfortunate chance. Caro did not believe it to be mere coincidence, but there was no point continuing to argue the matter with Lady Denby.

Her stepmother's genuine concern for her future usually kept Caroline from resenting—too much—Lady Denby's increasingly determined efforts to push her towards matrimony…as long as the discussion didn't drag on too long. Time to end this now, before her patience, always in rather short supply when discussing this disagreeable topic, ran out altogether.

'Enough, then. I promise I will view the company with an open mind. Now, I must change if I am to get that ride in before dinner.' She gave Lady Denby an impish grin. 'At least I'll don a habit, instead of my usual breeches and boots.'

Caroline was chuckling at her stepmother's shudder when suddenly the chamber door was thrown open. Caro's stepsister, Eugenia, rushed in, her cheeks flushed a rosy pink and her golden curls tumbled.

'Mama, I've heard the most alarming news! Indeed, I fear we may have to repack the trunks and depart immediately!'

'Depart?' Lady Denby echoed. With a warning look at Eugenia, she turned to the maids. 'Thank you, girls; you may go now.'

After the servants filed out, she faced her daughter. 'What calamity has befallen that would require us to leave when we've only just arrived? Has Mrs Ransleigh fallen ill?'

'Oh, nothing of that sort! It seems that her son, Mr Alastair Ransleigh, just arrived here unexpectedly. Oh, Mama, he has the most dreadful reputation! Miss Claringdon says he always has an actress or high-flyer in keeping, or is carrying on a highly publicised affair with some scandalous matron! Sometimes both at once!'

'And what would you know of high-flyers and scandalous matrons, Eugenia?' Caro asked with a grin.

'Well, nothing, of course,' her stepsister replied, flushing. 'Except what I learned from the gossip at school. I'm just relating what Miss Claringdon said. Her family is very well connected and she spent the entire Season in town last spring.'

'Poor Mrs Ransleigh!' Lady Denby said. 'What an embarrassing development! She can hardly forbid her son to enter his own home.'

'Yes, it's quite a dilemma! *She* cannot send him away, but if any of us should encounter him…why, Miss Claringdon said merely being seen conversing with him is enough for a girl to be declared *fast*. How enormously vexing! I was so looking forward to becoming acquainted with some of the ladies and gentlemen that I shall meet again next Season in London. But I don't want to remain and have my reputation tarnished before I've even begun.' She sighed, a frown marring her perfect brow. 'And that's not all!'

'Goodness, more bad news?' Lady Denby asked.

'I'm afraid so. Accompanying Mr Ransleigh is his cousin, the Honourable Mr Maximillian Ransleigh.'

'Why is that a problem?' Caro asked, dredging out of memory some of the details about the *ton* Lady Denby had drummed into her head during her short stay in London. 'Isn't he the Earl of Swynford's younger son? Handsome, wealthy, destined for a great career in government?'

'He *was*, but his circumstances now are sadly changed. Miss Claringdon told me all about it.' Eugenia gave Caroline a sympathetic look. 'It's no wonder you didn't hear about the scandal, Caro, with Sir Martin falling ill and you having to rush back home. Such a dreadful time for you both!'

'What happened to Mr Ransleigh?' Lady Denby asked.

'"Magnificent Max", they used to call him,' Miss Claringdon said. 'Society's favourite, able to persuade any man and charm any lady. He'd served with distinction in the army and was sent to assist General Lord Wellington during the Congress of Vienna—the perfect assignment, everyone believed, for someone poised to begin a brilliant diplomatic career. But then came the affair with the mysterious woman and the attack on Lord Wellington, and Mr Ransleigh was sent home in disgrace.'

Caroline frowned, remembering now that Harry had told her before leaving for Calcutta how the English commander, then in charge of all the Allied occupation troops in Paris after Napoleon's first abdication, had been forced to station a personal guard because of assassination threats. 'How did it happen?'

'Miss Claringdon didn't know the details, only that he returned to London under a cloud. Then, if that wasn't bad enough, when Napoleon escaped from Elba and headed to Paris, gathering an army as he marched, Mr Ransleigh disobeyed a direct order to remain in London until the Vienna matter was investigated and sailed to Belgium to rejoin his regiment.'

'Did he fight at Waterloo?' Caroline asked.

'I suppose so. There's still talk of a court-martial, though. In any event, Miss Claringdon says his father, the Earl of Swynford, was so incensed, he ordered his son out of the house! Lady Mary Langton, whom everyone thought he would marry, refused to see him, which ought to have been a vast good fortune for some other lucky female. Except that it's now said that he has vowed never to marry and has been going about London with his cousin Alastair, always in the company of some actress or…or lady of easy virtue!'

A glimmer of a memory stirred in Caroline's mind…Harry, talking about the 'Ransleigh Rogues', four cousins who'd been at school with him before they all joined the army and served in assorted regiments on the Peninsula. Brave, strapping lads who could always be found in the thick of the fight, Harry had described them approvingly.

'Miss Claringdon was nearly in tears as she told me the story,' Eugenia continued. 'She'd quite thought to set her cap at him before he began making up to Lady Mary…but now, with him dead set against marriage and keeping such scandalous company, no well-bred maiden would dare associate with him.'

'An earl's son, too.' Lady Denby sighed. 'How vexing.'

'Well, Mama, must we leave? Or do you think we can remain and avoid the Ransleigh gentlemen?'

For a moment, Lady Denby stared thoughtfully into the distance. 'Mrs Ransleigh and her elder daughter, Lady Gilford, are both eminently respectable,' she said at length. 'In fact, Lady Gilford is the most influential young hostess in the *ton*. I'm sure they will talk privately with the gentlemen who, once the situation has been explained, will either take themselves off, or remain apart, so as not to compromise any of Mrs Ransleigh's guests.'

'So they don't inadvertently ruin some young innocent before she even begins her Season?' Caro asked, winking at Eugenia.

'Exactly.' Lady Denby nodded. 'Though I'm convinced it will be handled thus, just to make certain, I shall go at once in search of Mrs Ransleigh and make enquiries.'

Caroline laughed. 'Goodness, Stepmama, how are you to phrase such a question? "Excuse me, Mrs Ransleigh, I just wished to make sure your reprobate son and disgraceful nephew aren't going to hang about, endangering the reputation of my innocent girls!"'

Eugenia gasped, while Lady Denby chuckled and batted Caroline on the arm. 'To be sure, it will be more than a little awkward, but I'll word my question a good deal more discreetly than that!'

'Perhaps she will lock the gentlemen in the attic—or the wine cellar, so none of the young ladies are at risk of irretrievable ruin,' Caroline said.

'Caro, you jest, but it is a serious matter,' Eugenia insisted, a worried frown on her face. 'A girl's whole future depends upon her character being thought above reproach! A ruined reputation *is* irretrievable, and I, for one, don't find the discussion of so appalling a calamity amusing in the least... especially after Miss Claringdon told me Lady Melross arrived this afternoon.'

Lady Denby groaned. 'The worst gossip-monger in the *ton*! What wretched luck! Well, you must both be extremely careful. Lady Melross can winkle out a scandal faster than a prize hound scents a fox. She'd like nothing better than to uncover some misdeed she can report back to her acquaintances in town.'

'Very well,' Caroline said, sobering at the sight of her stepmother's agitation. 'I shall behave myself.'

'And I shall go and make discreet enquiries of our hostess,' Lady Denby said. 'Eugenia, let me escort you to your room, where you should remain until dinner, while I...acquaint myself with the arrangements.'

'Please do, Mama. I shan't stir a foot from my chamber until you tell me it is *safe*!'

'You'd best make haste,' Caroline said, anxious to see them out of the door before her stepmother recalled her intention to ride and forbade *her* to leave her room. She didn't intend to let adherence to some silly society convention get in the way of riding the best horse she'd ever trained.

The two ladies safely dispatched, Caroline tugged the bell pull to summon Dulcie to help her into her habit. Extracting the garment from the wardrobe, she sighed as she thought of the much more comfortable breeches and boots she'd sneaked into her portmanteau. Though she was sensible enough not to don them when her hostess or the guests might be about, she did intend to wear them on her daily dawn rides.

Might she encounter one of the scandalous Ransleigh men this afternoon? If Mrs Ransleigh was going to banish them from the house, the stables were a likely place for them to retreat.

Despite Eugenia's alarm, Caroline felt no apprehension about encountering either Alastair or Max Ransleigh. She doubted either would be so overcome by her charms that they'd try to ravish her in the hayloft. As for having her reputation ruined merely by chatting with them, Harry would consider that nonsense, and his was the only opinion besides her own that mattered to her.

A knock at the door heralded Dulcie's arrival. Caroline

hurried into her habit, anxious to be changed and gone before her stepmother finished her errand and returned, possibly to ban her from riding for the duration.

She didn't slow her pace until she'd escaped the house and made it safely down the lane leading to the stables. Curious now, she looked about the grounds as she walked and peered around the paddock, but saw no sign of anyone besides the groom who had saddled Sultan for her.

She had enjoyed the ride tremendously, thrilled as always to order Sultan through his paces and receive his swift and obliging responses. As she turned him back towards the stables, she had to admit she was a bit disappointed she hadn't caught so much as a glimpse of the infamous Ransleigh men.

It would be interesting to come face to face with a real rogue. Her stepmother, however, would be aghast if she were to converse with either of them, given their terrible reputations and the fact that Lady Melross was now in residence. Were that woman to observe her exchanging innocuous comments about the weather with either Mr Ransleigh, she'd probably find herself branded a loose woman by nightfall.

Although, Caroline thought with a grin as she guided Sultan back into the stable yard, being pronounced 'ruined' in the eyes of society might be positively advantageous, if it relieved her of having to suffer through another Season and made her unacceptable as a bride to anyone save Harry.

The idea struck her then, so audacious that her heart skipped a beat and her hands jerked on the reins, causing Sultan to toss his head. Soothing him with a murmur, she took a deep breath, her pulse accelerating. But outrageous as it was, the idea caught and would not be dislodged.

For the rest of the way back to the stables and from there to her chamber, she examined the idea from every angle. Stepmother would probably be appalled at first, but soon enough, she and Eugenia would be off to London, where Caro's small scandal would be swiftly forgotten in the excitement and bustle of Eugenia's first Season.

By the time she'd summoned Dulcie to help her change out of her habit into one of the unattractive dinner gowns, she'd made up her mind.

Now all she needed to do was track down one of the Ransleigh Rogues and convince him to ruin her.

Chapter Three

In the late afternoon three days later, Max Ransleigh lounged, book in hand, on a bench in the greenhouse, shaded from the setting sun by a bank of large potted palms, his nose tickled by the exotic scents of jasmine and citrus. Alastair had gone off to see about purchasing cows or hens or some such for the farms; armed with an agenda prepared by his aunt that detailed the daily activities of her guests, he'd chosen to spend his afternoon here, out of the way.

A now-familiar restlessness filled him. Not that he wished to participate in this petticoat assembly, but Max missed, and missed acutely, being involved in the active business of government. His entire life, he'd been bred to take part in and take charge at a busy round of political dinners, discussions and house parties. To move easily among the guests, soliciting the opinions of the gentlemen about topics of current interest, drawing out the ladies, setting the shy at ease, skilfully managing the garrulous. Leaving men and women, young or old, eloquent or tongue-tied, believing he'd found their conversation engrossing and believing him intelligent, attentive, masterful and charming.

Skills he might never need to exercise again.

Anguish and anger stirred again in his gut. Oblivious to

the amber beauties of the sunset, he stared at the narrow iron framework of the glasshouse. Somehow, somewhere, he had to find a new and worthwhile endeavour to which he could devote his energy.

So abstracted was he, it was several minutes before he noticed the muffled pad of approaching footsteps. Expecting to see Alastair, he pasted on a smile and turned towards the sound.

The vision confronting him made the jocular words of greeting die on his lips.

Instead of his cousin, a young woman halted before him, garbed in a puce evening gown decorated with an eruption of lace ruffles, iridescent spangles and large knots of pink-silk roses wrapped in more lace and garnished with pearls. So over-trimmed and vulgar was the dress, it was some minutes before his affronted senses recovered enough for him to meet the female's eyes, which were regarding him earnestly.

'Mr Ransleigh?' the lady enquired, dipping him a slight curtsy.

Only then did he remember, being young and female, she must be one of Aunt Grace's guests and therefore should not be here with him. Especially unchaperoned, which a quick glance towards the door of the glasshouse revealed her to be.

'Have you lost your way, miss?' he asked, giving her the practised Max smile. 'Take the leftmost path to the terrace; the French doors will lead you into the drawing room. Hurry, now; I'm sure your chaperon must be missing you.'

He made a little waving motion towards the door, wishing her on her way quickly before anyone could see them. But instead of turning around, she stepped closer.

'No, I'm not looking for her, I'm looking for you and very elusive you've proven to be! It's taken me three days to run you to ground.'

Max stirred uneasily. Normally, when attending a gathering such as this, he'd have taken care never to wander off alone to a location that screamed 'illicit assignation' as loudly as this secluded conservatory. He couldn't imagine that he and Alastair had not been the topic of a good deal of gossip among the attendees—hadn't the girl in the atrocious gown been warned to stay away from them?

Or perhaps she was looking for Alastair? Though he couldn't imagine why a respectable maiden would agree to a clandestine rendezvous with as practised a rogue as his cousin—or why his cousin, whose tastes ran to sensual and sophisticated ladies well skilled in the game, would trouble himself to lead astray one of his mother's virginal guests.

'I'm sorry, miss, but I'm not who you are seeking. I'm Max Ransleigh and it would be thought highly inappropriate if anyone should discover you'd spoken alone with me. For your own good, I must insist that you depart imm—'

'I know which Ransleigh you are, sir,' the young woman interrupted. 'That's why I sought you out. I have a proposition for you. So to speak,' she added, her cheeks pinking.

Max blinked at her, sure he could not have heard her properly. 'A *"proposition"*?' he repeated.

'Yes. I'm Caroline Denby, by the way; my father was the late Sir Martin Denby, of Denby Stables.'

Thinking this bizarre meeting was getting even more bizarre, Max bowed. 'Miss Denby. Yes, I've heard of your father's excellent horses; my condolences on your loss. However, whatever it is you wish to say, perhaps Mrs Ransleigh could arrange a meeting later. Truly, it's most imperative that you quit my presence immediately, lest you put your reputation at risk.'

'But that's exactly what I wish to do. Not just risk it, but ruin it. Irretrievably.'

Of all the things the lady might have said, that was perhaps the most unexpected. The glib, never-at-a-loss Max found himself speechless.

While he goggled at her, jaw dropped, she rushed on, 'You see, the situation is rather complicated, but I don't wish to marry. However, I have a large dowry, so any number of gentlemen want to marry *me*, and my stepmother believes, like most of the known world—' her tone turned a bit aggrieved at this '—that marriage is the only natural state for a woman. But if I were to be found in a compromising situation with a man who then refused to marry me, I would be irretrievably ruined. My stepmother could no longer drag me about, trying to introduce me to prospective suitors, because no gentleman of honour would consider marrying me.'

Suddenly, in a blinding flash of comprehension, he understood her intentions in seeking him out. Chagrin and outrage held him momentarily motionless. Then, with a curt nod, he spat out, 'Good day, Miss Denby', turned on his heel and headed for the door.

She scurried after him and snagged his sleeve, halting his advance. 'Please, Mr Ransleigh, won't you hear me out? I know it's outlandish, and perhaps insulting, but—'

'Miss Denby, it is without doubt the most appalling, outlandish, insulting and crack-brained idea I've ever heard! Naturally, I shall say nothing of this, but if your doubtless long-suffering stepmother—who has my deepest sympathies, by the way—should ever learn of it, you'd be locked up on bread and water for a month!'

The incorrigible female merely grinned at him. 'She is long suffering, the poor dear. Not that it would do her any good to lock me up, for I'd simply climb out of a window. You've already been outraged and insulted. Could you not allow me a few more moments to explain?'

He ought to refuse her unconditionally and beat a hasty exit. But the whole encounter was so unexpected and preposterous, he found himself as intrigued as he was affronted. For a moment, curiosity arm-wrestled prudence…and won.

'Very well, Miss Denby, explain. But be brief about it.'

'I realise it's an…unusual request. As I said, I possess a substantial dowry and I'm already past the age when most well-dowered girls are married off. It wasn't a problem while my father lived—' sorrow briefly shadowed her brow '—for he never pressed me to marry. Indeed, we've worked together closely these last ten years, building the reputation of the Denby Stables. My only desire is to continue that work. But since Papa's death, my stepmother has grown more and more insistent about getting me wed. Because of my dowry, she has no trouble coming up with candidates, even though I possess almost none of the attributes most gentleman expect in a wife. If I were ruined, the suitors would disappear, my stepmother would be forced to give up her efforts and I could remain where I wish to be, at Denby Lodge with my horses.'

'Do you never want to marry?' he asked, curious in spite of himself.

'I do have a…particular friend, but he is in India with the army, and won't return for some time.'

'Wouldn't this "particular friend" be incensed if he were to discover you'd been ruined?'

She waved a hand. 'Harry wouldn't mind. He says most society conventions are contrived and ridiculous.'

'He might feel differently about something that sullied the honour of the woman he wished to marry,' Max pointed out.

'Oh, I'd have to explain, of course. But Harry and I have been the closest of friends since we were children. He'd understand that I only meant to…to save myself for him,' she finished.

'Let me see if I understand you correctly. You wish to be found in a compromising situation with *me*, then have me refuse to marry you, so you would be ruined, which would prevent any honourable gentleman but your friend Harry from ever seeking your hand in wedlock?'

She nodded approvingly, as if he'd just worked out a particularly difficult proof in geometry. 'Exactly.'

'First, Miss Denby, let me assure you that though the world may call me a rogue, I am still a gentleman. I do not ruin innocents. Besides, even if I were obliging enough to agree to this scheme, how could I be sure that in the ensuing uproar—and there would be considerable uproar, I promise you—that you would not change your mind and decide you had better wed me after all? Because—no offence meant to present company—I have no wish at all to marry.'

'Nor do I—no offence meant either—wish to marry you. But no one can *force* us to marry.'

Leaving aside that dubious claim, he said, 'If it's ruination you seek, why did you not approach my cousin Alastair? His reputation is even more scandalous than mine.'

'I considered him, but thought he wouldn't suit. For one, it's his mother's house party and he wouldn't wish to embarrass her. Second, I understand that since being disappointed in love, he's held females in aversion, whereas you are said to genuinely like women. And finally, since your plans for your career were recently shattered, I thought perhaps you would understand what it is like to have your future dictated by the decisions of others, with little control over your own destiny.'

His eyes widened, for the observation struck home. Despite the impossible nature of her request, he felt a rush of sympathy for this young woman who'd lost the only advocate who could guarantee her the life she wanted, while everyone else was trying to force her into a role not of her choosing.

She must have seen the realisation in his eyes, for she said, 'You do understand, don't you? Despite the setback in your choice of career, you are a man; you can make new plans. But when a woman marries, everything she owns, even power over her very body, becomes the possession of her husband, who can sell it, game it away, or ruin it, as he pleases. You must admit, few gentlemen would permit their wives to run a horse-breeding farm. I don't want to see Papa's lifetime of work pass into the hands of a man who would forbid me to manage it, who might neglect, ruin—or even sell it! *My* horses! There's no one I trust with Papa's legacy, except for Harry. So…won't you help me?'

The whole idea was outlandish, as she herself had admitted. He ought to refuse categorically and send her on her way…before someone discovered them and she was compromised in truth. But he hadn't been so intrigued and amused for a very long time. 'You're in love with this Harry, I suppose?'

'He's my best friend,' she said simply, her gaze resting on the glass panes behind them. 'We're comfortable together and we understand each other.'

'What, no passionate declarations, or sighs, or sonnets to your eyebrows? I thought all females dreamt of that.'

She shrugged. 'It might be lovely, I suppose. Or at least my stepsister, who always has her nose in a Minerva Press novel, says so. But I'm not a beauty like Eugenia, the sort of delicate, clinging female who inspires gentlemen to poetry. Harry will marry me when he gets back from India, but that's no help now.'

'Why don't you just contact him about entering into an engagement?'

She sighed. 'If I'd been thinking rationally at the time, I would have asked him to announce we were affianced before he left for India. But Papa had just died unexpectedly and I…' her voice trembled for a moment '…I wasn't myself. Not until weeks later, when my stepmother, fearing Harry might never return, began pressing me to marry, did I realise what Papa's demise would mean to my work and my future.

Meanwhile, Stepmama keeps trying to thrust me into society, hoping I will meet another gentleman I might be persuaded to marry. I shall not.'

'I sympathise—' and he truly did '—with your predicament, Miss Denby. But what of your family, your stepmother and stepsister? Do you not realise that if I were to agree to ruin you, the scandal would devastate them as well? Surely you wouldn't wish to subject them to that.'

'If we were discovered embracing in the garden at a London ball during the height of the Season and refused to marry, it might embarrass Stepmother and Eugenia,' she allowed. 'But I can't believe anything that happens here would even be remembered by the time next Season begins. In any event, Eugenia's a Whitman, not a Denby, so there'll be no contagion of blood and her dowry is handsome enough to make gentlemen overlook her unfortunate connection of a stepsister. By next Season, any stain on your honour for not marrying a girl you were thought to have compromised would have faded also.'

Max shook his head. 'I'm afraid you don't know society at all. So, though I am, ah, honoured that you considered me for your…unusual proposal—'

She chuckled, that unexpected reaction throwing him off the polite farewell he'd been about to utter.

'It's rather obvious you were not *"honoured"*,' she retorted. 'But speaking of honour, did you serve with the Foot Guards at Waterloo?'

'Yes, in a Light Guard unit,' he replied, wondering where she meant to go now with the conversation.

'Then you were at Hougoumont,' she said, nodding. 'The courage and valour of the warriors who survived that engagement will have earned you many admirers. Once most of the army returns home, you will have supporters aplenty to champion your cause. If you cannot be a diplomat, why not rejoin the service? But while you are lounging about, being naught but a rogue, why not do something useful and rescue me?'

'Rescue you by ruining you?' he summarised wryly, shaking his head. 'What an extraordinary notion.' But even as the words left his lips, he recalled how he'd told Alastair earlier that he'd be glad if his aborted career were good for *something*.

Despite the dreadful dress, Miss Denby was an appealing chit, perhaps the most unusual female he'd ever encountered. Spirited and resourceful, too, both factors that tempted him to grant her request, no matter how imprudent. Because despite what she seemed to believe, compromising her *would* cause an uproar and he *would* be honour-bound to marry her.

A realisation that should speed him into giving her a firm refusal and sending her away. But as his thoughtful gaze travelled from her hopeful face downwards, he suddenly discovered the hideous dress's one redeeming feature.

Miss Denby might be a most unusual young woman, but the full, finely rounded bosom revealed by the low-cut bodice of her evening gown was lushly female.

His senses sprang to the alert, flooding his body with sensation and filling his mind with images of ruining her... the scent of orange trees and jasmine washing over them as he tasted her lips...caressing the full breasts straining at her bodice, rubbing his thumb over the pebbled nipples while she moaned with pleasure...

He jerked his thoughts to a halt and his gaze back to her face. She might be startlingly plainspoken, but she was unquestionably an innocent. Did she have any idea what she was asking, wanting him to compromise her?

Instead of bidding her goodbye, he found himself saying, 'Miss Denby, do you know what you must do to be ruined?'

Confirming his assessment of her inexperience, she

blushed. 'Being found alone in a compromising position should be enough. You being a gentleman of the world, I thought you would know how to manage that part. As long as you don't go far enough to get me with child.'

For an instant, he was again speechless. 'Have you no maidenly sensibility?' he asked at last.

'None,' she replied cheerfully. 'Mama died giving birth to me. I was my father's only child and he treated me like the son he never had. I'm more at home in breeches and top-boots than in gowns.' Catching a glimpse of herself reflected in the glass wall, she shuddered. 'Especially gowns like this.'

He couldn't help it; his gaze wandered back to that firm, rounded bosom. Despite the better judgement urging him to dismiss her before someone discovered them and the parson's mousetrap snapped around him, a pesky thought started buzzing around in his mind like a persistent horsefly, telling him that compromising the voluptuous Miss Denby might almost be worth the trouble. 'Some parts of the gown are quite attractive,' he murmured.

He hadn't really meant to say the words out loud, but she glanced over, her eyes following the direction of his gaze. Sighing, she clapped a hand over the exposed bosom. 'Fiddle—I shall have to add a fichu to the neckline. As if the garment were not over-trimmed enough!'

The shadowed valley of décolletage just visible beneath her sheltering fingers was even more arousing than the unimpeded view, he thought, his heartrate notching upwards. Adding a fichu to mask that delectable view would be positively criminal.

Shaking his head to try to rid himself of temptation, he said, 'Your speech is so forthright, I would have expected your dress to be…simpler. Did Lady Denby press the style upon you?'

She laughed again, a delightful, infectious sound that made

him want to share her mirth. 'Oh, no, Stepmama has excellent taste; she thinks the gown atrocious. But I put up such a fuss about being forced to waste time shopping, she let me purchase pretty much whatever I selected. Although I couldn't manage to talk her into the yellow-green silk that made my skin look so sallow.'

The realisation struck with sudden clarity. 'You are deliberately dressing to try to make yourself unattractive?' he asked incredulously.

She gave him a look that said she thought his comment rather dim-witted. 'Naturally. I told you I was trying to avoid matrimony, didn't I? The dress is bad enough, but the spectacles are truly the crowning touch.' Slanting him a mischievous glance, from her reticule she extracted a pair of spectacles, perched them on her nose and peered up at him.

Huge dark eyes stared at him, so enormously magnified he took an involuntary step backwards.

At his retreat, she burst out laughing. 'They make me look like an insect under glass, don't you think? Of course, Stepmama knows I don't wear spectacles, so I can't get away with them when she's around, which is a shame, because they are wondrous effective. All but the most determined fortune hunters quail at the sight of a girl in a hideously over-trimmed dress wearing enormous spectacles. I shall have to remember about the fichu, however. The spectacles can't do their job properly if gentlemen are staring at my bosom.'

Especially when the bosom was as tempting as hers, Max thought. Still, the whole idea was so ridiculous he had to laugh, too. 'Do you really need to *frighten* away the gentlemen?'

Probably hearing the scepticism in his tone, she coloured a bit. 'Yes,' she said bluntly, 'although I assure you, I realise it has nothing at all to do with the attractions of my person. Papa's baronetcy is old, the whole family is excessively well-connected and my dowry is handsome. As an earl's son, do you not need stratagems to protect yourself from matchmaking mamas and their scheming daughters?'

She had him there. 'I do,' he acknowledged.

'So you understand.'

'Yes. None the less,' he continued with genuine regret, 'I'm afraid I can't reconcile it with my conscience to ruin you.'

'Are you certain? It would mean everything to me and I'd be in your debt for ever.'

Her appeal touched his chivalrous instincts—the same ones that had got him into trouble in Vienna. Surely that experience had cured him for ever of offering gallantry to barely known females?

Despite his wariness, he found himself liking her. The sheer outrageousness of her proposal, her frank speech, disarming candour and devious mind all appealed to him.

Still, he had no intention of getting himself leg-shackled to some chit with whom he had nothing in common but a shared sympathy for their inability to pursue their preferred paths in life. 'I'm sorry, Miss Denby. But I can't.'

As if she hadn't heard—or couldn't accept—his refusal, she continued to stare at him with that ardent, hopeful expression. Without the ugly spectacles to render them grotesque, he saw that her eyes were the velvety brown of rich chocolate, illumined at the centre with kaleidoscope flecks of iridescent gold. A scattering of freckles dusted the fair skin of her nose and cheeks, testament to an active outdoor life spent riding her father's horses. The dusky curls peeping out from under an elaborate cap of virulent purple velvet glowed auburn in the fading light of the autumn sunset.

Miss Denby's ugly puce 'disguise' was very effective, he realised with a something of a shock. She was in fact quite a lovely young woman, older than he'd initially calculated, and far more attractive than he'd thought upon first seeing her.

Which was even more reason not to destroy her future—
or risk his own.

'You are certain?' she asked softly, interrupting his contemplation.

'I regret having to be so disobliging, but…yes.'

For the first time, her energy seemed to flag. Her shoulders slumped; weariness shadowed her eyes and she sighed,
so softly that Max felt, rather than heard, the breath of it
touch his lips.

Those signs of discouragement sent a surge of regret
through him, ridiculous as it was to *regret* not doing them
both irreparable harm. But before he could commit the idiocy of reconsidering, she squared her shoulders like a trooper
coming to attention and gave him a brisk nod. 'Very well, I
shan't importune you any longer. Thank you for your time,
Mr Ransleigh.'

'It was my pleasure, Miss Denby,' he said in perfect truth.
As she turned to go, though it was none of his business, he
found himself asking, 'What will you do now?'

'I shall have to think of someone else, I suppose. Good
day, Mr Ransleigh.' After dipping a graceful curtsy to his
bow, she walked out of the conservatory.

He listened to her footfalls recede, feeling again that curious sense of regret. Not at refusing her absurd request, of
course, but he did wish he could have helped her.

What an unusual young woman she was! He could read-
ily believe her father had treated her like a son. She had the
straightforward manner of a man, with her frank, direct gaze
and brisk pace. She took disappointment like a man, too.
Once he'd made his decision final, she'd not tried to sway
him. Nor had she employed anything from the usual womanly
arsenal of tears, pouts or tantrums to try to persuade him.

He'd always prided himself on his perception. But so well
did she play the overdressed spinster role, it had taken an un-

accountably long time for him to realise that she was a potently alluring female.

She didn't seem to realise that truth, though. In fact, it appeared she hadn't the faintest idea that if she wished to tempt a man into ruining her, her most powerful weapons weren't words, but that generous bosom and that kissable mouth.

Now, if she'd slipped into the conservatory and caught him unawares, still seated on the bench…pressed against him to whisper her request in his ear, leaning over to place those mounded treasures but a slight lift of his hand away…lowered her face in invitation…with the potent scent of jasmine washing over him, he'd probably have ended up kissing her senseless before he knew what he was doing.

At the thought, heat suffused him and his fingers tingled, as if they could already feel the softness of her skin. Damn, but it had been far too long since he'd last pleasured, and had been pleasured by, a lady. He reminded himself that he didn't debauch innocents—even innocents who asked to be debauched.

If only she were not gently born and not so innocent. He could easily imagine whiling away the rest of his time at Barton Abbey with her in his bed, awakening to its full potential the passion he sensed in her, tutoring her in every delicious variety of lovemaking.

But she *was* gently born and marriage was too high a price to pay for a fortnight's pleasure.

The ridiculousness of her request struck him again and he laughed out loud. What an outrageous chit! She'd made him smile and forget his own dissatisfaction, something no one had done for a very long time. He hoped she found a solution to her dilemma.

Her last remark echoed in his ears then, dashing the smile from his lips. Had she said she meant to try some*thing* else? Or some*one* else?

The last of his warm humour leached away as quickly as if he'd jumped into the icy depths of Alastair's favourite fishing stream. Her proposal could be considered merely outlandish…if delivered to a gentleman of honour. But Max could think of any number of rogues who'd be delighted to take the luscious Miss Denby up on her offer…and would be deaf to any pleas that they halt the seduction to which she'd invited them short of 'getting her with child'.

Were there any such rogues present at this gathering? Surely Jane and Aunt Grace would not have invited anyone who might take advantage of an innocent. He certainly hoped not, for he had no doubt, with the same single-minded directness she'd employed with him, Miss Denby would not flinch from making her preposterous offer to someone else.

He tried to tell himself that Miss Denby's situation was not his concern and he should put her, enchanting bosom and all, from his mind. But despite the salutary lesson of Vienna, he found he couldn't completely ignore a lady in distress.

Not that he meant to accept her offer, of course. But while he remained at Barton Abbey, shooting, fishing with Alastair, reading and contemplating his future, he could still keep an eye—from a safe distance—on Miss Caroline Denby.

Chapter Four

Still brooding over her failed interview with Mr Ransleigh, Caroline rose at the first faint light of dawn, quickly donned the hidden boots and breeches, and crept silently to the stables before the tweenies were up to light the fires. She encountered only one sleepy groom, rousted from his bed above the tack room when she went in to retrieve Sultan's saddle.

After last night's dinner, the guests had stayed up playing interminable rounds of cards, so she felt fairly assured they would all be abed late this morning. Her peep-of-dawn start should give her at least an extra hour to ride Sultan before prudence required her to slip back to the house and change into more acceptable clothing.

He flicked his ears and nickered at her as she entered the stables, then nosed in her pockets for his usual treat as she led him from his stall. She fed him the bit of apple, quickly saddled him and led him to the lane, then gave him his head. Eagerly the gelding set off at a gallop, the calming effects of which she needed even more than the horse.

For the next few moments, she gave herself over to the unequalled delight of bending low over the neck of the magnificent animal beneath her, heart, mind and soul attuned to his effort as the ground flew by beneath his pounding hooves.

All too soon, it was time to pull up. Crooning her approval, she schooled him to a cool-down walk while her attention, no longer distracted by the pleasure of riding, returned inexorably to her dilemma.

Unwise as it was, it seemed she'd pinned her hopes on the mad scheme of being ruined. She hadn't realised until after he had turned her down just how much she'd been counting on coaxing Max Ransleigh to accept her offer and put an end to her matrimonial woes.

Though she had to admit to being a little relieved he *had* refused. Miss Claringdon had called him 'charming', but he exuded more than charm. Though she'd rather liked his keen wit, some prickly sense of awareness had flooded her as she'd stood under his gaze, some connection almost as real as a touch, that made her feel nervous and jittery as a colt eyeing his first bridle. When he'd asked her if she knew what he must do to compromise her, she'd blushed like a ninny, while visions of him drawing her close, covering her mouth with his, flashed through her mind. Thank heavens her garbled reply had made him laugh, but though the fraught moment had passed, she'd still felt his eyes examining her, heating her skin even as she walked away from him.

He certainly did not inspire her with the same ease and confidence Harry did.

Perhaps that's why she'd remained so tense and sleepless last night, tossing and turning in her bed as she ran through her mind all the gentlemen present at the house party who might be possible alternatives to Max Ransleigh.

Only Mr Alastair's reputation was scandalous enough to guarantee that being found in his presence would be enough to ruin her. She supposed she could try her luck with him, but she doubted he could be persuaded to throw his mother's house party into an uproar by compromising one of her guests.

She could approach him back in London next spring. But though she was fairly confident ruining herself here wouldn't create any long-lasting problems for her family, doing so at the height of the Season probably would, as Max Ransleigh had asserted. She certainly didn't wish to repay the kindness Lady Denby and Eugenia had always shown her by spoiling in any way the Season that her stepsister anticipated so eagerly.

Which brought her back to the guests at this house party.

Unless she could work out some way to turn one of them to account, the future stretched before her like a grimly unpleasant repetition of her curtailed London Season: evening after evening of dinners, musicales, card parties, balls and routs, crowded about by men eager to relieve her of her fortune.

Was there any way she could avoid being dragged through all that? Maybe she should write to Harry after all, proposing a long-distance engagement. But would Lady Denby consider such an informally made offer binding?

By the time they reached the end of the field bordering the paddock, she was no closer to finding an answer to her problem. Thrusting it aside in disgust, she turned her attention back to putting Sultan through his paces.

If only, she thought as she commanded him to a trot, life could be schooled to such perfection as a fine horse.

Blinking sleep from his eyes, Max shouldered creel and rod and followed Alastair to the stables. His cousin, having learned from his factor in the village that the fish were running well in the river, had dragged him from his bed before first light so they might try their luck at snagging some trout.

They were tromping in companionable silence down the path leading to the river when Alastair suddenly halted. 'By Jove, that's the finest piece of horseflesh I've seen in a dog's age, trotting there in the paddock,' he declared, pointing in that direction. 'Whose nag is it, do you know?'

Max peered into the distance, where a stable boy was guiding a showy bay hack in a series of high-stepping motions. His eyes widening in appreciation, he noted the horse's deep chest, broad shoulders, glossy sheen of coat and steady, perfect rhythm. His interest piqued as well, he said, 'I have no idea. The bay is a magnificent beast.'

'That's not one of our grooms, either. Horse must belong to one of Mama's guests, who brought his own man to exercise it.' Alastair laughed. 'I might resent providing the food and drink these man-milliners consume while they loiter here, but an animal as magnificent as that is welcome to my largesse.'

'Aunt Grace's largesse, to be fair.'

'Not that I truly begrudge Jane the expense of their party. I just wish the guests were less tedious and the timing not so inconvenient.'

At least one guest, Max thought, had not been 'tedious' in the least. He smiled as images of Miss Denby ran through his head: staring up at him with a grin, bug-eyed in her spectacles; the atrocious puce gown she'd employed to 'disguise' her loveliness; and ah, yes, the luscious breasts whose rounded tops enticed him above the low neckline of her dinner dress…

Desire rose in him, surprising in its intensity. Reminding himself that seducing Miss Denby was not a possibility, he thrust the memories of her from his mind and turned his attention back to the horse, now being put through several intricate manoeuvres.

Finally, the groom pulled up and leaned low over his mount's head, probably murmuring well-deserved compliments in his ear. Straightening, the lad kicked him to a trot across the paddock towards the lane leading back to the stables.

'I'd like a closer look at that horse,' Alastair said. 'If we cut back at the next crossing, we should reach the stable lane about the same time as the groom.'

Max nodding agreement, the two cousins set off. Confirming Alastair's prediction, after hurrying down the path, they emerged from behind a stand of trees just as the rider trotted past.

Apparently startled by their unexpected appearance, the horse neighed and reared up. With expert ease, the lad controlled him.

'Sorry to have frightened your mount,' Alastair told him. 'We've been admiring him from the other side of the paddock.'

Max was about to add his compliments when his assessing eyes moved from the horse to the rider. With a shock, he realised the 'groom' was in fact no groom at all, but Miss Caroline Denby.

Alastair, no sluggard where the feminine form was concerned, simultaneously reached the same conclusion. 'Devil's teeth! It's a girl!' he muttered to Max, even as he swept his hat off and bowed. 'Good morning, miss. Magnificent horse you have there!'

Miss Denby's alarmed gaze leapt from Alastair to Max. As recognition dawned in her eyes, her face flamed. 'Stepmother is going to be furious,' she murmured with a sigh. Apparently accepting that she'd been well and truly caught, she nodded to him. 'Good morning, Mr Ransleigh.'

Alastair's brows lifted as he looked enquiringly from Miss Denby back to Max, then gestured to him to perform the introductions. Bowing to the inevitable, Max said, 'Miss Denby, may I present my cousin, your host, Mr Alastair Ransleigh.'

She made a rueful grimace. 'I wish you wouldn't. I thought surely I'd be able to return before anyone but the grooms were stirring. Couldn't you just pretend you hadn't seen me?'

'Don't fret, Miss Denby,' Max said. 'We're not supposed to let *you* see *us*, either. Shall this unexpected encounter remain our secret?'

She smiled. 'In that case, I shall be pleased to meet you, Mr Ransleigh.'

'And I am absolutely charmed to meet you, Miss Denby,' Alastair replied, his rogue's eyes avidly roving her form.

Max restrained the strong desire to smack him. Hitherto he'd thought nothing could accentuate a lady's body like a silk gown, preferably thin and cut low in the bosom. But though he'd be delighted to see Miss Denby garbed only in the sheerest of materials, there was no escaping the fact that, in male riding attire, she looked entirely delectable.

Tight-knit breeches hugged her slender thighs and the curve of her trim *derrière* upon the saddle, while riding boots outlined her shapely calves. Beneath her unbuttoned tweed jacket, her shirt, open at the top since she wore no cravat, revealed a swan's curve of neck, kissable hollows at her throat and collarbones, and a lush fullness beneath that made his mouth water. Several lengths of the glossy dark hair she'd thrust up under her cap had tumbled down during the ride and lay in damp, tangled curls upon her face and neck—looking much as they might, he thought, if she were reclining against her pillows after a night of lovemaking.

The heated gleam in Alastair's eyes said he was envisioning exactly the same scene, damn him.

'Bargain or not, I'd best return immediately and get into more proper clothing,' Miss Denby said, pulling Max from his lusty imagining. 'Good day, gentlemen.'

'Wait, Miss Denby,' Alastair called. 'There wasn't a soul stirring when we left the house but a short time ago. Tarry with us a minute, please! I'd like to ask about your mount. You were training him, weren't you?'

She'd been looking towards the stables, obviously anxious to be away, but at Alastair's expression of interest, she turned back, her eyes brightening. 'Yes. Sultan is the most promising of our four-year-olds. Father bred him, Cleveland

Bay with some Arabian for stamina and Irish thoroughbred for strength in the bone. Easy-going, with wonderful paces. He'll make a superior hunter or cavalry horse…although I've about decided I cannot part with him.'

'Your father…you mean Sir Martin Denby, of the Denby Stud?' Alastair asked. When she nodded, he said, 'No wonder your mount is so impressive. Max, you remember Mannington brought several of Sir Martin's horses to the Peninsula. Excellent mounts, all of them.'

'Lord Mannington?' Miss Denby echoed. 'Ah, yes, I remember; he purchased Alladin and Percival. Geldings who are kin to Sultan here, having the same dam, but a sire with a bit more Arabian blood. I'm so pleased to know they performed well.'

'Mannington said their stamina and speed saved his neck on several occasions,' Alastair said. After giving her a second, more thorough appraisal, he said, 'You seem very knowledgeable about your father's operation.'

'I've helped him with it since I mounted my first pony,' she responded, pride in her voice. 'In addition to training the foals, I kept the stud books and sales records, as Papa was more concerned with charting bloodlines than plotting numbers.'

Sympathy softened Alastair's face. 'You must miss him very much. My condolences on your loss.' While, her lips tightening, she nodded a quick acknowledgement, Alastair said, 'A sad loss for the stud as well. Who is running it now?'

'I am,' she replied, lifting her chin. 'Papa involved me in every aspect of the business, from breeding the mares to weaning the foals to breaking the yearlings and beginning the training of the two-year-olds.' Her chin notched higher. 'Denby Stud is my life. But…' she gestured toward the fishing gear looped across their shoulders '…I mustn't keep you from the trout eager to sacrifice themselves to your lures.'

She turned her mount's head towards the stable, then paused. 'I *can* count on your discretion, I trust?'

'Absolutely,' Alastair assured her.

Giving them a quick nod, she touched her heels to the gelding and rode off. Alastair, Max noted with disgruntlement, was following the bounce of her shapely posterior against the saddle as closely as he was, devil take him.

After she disappeared around the curve in the lane, Alastair turned to Max, grinning. 'Well, well, well. Don't think I've ever seen you so silent around a female. Here I thought you'd been moping about, mourning your lost career. Instead, you're been perfecting your credentials as a rogue, sneaking off to secret assignations with a tempting little morsel like that.'

Max struggled to keep his temper in check. 'Let me remind you,' he said stiffly, 'that "morsel" is one of your mother's guests and an innocent maid.'

'Is she truly innocent?' Alastair shook his head disbelievingly. 'Lord have mercy, riding astride in breeches like that! I can't believe I didn't immediately realise she was female. Just shows how one doesn't recognise what is right before one's eyes when one's not expecting it. Though she *is* an excellent rider: fine hands, great seat.' With a chuckle, he added, 'Wouldn't mind having her in the saddle, those lovely long legs wrapped around *me*.'

A flash of fury surging through him, Max whacked his cousin with his fishing pole. 'Stubble it! That's a *lady* you're insulting.'

'Fancy her for yourself, do you?' Alastair asked, unrepentant. 'With her going about like that, her limbs and bottom outlined for any red-blooded man to ogle, it's not my fault she evokes such thoughts. Nor are we the only ones watching.' He pointed toward the opposite side of the field. 'Some bloke over there is ogling her, too.'

His gaze following the direction of his cousin's extended arm, Max squinted into the morning sunlight. 'Who is it?'

'How should I know? Probably another one of those damned macaroni merchants hanging about, measuring up the female flesh on display. Not a man's man among them— petticoat-string dandies all,' he concluded in disgust. 'But this girl…she's truly an innocent, you say?'

'Absolutely.'

'How do you know so much about her?'

Knowing he'd have to explain, but not wishing to reveal too much—certainly not her scandalous proposition—Max gave Alastair an abbreviated version of his meeting with Miss Denby in the conservatory.

'Devil's teeth, she's a luscious armful in breeches. What a mistress she'd make!' Alastair exclaimed, then waved Max to silence before he could deliver another rebuke. 'Don't get your cravat in a knot; I know there's no chance of that. She is a "lady", amazing as that seems to a man seeing her for the first time garbed like that. If *marriage* is her stepmother's object, pulling it off is going to be difficult if word gets out of her offending the proprieties by riding about in boy's dress. Though it would almost be worth wedlock, to get one's hands on the Denby Stud.'

'So she fears. She doesn't want to marry, she said, and risk losing control over it.'

Alastair nodded. 'I suppose I can understand. One wouldn't wish to turn such a prime operation over to some hamfisted looby who couldn't housebreak a puppy.'

'How infuriating to see everything you'd worked on, worked for, the last ten years of your life given over to someone else. Ruined, perhaps, and you unable to do anything about it.'

Alastair gave him a searching look, as if he thought Max were speaking more about himself than Miss Denby. 'Well,

I wish her luck. She's an odd lass, to be sure. But undeniably attractive, even without the inducement of the Denby Stud. Now, if we're going to catch breakfast, we'd better be going.' At that, Alastair kicked his mount into motion.

Lagging behind for a moment, Max studied the man across the field, who was now striding back toward the stables. He'd better find out who that was. And continue to keep an eye on Miss Denby.

Chapter Five

After a most satisfactory session at the stream, Max and Alastair returned the trout to the kitchen for Cook to turn into breakfast. While Alastair went on to change out of his fishing garb, Max hesitated by the door to his aunt's room.

All during their mostly silent camaraderie at the river, rather than concentrate on fish, Max had thought about his aunt's unusual guest. He'd had, he was forced to admit, to exercise some considerable discipline to keep his thoughts from turning from the serious matter of her situation and the man watching her to memories of her inviting gurgle of a laugh, that enticing bosom and the wonderfully suggestive up-and-down motion of her *derrière* on the saddle.

Making enquiries of Aunt Grace might seem odd, but while Alastair was otherwise occupied, he probably ought to risk it. If he discovered that the gentleman guests included none but paragons of honour and virtue, he could stop worrying about Miss Denby and dismiss her situation from his mind.

Decision made, he knocked and was bid to enter. 'Max! This is a pleasant surprise!' Mrs Ransleigh cried, her expression of mild curiosity warming to one of genuine pleasure.

'Will you take chocolate with me, or some coffee? I confess, I do feel terrible, I've been so poor a hostess to you.'

'Nonsense,' he said, waving away her offer. 'I'll not stay long enough for coffee; we're just back from the river, and I'm sure you'd as lief I not leave fish slime on your sofa. You know Alastair and I are quite able to keep ourselves well entertained.'

She flushed. 'I do appreciate your…discretion. Even as I absolutely deplore the necessity for it! Is there truly no hope of your finding another diplomatic position?'

'I have some ideas, but there's no point initiating anything yet while Father is still so angry. You know he has the influence to block whatever I attempt, should he wish to.'

'That's so *James*!' she cried. 'Brilliant orator and skilled politician your father may be, but he can be so bull-headed and unreasonable sometimes, I'd like to shake him!'

Though he appreciated his aunt's sympathy, he'd just as soon not dwell on the painful topic of his ruined prospects. 'I didn't stop by to talk about me,' he parried. 'How goes your party? Has Jane succeeded in leg-shackling any of the guests? Has Lissa found her ideal mate?'

'Felicity is enjoying herself immensely, which is all I wished for her, since I have no desire to give her up to a husband just yet! Among the other guests, there are some promising developments, though it's too early to tell yet whether they will result in engagements.'

Trying for a nonchalant tone, Max said, 'I happened to encounter one of your young ladies. No, nothing scandalous about it,' he assured her hastily before, her eyes widening in alarm, she could speak. 'I met her briefly and by chance one afternoon in the conservatory, where she darted in, she told me, to escape some suitor. A most unusual young woman.'

Aunt Grace laughed. 'Oh, dear! That must have been Miss Denby! Poor Diana—her stepmother, Lady Denby, an old friend of mine—is quite in despair over the girl. Perhaps you didn't notice in your quick meeting, but the lady is rather… old.'

Were he pressed to describe what he'd noticed about Miss Denby during that first meeting, Max thought, 'old' would not be among the adjectives that came to mind. 'I must confess, I didn't notice,' he replied in perfect truth.

'She should have had her first Season years ago,' his aunt continued. 'But she was her widowed father's only child. Now that I face having *my* last chick leave home, I can perfectly understand why he didn't wish to lose her. She's a great heiress, though, so Diana hasn't given up hope yet of her making an acceptable match, even though at five-and-twenty she's practically on the shelf.'

'A doddering old age, to be sure.'

'For a female of good birth and fortune to remain unwed at such an age *is* unusual,' his aunt said reprovingly. 'With her being practically an ape-leader, you'd think she'd be eager to wed, but apparently it's quite the opposite! Though the poor dear seems intelligent enough, she's terribly shy in company and possesses not a particle of conversation unrelated to hunting and horses. To make matters worse, though I hesitate to say something so uncharitable about a guest, her taste in clothing is atrocious. I expect, arbiter of fashion that you are, you did notice the dreadful gown.'

'I did,' he said drily. *Though my attention focused more on the neckline than the trimming.* 'So, there is no one here who wishes to coax her into matrimony?

'I had high hopes of Lord Stantson. A very knowledgeable horseman, he's a mature man with a calm demeanour I thought might appeal to her.' At Max's raised eyebrow, she said, 'Many young ladies prefer to entrust their future to the steady hand of an older gentleman, rather than risk all with such dashing young rakes as *some* I might mention!

Mr Henshaw has also been pursuing her, though I have to admit,' his aunt concluded, 'she has given neither man any encouragement.'

Henshaw! That was the man who'd been watching her in the paddock this morning, Max realised.

Aunt Grace sighed. 'Lady Denby is quite determined to get her settled before her own daughter Eugenia makes her début next spring. The poor girl's chances for making a good match will diminish drastically if she must share her Season with her stepsister, for Eugenia Whitman is nearly as wealthy as Miss Denby and far outshines her in youth, wit and beauty.'

Miss Denby was hardly an antidote, Max thought, indignant on her behalf before he recalled the great pains she'd been taking to ensure she created just the sort of negative impression his aunt was describing.

'If she seems so unwilling and unsuitable, I wonder that her stepmother keeps pushing her to wed. Why not let her remain at Denby Lodge, with her horses?'

'Well, she must marry *some time*,' Mrs Ransleigh said. 'What else is she to do? And she's very, very rich.'

'Which explains the gentlemen's pursuit of someone who gives them no encouragement.' Max had been feeling more hopeful, but some niggle of memory made him frown.

Having spent so much time away with the army, he hadn't visited London very often the last few years, but he vaguely recalled from his clubs the tattle that Henshaw was always pursuing some heiress or other. 'Is Henshaw a fortune hunter?'

Aunt Grace coloured. 'I should never describe him in such uncomplimentary terms. Mr Henshaw comes from a very good family and is perfectly respectable. If he wishes to marry a wealthy girl, such a desire is hardly unusual.'

Definitely a fortune hunter, Max concluded. 'Anyone else angling for the reluctant Miss Denby?'

His aunt fixed him with an assessing look. 'Did the young lady catch your interest?'

'Does she look like a lady who would attract me?' Max asked, feeling somehow guilty for disparaging a woman he admired even as he imbued his voice with the right note of disdain.

Fortunately, his previous flirts had always been acknowledged beauties, so the hopeful light in his aunt's eyes died. 'No,' she admitted.

'I merely found her amusingly unconventional.'

Aunt Grace laughed ruefully. 'She is certainly that! Poor Lady Denby! One can only sympathise with her difficulties in trying to get the girl married.'

Having discovered what he'd come for, he'd best take his leave, before Aunt Grace tried to spin some matrimonial web around *him*. 'I'll leave you to your dresser and return to my breakfast, which Cook is now preparing.'

'Go enjoy your fish, then. I'm so glad you stopped by. I do hope you'll stay long enough that we can have a good visit, after all the guests leave. Felicity and Jane are eager to have more from you than a few hurried words.'

'I would like that.'

'Enjoy your day, then, my dear.'

Max kissed her hand. 'Enjoy your guests.'

After bowing himself out, Max walked towards the study he and Alastair had turned into their private parlour, running over in his mind what he'd learned from Aunt Grace about Miss Denby.

So none but Stantson and Henshaw had set their sights on the heiress. If Aunt Grace believed both to be gentlemen, he had nothing to worry about. He might enquire and see what Alastair knew about the men, just to be sure, but unless his cousin disclosed something to their discredit, he had no reason to involve himself any further in the matter of her future.

Though, as he'd assured his aunt, the lady was nothing at all like the women who usually attracted him, he had to admit to a feeling of regret at the idea that he'd seen the last of Miss Denby, the only unusual member of what was otherwise a stultifyingly conventional gathering of females.

Several days later, while Alastair occupied himself in the estate office, Max repaired to his bench in the conservatory to while away the afternoon with some reading.

No sun gilded the tropical plants today, but the morning's rain had left a soft mist dewing the grass, greying the greens of the trees, shrubs and vines. Within the warm, heated expanse of the glasshouse, the soft swish of swaying palms and ferns and the sweet exotic scent of citrus and jasmine were infinitely soothing.

Alastair had informed him the previous evening that he'd heard the colonel of Max's former regiment had just returned from Paris. He'd recommended that Max speak with him about a position, sound advice Max meant to follow. The calm and beauty surrounding him here further lifted his spirits, filling him with the sense that much was still possible, if he were patient and persistent enough.

He was absorbed in his book when, some time later, a lavender scent tickled his nose. At the same moment, a soft 'Oh!' of surprise brought his head up, just in time to see Miss Denby halt abruptly a few yards away down the pathway.

A warm wave of anticipation suffused him, even as she hastily backed away. 'I'm so sorry, Mr Ransleigh! I didn't mean to disturb you!'

'Then you didn't come here to seek me out?' he asked, his tone teasing.

'Oh, no! I wouldn't have intruded on your privacy, sir. Your cousin Miss Felicity, who has become great friends with my stepsister, Eugenia, told her you and Mr Alastair would be away all day.'

'You truly are not pursuing me, then?' He clapped a hand to his chest theatrically. 'What a blow to my self-esteem.'

For an instant, her brow furrowed in concern, before her ear caught his ironic tone and she grinned. 'I dare say your self-esteem can withstand the injury. But I told you I would not tease you and I meant it. I shall leave you to your book.'

It was only prudent that she leave at once…but he didn't want her to, not just yet.

'Since you've already interrupted my study, do stay for a moment, Miss Denby.'

She raised her eyebrows. 'For a chat that will become another of our little secrets?'

He grinned, pleased that she would joke with him. 'Exactly.' Come, sit.'

He motioned her to the bench…and found himself holding his breath, hoping she would come to him. Already his pulse had kicked up and all his senses sharpened, his body quickening at her nearness—which should have been warning enough that urging her to linger was not wise. He thrust the cautionary thought aside.

And then in a graceful swish of fabric, she sat down beside him. Max inhaled deeply as her faint lavender scent washed over him. It must be soap; he'd be astonished if she wore perfume. She was garbed against the misty chill in a cloak that covered her from head to toe, masking whatever hideous gown she'd selected along with, alas, that fine bosom. Even so, close up, he was able to drink in the fine texture of her face, the soft glow of her skin, the perfect shell of ear outlined by a mass of auburn-highlighted brown curls, tamed under her hat on this occasion. She tilted her face up to him and he lost himself in her extraordinary eyes, watching the golden centres shimmer within their dark-velvet depths.

Her lips, full and shapely, bore no trace of artificial gloss or colour. Would her mouth taste of wine, of apple, of mint?

Make conversation, he reminded himself, pulling back abruptly when he realised he'd been lowering his head toward their tempting surface. Devil's teeth, why did this young woman of no outstanding beauty evoke such a strong response from him?

'How goes your campaign?' he managed.

She made a moue of distaste, curving back the ripe fullness of her mouth. He wanted to trace the twin dimples that flanked it with his tongue.

'Not well, I'm afraid. As one might expect, all the men—the ones your aunt *invited*, in any event,' she added, tossing him a mischievous glance, 'are unmistakably gentlemen. I've considered each of them, but some are actively pursuing other ladies. Of the two pursuing *me*, neither is likely to refuse to marry, should I find some way to get myself compromised. Then there's the inhibiting presence of Lady Melross, whom I suspect Lady Claringdon inveigled to be present just to ensure that if any gentleman coaxed a maiden to stroll with him where she shouldn't, he'd be fairly caught—unless he was too dishonourable to do the proper thing and abandoned the girl to her ruin.' She sighed. 'Would that I might be!'

'Lady Melross is a dreadful woman, who delights in spreading bad news,' Max said feelingly. She'd been the first to trumpet the rumours of his disgrace, even before he reached London after leaving Vienna, then to whisper that his father had banished him. Though he knew she was zealous about reporting the failings of anyone of prominence whose missteps happened to reach her ears, it seemed to him she took a particularly malevolent interest in his affairs.

If he ever managed to secure a prominent position in government, hers would be the first name he would see struck from the invitation list at any function he attended.

Miss Denby drummed her fingers absently on the bench. 'I wish I could marry my horse. He's the most interesting male here, present company excepted, of course. Even if he has, ah, been deprived of the tools of his manhood.'

Surprised into a bark of laughter, Max shook his head. 'You really do say the most outlandish things for a lady.'

She shrugged. 'Because I'm not one, really. I wish I could convince all the pursing gentlemen of the fact that I'd make them a sadly deficient wife.'

With her seated there, tantalising his nose with her subtle lavender scent and his body by her nearness, Max thought that, for certain of a wife's duties, she would do admirably.

Before his thoughts could stampede down that lane, he reined himself back to more proper conversational paths. 'Still training your gelding every morning?'

'Yes.'

'In breeches and boots?' *A lovely image, that!*

'No more breeches and boots, alas; you and your cousin taught me to be more cautious. Though I still ride early, it's getting more difficult to avoid company. Lord Stantson has been pressing me to let him ride with me of a morning, but thus far has honoured my wishes when I firmly decline. He's a fine enough gentleman, but I've heard he came here specifically looking for a second wife. Since I'm not angling for the position, I'm trying to give him no encouragement.'

Wrinkling her nose in distaste, she continued, 'Mr Henshaw, however, not only requires no encouragement, he positively refuses to be *dis*couraged! He's turned up each of the last two mornings, despite my continued insistence that I prefer to ride alone. How am I to train Sultan properly, with him interrupting us?'

For a moment, her eyes focused unseeing on the glasshouse wall and she shivered. 'Though I was garbed in a stiflingly proper habit, he seems to be always *staring* at me. I don't care for his expression when he does so, either—as if I were a favourite pudding he meant to devour.'

Max frowned. She might have worn a proper habit every day since that first one, but she hadn't been the morning he'd seen Henshaw watching her. How close a look at her had the man got? Close enough to get an eyeful of the shapely form he and Alastair had so appreciated?

If so, Max could hardly fault any man for staring at her like a 'pudding one meant to devour'. Which didn't reduce one whit the strong desire rising in him to blacken both Henshaw's eyes for making her feel uncomfortable.

'He insisted on riding with me, despite the fact that I was quite obviously trying to work with Sultan,' Miss Denby continued. 'Honestly, he possesses terrible hands and the worst seat I've ever been forced to observe. I've taken to riding even earlier to avoid him.'

'I've never seen him astride, only observed his…remarkably inventive dress. He must make his tailors very rich.'

She chuckled. 'A man milliner indeed. One would think, with his exacting tastes in garments, sheer disgust over my atrocious gowns would be enough to dissuade him from pursuing me.'

She looked up at him, smiling faintly, those great dark eyes inviting him to share her amusement. Her lavender scent wrapped itself around him like a silken scarf, pulling him closer. He wanted to trace the scent to its origin, lick it from her neck and ears and the hollows of the collarbones he'd seen that day she'd ridden in an open-collared shirt and breeches.

As he gazed raptly, her dark eyes widened and her smile faded. She seemed as mesmerised as he, her lips parting slightly, giving him the tiniest glimpse of pink tongue within the warmth of her mouth.

Desire shot through him, pulsing in his veins, curling his fingers with the itch to cup her chin and taste her.

'Well,' she said, her voice a bit breathless, 'I suppose I should leave you now, lest someone come by and see us. Unless…' she smiled tremulously, brushing a curl back from her forehead as her cheeks pinked '…you'd like to…reconsider my proposition?'

Her cloak fell open at that movement. Beneath the fabric of another overtrimmed, pea-green gown, he saw the rapid rise and fall of her breasts as her breathing accelerated.

His certainly had. All over his body, things were accelerating and rising and pulsing. The need to kiss her, learn the taste of her mouth, the contour of her ears and shoulders and the hollow of her throat, thrummed in his blood. His gaze wandered back to the mesmerizing shimmer of gold in her eyes and halted.

In his head, that persistent fly of temptation buzzed louder, almost drowning out good sense.

Almost.

It took him a full minute to shoo it away and find his voice.

'A tempting offer. But I fear I must still decline.'

Despite the words, he couldn't make himself stand, bow, put an end to this interlude, as prudence demanded.

She, too, remained motionless, her eyes studying his, the current of attraction pulsing between them almost palpable. As he watched intently, the embarrassment she'd displayed upon repeating her offer changed to uncertainty and then, yes, he was certain, to desire. Confirming that assessment, slowly she leaned towards him and tilted her face up, bringing her lips tantalisingly close.

Max forced himself to remain motionless, while every nerve and sense screamed at him to lower his head and take her mouth. In some distant corner of his brain, honour and common sense was nattering that he should move away, end this before it began.

But he couldn't. He would not cross that slight boundary

and touch her first, but, shutting out the little voice insisting this was madness, he waited, aflame with anticipation, confident she would close the distance between them and kiss him.

Her eyelashes feathered shut. His eyes closed, too, as her warm breath washed over him, the first tentative wave from an incoming tide of pleasure.

Just as his eager body whispered 'now, now', she straightened abruptly and scooted backwards on the bench.

'I—I should go,' she said unsteadily.

Max shook his head, trying to drown out the buzzy little voice that urged him to lure her into remaining.

And he could do it; he knew he could.

Over the protest of every outraged sense, he wrestled his desire back under control. 'That would be wisest…if not nearly so pleasant.'

'Wisest…yes,' she repeated and belatedly bobbed to her feet. 'Thank you for the, ah, chat. Good day, Mr Ransleigh.'

He stood as well and bowed. 'Good day, Miss Denby.'

Regretfully, while his body yammered and scolded at him like a disgruntled housewife cheated by a market vendor, he watched her retreat down the pathway. Just before turning the corner to exit the glasshouse, she halted.

Looking back over her shoulder, she said softly, in tones of wonder, 'You tempt me too, you know.'

A surge of delight and pure masculine satisfaction blazed through him. Before he could reply, she turned and hurried out.

He jumped to his feet and paced after her. Fortunately, by the time he reached the door to the glasshouse, sanity had returned.

Good grief, if he couldn't rein in his reaction to her, he'd better avoid her altogether, lest he find himself being quick-stepped to the altar. Had he not committed idiocies enough for one lifetime?

So he made himself stand there, watching her trim figure retreat through the mist down the pathway back to the house. But as she took the turn leading to the drawing-room terrace, a man stepped out.

Henshaw.

Max gritted his teeth. Frowning, he watched the exchange, too far away to hear their voices, as Henshaw bowed to Miss Denby's curtsy. Offered his arm, which she declined with a shake of her head and a motion of her hand in the direction of the stables. Henshaw, giving a dismissive wave, offered his arm again, which, after a few more unintelligible words, she reluctantly accepted.

They'd just set off on the path to the house when Alastair came striding up. Putting a hand to his forehead, he peered into the distance and declared, 'That looks like the chap who was watching Miss Denby ride the other morning.'

'It is. David Henshaw. Do you know him?'

'Ah, yes, that's why he looked familiar. He's a member at Brooks's. Too concerned with the cut of his coat and the style of his cravat for my taste. He the front runner for Miss Denby's affections?'

'Not if she has anything to say about it.'

'Ah, had another little chat with the lady, did you? Sure you don't fancy her for yourself?'

He made himself give Alastair a withering look. 'Does she look like a woman I'd fancy?' he drawled, feeling more uncomfortable about uttering the disparaging remark this time, after he'd practically devoured her on the greenhouse bench, than when he'd been trying to throw Aunt Grace off the scent.

'Not in your usual style,' Alastair allowed, 'but there is *something* about her. Devilishly arousing in her own way... like when riding astride in breeches! What a shame she's an innocent; don't forget, my friend, that the price for tasting *that* morsel is marriage.'

'So I keep reminding myself,' Max muttered, grimly aware that the moment she'd sat down beside him, his instincts for self-preservation had gone missing.

'I'm not surprised Henshaw is on the scent,' Alastair continued. 'The latest word at the London clubs was he's run so far into debt, he can't even go back to his town house for fear of meeting the bailiffs. The Denby girl's fat dowry would put all his financial problems to rest.'

Max had never given much thought to the fact that a husband gained control over all his wife's wealth, but after hearing Miss Denby lament the fact, such an arrangement now struck him as little short of robbery. 'Doesn't seem quite sporting that he could float himself down River Tick and then use her money to paddle out of danger.'

Alastair shrugged. 'It's done all the time.'

The fact that it was didn't make it any more palatable, Max thought. 'Does Aunt Grace know about Henshaw's current monetary difficulties?'

'I don't know. But he's been angling to marry a fortune ever since he came up from Cambridge, so there's nothing new about it, except perhaps the degree of urgency. Come now, enough about Henshaw. The man's a pretentious, ill-dressed bore. How about a game of billiards before dinner? If any guests approach the room, I'll have Wendell scare them off.'

Absently Max agreed, but as they walked back to the house, he couldn't get out of his mind the image of Henshaw compelling Miss Denby to take his arm.

Were Henshaw's circumstances difficult enough that he'd be willing to coerce an heiress into matrimony?

Most likely, he was letting his dislike for the dandified Henshaw colour his perceptions. The man *was* a gentleman of good family and Aunt Grace would never have invited him if there were any doubt about his integrity.

However, just to be safe, he'd ride out early tomorrow and warn Miss Denby to be on her guard with him.

Feeling better about the matter, he followed his cousin into the house and focused his mind on the best strategy for beating Alastair for the third evening in a row.

Chapter Six

The next morning, Max rose before dawn and headed to the stables before even a glimmer of dawn lightened the treeline, determined not to risk missing Miss Denby. But though he trotted his mount up and down the stable lane for so long that the grooms must have wondered what in the world he was doing, she did not appear.

Perhaps she was being prudent, abstaining from her morning ride so as not to be pounced upon by Henshaw. Alastair had told him over billiards the previous evening that his mother said the party was wrapping up; Jane had boasted to him of its successes, two matrons having managed to get offers for their daughters. Felicity, she added, had made a great new friend of Miss Denby's stepsister, Eugenia Whitman, and was giddy about the prospect of sharing her upcoming Season with the girl.

The same Miss Whitman who, his Aunt Grace had informed him, 'far outshines her stepsister in youth, wit and beauty'. Max still resented that comment on Miss Denby's behalf.

In any event, it appeared she would soon be relieved of Mr Henshaw's pursuit, Max concluded, turning his probably puzzled mount to the stable and returning to the house.

But what of next spring? Would she, as she feared, have to suffer through another Season, dragged off to participate in a round of social activities for which she had no inclination, forced to neglect her beloved horses?

What a shame her childhood beau Harry was so far away. She deserved to marry a man who appreciated her unique talents and interests, who supported rather than discouraged her desire to carry on her father's legacy.

He toyed with the idea of trying to seek her out and bid her goodbye, but couldn't come up with a way to do so that would not shock the gathering by revealing she was well acquainted with a man she wasn't supposed to know. Perhaps, once he had his life sorted out, he could call on her in London, maybe even seek her out at Denby Lodge and purchase some of her horses.

With Alastair away on another of his lord-of-the-manor errands, Max fetched his book and headed for what might be his last afternoon hidden away at the conservatory. He'd rather miss the place, whose warm scented air and soothing palm murmurs he would probably never have discovered had he not been forced to vacate the house. With the guests soon departing, he and Alastair would have free run of the estate again.

He halted just inside the threshold of the glasshouse, inhaling the tangy-sweet scent of jasmine that seemed always to hang in the air, insubstantial as a whisper. He was about to proceed to his usual bench when a murmur of voices reached his ears, the words as indistinct as the gurgling of a brook over rocks.

He halted, trying to identify the speakers. Aunt Grace, conferring with the gardener? Or one of the affianced couples, stealing one last tryst before the party broke up?

In either case, his presence would be an impediment. He was silently retracing his steps when a feminine voice reached his ears, its increased volume making the words suddenly clear.

'Mr Henshaw, I *do* appreciate the honour of your offer, but I'm absolutely convinced we will not suit!'

Miss Denby's voice, Max realised, halting in mid-step. Had Henshaw tracked her there?

His first impulse was to set off in her direction, but she'd probably not thank him for interfering. Still, though he felt confident she could handle her disappointed suitor without his assistance, some deep-seated protective instinct made him linger.

After a masculine murmur whose words he could not make out, Miss Denby said, 'No, I shall not change my mind. You must admit, sir, that I have tried in every possible way to discourage you, so my refusal can hardly come as a surprise. You will oblige me by leaving now.'

'Waiting here for someone else, were you?' Henshaw replied, his angry tones now comprehensible. 'Max Ransleigh, perhaps? He'd never marry you. Despite his father's banishment, he has money enough, and if he ever does wed, it will be a woman from a prominent society family. In any event, his taste runs to sophisticated beauties, which you, I'm forced to say, are not. Nor are you getting any younger. If you've any hopes at all of marrying, you'd better accept my offer.'

Why, the mercenary little weasel, Max thought, incensed. Only the certainty that Miss Denby would not appreciate having him witness this embarrassing scene kept him from setting off down the pathway to plant a fist squarely on the jaw of that overdressed excuse for a gentleman.

'You're quite correct,' she was saying. 'I possess none of the virtues and talents a gentleman looks for in a wife. As you so kindly noted, I'm hardly a beauty and am hopeless at making the sort of polite chat that makes up society conversation. Worst of all, I fear I have no fashion sense. You can do so much better, Mr Henshaw! Why not wait until the Season and find yourself a more suitable bride?'

Despite his ire, Max had to grin. Had any female ever so thoroughly disparaged herself to a prospective suitor?

'I'm afraid, my dear, the press of creditors don't allow me the luxury of waiting. Though admittedly you possess neither the style nor the talents I would wish for in a wife, you do have…a certain charm of person. And wealth, of which I'm in desperate need.'

No style? No talent? His mirth rapidly dissipating, Max reconsidered the prospect of cornering Henshaw, shaking him like a dog with a ferret and then tossing him out of the glasshouse like the refuse he was.

But alerting them to his presence would not only distress Miss Denby, it might give the thwarted suitor an opportunity to claim he'd caught *Max and Miss Denby* alone together. His self-protective instincts on full alert now that Miss Denby wasn't within touching distance, Max didn't want to risk that.

His decision not to intervene, however, wavered when he heard a sharp, cracking sound that could only be a slap.

'Keep your hands to yourself,' Miss Denby cried. 'You followed me without my leave or encouragement. If you will not quit this place, then I will do so. Since I do not anticipate seeing you again before the party ends, I will say goodbye, Mr Henshaw.'

'Not so hasty, my dear. It might not be an arrangement either of us want, but you *will* marry me.'

'Let go of my arm! It's useless for you to detain me, for I promise you, nothing on earth would ever induce me to marry you!'

'I'd hoped you would consent willingly, but if you will not, you force me to employ…other measures. Before you leave this spot, you'll be fit to be no one's wife but mine.'

At that threat, Max abandoned discretion and set off at

a run. If he hadn't already been prepared to tear Henshaw limb from limb, the scuffling, panting sounds of a struggle that reached him as he rounded the last corner, followed by the unmistakable rip of fabric, had him ready to do murder.

Seconds later, he lunged over a potted fern to find Henshaw trying to pin a wildly struggling Miss Denby down on the bench, his free hand clawing up her skirts. As a clay pot fell over and shattered, Henshaw looked up, his hands stilling.

The smirk on his face and the lust in his eyes turned to surprise, then alarm as he recognised Max. But before Max could seize him, Miss Denby, taking advantage of Henshaw's distraction, kneed him in the groin, then caught him full on the nose with a roundhouse left jab of which Gentleman Jackson would have been proud.

Howling, Henshaw released Miss Denby and staggered backwards, one hand on his breeches front, the other holding his nose. Blood oozing through his fingers, he snarled, 'Bitch! You'll regret that!'

Max grabbed him by the arm and slammed him against the wall, regrettably with less force than he would have liked, but he didn't want to break a glass panel in Aunt Grace's conservatory.

Securing him against it with a stranglehold on his cravat, Max growled, 'Miss Denby will not regret her rejection. But you, varlet, will regret this episode for the rest of your life unless you do exactly what I say. You will apologise to Miss Denby, then pack your bag and leave immediately, before I tell the world and Lady Melross how you tried to attack an innocent and unwilling young lady.' Giving Henshaw's cravat a final twist, he released the man.

Henshaw shook his arms free and retreated several steps, trying to repair his ruined cravat before giving it up as hopeless. 'You dare to threaten me?' he blustered. 'Who will believe you? A flagrant womaniser, sent away from Vienna in disgrace, disowned by your own father!'

'Who will believe me?' Max echoed, his voice silky-soft. 'Your hostess, my aunt, perhaps? Or Lady Melross, seeing your elegant attire as it now appears?'

Fury and desperation might have briefly clouded Henshaw's judgement, but the reference to his dishevelled clothing snapped him back to reality. Obviously realising he could not hope to prevail over the nephew of his hostess, especially in his present incriminating state of disorder, he clamped his lips shut and looked down the pathway, eyeing the exit.

More concerned with assisting the lady, Max resigned himself to letting him go. 'Are you unharmed, Miss Denby?' he asked, stepping past Henshaw to her side.

'Y-yes,' she replied, her voice breaking a little.

The path to the doorway free, Henshaw backed cautiously away, his wary gaze fixed on Max. After retreating a safe distance, he tossed back, 'I won't forget this, Ransleigh. I'll have retribution some day…and on the bitch, too.'

'You don't follow instructions very well,' Max said softly, an icy contempt filling him. 'Now I'm going to have to thrash you like the cur you are.'

But before he could take a step, abandoning any pretence of dignity, Henshaw bolted for the door. Much as he would have liked to give chase and thrash the man, Max concluded his more urgent duty was to see to Miss Denby, who stood trembling by the bench, holding together the ripped edges of her bodice.

Her cloak had fallen off during the struggle and her pelisse, now lacking its buttons, gaped open over her white-knuckled hands. Her beautiful dark eyes, wide with shock and outrage, looked stricken.

Max cursed under his breath, wishing he'd tossed the bounder through the glass wall after all. 'I entered a few minutes ago and heard voices, but didn't realise what was transpiring until…it was almost too late. I'm so sorry I didn't intervene earlier and spare you that indignity. Say the word and I'll track down Henshaw and give him the drubbing he deserves.'

'Beating him further will serve no useful purpose,' she said, attempting a smile, which wobbled badly. 'Though I might wish to hit him again myself. He has ruined one of my best ugly gowns.'

Thankfully, some colour was returning to her pale cheeks and her voice sounded stronger, so Max might not have to pursue the man and rearrange his skeleton after all. 'You did quite a capital job on your first round, though I don't believe you succeeded in breaking his nose, more's the pity. Who taught you to box? That roundhouse jab was worthy of a professional.'

'Harry. He took lessons with Jackson in London while he was at Winchester. Satisfying as it was to land the blow exactly where I wished—on both parts of his anatomy—that won't help my biggest problem now, which is how to get back to my chamber and out of this gown. My stepmother would have palpitations if she saw me like this. Not that I would mind being ruined, but I should be indignant if anyone were to try to force me to marry *Henshaw*.'

'That sorry excuse for a man?' Max said in disgust. 'I should think not.'

'A sorry excuse indeed, but stronger than I anticipated,' she said, looking down at the fingers clutching her torn bodice. 'I thought I could handle him, but…' She took a shuddering breath, as if shaken by the evidence of how close she'd come to being ravaged. 'If only *you* had accepted my first offer! I'm certain you would have c-compromised me much more g-genteelly.'

She was trying to put on a brave face, but tears had begun slipping down her cheeks and she started to tremble again.

Making a vow to seek out Henshaw wherever he went to ground and pummel him senseless, Max abandoned discretion and drew Miss Denby into his arms. 'If *I* were to compromise you, I would at least make sure you *enjoyed* it,' he said, trying for a teasing tone as he cradled her, gently chafing her hands and trying to use his warmth to heat her chilled body. 'And it would have been done with much more expertise and finesse. Like this,' he said and kissed just the freckled tip of her nose.

The last time he'd encountered her in the conservatory, he'd burned to plunder her mouth and let his lips discover every wonder of nose, chin and eyelids. As indignant as his aunt would be that a guest of the Ransleighs had been assaulted, all he wished for now was to erase from her memory the outrage that had just been perpetrated against her.

To his relief, she gave herself into his hands, snuggling with a broken little gasp against his chest. For long moments, he simply held her, one finger gently stroking her cheek, until at last the tremors eased and she pulled back a bit, still resting in the circle of his arms.

'You do compromise a lady most genteelly,' she said. 'Thank you, Mr Ransleigh. I shall never forget your kind assistance.'

'Max,' he corrected with a smile. 'I should be honoured to have you call on me at any time.'

Before she could reply, a loud shriek split the air. *'Miss Denby!'* a shrill female voice exclaimed. 'Whatever are you about?'

A sense of impending disaster stabbing in his gut, Max looked over Miss Denby's head to see Lady Melross hurrying toward them.

Chapter Seven

Clutching the ragged edges of her bodice, Caroline stared in horror as Lady Melross marched up to them, her eyes widening with shock, then malicious glee as she perceived Caro wrapped in Ransleigh's arms, her bodice in ruins.

A sick feeling invaded Caro's stomach. How could things have gone so hideously wrong? In Lady Melross's accusing eyes, Mr Ransleigh, who had protected and comforted her, must now appear to be the one who'd tried to ravish her. And the old harpy would lose no time in trumpeting the news to all and sundry.

'This isn't what you think!' Caro cried, furious, frustrated, knowing the denial was hopeless. Oh, that she might run after Henshaw and rake her fingers down his deceitful face!

Ransleigh had never wanted to compromise her. Now, through the hapless intervention of the detestable Henshaw, the scandal he'd scrupulously avoided would fall full upon him.

It was all her fault…and she couldn't think of a single way to stop it.

'Not what I think?' Lady Melross echoed. 'Gracious, Miss Denby, do you believe me a simpleton, unable to comprehend what I see right before my eyes? No wonder a little bird told me I might find something interesting in the conservatory.'

'A little bird?' Caro echoed. 'What do you mean?'

'Oh, I had a note…from someone who knew about your rendezvous. Or maybe you sent it yourself, Miss Caroline?'

'Henshaw,' Caro whispered, her eyes pleading with Max, who'd already stepped away from her, his face going grim and shuttered the moment he saw Lady Melross charging toward them down the glasshouse path, Lady Caringdon trailing behind.

Henshaw must have sent the note, wanting Lady Melross to find them with her gown in tatters, ensuring a scandal public enough that they'd be forced to marry.

Surely Max Ransleigh understood that?

'You, Ransleigh,' Lady Melross said, turning to Max, 'I wouldn't have expected something this lacking in taste and finesse…although after Vienna, I suppose maybe I should have. What a sly thing you turned out to be, Miss Denby,' she continued as she snatched up Caroline's cloak and tossed it over her shoulders. 'There, you're decent again.'

Lady Caringdon stared at them both accusingly. 'Aren't you a rum one, Ransleigh, sneaking around, keeping your distance from the company while you plotted to seduce an innocent right under the nose of her chaperone! And you, young lady, have got exactly what you deserve!'

'Indeed!' Lady Melross crowed. 'Don't you understand, you stupid girl? Ruining yourself with Ransleigh won't earn you the elevated position in society you expect, for his father isn't even receiving him! While you were immured in the country at that dreary horse farm, he was creating a scandal—'

'Lady Melross,' Max broke in on the lady's tirade, 'that is quite enough. Abuse me as you will, but I cannot allow you to harass Miss Denby. She has suffered a shock and should return to the house at once to recover. Miss Denby,' he continued, turning to Caroline, his voice gentling, 'will you allow these ladies to escort you back to your chamber? We will talk of this later.'

'I should like to settle it now—' Caro said.

'No, in this at least, Ransleigh has the right of it,' Lady Melross broke in. 'You cannot stand there chatting in that disgrace of a garment! Come along, both of you. Though I cannot imagine what you could say that might excuse your behavior, Ransleigh, before you present yourself to Lady Denby, you'd best go and make yourself respectable.'

'Perhaps it would be better if I talk with Stepmother first,' Caroline conceded. Poor Lady Denby would be close to hysterics if the outcry about this disaster reached her before Caro did. She'd need to explain and calm her down before Max called on her.

Lady Caringdon sniffed. 'Poor Diana. What a tawdry, embarrassing predicament—and with dear Eugenia set to make her bow next spring! Dreadful!'

'Dreadful indeed,' Lady Melross said, sounding not at all regretful. 'Come along now, and wrap that cloak tight about you, miss. I shouldn't want to shock any of the *proper* young ladies we might encounter on the way. Doubtless Lady Denby will summon you later, Ransleigh. Perhaps you'd better go and acquaint your aunt with the débâcle you've created in the midst of her party.'

'Don't worry,' Ransleigh said to Caro, ignoring Lady Melross's disparaging remarks. 'Get some rest. I'll see you later and make everything right.' Giving her an encouraging smile, he stepped back to allow Lady Melross to take her arm.

Having a sudden change of heart, Caroline almost reached out to snag his sleeve and beg him to walk in with her. If only they could face Lady Denby now, together, and explain what had happened, surely they could sort it out and keep the dreadful Lady Melross from spreading her malicious account of the events!

But she suspected Ransleigh wouldn't deign to explain himself with Lady Melross present, and there was no chance whatsoever that the lady would let herself be manoeuvred out of escorting her victim into the house.

'I will call on Lady Denby soon,' he told Caro, then moved aside to let them pass.

'Speak with me first!' she tossed back as, Lady Caringdon seizing her other arm, the two women half-led, half-dragged her down the path.

They marched her into the house and up the stairs, relentless as gaolers. Initially they peppered her with questions, but her refusal to provide any details eventually convinced them she intended to remain silent.

With a final warning that it was useless to turn mute now, as her character was already ruined, they ignored her and spent the rest of the transit speculating about how devastated Lady Denby and Mrs Ransleigh would be and how fast the scandalous news would spread.

While they chattered, Caro's mind raced furiously. Should she ask Max Ransleigh to seek out Henshaw, drag him in so they might jointly accuse him? Was Henshaw still at Barton Abbey to be accused?

Trapped between the two dragons, she had no way of determining that. Should she try to explain immediately to Lady Denby, or wait until after she'd consulted with Mr Ransleigh?

She had only a short time to figure out what *she* wanted, while her whole life and future hinged on her making the right decision.

When she reached her rooms and her erstwhile 'rescuers' discovered neither her stepmother nor her sister was present, they finally stopped plaguing her and rushed off. Doubtless

anxious to compete over who could convey the interesting
news to the most people the fastest, Caro thought sardoni-
cally.

She hoped her stepmother would not be one of those so
informed, vastly preferring to break the dismal story herself.
In any event, Lady Denby's absence gave her the opportunity
to summon Dulcie and change before the tattered evidence of
the disaster could further upset her stepmother. Reassuring
her maid, who gasped in alarm upon seeing her in the ruined
gown, that she was quite unharmed and would explain later,
Caro sent her off to dispose of the garment.

Watching the girl carry out the shreds, Caro smiled grimly.
It certainly wasn't the way she would have chosen to do it,
but the escapade in the glasshouse *had* effectively ruined
her. At least now she'd be able to purchase gowns that didn't
make her wince when she saw her image in a mirror. With
that heartening thought, she scrawled a note asking Mr Ransleigh to meet her in Lady Denby's sitting room at his earliest convenience.

As she waited for her stepmother to return, she tried to
corral the thoughts galloping about in her mind like colts set
loose in a spring meadow. How could she turn Henshaw's despicable conduct to best advantage, managing the scandal so
she would be able to return to Denby Lodge and her horses,
while leaving Mr Ransleigh's good name unblemished?

Only one thought truly dismayed her: that having heard
Lady Melross testify that she'd received a note bidding her
come to the conservatory, Max might think, in blatant dis-
regard of his wishes, *she* had arranged for Lady Melross to
find them, trapping him with treachery into compromising
her after persuasion had failed.

Trapping herself?

How to avoid that fate? Too unsettled to remain seated,
she paced the room. In the aftermath of Henshaw's unex-

pected attack, her still-jangled nerves were hampering her ability to think clearly. The bald truth was she'd underestimated the man, dismissed him as a self-indulgent weakling she could easily handle.

It shook her to the core to admit that, had Max Ransleigh not rushed to her rescue, she probably could not have successfully resisted Henshaw.

How understanding Max had been, lending her his warmth and strength as she had struggled to compose herself. Bringing her back from the horror of what might have been to a reassuring normalcy with his gentle teasing. Renewed gratitude suffused her.

They must find some way out of this conundrum. She refused to repay his generosity by trapping him in a marriage neither of them wanted.

But when she recalled his parting words, a deep sense of unease filled her.

'I'll make everything right,' he'd said. Initially, she'd thought he meant to track down Henshaw and force him to confess his guilt. However, if Henshaw had already scuttled away from Barton Abbey, leaving Max bearing the blame for her disgrace, Ransleigh's sense of honour might very well force him into making her an offer.

And that wouldn't do at all. For one, he'd told her quite plainly he had no wish to marry and she could think of few things worse than being shackled to an uninterested husband. The image of her cousin Elizabeth came forcefully to mind.

Nor did she want to cobble her future to a man with whom she had little in common, whose wit engaged her but who agitated and discomforted her every time she was near him, filling her with powerful desires she had no idea how to manage.

Before she could analyse the matter any further, a rapid patter of footsteps in the hallway and the buzz of raised voices announced the imminent return of her stepmother.

Praying Lady Melross had not accompanied her, Caro braced herself for the onslaught.

A moment later, the door flew open and Lady Denby burst into the room, Eugenia at her elbow. 'Is it true?' her stepsister demanded. 'Did Mr Ransleigh truly…debauch you in the conservatory, as Lady Melross claims?'

'He did not.'

'Oh, thank heavens!' Lady Denby exclaimed. 'That dreadful woman! I knew it had to be naught but a malicious hum!'

'There was an…altercation,' Caro allowed. 'But events did not unfold as Lady Melross supposed.'

'Surely she didn't find you wrapped in Mr Ransleigh's arms, your gown in disarray, your bodice torn?' Eugenia asked.

'My gown had been damaged, but it was not—'

'Oh, no!' Eugenia interrupted with a wail. 'Then you *are* ruined. Indeed, we are *both* ruined! I shall never have my Season in London now!' Clapping a hand to her mouth, she burst into tears and rushed into her adjoining room, slamming the door behind her.

Lady Denby stood pale-faced and trembling, tears tracking down her own cheeks as she looked at Caro reproachfully. 'Oh, Caro,' she said faintly, 'how *could* you? Even if you had no concern about your own future, how could you jeopardise Eugenia's?'

'Please, ma'am, sit and let me explain. Truly, it is not as bad as you think. I'm certain that virtually nothing the detestable Lady Melross told you is accurate.'

Lady Denby allowed herself to be shown to a seat and accepted a glass of sherry, which she sipped while Caro related what had actually transpired. When she got to the part about how Mr Ransleigh's timely arrival had prevented Henshaw from overpowering her, Lady Denby cried out and leapt to her feet, wrapping Caro in her arms.

'Oh, my poor dear, how awful for you! Bless Mr Ransleigh for having the courage to intervene.'

'I owe him a great debt,' Caro agreed, settling her stepmother back in her chair. 'Which is why we need to somehow stop Lady Melross from circulating the falsehood that he compromised me. I can hardly repay Mr Ransleigh's gallantry by forcing him to offer for me, a girl he hardly knows. That would not be fair, would it?'

'It doesn't seem right,' Lady Denby admitted. 'But if you don't marry *someone*…how are we to salvage anything? And my dear, the truth is, this scandal could ruin Eugenia's Season as well!'

'Surely not! She's not even a Denby! Once Lady Gilford and Mrs Ransleigh learn the truth, I'm certain they will enlist their friends to ensure my difficulties do not reflect badly on my stepsister.'

That hope seemed to reassure Lady Denby, for she nodded. 'Yes, perhaps you are right. Grace and Jane would think it monstrous for poor Eugenia to suffer for Henshaw's villainy. But how are we to salvage your position, my dear?'

'I don't know yet,' Caro evaded, guiltily aware that she had no desire to 'salvage' it. 'Will you allow me to discuss this alone with Mr Ransleigh first, before he speaks with you? I expect him at any moment.'

'Very well,' Lady Denby agreed with a sigh. 'It's all so very distressing! I must go and comfort Eugenia.'

After giving her a final hug, Lady Denby walked out. Knowing that she would be meeting Max Ransleigh again any moment set every nerve on edge.

The fact that, despite her agitation, an insidious little voice was whispering that wedding Max might not be so disastrous after all filled her with a panicky agitation that drove her once again to pace the room.

From the very first, he'd affected her differently than any

other man she'd ever met. Being near him filled her with a tingling physical immediacy, a consciousness of her breasts and lips and body she'd never previously experienced.

Yesterday in the conservatory, that strange but powerful attraction had urged her to touch him, kiss him, feel his mouth and hands on her. Thought and reason vaporised into heat and need, into a burning, irresistible desire to know him, to let him know her. She'd *craved* that contact with a force and single-mindedness she would never have believed possible.

Even with the threat of the Curse hanging over her, she wasn't sure she would have been able to bring her rioting senses under control and walk away if he'd made any move at all to entice her to stay.

The power Henshaw had exerted over her while she struggled to escape him had frightened her, but what Max inspired in her was even more terrifying…because she hadn't wanted to escape it. Indeed, recalling him poised motionless on the bench, inviting her kiss, making no move to cajole or entice, letting her own desire propel her to him, was more coercive than any force he could have employed.

She'd been as powerfully in his thrall as…as her cousin Elizabeth had once been to Spencer Russell, the reprobate she'd married. The man who'd charmed and wed and betrayed, and almost bankrupted her cousin before a fortuitous racing accident had brought to an end Elizabeth's humiliating existence as a disdained and abandoned wife.

Caro did not want to be ensnared by an emotion that dazzled her out of her common sense, nor be held captive by a lust so strong it paralysed will and smothered rational thinking.

Just as she reached that conclusion, a rap sounded at the door.

Her heartbeat stopped, then recommenced at a rapid pace

as a stinging shock rippled through her, setting her stomach churning. Wiping her suddenly sweaty palms on her gown, she took a deep breath and walked to open the door.

Chapter Eight

As expected, Max Ransleigh stood on the threshold. Looking solemn, he took her hand and kissed her fingers.

A second wave of sensation blazed through her. Clenching her fists and jaw to try to dampen the effect, she mumbled an incoherent welcome and led him to a chair. Though she was still too agitated to want to sit, knowing he would not unless she did so, she forced herself into the place opposite him.

'I'm so sorry to have involved you in this,' she began before he could speak. 'Though I did invite you to compromise me, I hope you realise I had no part in setting up the situation in the conservatory today! I would never have gone behind your back to create a scandal in which you'd already assured me you wanted no part.'

'I believe you,' he said, calming her fears on that matter, at least. 'I expect it was Henshaw who sent Lady Melross the note, wanting her to find you with him in a state dishevelled enough to ensure you'd be coerced to wed him.'

'Thank you. I would hate to have you think I'd use you so shabbily. Lady Denby has agreed to let me speak with you privately before she comes in, so shall we discuss what is to be done?'

'Let us do so. You did get your wish, you know. You are quite effectively ruined.'

'Yes, I know. I certainly didn't enjoy being mauled by Henshaw, but it might turn out for the best. We need only tell people what really happened, establishing that you had no part in it, and all will be well. I'll still be ruined, but with Henshaw showing his character to be so despicable, no one could fault me for refusing to marry him.'

Frowning, Ransleigh shook his head. 'I'm afraid that is not the case. Society would still believe the only way to salvage your reputation would be for you to marry your seducer. However deplorable his present conduct, Henshaw was *born* a gentleman, so much would be forgiven as long as you end up wed.'

'But that's appalling!' Caro cried. 'The *victim* is expected to marry her attacker?'

'Rightly or wrongly, the blame usually attaches itself to the female. But it won't come to that. Accusing Henshaw isn't possible; he's already left Barton Abbey. Any evidence that might confirm he was your attacker—bloody nose, ruined cravat—will have been put to rights by the time I could run him to ground. Since he can now have no doubt that you'd refuse to marry him, he has no reason to corroborate the truth, especially since Lady Melross is circulating a version of events that relieves him of responsibility. Indeed, he will probably think it a fine revenge to see me blamed for his transgressions.'

Caro nodded, distressed but not surprised that Ransleigh's assessment of Henshaw's character matched her own. 'I imagine he would, though I have no intention of allowing him the satisfaction. Whether he admits his guilt or not, I still intend to accuse him. Why should you, who intervened only to help me, suffer for his loathsome behaviour?'

'I don't think accusing him would be wise.'

Puzzled, Caro frowned at him. 'Why not?'

'You were discovered in *my* embrace. I'm the son of an earl who exerts a powerful influence in government; you are the orphaned daughter of a rural baron. If you accuse Henshaw, who will justly claim he was in his room, preparing to depart when Lady Melross found us, there will be many who will whisper that I coerced you into naming another man to cover up my own bad conduct. Lady Melross in particular will be delighted to embellish the details of my supposed ravishment and assert such behaviour is only to be expected after my…previous scandal.'

'You really think no one would believe me if I tell the truth?' Caro asked incredulously.

'What, allow such a salacious act to be blamed on some insignificant member of the *ton* rather than titillate the masses by accusing the well-known son of a very important man? No, I don't think anyone would believe you. I can see the scurrilous cartoons in the London print-shop windows now,' he finished bitterly.

'But that's so…unfair!' she burst out.

He laughed shortly, no humour in the sound. 'I have learned of late just how unfair life can be. Believe me, I like the solution as little as you do, but with your reputation destroyed and the blame for it laid at my door, the only way to salvage your position is for you to marry me.'

Alarmed as she was by his conclusion, Caro felt a flash of admiration for his willingness to do what he saw as right. 'A noble offer and I do honour you for it. But I think it ridiculous to allow society's expectations—based on a lie!—to force us into something neither of us desire.'

'Miss Denby, let me remind you that you are *ruined*,' he repeated, his tone now edged with an undercurrent of anger and frustration. 'Fail to marry and you risk being exiled altogether from respectable society. Being cast out of the company of those with whom you have always associated is not a pleasant condition, as I have good reason to know.'

'First, I've never really "associated" with the *ton*,' she countered, 'and, as I've assured you several times, polite society's opinion does not matter to me. Certainly not when compared with losing the freedom to live life how—and with whom—I choose.'

'But Lady Denby does live and move in that society and Miss Whitman's future may well depend upon its opinions. We may be far removed from London here, but I assure you, Lady Melross will delight in dredging up every detail of this scandal when your relations arrive in London next spring.'

Caroline shook her head. 'I've already discussed that problem with my stepmother. If they band together, I'm certain Lady Denby, your aunt and Lady Gilford can manage this affair so that no harm comes to Eugenia's prospects. Since you are already accounted a rake, it shouldn't much affect your reputation and ruining mine has been my goal from the outset.'

She'd hoped to persuade Max to accept her argument. Far from looking convinced, though, his expression turned even grimmer and his jaw flexed, as if he were trying not to grit his teeth.

'Miss Denby,' he began again after a moment, 'I don't mean to seem overbearing or argumentative, but the very fact that you have not much associated with society means you are in no position to accurately predict its reaction. I have lived all my life under its scrutiny and I promise you, once Lady Denby has thought through the matter, she will agree with me that our marriage is the only solution that will safeguard the reputations of everyone involved.'

He paused and took a deep breath, as if armouring himself. 'So you may assure her that I have done the proper thing and made a formal offer for your hand.'

If the situation had not been so serious, Caro might have laughed, for he spat out the declaration as if each word were a hot coal that burned his tongue as he uttered it. His obvious reluctance might even have been considered insulting, if her own desire to avoid marriage hadn't exceeded his.

But then, as if realising that his grudging offer was hardly lover-like, he shook his head and sighed. 'Let me try this again,' he said, then reached over to tangle his fingers with hers.

Immediately, heat rushed up her arm, while her heart accelerated so rapidly, she felt dizzy.

'Won't you honour me by giving me your hand?' he said. 'I know neither of us came to Barton Abbey with marriage in mind. But during our brief acquaintance, I've come to admire and respect you. I flatter myself that you've come to like me, too, at least a little.'

'I do like and…and admire you,' she replied disjointedly, wishing he'd release her fingers. They seemed somehow connected to her chest and her brain, for she was finding it hard to breathe and even harder to think as he retained them.

His thumb was rubbing lazy circles of wonderment around her palm, setting off little shocks of sensation that seemed to radiate straight to the core of her.

She should pull free, but she didn't seem able to move. So he continued, his touch mesmerising, until all the clear reasons against marriage dissolved into a porridge-like muddle in her brain. She couldn't seem to concentrate on anything but the press of his thumb and the delights it created.

'I think we could rub together tolerably well,' he went on, obviously not at all affected by the touch that was wreaking such havoc in her. 'I admire you, too, and from what I've seen of your Sultan, you are excellent with horses. You could run Denby Stud with my blessing.'

That assurance was as seductively appealing as the thumb

caressing her palm, which was now making her body hot and her nipples ache. An insidious longing welled up within her, a yearning for him to kiss her, for her to kiss him back.

Without question, he knew society better than she did, and, for a moment, her certainty that she ought to refuse him wavered. She struggled to recapture her purpose and remember why marrying him was such a bad idea.

Unable to order her thoughts in Max's disturbing presence, she pulled her fingers free, sprang up and paced to the window.

How could she become his wife and not let him touch her? Was she really ready to test the power of the Curse for a man who merely 'admired' her? Besides, the experience of their last two meetings suggested that her ability to resist him, if he did make overtures toward her, would be feeble at best, regardless of how tepid his feelings for her might be.

She could tell him why she was so opposed to marriage. But after his courage in rescuing her and resolutely facing the consequences, she really didn't wish to appear a coward by admitting that it was the strong probability that she would die in childbed, as so many of her maternal relations had, that made her leery of wedlock.

No, the very fact that he affected her so strongly was reason enough not to marry Max Ransleigh.

Reminding herself of her conviction that Lady Denby could protect Eugenia, she said, 'I know you make your offer hastily and under duress. If you will but think longer about it, you will agree that it isn't wise to take a step that will permanently compromise our futures in order to avoid a scandal that will soon enough be overshadowed by some other.'

'It will have to be some scandal,' he said drily.

'Only think if I were to accept you!' she continued, avoiding his gaze in the hope that not meeting his eyes might lessen the disturbing physical hold he exerted over her. 'I'm not being modest when I assert that a huge divide exists between Miss Denby, countrified, unfashionable daughter of minor gentry, and Max Ransleigh, an earl's son accustomed to moving in the first circles of society. I have neither the skills nor the background to be the sort of wife you deserve.'

Before he could insert some patently false reassurance, she rushed on, 'Nor, frankly, do I wish to acquire them. My world isn't Drury Lane, but the lane that leads from the barns to the paddocks. Not the odour of expensive perfume, but the scent of leather polish, sawdust and new hay. Not the murmur of political conversation, but the jingle of harness, the neighing of horses, the clang of the blacksmith's hammer. I have no desire to give that up for your world, London's parlours and theatre boxes and its endless round of dinner parties, routs and balls.'

His expression softened to a smile. 'You are quite eloquent in defence of "your world", Miss Denby.'

'I don't mean to disparage yours!' she said quickly. 'Only to point out how different we are. All I want is to remain at Denby Lodge, where I belong, sharing my life with someone who loves and appreciates that world as I do.' *Someone to whom*, she added silently, *I have long been bound by a comfortable affection, not a man as disturbing and far-too-insidiously appealing as you.*

Turning from the window, she said, 'Though I am fully conscious of the honour of your offer, as I told you from the beginning, I wish to marry Harry. By the time he returns from India, this furore will have calmed. And even if it has not, Harry will not care.'

'I don't know that you can be certain about that,' he objected. 'If it doesn't, and he marries you, he will share in your notoriety. Being banished from society is no little thing. Would you choose exile for him? Would he suffer it for you?'

'Harry would suffer anything for me.'

'How can you commit Harry to such a course without giving him a choice?'

'How can you ask me to give him up without giving him a chance? No, Mr Ransleigh, I will not do it. I will leave it to ladies better placed than I to protect my stepsister and to Harry to settle my future when he returns. And lest you think to argue your position with her, Lady Denby would not compel me to marry against my will.'

Hoping to finally convince him, she chanced gazing into his eyes. 'It really is more sensible this way, surely you can see that! Some day you, too, will encounter a lady you *wish* to marry, one who can be the perfect helpmate and government hostess. You'll be happy then that I did not allow you to sway me. So, though I am sorry to be disobliging, I must refuse your very flattering offer.'

He studied her a long moment; she couldn't tell from his face whether he felt relief or exasperation. 'You needn't give me a final answer now. Why not think on the matter for a few days?'

'That won't be necessary; I am resolved on this. As soon as my stepmother recovers from the shock, we will pack and leave for Denby Lodge.'

For another long moment he said nothing. 'I am no Henshaw to try to force your hand, even though I believe your leaving here without the protection of an engagement is absolutely the wrong course of action. However, if you insist on refusing it, know that if at any time you decide to reconsider, my offer will remain open.'

Truly, he was the kindest of men. The shock and outrage and dismay of the day taking its toll, she felt an annoyingly missish desire to burst into tears.

'I will do so. Thank you.'

He bowed. 'I will send a note to Lady Denby, offering to

call and tender my apologies if she permits. Will you let me know before you leave, so I might bid you goodbye?'

'It would probably be wiser if we go our separate ways as quickly as possible.'

'As you wish.' He approached her then, halting one step away. Her body quivered in response to his nearness.

'It has been a most…interesting association, Miss Denby.' He held out his hand and reluctantly she laid hers in his as he brought her fingers to his lips. Little sparks danced and tingled and shivered from her fingernails outwards.

'I will remain always your most devoted servant.'

Snatching back the hand that didn't want to follow her instructions to remove itself from his grasp, she curtsied and watched him stride out of the room, telling herself this was for the best.

And the sooner she got back to Denby Lodge, the better.

Chapter Nine

Max stalked from Lady Denby's sitting room towards the library, anger, outrage and frustration churning in his gut. Encountering one of the guests in the hallway, avid curiosity in his eyes, Max gave him such a thunderous glare, the man pivoted without speaking and fled in the opposite direction.

Stomping into his haven, he went straight to the brandy decanter, poured and downed a glass, then poured another, welcoming the burn of the liquor down his throat.

What a calamity of a day.

Throwing himself into one of the wing chairs by the fire, he wondered despairingly how everything could have gone so wrong. It seemed impossible that, just a few bare hours ago, he'd halted on the threshold of the conservatory and breathed deeply of the fragrant air, his spirits rising on its scented promise that life was going to get better.

Instead, events had taken a turn that could end up anywhere from worse to disastrous.

Reviewing the scene in the glasshouse, he swore again. Hadn't Vienna taught him not to embroil himself in the problems of females wholly unrelated to him? Apparently not, for though, unlike Madame Lefevre, he acquitted the Denby girl of deliberately drawing him into this fiasco, by watching over her he'd been dragged in anyway.

And might very well be forced into wedding a lady with whom, by her own admission, he had virtually nothing in common.

True, Miss Denby had turned down his offer. But he placed no reliance on her continuing to do so, once her stepmother brought home to her just how difficult her situation would be if they didn't marry.

His wouldn't be as dire, but the resulting scandal certainly wouldn't be helpful. With a sardonic curl of his lip, he recalled Miss Denby's blithe assumption that since he already had a reputation as a rake, the scandal wouldn't affect him at all. He'd been on the point of explaining that, even for a rake, there were limits to acceptable behaviour and ruining a young lady of quality went rather beyond them.

But if the danger to her own reputation wasn't enough to convince her, he wasn't about to whine to her about the damage not wedding her would do to his own.

There might be some small benefit to be squeezed from disaster: if he were thought to be a heartless seducer, he'd no longer be a target for the schemes of matchmaking mamas and their devious daughters. However, for someone about to go hat in hand looking for a government posting, the timing couldn't be worse. Being branded as a man unable to regulate his behaviour around women certainly wouldn't help his chances of finding a sponsor…or winning back Wellington's favour.

He seized his empty glass and threw it into the fireplace.

He was still brooding over what to do when Alastair came in.

'Devil's teeth, Max, what fandango occurred while I was

out today? Even the grooms are buzzing with it—some crazy tale of you trying to ravish some chit in the conservatory?'

Max debated telling Alastair the truth, but his hot-headed cousin would probably head out straight away to track down Henshaw and challenge him to a duel, pressing the issue until the man was forced to face him or leave the country in disgrace.

Of course, being an excellent shot as well as a superior swordsman, if Alastair prevailed upon Henshaw to meet him, his cousin would kill the weasel for certain—and then *he*'d be forced to leave England.

He'd complicated his own life sufficiently; he didn't intend to ruin Alastair's as well.

'I...got a bit carried away. Lady Melross and her crony came running in before I could set the young lady to rights.'

Alastair studied his face. 'I heard the chit's bodice was torn to her bosom, the buttons of her pelisse scattered all over the floor. Devil take it, Max, don't try to gammon me. You've infinitely more finesse than that...and if you wanted a woman, you wouldn't have to rip her out of her gown—in a public place, no less!'

Wishing he hadn't tossed away his perfectly good glass, Max rummaged for one on the sideboard and poured himself another brandy. 'I'm really not at liberty to say any more.'

'Damn and blast, you can't think I'd believe that Banbury tale! Did the Denby chit deliberately try to trap you? Dammit, I *liked* her! Surely you're not going to let her get away with this!'

'If by "getting away with it", you mean forcing me to marry her, you're out there. I made her an offer, as any gentleman of honour would in such a situation, but thus far, she's refused it.'

Alastair stared at him for a long moment, then poured himself a brandy. 'This whole story,' he said, downing a large swallow, 'makes no sense at all.'

'With that, I can agree,' Max said.

Suddenly, Alastair threw back his head and laughed. 'Won't need to worry about the Melross hag blackening your character in town. After bringing her party to such a scandalous conclusion, *Jane*'s going to murder you.'

'Maybe I'll hand her the pistol,' Max muttered.

'To women!' Alastair held up his glass before tossing down the rest of the brandy. 'One of the greatest scourges on the face of the earth. I don't know what in hell happened today in the conservatory and, if you don't want to tell me, that's an end to it. But I do know you'd never do anything to harm a female and I'll stand beside you, no matter what lies that dragon Melross and her pack of seditious gossips spread.'

Suddenly a wave of weariness come over Max...as it had in the wake of the Vienna disaster, when he'd wandered back to his rooms, numbed by shock, disbelief and a sense of incredulity that things could possibly have turned out so badly when he'd done nothing wrong. 'Thank you,' he said, setting down his glass.

Alastair poured them both another. 'Ransleigh Rogues,' he said, touching his glass to Max's.

Before Max could take another sip, a footman entered, handing him a note written on Barton Abbey stationery. A flash of foreboding filled him—had Miss Denby already reconsidered?

But when he broke the seal, he discovered the note came from Lady Denby.

After thanking him for his offer to apologise and his assurance that he stood by his proposal to marry her stepdaughter, since Miss Denby informed her she had no intention of accepting him, there was really nothing else to be said. As both Miss Denby and her own daughter were most anxious to depart as soon as possible, she intended to leave immediately, but reserved the privilege of writing to him again when she'd had more opportunity to Sort Matters Out, at which time she trusted he would still be willing, as a Man of Honour, to Do The Right Thing.

An almost euphoric sense of relief filled Max. Apparently Lady Denby hadn't managed to convince her *stepdaughter* to 'Do the Right Thing' before leaving Barton Abbey. With Miss Denby about to get everything she wanted—a return to her beloved Denby Lodge and a ruination that would allow her to wait in peace for the return of her Harry—Max was nearly certain no amount of Sorting Things Out later would convince Miss Denby to reconsider.

He'd remain a free man after all.

The misery of the day lightened just a trifle. Now he must concentrate on trying to limit the damage to his prospects of a career.

'Good news?' Alastair asked.

Max grinned at him. 'The best. It appears I will not have to get leg-shackled after all. Amazingly, Miss Denby has resisted her stepmother's attempts to convince her to marry me.'

Alastair whistled. 'Amazing indeed! She must be dicked in the nob to discard a foolproof hand for forcing the Magnificent Max Ransleigh into marriage, but no matter.'

'There's an army sweetheart she's waiting to marry.'

'Better him than you,' Alastair said as he refilled their glasses. 'Here's to Miss Denby's resistance and remaining unwed!'

'Add a government position to that and I'll be a happy man.'

Max knew the worst wasn't over yet. Whispers about the scandal in the conservatory would doubtless have raced through the rest of the company like a wildfire through parched grass. At some point, Aunt Grace would summon him in response to the note he'd sent her, wanting to know why he'd created such an uproar at her house party.

The two cousins remained barricaded in the library, from which stronghold they occasionally heard the thumps and bangs of footmen descending the stairs with the baggage of departing guests. But as the hour grew later without his aunt summoning him, Max guessed that some guests had chosen to remain another night, doubtless eager to grill their hostess for every detail over dinner, embarrassing Felicity, making Jane simmer and contemplate murder.

Alastair, ever loyal, kept him company, playing a few desultory hands of cards after he'd declined the offer of billiards. He wasn't sure he'd trust himself with a cue in hand without trying to break it over someone's head.

Probably his own.

So it was nearly midnight when a footman bowed himself in to tell him Mrs Ransleigh begged the indulgence of a few words with him in her sitting room.

Max swallowed hard. Now he must face the lady who'd stood by him, disparaging his father's conduct and insisting he deserved better. And just like Vienna, though all he had done was assist a woman in distress, this time he'd ended up miring not just himself, but also his aunt, in embarrassment and scandal.

He'd not whined to Miss Denby about the black mark that would be left on his character by her refusal to wed; he wasn't going to make excuses to his aunt, either. Girding himself to endure anger and recriminations, he crossed the room.

Alastair, who knew only too well what he'd face, gave him an encouraging slap on the shoulder as he walked by.

He found his aunt reclining on her couch in a dressing gown, eyes closed. She sat up with a start as the footman announced him, her eyes shadowed with fatigue, filling with tears as he approached.

His chest tightening, he felt about as miserable as he'd ever felt in his life. Rather than cause his aunt pain, he almost wished he'd fallen with the valiant at Hougoumont.

'Aunt Grace,' he murmured, kissing her outstretched fingers. 'I am so sorry.'

But instead of the reproaches he'd steeled himself to endure, she pushed herself from her seat and enveloped him in a hug. 'Oh, my poor Max, under which unlucky star were you born that such trouble has come into your life?'

Hugging her back, he muttered. 'Lord knows. If I were one of the ancients, I'd think I'd somehow offended Aphrodite.'

'Come, sit by me,' she said, patting the sofa beside her.

Heartened by her unexpectedly sympathetic reception, he took a seat. 'I'd been prepared to have you abuse my character and order me from the house. I cannot imagine why you have not, after I've unleashed such a sordid scandal at your house party.'

'I imagine Anita Melross was delighted,' she said drily. 'She will doubtless dine out for weeks on the story of how she found you in the conservatory. Dreadful woman! How infuriating that she is so well connected, one cannot simply cut her. But enough about Anita. Oh, Max, what are we to do now?'

'There isn't much that can be done. Lady Melross and her minions will have already set the gossip mill in motion, thoroughly shredding my character. Frankly, I expected you to take part in the process.'

'Frankly, I might have,' his aunt retorted, 'had Miss Denby not insisted upon speaking with me before she left.'

Surprise rendered him momentarily speechless. 'Miss Denby spoke with you?' he echoed an instant later.

'I must admit, I was so angry with both of you, I had no desire whatsoever to listen to any excuses she wished to offer. But she was quite adamant.' His aunt laughed. 'Indeed, she told Wendell she would not quit the passage outside my chamber until she was permitted to see me. I'm so glad now that she persisted, for she confessed the whole to me—something I expect that you, my dear Max, would not have done.'

'She…told you everything?' Max asked, that news surprising him even more than his aunt's unexpected sympathy.

His aunt nodded. 'How Mr Henshaw made her an offer, so insistent upon her acceptance he was ready to attack her to force it! I was never so distressed!' she cried, putting a hand on her chest. 'Is there truly no way to lay the blame for that shocking attack where it belongs, at Henshaw's feet?'

'If Miss Denby disclosed the whole of what happened, you must see that there is virtually no chance we could fix the responsibility on him.'

'Poor child! I feel wretched that someone I invited into my home would take such unspeakable liberties! With her shyness and lack of polish, she would never have found much success in the Marriage Mart, but to have her ruined by that… that infamous blackguard! And then, to have *you* wrongfully accused for her disgrace! 'Tis monstrous, all of it!'

Max sat back, his emotions in turmoil. Though he hadn't truly blamed Miss Denby for what had happened, he'd resented the fact that, at the end of it all, *she* had got what she wanted, while *he* was left a position that made obtaining his goal much more difficult.

Still, he could work relentlessly until he achieved what he wanted; her ruination couldn't be undone. It had taken courage to insist on braving the contempt of her hostess so she might explain what had really transpired, thereby exonerating him to a woman whose good opinion she must know he treasured.

In refusing to allow herself to be forced into something she did not want, regardless of the personal cost, and in remaining steadfastly loyal to her childhood love, she'd displayed a sense of honour as unshakeable as his own. He couldn't help admiring that.

'I hardly expected her to tell you the truth…but I'm glad she did,' he said at last.

'Oh, Max, you would have said nothing and simply shouldered all the blame, would you not?' she asked, seizing his hands.

He shrugged. 'With Henshaw showing himself too dishonourable to admit to his actions, I don't see how I could avoid it. There was no point making accusations we have no way of proving.'

'Are you certain that's the right course? It seems monstrous that you both must suffer, while the guilty party escapes all blame!'

'We'll have to endure it, at least for the present. I intend to quietly search for evidence that might incriminate Henshaw, but I'm not hopeful anything useful will turn up. In the interim, I'd rather Alastair not learn the truth. He's already suspicious of Lady Melross's story. If he were to find out what really happened, he might go after Henshaw and—'

'—tear him limb from limb, or something equally rash,' Mrs Ransleigh finished for him. 'Although it will chafe him to be kept in the dark, I appreciate your doing it. Ever since… That Woman, he's been so reckless and bitter. Even after all those years in the army, he's still spoiling for a fight, still heedless of the consequences.'

'It shall remain our secret, then.'

She sighed. 'If there is any way I might be of assistance, let me know. I can think of little that would give me more pleasure than being able to show up Anita Melross for the idle, malicious gossip she is.'

'If the opportunity arises, I will certainly call on your help.

By the way…did Miss Denby also tell you I'd asked for her hand and she'd refused me?'

'She did. Bless the child, she even said that after you had been everything that was gentlemanly, preventing Henshaw from ravishing her and comforting her afterwards, she simply could not repay your kindness by shackling you to a girl you didn't want. She insisted you must remain free to take a wife of your own choosing, who would be the suitable hostess and companion to a man in high position that she could never be.'

Max smiled, his spirits lightened by the first glimmer of amusement he'd felt since Lady Melross burst into the conservatory. 'Difficult to be angry with someone who rejects you with such glowing compliments.'

'And such absolute sincerity! It was the longest and most eloquent speech I've got from her since her arrival. Perhaps she isn't quite as hopeless as I'd thought.'

Max resisted the impulse to defend Miss Denby. How well she'd cultivated the image of an awkward, ill-spoken spinster! If only his aunt could have seen her, fierce determination in her eyes as she'd vividly described her world at Denby Lodge.

She'd been quite magnificent. Even had he wished to wed her, he would have felt compelled to let her go.

'I must say, I was relieved to discover she has an army beau who will marry her when he returns,' Mrs Ransleigh continued. 'Having been the unwitting instrument of her disgrace, it makes me feel a bit better to know she won't be condemned for ever to live without the care and protection of a good man.'

Max nodded. 'That's the only reason I didn't push her harder to marry me. Not that I'd ever force myself on a woman.'

'Of course you would not. Well, I'm off to bed. Calamities such as the events that transpired today exhaust me! But I did not wish to sleep before telling you I knew everything, lest you take it in your head to lope off somewhere in the night, still believing I thought ill of you.'

'I'm so glad you do not. And I've no plans to take myself off as yet.'

'Stay as long as you like,' his aunt said as she offered him her cheek to kiss. 'By the way, I should like to reveal the truth to Jane. She is perfectly discreet and, as she is now quite an influential hostess in London, she might find the means to be of some help.'

'Miss Denby already mentioned that Lady Denby hoped to enlist you and Jane in defending her stepsister; I'd appreciate anything you might do to assist Miss Denby as well. Of all the unwilling participants in this débâcle, she is the one who loses the most.'

Mrs Ransleigh nodded. 'We will certainly give it our best efforts.'

'I'll leave you to your slumber, then. Thank you, Aunt Grace. For still believing in me.'

'You're quite welcome,' she replied with a smile. 'You might want to thank Miss Denby, too, for believing in you as well.'

Bidding her goodnight, Max walked out. Though he hadn't yet worked out how he was going to work around this check to his governmental aspirations, he felt immeasurably better to know that he had not, after all, disappointed and alienated his aunt.

That happy outcome he owed to Miss Denby. He found her courage in risking censure to defend him to his family as amazing as her fortitude in refusing a convenient marriage.

Aunt Grace was right. He did owe her thanks. But given the disastrous events that seemed to happen when she came near him, he didn't think he'd risk delivering it in person any time soon.

Chapter Ten

In the late afternoon a month later, Caroline Denby turned the last gelding over to the stable boy and walked out of the barn. After returning from the disaster at Barton Abbey, she'd thrown herself into working with the horses, readying them for the upcoming autumn sale. But as she'd suspected, though she'd left the scandal behind, its repercussions continued to follow her.

In the last two weeks, several gentlemen who'd not previously purchased mounts from the stud had journeyed into Kent, claiming they wished to view and evaluate the stock. Since the gentlemen had spent more time gawking at her than at the horses, she suspected their real interest had been to inspect for themselves the subject of Lady Melross's most titillating gossip—the hoyden who'd been discovered half-naked with Max Ransleigh.

If they'd been expecting some seductive siren, she'd doubtless sent them away disappointed, Caro thought with a sigh.

At least there was no question of her returning to London for another Season, and after a week of fruitless attempts, Lady Denby had given up trying to convince her to marry Max Ransleigh as well. Though Eugenia still hadn't entirely forgiven her for the débâcle which had put such an unpleasant end to the house party, when Caro had explained during the drive home what had really happened, her stepsister had been first shocked, then indignant, then had wept at the outrage she had suffered.

So it now appeared, Caro thought with satisfaction as she paced up the steps into the manor and tossed her gloves and crop to the butler, that she'd gained what she'd wanted all along: to be left in peace to run her farm.

She was hopeful that Eugenia would also get what she wanted, the successful Season she'd dreamed of for so long. While Caro worked with her horses, Lady Denby had been busy with correspondence, consulting with Lady Gilford and Mrs Ransleigh and writing to her many friends to ensure enough support for Eugenia's début that her prospects would not suffer because of Caro's scandal.

Grateful for that, Caroline refused to regret what had happened. And if she sometimes woke in the night, her soul awash with yearning as she recalled being cradled against a broad chest, while a strong finger gently caressed her cheek and a deep masculine voice murmured soothingly against her hair, she would, in time, get over it.

Garbed in her usual working attire of breeches and boots, she intended to tiptoe quietly up to her chamber and change into more conventional clothing before dinner. But as she crept past the parlour, Lady Denby called out, 'Caroline, is that you? I must speak to you at once!'

Wondering what she could have done now to distress Lady Denby, she changed course and proceeded into the room. 'Yes, Stepmama?'

In her agitation, Lady Denby didn't so much as frown at Caro's breeches. 'Oh, my dear, I fear I may have inadvertently done you a grave disservice!'

Foreboding slammed like a fist into her chest. 'What are you talking about?'

Lady Denby gave her a guilty look. 'Well, you see, after the events at Barton Abbey, I wrote to the trustees of your father's estate, informing them you were to be married and asking that the solicitors begin working on marriage settlements.' Before Caroline could protest, she rushed on, 'I was so very sure you would, in the end, be convinced to marry! Then last week, after finally conceding there would be no wedding, I wrote back to them, telling them you had refused Mr Ransleigh's offer. In today's post, I received a reply from Lord Woodbury.'

'Woodbury?' Caro gave a contemptuous snort. 'I can only imagine what *he* had to say about it. How I wish Papa had not made him head of the trustees!'

'Well, dear, he was one of your papa's closest friends and his estate at Mendinhall is very prosperous, so it's not unreasonable that Papa thought Woodbury would take equal care of yours.'

'I won't deny that he's a good steward,' Caro replied, 'but Woodbury never approved of my working the stud. The last time they met, he told Papa he thought it well past time for me to put on proper dress and start behaving like a woman of my rank, instead of racketing about the stables, hobnobbing with grooms and coachmen.'

When Lady Denby remained tactfully silent—probably more in agreement with Lord Woodbury's views than with her own—Caroline said, 'What did Lord Woodbury write, then?'

Her stepmother sighed. 'You're not going to like it. Apparently he heard about the events at Barton Abbey. He claims the shock of it must have unbalanced your mind for, he wrote, no young lady of breeding in her right senses, caught in such a dire situation, would ever turn down a respectable offer of marriage. He's convinced your, um, "unnatural preoccupation" with running the stud has made you unable to realise how badly the scandal reflects upon you and the entire family. So, to protect you and the Denby name, he's convinced the other trustees to agree to something he's long been urging: the sale of the stud.'

Shock froze her in place, while her heart stood still and blood seemed to drain from her head and limbs. Dizzy, she grabbed the back of a wing chair to steady herself. 'The sale of the stud?' she repeated, stunned. 'He wants to sell *my horses*?'

'Y-yes, my dear.'

It was impossible. It was outrageous. Aside from Lady Denby's generous widow's portion, the rest of the estate, including Denby Lodge, the Denby Stud and the income to operate it, had been willed to her. Papa had always promised the farm and the land would remain hers, for her use and then as part of her dowry.

She shook her head to clear the faintness. 'Can they do that?' she demanded, her voice trembling.

'I don't know. Oh, my dear, I'm so sorry! I know how much the stud means to you.'

'How much… Why, it means *everything*,' Caro said, feeling returning to her limbs in a rush of fury. 'Everything I've worked for these last ten years! Has it been done yet? May I see the note?'

Silently, her stepmother held it out. Caroline snatched and read it through rapidly.

'It does not appear the sale has gone through yet,' she said, when she had finished it. 'There must be some way to stop it. The stud belongs to me!'

But even as she made the bold declaration, doubt and dread rose up to check her like a ten-foot gate before a novice jumper.

Did she have control of the stud? Numb, shocked and trying to cope with the immensity of her father's sudden death, she'd sat silent and vacant-headed during the reading of his will. Thinking back, she knew the assets of the estate had been turned over to trustees to manage for her, but no details about how the trust was to be administered, or the extent of the powers granted the trustees, had penetrated her pall of grief and pain.

'What will you do?' Lady Denby asked.

'I shall leave for London tomorrow at first light and consult Papa's solicitor. Mr Henderson will know if anything can be done.'

Lady Denby shook her head. 'I'm so sorry, Caroline. I would never have written if I'd had any suspicion Lord Woodbury would do such a thing.'

Absently Caroline patted her hand. 'It's not your fault. According to the note, Woodbury has been trying to convince the other trustees to sell the stud for some time.'

Anguish twisted in her gut as the scene played out in her head: some stranger arriving to lead away Sultan, whom she'd eased from his mother's body the night he was born. She'd put on him his first halter, his first saddle. Turning over Sultan, or Sheik's Ransom or Arabian Lady or Cleveland's Hope or any of the horses she'd worked with from foal to weaning to training, would be like having someone confiscate her brothers and sisters.

'Thank you for telling me at once,' she said, brisk purpose submerging her anxiety—at least for the moment. 'Now, you will please excuse me. I must confer with Newman in the stables, so he may continue the training while I'm gone.' She dismissed the flare of panic in her belly at the thought that when she came back, she might no longer be giving the orders. 'Would you ring Dulcie for me and ask her to pack some things?'

'While you're at the stables, be sure to tell John Coachman to ready the travelling barouche.'

Already pacing towards the door, Caro shook her head impatiently. 'No, I'll go by mail coach; it will be faster.'

'By mail coach!' Lady Denby gasped. 'But…that will not be at all proper! If you don't wish to take the barouche, at least hire a carriage.'

'My dear Stepmama, I don't wish to make the journey in the easy stages required if I'm forced to hire horses along the way! I'll take Dulcie to lend me some countenance,' she added. Despite her agitation, she had to grin at the dismay the maid would doubtless feel upon being informed she would be rattling around in a public vehicle, probably stuffed full of other travellers, that broke its journey at the inns along the route only for the few minutes required to change the horses.

'Where will you stay in London?' Lady Denby cried, following her out into the passage.

'With Cousin Elizabeth. Or at a hotel, if she's not in town. If necessary, Mr Henderson will find me something suitable. Now I must go. I have a hundred things to do before the Royal Mail leaves tomorrow.'

Giving her stepmother's hand a quick squeeze, Caro strode through the entry, trotted down the steps and, once out of her stepmother's sight, set off at a run for the stables.

It was long past dark by the time she'd concluded her rounds of the stalls with Newman, her head trainer, reviewing with him the regimen she wished him to follow with each horse.

'Don't you worry, Miss Caroline,' he told her when they'd finished. 'Your late father, God rest 'im, trained me and every groom at Denby Stables. We'll do whatever's needful to carry on. You go up to London and do what you must. And, miss…' he added gruffly, giving her arm an awkward pat, 'best of luck to you.'

With a wisp of a smile, Caro watched him go. Even after

so many years of living in a large household, it never ceased to amaze her how quickly news travelled through invisible servants' networks. Although she'd told Newman nothing beyond the fact that urgent business called her away to London, somehow he must have discovered the true reason behind her journey.

Her final stop before returning to the house was Sultan's box. 'No, my handsome boy, I'll not take you with me this time,' she told him as she stroked the velvet nose. 'You're too fine a horse to risk having you turn an ankle in some pothole, racing through the dark to London. Though you would fly to take me there, if I asked you.'

The gelding nosed her hand and nickered his agreement.

The darkness seemed to close around her, magnifying the fear and anxiety she'd been struggling to hold at bay. Sensing her distress, Sultan nosed her again and rubbed his neck against her hand. Trying to give her comfort, it seemed.

What comfort would she have, if she lost him, lost them all? She had no siblings, no close neighbours other than Harry, and he was off in India. All her life, her horses had been her friends and playmates. She'd poured out her problems and told them her secrets, while they listened, nickering encouragement and sympathy.

Denby Lodge was a vast holding, its wealth derived from farms, cattle and fields planted in corn and other crops. Like her father, she'd been content to let the estate manager—and then the trustees in London—concern themselves with the other businesses, as she let the housekeeper manage the manor itself and its servants, while she focused solely on managing the stud.

She'd not been dissembling when she told Henshaw she possessed no feminine talents. She didn't sew or embroider, paint, sing, or play an instrument. What was she to do with herself without her horses to birth, raise and train?

It was all she knew. All she had ever done. All she had ever wanted to do. What could she find to replace the long hours spent in these immaculately kept barns with their rows of box stalls, where every breath brought the familiar scents of hay and bran and horse, saddle leather and polished brass? What could replace the thrill of feeling a thousand pounds of stallion thundering under her as he galloped across a meadow, responding to signals she'd ingrained in him after hours and hours of patient, careful training?

After all she had done to keep the stud, it was intolerable that some self-important peer, who wished to dictate to her what a woman's place should be, might have the power to strip it all from her.

What was to become of her if Woodbury succeeded?

Weary, anxious, desperate, she wrapped her arms around Sultan's neck and wept.

Chapter Eleven

Little more than thirty hours later, Caroline climbed down from the hackney that had brought her back from the solicitor's office and walked slowly up the stairs into her cousin Elizabeth's modest town house. A house that been part of her cousin's marriage settlements, fortunately, Caro thought, making it one of the few assets her profligate husband hadn't been able to squander.

Oh, fortunate Elizabeth.

A dull ache in her head, she felt the weariness of every sleepless hour she'd endured, from her last night at Denby Lodge, briefing the trainer and preparing for the journey, to the long dusty, uncomfortable transit into London. She'd barely taken the time to greet Elizabeth and inform her about her urgent mission before leaving for Mr Henderson's office.

Where she was met by the chilling news that her trustees, approved by the Court of Chancery under her father's will to care for her inheritance, definitely had the legal right to sell off any land or assets they saw fit, for the good of the estate.

Lady Elizabeth was out, the butler told her as he let her in. Her chest so tight with pain and outrage she could barely breathe, too exhausted to sleep, Caroline went to the small

study, took paper and scrawled a letter to Harry, pouring into
it all her anguished desperation.

Not that it would make any difference; she probably
wouldn't even post it. By the time the letter reached Harry,
even if he wrote back immediately, agreeing to marry her by
proxy, it would be too late. The sale, Mr Henderson had advised her this afternoon, was already near to being concluded.

She was going to lose the stud.

That awful fact echoed in hollowness of her belly like a
shot ricocheting inside a stone building, chipping off pieces
that could wound and maim. She felt her heart's blood oozing out even now.

She might as well shoot herself and get it over with, she
thought bleakly.

A rustling in the passageway announced her cousin Elizabeth's return. Not wishing to leave the letter there, where
some curious servant might read her ramblings, she quickly
sanded and folded it and scrawled Harry's name on the top.
Setting it to the side of the desk, she rose to meet her cousin.

Elizabeth took one look at her face and gathered her into
a hug.

'Men!' she said bitterly, releasing Caro before linking arms
and leading her to the sofa. 'They shape our world, write its
laws and pretend we are helpless creatures who cannot be
trusted to manage our own lives. So they can take it all.'

'At least you have your house. Maybe I can come and reside with you, once…once it's gone. I don't think I can bear
to live at Denby Lodge, afterwards.'

'You'd certainly be welcome. I don't have nearly the income I once did, but it's enough for us to manage.'

'Oh, I should have wealth aplenty for us both, especially
after the sale. My kind trustees are managing the estate so
brilliantly, I should be awash in guineas. Lord Woodbury
would doubtless approve my buying every feminine frip-

pery under the sun…as long as I don't do the only thing in life I care about.'

Elizabeth poured them wine and handed Caro a glass. 'Come and live with me, then. We'll be two eccentric blue-stockings, keeping pugs, reading scientific tracts and nattering on about the rights of working women and prostitutes, like that Mary Wollstonecraft creature.'

Caro attempted a smile, but with her whole world disintegrating around her, she didn't have the heart to appreciate her cousin's attempt at humour. 'You should think twice before making such an offer. I'm a social pariah now, remember.'

Her cousin merely laughed. 'Oh, yes, I've heard the fantastical tale Lady Melross has been spreading. You, baring your bosom to snag a gentleman? Max Ransleigh, rake though he be, mauling a gently born girl in his own aunt's conservatory? No one who knows either of you could possibly believe it.'

In no mood to recount the story again, despite the curiosity in her cousin's eyes, Caro merely shrugged.

Tacitly accepting her reluctance, Elizabeth sighed. 'Is there no way to get around Lord Woodbury?'

'Only if I could find a fortune hunter desperate enough to escort me to Gretna Green tonight.'

Elizabeth shuddered. 'Don't even joke of such a thing! Besides, wouldn't Woodbury put a stop to that, too?'

'He couldn't; I'm of age. And, once married, my new husband would take ownership of everything from the trustees, with the power to cancel the sale.'

'I trust you are only jesting,' Elizabeth said, looking at her with concern. 'Gaining a husband would give you no more control over your wealth than your trustees do, as I learned to my sorrow. Oh, if only Harry were not so far away in India!'

'I know,' Caro said, feeling tears again prick her eyes. She'd never expected that at the most desperate hour of her life her closest childhood friend would be too far away to help

her. 'I wrote to him tonight, useless as that was. But the plain
fact is he's not here, nor could he possibly return before the
sale goes through…and then the stud is lost to me for ever.'

Merely saying the words sent a knife-like pain slashing
through her. Lips trembling, she pushed the image of Sultan
from her mind.

'That soon?' Elizabeth was saying. 'I'm almost willing to
draw up a list of eligible gentlemen.'

'He could have all my money, as long as he left me enough
to maintain the stud. If only I knew someone besides Harry
who'd be honourable enough to make such a bargain and
keep—' Caroline broke off abruptly as Max Ransleigh's
words echoed in her ears: *You could run the stud with my
blessing…*

A near-hysterical excitement blazing new energy into her,
she seized her cousin's arm. 'Elizabeth, you are acquainted
with the Ransleighs, aren't you?'

'I haven't moved in their circles since my début Season,
but I still count Jane Ransleigh as a friend. She's Lady Gilford now, one of society's most important—'

'Yes, yes, I know her,' Caroline interrupted. 'Is she in
town? Could you get a message to her?'

'I suppose so. What is it, Caro? You're as white as if you
were about to faint—and you're hurting my arm.'

'Sorry,' she mumbled, releasing it at once. Lightheaded,
desperate, feeling every hour she'd gone without food and
sleep and rest, she said, 'I must get a message to her cousin,
Max Ransleigh. Tonight, if possible.'

'Max Ransleigh? Ah, the man who…' Comprehension
dawned in Elizabeth's eyes. 'Are you sure?'

'I am. Though I'm not at all sure, after the scandal I
dragged him into, that Lady Gilford would agree to give me
his direction.'

'You don't have to ask her. Max is here now, in London.

Jane told me at tea last week that he'd come to town to meet with the colonel who used to command his regiment.'

'Do you know where he is staying?

'No, but Tilly, my maid, could find out. A friend of hers is the housekeeper's assistant for Lady Gilford.'

'Could you ask her to go to Lady Gilford's at once?'

Elizabeth studied her. 'Are you sure you want to do this?'

'No,' Caro replied, panic and hope coursing through her in equal measure. 'Nor have I any assurance he would even agree to see me, if I can locate him. But it's the only chance I've got. The sale will be final before the month's end.'

'What about the Curse? Your mother, aunt, cousin, grand-mother—every female on your mother's side, for the last two generations has died in childbed. I thought you intended never to risk that.'

Putting out of her mind the heat that had flared between them in the glasshouse, Caro said, 'Mr Ransleigh's only seen me in atrocious gowns and in breeches, so maybe he won't want that from me. By all accounts, he prefers beautiful, sophisticated women and I'm hardly that. I'd give him free rein, with my blessing, to pursue and bed any other woman he wished.'

Elizabeth's eyes shadowed; Caro knew her husband had availed himself of that privilege without his wife's blessing. And despite her passionate love for him.

Maybe there was something to be said for wedding with cool calculation, with no emotions involved.

'Even if he took his pleasure elsewhere, he'd want to couple with his wife. Like every other man, he'll want an heir.'

'Perhaps. I'll worry about that later, after I save the stud.'

'What about Harry?' Elizabeth persisted.

A bittersweet pang went through her. She'd never imagined a future that did not include working the stud with Harry, the two of them linked by the same companionable affection they'd shared since childhood.

Pushing away the doubts, she said, 'What good would it be to have Harry, with no stud to run? Once the horses are sold and scattered, it would be nearly impossible to reassemble the breeding stock. As for the Curse, what good is hanging on to life if I've already lost what I love the most? No, Elizabeth, if there is a single chance of saving my horses, I simply must take it.'

Elizabeth hesitated another moment, frowning. 'I'm not at all sure this is wise, but…very well, I'll send Tilly to Lady Gilford's.'

Caroline crushed her cousin in a hug, hope and fear and desperation racing through her with the speed of a thoroughbred galloping towards the finish line at Newmarket. 'I'm not sure it's wise either. But ask her to hurry.'

On the other side of Mayfair, Max Ransleigh was sharing a brandy with the colonel of his former regiment at his lodgings at Albany.

'I appreciate your support, sir,' Max told him.

Colonel Brandon nodded brusquely. 'Can't trust these civilians not to muck things up. Foreign Office!' He snorted. 'If any of them had ever faced down fire in the heat of battle, they'd know the mettle of the men who fought beside them beyond any doubt. The very idea that you could have anything to do with that attempt against Wellington would be considered insulting and ridiculous by any soldier who ever served with you. As the scurvy diplomats should have realised.'

'If my own father wasn't willing to go to my defence, I don't suppose I can complain about the Foreign Office's lack of support,' Max countered, trying to keep the bitterness from his tone.

'Your father's a political type and they are even worse than the Foreign Office. I suppose policy making requires compromise, but hell's teeth, give me a battlefield any day! No wrangling over this clause or that provision, just the enemy before you, your men around you, and duty, clear and simple.'

'After my brief time in Vienna, I must agree,' Max said.

'I've no doubt we can find you some position where you belong, in the War Department. Though I must warn you, Ransleigh, you've certainly muddied the waters with this heiress business. Not that I credit any of the wild stories floating about, but the fact that you are believed to have compromised a well-born girl and then refused to marry her won't make finding a post any easier. Especially not coming on the heels of that Vienna affair.'

So, just as he'd feared, he was being blamed for the fiasco. The anger, resentment and frustration with his situation—and Caroline Denby—that simmered just beneath the surface fired hotter and Max had to rein in the strong desire to explain what had happened and defend himself.

But the colonel wasn't interested in excuses. 'I'm well aware of that,' he said shortly.

'I cannot help but advise that it would improve your prospects if you'd just marry the chit. Or you might try to locate that damned female who tried to cozen up to you in Vienna.'

'I intended to do so right after I returned from Waterloo. But the Foreign Office gave me to understand it wouldn't make any difference.

'The Foreign Office prefers concealing dirty linen to laundering it,' the colonel said acidly. 'No, I'm convinced that if you could get her to confess to the plot, it would go a long way towards redeeming your reputation. I might even be able to talk Wellington around.'

'Do you think so?' Max tried to stifle the hope that flared within him. 'It would mean a lot to know I'd regained his trust.'

'Old Hookey is notoriously intolerant of error, but he has a soft spot for the ladies. He might be induced to see there was no other course that you, as a gentleman, could have taken but to help a female in distress.'

Max tried to curb a rising excitement. 'Then perhaps, while you look around for a posting, I'll head back to Vienna and see what I can turn up.'

'Couldn't hurt,' the colonel said. 'Those lackwits in the Foreign Office bungled their chance to have you, the fools. The War Office's a better place for the man who led the counter-charge and saved the colours at Hougoumont! Had the chateau fallen, we might have lost the whole damn battle, and now be watching Bonaparte march through Europe again. Report back to me in a month and I'll see what I can do.'

'Thank you, Colonel. I'm much in your debt.'

Brandon waved off Max's thanks. 'It's a commander's job to watch out for his men. Only wish I'd returned to London sooner, so you'd not have been left twisting in the wind for so long. Drinking and wenching is all good and well, eh?' he said, giving Max a wink. 'But a man of your talents should occupy his time with something more challenging.'

Max grinned. 'Amen to that, sir.'

After an exchange of courtesies, Max bowed and took his leave, fired with more purpose than he'd felt since leaving his unit after Waterloo. The colonel's optimism provided him the first real glimmer of hope he'd had since that awful day in Vienna, when the world as he'd known it had shattered around him like the windows of Hougoumont under French artillery fire.

After nearly a year of drifting idly about—drinking and wenching, as the colonel had said—he might finally be on the threshold of the new career for which he longed.

He might even win back Wellington's approval.

That happy thought cheered him as the hackney he'd hailed

carried him towards the lodgings in Upper Brook Street that, being barred from his own family's home in London, he'd borrowed from Alastair.

With a respectable position, he'd be able to hold his head up again when he visited his mother.

He wasn't sure when, or if, he'd seek out his father. The earl had made clear during their one meeting that his son was no longer of any use to him in the Lords and a person of no use to the earl was no longer of any importance either. The truth of that fact stung less now than it had when he'd first had to face it, after Vienna.

A short time later, the hackney halted in front of Alastair's town house. Paying off the driver, Max paced to the entry, the cold sharp night air as invigorating as the renewed hope within him.

He was about to mount the steps when, in the darkness beside the entry stairs, something stirred. Reflexes honed by years on a battlefield had him instantly whipping out the blade hidden in his boot. Half-crouched and prepared to strike, he called out, 'Who's there? Come out where I can see you!'

While he poised, knife extended, a shadow straightened and walked toward him. In the dim illumination of the streetlamp, she pulled off the hood of her cloak.

For a shocked moment he thought he must be hallucinating. 'Miss *Denby*?' he said incredulously.

'Mr Ransleigh,' she acknowledged with a nod. 'Although I may be the last person in England you wish to see, may I beg a moment of your time?'

Max blinked, still not quite believing she was standing beside his doorstep. What could have possessed her to come alone to his lodgings and wait for him in the fair middle of night?

A strong protective instinct surfaced, warning whatever brought her would likely mean yet more scandal and he'd had enough already.

'You shouldn't be here,' he said flatly, his eyes sweeping the street, which mercifully appeared to be deserted. 'Where are you staying? Give me your direction and I'll call on you tomorrow.'

'I know it's highly irregular to come here, but it's not as if I have any reputation left to lose. The matter about which I must consult you is so pressing I don't want to wait until tomorrow. That is, if…if you will consent to speak with me.'

Whatever it was, his first imperative was to get her away from his front door and out of sight of the neighbours or any passers-by returning home from some *ton* party.

'Very well. Please, do come in,' he urged, hurrying her up the stairs and through the doorway.

The sleepy footman within snapped to attention, closing his gaping mouth at Max's warning frown when he perceived Max was accompanied by a female. At Max's pointed glance, he stepped out of the way and handed over his candle.

Just what he needed, Max thought, his anger and frustration surfacing again, Miss Denby turning up to cause more problems just when Colonel Brandon was about to begin delicate negotiations to secure his future.

Max hustled her past the servant down the hall and into the back sitting room, where the glow of the light wouldn't be visible to any neighbours on the other side of Upper Brook Street. Now to discover her mission and hustle her back out again before she caused any more damage.

Chapter Twelve

Torn between irritation and curiosity over Miss Denby's audacity in sitting beside his steps like a forgotten parcel, Max tried to muster up a cordial tone. 'Perhaps you'd better explain and be on your way.'

She took a deep breath. 'When I refused your offer at Barton Abbey, you assured me that if I should ever change my mind, I should let you know.'

Max swallowed hard, her words like a noose tightening around his neck. Now, when it finally looked like he might work out the future he wanted, was she suddenly going to hold him to that honour-coerced offer?

Grasping at something to deflect her, he said, 'I seem to remember that you were quite adamant about refusing it. You insisted you would marry no one but your Harry.'

'So I was, but I've just encountered circumstances that force me to revise those plans. Upon my father's death, trustees were appointed to oversee the management of the estate he bequeathed to me. As long as they did not interfere in the running of the stables, I was perfectly content with the arrangement.'

He recalled the great lengths she had gone to, willing to sacrifice her reputation—and sully his—to maintain control over the stud. 'And now they are interfering?' he guessed.

'Worse than interfering. I've just learned they intend to sell it. A buyer has been found and, unless something happens to prevent it, in about two weeks' time the estate will no longer own the stud.'

'And you can do nothing to stop this?' he asked, appalled despite himself and keenly aware of what the loss of Denby stables would mean to her.

'Lord Woodbury, the head trustee, has never approved of my involvement with the stud. When he learned that, despite becoming embroiled in a scandal that threatened my reputation, I refused to marry, he convinced the other trustees that my unnatural position running the stud had so corrupted my feminine nature, they should sell it to "protect" me and the good name of the family from further harm. Believing that, he's unlikely to listen to any plea I might make begging him to halt the sale. The only way—'

'—is to marry and have control over your assets pass to a husband,' Max finished, understanding now why she had come to him.

'I'm desperate, or I would never be going back on my promise to leave you free to wed a woman of your choice. But you did once tell me you thought we might rub along well together, so if you would consider renewing your very kind offer, wedding me could offer you a few advantages.'

Her words tumbled over each other, as if she'd stood there in the dark rehearsing the speech over and over. Pausing only to drag in a ragged breath, she continued, 'I know you are already comfortably circumstanced, but I am a very wealthy woman. As long as you guarantee me sufficient funds to maintain the stud, you are welcome to the rest. Buy a higher rank in the army, purchase an estate, make investments on the 'Change. Travel to Vienna and hunt down the conspirators who engineered the attack on Lord Wellington. Whatever you wish that coin can buy, it can be yours.'

As if she didn't dare give him the opportunity to utter a syllable, she rushed on, 'Wedding me would also help to re-establish your reputation since, as you asserted from the first and I now recognise, my refusal to marry has most unfairly layered blame upon you. Indeed, if you truly wish to spike the guns of Lady Melross's malicious gossip, you might have Lady Gilford put it about that we've been acquainted for some time and the wedding long planned. No one would think it remarkable that the son of the Earl of Swynford, discovered caressing his almost-betrothed in a secluded conservatory, would feel no need to justify his actions or explain the nature of his relationship to a mere Lady Melross.'

The idea was so ingenious that, despite the turmoil of thoughts whirling in his brain, Max had to laugh. 'Brilliant! An audacious lie—but plausible.'

'We'd have to wed by special license, but many prominent individuals do so, to avoid the vulgar publicity of having the banns called. If Lady Gilford and her friends seemed to find nothing exceptional about it, society would accept it as well.'

'You mis-spoke, Miss Denby,' Max said, shaking his head with rueful admiration. 'You are quite diabolical. I begin to believe you'd make a master politician.'

That earned him a wisp of a smile before, clutching her hands together, she dropped her eyes, avoiding his gaze. 'As for intimacy,' she continued, her cheeks colouring, 'I should prefer a marriage in name only, for reasons I would rather not discuss. Since you aren't the eldest son, there's no title to pass along. Having already asked so huge a favour, I should make no other claim upon your time or your affections. Although, obviously, you would not be free to marry, I will neither in-terfere in nor protest at any other relationship you choose to enter. Although if…if you felt for some reason that you *must* exercise your marital rights…well, I realise I would have no grounds to refuse you.'

Taking another deep breath, she raised her chin and faced him squarely. 'So that is the bargain. I don't expect you to give me an answer tonight, but I will need your reply within a few days. I know I have no right to intrude upon you with my dilemma…but the stud is my life. With everything I am and everything I love about to be stripped away, I simply had to seize any possible chance to prevent it.'

She fell silent, watching him, her dark eyes huge and imploring in a face lined with weariness. Tears had gathered at the corners of her eyes, he noted, sparkling like brilliants in the candlelight.

A host of questions crowded to his lips, even as his startled wits tried to sort out the preposterous new scheme she'd just laid in front of him. But before he had a chance to ask any of them, she sighed and hoisted herself unsteadily to her feet.

'I'll go now, through the kitchen if the footman will lead me out, so it's less likely any of your neighbours might see me and make matters worse. If such a thing is possible.'

But as she took a step, she stumbled and fell forwards. Max jumped up to catch her before she tumbled to the floor, her slight frame swaying in his hands.

'You're not well,' he exclaimed, all the questions swirling in his mind slamming to a halt at that observation. 'Here, sit back down.'

He eased her into the chair, sure she would have collapsed had he not supported her weight. 'Where is Lady Denby? When did you arrive in London?'

She gave her head a small shake, as if the answer to so simple a question was a profound mystery. 'I arrived…this afternoon? Yes, it was this afternoon. Just myself and my maid. Stepmother got Lord Woodbury's letter two days ago; I travelled post yesterday and last night, arriving today to consult with Papa's solicitor and see if anything could be done.'

'You travelled post yesterday?' he repeated with a frown. 'When did you last sleep? Two nights ago? Three?'

'I don't recall.' She scrubbed a hand over her eyes, as if trying to clear the exhaustion from them. 'Something like that.'

'When did you last eat?'

'I'm not sure. The Royal Mail stops only to change horses, you know, not long enough to order a meal. Upon reaching London, I went directly to the solicitor's office, then back to my cousin Elizabeth's. And when I thought maybe you could help me, I came here.'

'Sit back in that chair before you fall out of it,' he ordered, pacing over to throw open the door. The footman he'd intended to call stood just beyond the threshold; from the flush on the man's face and his half-bending stance, Max suspected he'd been listening through the keyhole.

'Fetch some bread, cheese and ham,' he instructed. 'Brandy for me and some water.'

'No, you needn't entertain me,' Miss Denby protested as he closed the door. 'I've already trespassed enough on your time. I will await your reply at my cousin's house. Lady Elizabeth Russell, in Laura Place.'

She made another wobbly attempt to rise; gently he pushed her back into her chair. 'Miss Denby, there is no way I am sending you out of the kitchen door like some Whitechapel purse-snatcher to creep home through the midnight streets. By the way, please assure me you didn't walk here alone in the dark.'

'No, I did not.'

'Thank heavens for that!'

'I took a hackney to Hyde Park and walked from there. I didn't want the neighbours to see a carriage pull up and a female alight from it before your front door.'

Which meant she had traversed quite a distance through

the London night. Though Mayfair was one of its more prosperous sections, no area of the city was entirely safe after dark for a young woman alone.

Max uttered an exasperated oath. 'Are you always this much trouble?'

'I'm afraid so,' she replied, with an apologetic look that almost made him chuckle.

'Well, your nocturnal wanderings are over,' he pronounced, curbing his humour. 'You will sit by that fire and warm yourself, then take some nourishment while I consider what is to be done.'

A ghost of a smile touched her weary lips. 'So masterful, Mr Ransleigh. Spoken like an earl's son indeed.'

Despite himself, he had to grin—was there any situation into which he'd got with this girl that didn't become absurd? 'It's the army officer in me,' he corrected.

'I knew it couldn't be the diplomat. Never make up their minds about anything without debating it for weeks.'

But, too distressed and weary, he suspected, to give more than token protest, she settled into the wing chair with a sigh, leaning her head back and closing her eyes.

Wilson returned a moment later with the refreshments, nearly goggle-eyed with curiosity. Instructing the footman to venture out into the night and find a hackey, Max closed the door in his face. Probably not even Wilson's scandalous employer Alastair had ever escorted an obviously gently bred female into the house after midnight.

'So, let me see if I understand you correctly,' he said after she'd begun dutifully nibbling on some ham and a biscuit. 'You propose that we wed immediately so that I may take charge of your assets before Lord Woodbury can sell off the stud. I would agree to allow you sufficient funds to run it and go my own way, with the rest of your dowry to invest as I see fit.'

'Correct.'

'In addition, I am free to engage in such…relationships as I choose, with your full approval.'

'Yes,' she confirmed, meeting his eyes steadily, though a hint of a blush coloured her cheeks.

He turned away, considering. Though he found her unusual and quite attractive in an unconventional way, he had no more inclination to marry now than when honour had forced him to make her an offer at Barton Abbey. Sympathetic though he was to her dire situation, his first impulse was to refuse.

But then he recalled Brandon's advice that the most helpful thing he could do to speed the colonel's efforts would be to redress the scandalous situation with the heiress.

Wedding her would rub out the tarnish on his honour, especially if he prevailed upon Jane to circulate the myth of their prior relationship that Miss Denby had just invented. His lips twitched again with appreciation at that blatant falsehood. Oh, how satisfying it would be to rout the noxious Lady Melross!

More importantly, wedding Miss Denby was the only way she could salvage *her* reputation. Though he wanted to remain angry with her for embroiling him in this mess to begin with, in truth, she was as much an innocent victim of the scandal Henshaw had unleashed upon them as he was.

As a gentleman of honour, he didn't see how he could refuse her plea that they marry now, any more than he could have avoided making her an offer after the escapade in the glasshouse at Barton Abbey.

Dismayed by that conclusion, he stared into the fire, his mind furiously casting about for any feasible way out…and finding none. It seemed he might have to marry her after all. Could he make himself do it?

If he did, he vowed the relationship would have to be more than the cold-blooded alliance of convenience his parents had made. He already knew that even if they had nothing else in common, there was passion between them.

He stole a covert look at Miss Denby, who had, after presenting her first proposition, having laid out all her arguments, left him alone to ponder his decision, with no further effort to entreat or cajole.

Though she was certainly far lovelier than she gave herself credit for being, there was no getting around the fact that she was nothing like well-connected society beauty Lady Mary Langton, whom he'd vaguely imagined marrying back when he was thought to have a brilliant political future.

But there might be advantages to that. Since Miss Denby wanted to remain in the country, he would not have to torture himself escorting his wife through endless rounds of society amusements, when he'd much prefer being at the nearby political gatherings from which he was now barred.

But she would never bore him. Unless he was much mistaken about her character, she'd never beg him for trifles, demand that he dance attendance upon her, sulk or pout or importune him to get her way over some matter upon which they disagreed. Like a man, she'd discuss and reason and agree to compromise.

He'd be passing up his only chance to marry for love, but he wasn't sure he really believed in that poetic nonsense anyway. Of his closest friends, only Alastair had experienced it, and all that had got him was a desire to blow himself up on the nearest battlefield.

By now, Miss Denby had stopped eating and sat gazing glassy-eyed into the distance. Since she appeared too weary to notice, he indulged himself by openly inspecting her.

He'd thought it angular, but in fact her face was all soft curves and planes crowned by high cheekbones and finished with a determined little chin below full, soft lips he remembered all too well. Above that graceful arch of neck, another stray auburn curl caressed the edge of a delicious little shell of an ear.

How far down her back and breasts would that thick mass of curls tumble when he removed it from its pins? His fingers tingled and desire stirred, thick and molten in his blood.

She wore another of her dreadful, over-trimmed dresses. He imagined the kind of gown he might buy for her, that would show off to perfection her slender form…and luscious bosom.

His mouth grew dry as he remembered that, too.

This current appraisal confirmed his previous assessment that she was far lovelier than anyone at Barton Abbey had realised. Having gone about all her life thinking of herself almost as her father's son, she treated her womanly attractions as negligible. She seemed to have no inkling whatsoever of their potent power.

He could teach her that. Awaken her.

The zeal with which she pleaded for her horses, the fire he'd seen in her as she rode, the energy and determination that had driven her to travel halfway across England by coach and halfway across London by night all bespoke a passionate nature.

That passion and loveliness could be his, to arouse and enjoy. But, no, hadn't she also requested a marriage in name only?

Why would a woman of such obvious fire wish to enter a marriage without any? he wondered. Had one of her father's buyers cornered her in a stall one night, frightened her, manhandled her, as Henshaw had?

Anger boiled up at the thought. If she had been attacked, she'd not been violated; forthright as she was, she would have told him if she were not a virgin. He would certainly never force himself on her, but he had no right whatsoever to his reputation as Magnificent Max, able to charm any woman and persuade any man, if he couldn't manage to seduce his own bride. The fiery young woman who, he recalled with satisfaction, had already admitted in the conservatory at Barton Abbey that he tempted her.

A more unpleasant explanation occurred, chilling his ardour like the splash of a North Sea wave. Did she spurn fulfillment because she wanted to 'save herself' for the absent Harry? He was willing to risk many things, but not the possibility of being cuckolded.

'Despite our marriage vows, you offered me freedom of conduct if I agree to wed you, did you not, Miss Denby?' he asked, breaking the long silence.

Startled out of her abstraction, she looked up. As the meaning of his words penetrated, surprise widened her eyes. 'You might actually…consider doing this?'

'If I do, I'm afraid I'm not prepared to be as generous about your conduct. I require unquestioned faithfulness in my wife. What of Harry, when he eventually returns?'

'I promise you, upon my most solemn honour, that if you agree to marry me, I will pledge you my loyalty as well as my hand. I would never betray you with anyone else. Not even Harry.'

Another woman, seeing what she most desired within grasp, might dissemble at such a moment, but Miss Denby had never told him less than the absolute truth. Even when it didn't flatter her, he recalled ruefully.

He remembered her soldier's bearing as she straightened her shoulders and marched off with no tears or pleading after he refused her first offer. How she'd backed away, apologising for intruding upon his peace, when they'd met by accident in the conservatory the second time. How she'd stationed herself outside his aunt's door at Barton Abbey, refusing to leave until she had spoken with Mrs Ransleigh and exonerated him.

He knew in his bones she meant every word of her promise and intended to keep it.

That fact sealed his fate. Perhaps on some level he'd known, ever since they'd been caught by Lady Melross in the glasshouse, that eventually it would come to this, for his initial fury had subsided to a calm resignation.

Never one to put off what must be done, once he'd truly decided to do it, Max dropped to one knee before her. 'Miss Denby, would you do me the honour of accepting my hand in marriage?'

Her eyes widened further. 'Don't you want to consider this further?'

'I have considered it. I'm quite willing to proceed at once.'

A look of befuddled wonder came over her face. 'You'll really marry me, Mr Ransleigh?'

'If you will have me, Miss Denby,' he replied, amused and a little touched by the enormity of her surprise. It seemed she hadn't truly believed her last-minute, desperate appeal would succeed.

Did she count the wealth she brought him, her intriguing personality, that ferocious honour and sense of loyalty…that luscious body, of such little worth?

Max would have to show her differently. Marriage to Caroline Denby might even be…fun.

If she'd been so unprepared for his acceptance, though, maybe she hadn't considered the consequences very carefully. 'Are you sure *you* don't need to think it over further?'

'Absolutely!' she cried, one of the tears still lingering at the corners of her eyes spilling down her cheek. Tentatively, as if she couldn't quite believe she now had the right, she laid her hand on his. 'I should be honoured to accept your offer, Mr Ransleigh.'

'Please, my friends call me Max.'

'Yes, friends. I believe we can be very good friends…Max.'

Friendship was a beginning, he thought. But with any luck and a full measure of his celebrated charm, he hoped to become a good deal more. If he must wed, by heavens, he intended his union to be a passionate one.

'If you've finished, let me escort you back to your cousin's house—by way of the front door, if you please. Now that we are to marry, I'll have no more skulking alone about the back streets of London.'

She nodded, 'And if we're to wed without delay, there is much to be done.'

'I'll set about obtaining a special licence, but there doesn't need to be unseemly haste.'

'But we only have—'

'I'll speak with Lord Woodbury and the trustees, telling them I don't wish the stud to be sold. Once they know we are to wed, I'm sure they will respect that choice.'

Her lips twisted in distaste. 'I expect you're right. *My* desires mean nothing, but the trustees will bow to the wishes of my intended husband.'

'Who also happens to be the son of a powerful member of government, someone they would not want to offend. Might as well use Papa's position to our benefit.' *Since it has done me little other good of late*, Max thought cynically. 'Besides, I suspect Lady Denby would be hurt were we to rush off and marry without even informing her.'

To his satisfaction, her eyes lit at that observation. 'You are right again, of course. She's harangued and cajoled me toward matrimony so frequently, I know she would be disappointed not to be present when her fondest wish is finally realised.'

'Exactly. Once I obtain the licence, we can be married at Denby Lodge, if you prefer.'

'I'd rather do so here, as soon as Stepmama and Eugenia can get to London. I don't trust Lord Woodbury.'

'Would you like to accompany me when I call on him?'

'Only if you intend to make him grovel,' she retorted.

He grinned at her. 'That could probably be arranged.'

Her eyes scanned his face, weighing the seriousness of his offer. Finally realising he meant every word, she said, 'That, I would very much like to witness—galling as it will be to watch him treat you with every solicitude, when he has always dismissed my opinions out of hand.'

'He will never do so again,' Max promised. Having a female, especially a young female, run a horse farm might be unusual, but since it was Lord Woodbury's interference that had forced this situation upon them, Max was not inclined to be forgiving.

She smiled with genuine gratitude. 'Though I sorely wish I might be able to do it on my own, watching you vanquish Lord Woodbury will still be satisfying. Thank you for being so considerate. And waiting until I can have my family present for the wedding. It will make it seem more…real.'

'Legally, it's absolutely real, wherever it takes place.' Pushing away the faceless image of an army lieutenant serving in far-off India, he continued, 'You must be very certain this is what you want; there'll be no going back later.'

'No going back for you, either,' she countered soberly. 'I only hope you won't hate me one day…as you might well, should you ever fall in love with a woman you then can't marry.'

'I think I will be quite satisfied with our bargain,' he assured her…and, to his surprise, realised that if wedding her made obtaining a posting easier, he might actually mean those gallant words.

'I shall do my best to make sure you never regret it.'

Max brought the hand she'd given him to his lips. As he brushed them against her knuckles, he heard her quick intake of breath, felt the shiver that moved through her.

Desire rose in him, sharp, sudden. He wanted to taste her

skin, take her mouth, trace his thumb over the outline of her breasts, sure he would find the nipples taut and pebbled.

But not yet, not now, while fatigue clouded her eyes and worry over the loss of her home and her horses consumed her thoughts.

She tugged at her hand, confirming that caution. At once he released her.

At that moment, there was a knock at the door. Wilson peeked in to inform Max that a hackney awaited them.

'I'll return you to your cousin's, then,' Max said, helping her to her feet. 'You need your rest. Can't have my bride looking haggard, letting Lady Melross claim she had to be coerced into marrying me.'

'No, I must be radiant—if only to confound Lady Melross.'

Max escorted her out, reflecting that over his time as a privileged son, he'd had women from Diamonds of the *ton* to experienced courtesans try to entice him. None of them had sparked in him the combination of curiosity and desire inspired by the plain-spoken Caroline Denby—who'd made no attempt at all to entice him.

He had a sudden, lowering thought that he was about to marry a woman who might well fascinate him for the rest of his life…and she was marrying *him* to save her horses.

He'd just have to be up to the challenge of fascinating her, then. He might not be able to coerce an apology from the Foreign Office, but surely he could make one slip of a girl never regret marrying him.

Chapter Thirteen

Two days later, Max collected Caro at Laura Place and escorted her to the offices of Mr Henderson in the City, where Lord Woodbury, as spokesman for her father's trustees, was to meet them.

The solicitor, to whom Caro had already sent a note apprising him of her new status, greeted her warmly and treated Max, she thought, with just the right amount of deference, respectful of his status as an earl's son, but not fawning over him. After offering congratulations on their imminent nuptials, he said, 'I'm assuming you wanted to consult Lord Woodbury about transferring control over Miss Denby's inheritance?'

'Yes. Most urgently, though, I want to inform him that I do not wish for Denby Stud to be sold.'

'I'm so very glad to hear it!' Mr Henderson exclaimed. 'Having Miss Denby assume so active a role in the business might have been uncommon, but knowing how well she discharged those duties, I very much regretted the trustees' decision, an action I had no authority to countermand. I'm delighted you intend to retain ownership.'

'Anything that pleases my intended, pleases me as well,' Max said. 'I've been impressed by how highly Miss Denby has spoken of your services, Mr Henderson. If you will, I'd like you to work with my solicitors in drawing up the wedding settlements. We're both anxious to be wed as soon as possible,' he added, giving Caro a warm, lover-like look so believable that her face heated…and her body hummed.

Observing that glance, the lawyer smiled. 'So I see. I'm honoured by your confidence and will begin the necessary paperwork at once. Now, if I may show you into my private office? Lord Woodbury awaits you.'

Max offered his arm; Caro took it and together they walked into the office.

Lord Woodbury rose from his chair as they entered. After looking at Caro with some surprise, he recovered to say, 'Ah, the affianced couple! Allow me to wish you both every happiness.'

'Thank you,' Max said. 'As I mentioned in my note, I wish to briefly review the status of Miss Denby's estate.'

'Of course. Miss Denby, I'm sure Mr Henderson will make you comfortable elsewhere whilst Mr Ransleigh and I discuss these matters.'

'No, I wish her to be present,' Max said. 'The first item under review is halting the sale of the Denby Stud and Miss Denby knows the details of its operation much better than I.'

Woodbury looked as if he'd like to assert she knew them far too well—but after viewing Max's expression, swallowed those words and said instead, 'You wish the estate to retain ownership?'

'I don't want any major changes made to the estate's assets before my man of business and I have the opportunity to review the whole.'

To Caro's mingled outrage and chagrin, without a syllable of protest, Woodbury replied, 'Quite understandable, Mr Ransleigh. I must confess some surprise, however, that you have an interest in running the stud. I assumed you would prefer to return to a government post.'

'I probably shall accept another position. Since my bride has overseen the stud's operation with great competence for years, I see no reason to make any changes in its management.'

Though the approving light in Woodbury's eyes dimmed, to Caro's added irritation, whether out of respect for the Earl of Swynford's son or because a *man* made the statement, Woodbury did not argue. After a moment, he said only, 'I suppose you may order things as you like in your own household.'

'Indeed I shall. I shall also see that my bride is never again slighted or insulted by those into whose safekeeping her inheritance was entrusted.'

Woodbury had the grace to look a bit uncomfortable. 'Certainly not.'

'I regret to say I am most disappointed in your stewardship, my lord. Nay—' Max held up a hand when Woodbury, eyes widening in surprise, began to sputter a protest. 'I appreciate that, in the main, the estate has prospered. But I must wonder at the character of a man who would so carelessly injure the delicate sensibilities of a female under his protection.'

Woodbury stared at him. 'Delicate sensibilities of a female...you mean *Caro*?'

After a warning glance from Max, Caro stifled the protest automatically rising to her lips. Following his lead, she sighed heavily and dropped her gaze, trying her best to look like a fragile maiden in distress.

'I understand you were a close friend of Sir Martin. I cannot imagine he would have been happy to learn you intended to strip away from his poor orphaned daughter the great project upon which the two of them had worked closely for so many years, the sole reminder she possessed of the father for whom she still grieves.'

'Well, I certainly—' Woodbury sputtered.

'Then there's the matter of the letter you wrote to Lady Denby, making rather…regrettable remarks about my betrothed. I'm shocked that a gentleman of your standing would have given so much heed to scurrilous rumour, rather than discreetly enquiring of the families involved. Surely you don't expect the Earl of Swynford to post details about private family matters on a handbill in every print-shop window! Or that he would stoop to correct common gossip.'

'But Lady Denby herself wrote me that you were not to wed!' Woodbury protested.

Max shook his head pityingly. 'Perhaps you did not read her letter aright. She merely meant to inform you that, at the time of her missive, we were not planning an immediate wedding. We subsequently decided to advance the date of our nuptials. In any event, I was quite disappointed by the unnecessary haste with which you set about disposing of a major component of my betrothed's estate without even the courtesy of consulting me. As was my father, the earl.'

'Your father, the earl?' Woodbury echoed, his indignation visibly wilting at Max's mention of his father's disapproval.

'I suppose you were only doing what you thought best—'

'Indeed, I was!' Woodbury inserted hastily.

'Still, I think you owe Miss Denby an apology.'

Woodbury opened and closed his lips several times, indignation seeming to vie with prudence as he attempted to dredge up the appropriate words.

'My father, the earl, would think it a handsome gesture,' Max added softly.

The expression on his face as sour as if he had just swallowed a large bite of green apple, Woodbury turned to Caro.

'My apologies, Miss Denby, if I have given offence,' he said woodenly. 'It was certainly unintended.'

She nodded. 'Apology accepted, Lord Woodbury. We may have had our...disagreements, but I know you tried to serve the best interests of the estate.'

'Since your trusteeship will end within days anyway, you may consider yourself relieved of your duties now,' Max announced. 'Mr Henderson can oversee whatever needs to be done until our marriage. Thank you for your efforts on Miss Denby's behalf, Lord Woodbury, and a good day to you.' Gesturing towards the door, Max gave him a regal wave of farewell.

Caro doubted the Prince Regent himself could have sounded more dismissive. Stifling any reply he might have wished to make, Woodbury bowed and departed, looking like a resentful schoolboy who'd just been caned by the headmaster.

After he'd exited, Max turned to Caro. 'Satisfied?'

Caro jumped up and sank before him into a curtsy deep enough to do justice to the Queen's Drawing Room. 'Completely, my lord. How perfectly you play the "earl's son" when you wish! I was nearly intimidated myself.'

'I did study at the feet of a master,' Max said drily.

'You tell a falsehood with as much skill as I do.' She chuckled. 'I can only imagine the outrage of your father, could he have heard you invoking his name in this case! To give Lord Woodbury his due, he did manage the *other* assets of the estate quite competently.'

'Yes, but while doing so, he deeply wounded the delicate sensibility of the female under his protection. Made her desperate enough to travel through the night to reach London and then endanger herself crossing the city alone in darkness. She even offered herself in a marriage she did not want, to undo the damage he had done. That's not an injury I will easily forgive.'

She was about to protest the 'delicate sensibility' description...but, in truth, she *had* been desperate. Looking up to admit that, she met his gaze, so full of concern that it sent a shock through her.

The rout he'd just made of Lord Woodbury was more than a clever demonstration of his rhetorical power; it showed he was indeed prepared to defend what mattered to her. That he took seriously his promise to protect it, and her.

For the first time since her father's death, Caro felt...safe. A wave of affection and gratitude swept through her, brought the sting of tears to her eyes, made her want to throw her arms around his neck.

'Thank you for standing behind me to save the stud.' The last part of his comment suddenly registering, she added softly, 'As for that marriage, I'm daily coming to believe proposing to you was the wisest decision I've ever made.'

He took her hand and kissed it. 'I hope so. You are mine to protect now, Caro. I intend to do that to the very best of my abilities.'

As soon as he touched her, the clarity of her thoughts muddied, her mind disturbed by a rush of sensation, like the clash when the foam of a receding breaker meets the thrust of an incoming wave. Staring down at the hand he still held, distracted by the feelings coursing through her, she stuttered, 'I—I will t-try to prove myself worthy of that care.'

Then she looked up from her tingling fingers, became caught by his ardent gaze...and was lost.

She couldn't seem to either speak or look away. The attraction between them intensified, throbbing in her veins, humming in her ears, drowning out sound, paralysing thought.

That same strange, powerful compulsion she had felt in the conservatory at Barton Abbey welled up again, pulling her towards him. As if hypnotised, she found herself lifting her chin, stripped of everything but the need to feel his lips against hers.

He placed his warm, strong hand under her chin, drawing a murmur from her as she angled her head to feel the slide of his fingers against her skin. A maelstrom of desire began churning in her belly, tightening in her chest, as she raised her lips towards his.

Just as her eyelids fluttered shut, the door swung open. The sound acting upon her taut nerves like the crack of a whip, she pushed away from Max with a gasp, her heart pounding.

Henderson walked in, a stack of documents in his hands. 'I've begun the preliminary paperwork, Mr Ransleigh. If you'll have your solicitors contact me, I'm sure we can sort everything out quickly. If you have no further business here, may I offer you some refreshment before you leave?'

'Thank you, but we must be going. Let me again express my gratitude for the advice and support you have given my fiancée.'

Henderson bowed. 'Having known and esteemed Miss Denby since she was a child, I'm pleased to find that you intend to honour her wishes…and her.' Surprising Caro, he added, 'You might just be worthy of her.'

Grinning, Max returned the bow, the earl's son seeming not at all offended to have his conduct judged by a mere solicitor. Her nerves still jangled, Caro let him lead her back to the carriage, trying to stifle the yearning of a body that stubbornly regretted not getting that kiss.

Max had been not nearly as affected by it, she scolded herself. He'd probably kissed a score of girls, many of them prettier, every one of them more skilled in allurement than she. A simple little kiss was not for him the soul-shattering experience it promised to be for her.

Oh, this would never do. She simply had to wrestle this

unruly attraction under control. Certainly before the wedding…after which she would suddenly be cast into significantly closer proximity to him for a much longer interval.

She really was getting married. A *frisson* of alarm, underscored by a deeper, hot liquid excitement licked through her. Once she truly belonged to him, body and soul, how was she to resist the force driving her to yield to him?

By recalling that the power of the Curse loomed a mesmerised moment of forgetfulness away.

Caro sighed. If she had any hope of resisting him, she must concentrate more on that real danger and learn to deal better with his maddening, bewitching allure. And with the wedding a mere few days away, she'd better learn quickly.

Chapter Fourteen

A little over a week later, Caro stood before the glass in a guest bedchamber of Lady Gilford's London town house. Lady Denby stood behind her, instructing the maid who was adjusting the skirts of her pale-green wedding gown.

Wishing she could soothe away the anxiety in her stomach as easily as the maid smoothed down the soft silken skirts, Caro studied her reflection critically. She couldn't remember ever owning so flattering a garment. At home, she'd ordered a few gowns each year from the village seamstress, but they had been adequate rather than stylish, and during her aborted Season, she'd taken care to choose cuts and colours as unsuited to her as possible.

For her wedding, she'd wanted to wear something that at least wouldn't make Max regret his decision the minute he saw her at the altar.

Would he find her appealing? Anticipation and unease skittered across her skin. In the few rushed days since their trip to Mr Henderson's office, she'd not made any progress in bringing her response to him under control. She felt attraction curl in the pit of her stomach every time he handed her into a carriage or took her arm up the stairs. Each time, she longed to extend and lengthen the contact.

In fact, the more time she spent with him, the more powerful his allure seemed to become, to the point that she feared if he made any move to make their marriage a real one, even the threat of the Curse might not be enough to armour her against him.

Which made it all the more imperative for her to get this marriage business finished as soon as possible and leave him in London to tend his career while she returned to Denby Lodge.

'Enough, Dulcie, you may go,' Lady Denby was saying. As the maid departed, Lady Denby gave her a reproving look. 'How lovely you are! I can't believe you hoodwinked me into wearing those atrocious dresses!'

'You have forgiven me, I hope.'

'With you mending matters by marrying Mr Ransleigh after all, of course I have. I do hope you'll be very happy.'

'I hope to make him so,' Caro said, thinking guiltily how robbing him of the chance to marry a lady he truly loved would make that goal more difficult. With society holding him responsible for her ruin, honour had given him little choice but to agree to her bargain.

'You mustn't worry about tonight,' Lady Denby said, obviously noticing Caro's nervousness. 'You may know everything about breeding horses, but the human animal is quite different. I'm sure Mr Ransleigh will be gentle and careful with you.'

Would he? They'd said nothing more since the first night about that part of their agreement. Legally, she couldn't deny him if he decided to ignore her request that theirs be a marriage in name only. Would he choose to do so...or not?

She came back from her reverie to find Lady Denby staring at her. 'I'm not worried,' she said a bit too heartily.

'You must put out of your mind that silly business about "the Curse",' Lady Denby said, patting her hand soothingly.

'I admit, the experience of some of your relations was unfortunate, but your mama, Sir Martin told me, had always been delicate. You are young and in robust health; there's no reason not to believe your own experience won't be much happier. Indeed, when the midwife places that first babe in your arms, you'll know it was worth all the discomfort and danger.'

Not if the hands receiving the babe were dead and cold, Caro thought.

'In any event, Mr Ransleigh will hope for an heir, as all men do, and you can't mean to deny him,' Lady Denby concluded, with a sharp glance at Caro.

Having no intention of confessing her bargain to her stepmother, Caro said meekly, 'No, of course not.'

Blessing again the fact that Max bore no responsibility for passing on his father's title, Caro hoped, for the present at least, that he'd be content to dally with the ladies sure to flock about such a dynamic, handsome, charismatic man—especially once he'd been restored to some important government position. She squelched a little niggle of jealousy at the thought.

It was ridiculous for her to be jealous that he would doubtless share with other women the intimacy she needed to avoid—and had actively *encouraged* him to pursue elsewhere.

She had about as much luck banishing the emotion as she had at controlling her responses to Max. Sighing, she shook her head at her own idiocy. Her inability to think coolly and logically about this matter was yet another indication that the sooner they parted after the wedding, the better.

Before they could walk out, a beaming Eugenia hurried in. 'Caro, how lovely you look! Oh, Mama, I've just had the most wonderful talk with Lady Gilford and Miss Ransleigh. Lady Gilford said she was going to speak with you about having us stay with her for the whole Season, so Felicity and I can share the experience! How kind she is, inviting us and allowing Caro and Mr Ransleigh to have their wedding breakfast at her house.'

As well as quietly putting out the taradiddle Caro had constructed about a previous attachment between herself and Max Ransleigh. 'We owe her a great deal,' Caro said. 'I'm glad everything is going to work out for your Season.'

'How much better everything looks now than when we left Barton Abbey! Though…I am sorry about Harry, Caro. I hope you are not too unhappy about marrying Mr Ransleigh instead. Not that I can imagine any girl being unhappy to marry someone so handsome, charming and well connected! But I know Harry was your best and dearest childhood friend.'

'I am quite content to marry Mr Ransleigh,' Caro answered, trying to keep her voice even and mask the frantic agitation the mere thought set fluttering in her veins.

The busyness of the last week had made it possible for her to put out of mind the fact that she'd traded away the ease, long friendship and wordless understanding she'd always shared with Harry for the edgy uncertainty of marriage to a man whose mere presence in a room made her pulse race.

But though she might refuse to *think* about it, the fierce attraction continued to simmer between them, driving her at once to try to stay near him and to flee his hold over her. With her nerves constantly on edge, she'd barely slept and, despite Lady Denby's assurances, could scarcely contemplate the wedding night without a panicky feeling in her gut. Would he come to claim her? Could she make herself resist him if he did?

Oh, how much easier this would have been had Harry been the bridegroom with the right to enter her chamber tonight! A vision of his dear face rose up before her and she felt tears prick her eyes.

But it wouldn't be Harry tonight. It would never be Harry.

Facing the dilemma before her, she'd made the only choice she could. There was no use looking back; she could only go forwards.

As she reaffirmed that conclusion, Lady Gilford opened the door and beckoned to them.

'How charming you look, Miss Denby! Shall we go? Max and the clergyman will be awaiting us at the church.'

In the nave of St. George's, Hanover Square, Max paced, trying to settle down a few nerves of his own. Once the decision to wed Caro Denby had been finalised, he'd experienced surprisingly few qualms and only one minor regret. Despite his vaunted charm, he hadn't made much headway in seducing his bride; if anything, she seemed more skittish than ever.

Perhaps it was only maidenly nerves and inevitable; knowing nothing about virgins, Max couldn't tell. An experienced man did have the advantage; he knew what to expect of intimacy, where his innocent bride could only speculate. The stories reaching her ears must be lurid indeed, Max reflected, for as the day of their wedding grew nearer, Caro had grown as unsettled as a green-broke colt sidling in a paddock, eyeing the saddle about to be placed on its back. Each time he took her arm to assist her into a carriage or walk her into a room, she jumped as if scalded by his touch.

He shook his head ruefully and laughed. Bless her, did she think he was going to drag her into the bedchamber tonight and mount her with no regard for her fears or her comfort, like a stallion covering a mare?

The door to the sanctuary opened and his senses sprang to the alert. But instead of the priest leading in the bridal party, the figure striding in was his father, the Earl of Swynford.

Max sent a swift prayer of thanks that he had the space of several rows between them to collect his thoughts before he must greet the man with whom he'd had no contact since the morning he'd been dismissed from Ransleigh House. He'd taken Caro to call briefly on his mother—after making sure his father would be out. He'd left his sire only a terse note to inform him of his upcoming nuptials.

The man whose approval he'd once sought to win before all else halted before him. 'My lord,' Max said, bowing. 'I didn't expect you'd have the time to attend.'

'I shan't stay for the wedding breakfast, but I thought it wise to appear for this, so society would know I approved your choice. Despite the recent scandal over this girl, it seems you managed to land on your feet after all. "A previous attachment", indeed,' the earl said with a snort. 'I hope you thanked your aunt and Jane Gilford for their assistance in promoting that falsehood.'

'Yes, I've much appreciated all the efforts they expended on my behalf,' he said drily.

That barb hit home; his father frowned. 'You mean to imply that I have done nothing? You must remember, my son, at the time of your ill-advised liaison in Vienna, I was in the midst of very delicate negations to—'

Max held up a hand. 'I understand, Father.' The hell of it was, he *did* understand, though he still couldn't help resenting the fact that his father had not tried harder to find a way to intervene on his behalf.

'Well, however odd the path you followed to settle on this girl, it's a good choice. Better to have had a bride from a political family, but after Vienna, there's not much chance of that. At least you found yourself an heiress. Being rich will go a long way toward reconciling society to your lapses in judgement.'

Angry words rushed to his lips, but arguing with his father wouldn't set the proper tone for his wedding day. Restraining himself with effort, he said instead, 'I'm glad you approve my choice.'

'I expect you'll get her breeding and leave her in the country. I don't recall meeting her last Season, but Maria Selfridge told me she wasn't up to snuff, with little to recommend her beyond a good pedigree and a better dowry.'

'Indeed?' Max said, annoyed by this cavalier dismissal of Caro, even though he knew she'd taken great pains during her brief Season to create exactly that impression. 'I find her both intelligent and lovely. But, yes, I expect we will settle at her property in Kent, to which she is very attached.'

His father nodded. 'Probably a wise move. Live retired for a year or two, breed some sons, let the memory of the scandals die down. By that time, when you come back to London, I'll probably be able to find a position for you.'

A cold anger rose in him, surprising in its intensity. 'There's no need, Father. I'm sure whichever flunky with whom you're now working is performing quite adequately, else you'd have turned him off, too. In any event, Colonel Brandon is soliciting a post for me in the War Department. If you'll excuse me, I must see what is keeping the priest.'

With a nod to his father, Max strode across the room and out into the foyer.

He closed the door, his hands still shaking with the force of his fury and, acknowledging that, his lips curved in a wry smile. Apparently the resentment and hurt over his father's abandonment ran far deeper than he'd thought.

Taking a shaky breath, he was wondering if he should hide out in the gardens until the priest summoned him for the ceremony when the bridal party appeared at the entry door.

Then he saw Caro and his anger at his father was swept away by wonder.

He'd known since first discovering her 'disguise' that she was attractive. He'd been anticipating seeing her garbed in a more flattering gown—and taking her out of it. Still, he was not prepared for the enchanting vision that now met his appreciative eyes.

Vanished with the ugly gowns was any chance her unusual activities could lead one to find her mannish or unfeminine. Sunlight shining through the open doorway haloed her in gold, while its beams burnished to copper the artful arrangement of her auburn curls. The soft sage colour of her gown set off the cream of her shoulders and the rounded tops of her breasts that swelled up from beneath the fashionably low neckline. The long skirt and demi-train, mercifully unadorned, draped and flowed about her waist and hips, showing off her shapely, slender figure to perfection.

While he drank in the sight of her, she must have seen him, for she froze in mid-step on the threshold, her hand clutching at her stepmother's arm. With her dark eyes staring at him, she looked as uncertain and wary as a startled doe poised to flee.

This was no creature of salons and ballrooms, skilled in meaningless chat and empty flattery, but a pure, untamed soul whose words mirrored her actions and showed her to be exactly what she claimed: a woman who emanated a fierce independence and a feral energy that triggered a primitive response in him.

He wanted to devour her in one gulp.

But that would be for later…if the time was right. Max sighed. Nervous as she'd been this last week and still looked, that time probably wouldn't be tonight.

The priest entered and nodded at them both. 'Are you ready to proceed?'

Max walked over to claim her hand. He wasn't surprised to find it cold. 'Shall we do this?' he murmured, half-expecting her to say 'no'.

Taking a deep breath, she seemed to gather her composure. 'Yes. I'm ready.'

'Let us begin, then, Father Denton,' Max told him.

Within moments, they had taken their places before the altar. For Max, unable to wrench his wondering gaze from Caro, the ceremony afterwards was a blur. He barely registered his father watching sombrely, Lady Denby dabbing at her eyes, the delight on Felicity and Caro's stepsister's faces, the pleasure on Jane's and Aunt Grace's.

In some miraculous transformation, the nervous bride had disappeared, replaced by a serene lady lovelier than he could have imagined, who repeated her vows in a calm voice. From time to time, she glanced up at him shyly, golden motes dancing in huge dark eyes he could lose himself in.

Then the priest clasped hands together, pronouncing them husband and wife, and led them off to sign the parish register.

'Well, it's done,' she said quietly as she wrote her name in a firm hand.

'You look enchanting.'

She angled her head at him, apparently assessing the genuineness of his compliment. 'You truly think so?'

'I do.'

She smiled. 'Then thank you. Was that your father, glowering at us? I would think he'd approve of your marrying a fortune, at least. Will he be at the wedding breakfast?'

'No, thankfully. Mother should be and a handful of Jane's friends. I hadn't expected him here, either, or I would have warned you.'

She shrugged. 'I'm more nervous about your mother. Shock doubtless limited her conversation during the brief call we made on her; I fear she will want to corner me for a proper grilling this time, trying to discover how some country nobody made off with her son.'

'You needn't fear that. Aunt Grace has already told her what happened at Barton Abbey. She wants only to see me happy. Since you are now my wife, that means she wants you to be happy too.'

Caro gave him a dubious look, but had no time to reply before Lady Gilford came over to give them each a hug. 'A splendid wedding! Shall we return to the house? I expect guests will be arriving for the wedding breakfast soon.'

Looking a bit alarmed, Miss Denby—no, *Mrs Ransleigh*, a title it was going to take Max some time to adjust to, he admitted—said, 'There won't be many, will there? Stepmama said it was to be just a small reception.'

'Of course. In keeping with the story already circulating—which, Max tells me, was your invention, and very clever!—I thought it best to keep it very select, just immediate family and a few close friends.'

Caro nodded. 'Fewer people to gossip.'

Lady Gilford gave a peal of laughter. 'Oh, no, quite the opposite! With only the *crème de la crème* in attendance, those who weren't present will envy those who were and want to know everything about it…so they can discuss it as if they, too, had been invited. It will be quite the talk of the town.'

'Approving talk?' Caro asked.

'Definitely. Without wishing to sound arrogant, I do have a fair amount of influence. Where I and my friends approve, others follow…especially now that Max has done the sensible thing and got himself wed to a lady of intelligence and breeding.'

'And beauty,' Max said, pulling Caro's hand up for a kiss that set his lips—and other parts—tingling.

Blushing a bit, she pulled her hand free. 'And large dowry,' she added. 'How much more sensible could any gentleman be?'

So completely had Max concentrated on Caro's flustered reaction—and the brief moment when her hand had tightened on his before pulling away—the sound of his father's voice startled him.

'Congratulations, Mrs Ransleigh, and welcome to the family,' the earl was saying.

'It was good of you to attend, my lord,' Caro said, dipping him a curtsy.

'I wanted all of London to know I approve of my son's choice.'

'This time, you mean?'

In the sudden hush, Max could almost hear the gasp of indrawn breath; no one who knew the Earl dared risk inciting his famous temper. Max tensed, mentally scrambling for words to deflect what would probably be a stinging rejoinder.

It must be bridal luck, for the earl merely gave a thin smile. 'This choice, no one could dispute.'

'I'm glad you think so and I'm sure he appreciates your taking the time to attend the service. I'm sorry we shall not see you at Lady Gilford's breakfast, but as I understand your duties keep you excessively busy I shall bid you farewell here. Thank you again for attending, my lord.' She made the earl another graceful curtsy.

It was almost a...*dismissal*! Max thought, shocked. He'd assumed her initial, rather confrontational greeting to his sire was perhaps an awkward choice of words due to nervousness.

But she didn't appear nervous—quite the opposite. Her poised figure and cool manner seemed to indicate she neither feared, nor desired to impress, the powerful earl whose behaviour, her tone suggested, she disapproved of. Astounded, Max had to conclude she'd said exactly what she had wanted to say.

Since he wasn't sure how he might deflect a tongue-lashing from his father, thankfully the earl chose to be forbearing. With only a surprised lift of his eyebrow in Max's direction, he bowed and kissed Caro's hand. 'Let me wish you both happy.'

Max watched his father walk away. Still somewhat awed, he offered Caro his arm and led her to their waiting coach. As she settled into her seat, he said, 'I should warn you not to tweak my father. Few who do so emerge unbloodied.'

Caro merely shrugged. 'Unless the earl can sell off my stud, I've nothing to fear from him. His approval means nothing to me—nor are your future prospects held hostage to his patronage any longer. Which is fortunate, since it's certainly done you little enough good so far. I'm sorry if I sounded... ungracious; I do appreciate his recognition of you, however belated.'

A flush of gratitude warmed Max at this unexpected avowal of support. Before he could summon a reply, Caro continued, 'But how could he not approve? He'd look rather foolish if he refused to bless his son's marriage to a girl of impeccable birth who brought a fortune into the family. As I possess no ties of childhood affection that make me anxious for his favour, I'll not easily forgive him for refusing to assist you when you needed him most.'

She halted the protest he'd been about to utter with a lift of her hand. 'Oh, I understand he is a busy man with heavy responsibilities. But to my mind, there is no responsibility more important than helping your own kin.'

'Being his son has brought me many advantages,' Max replied, finding himself in the odd position of defending the man who'd hurt and angered him so deeply.

'He gave you the advantages of birth and his approval when it cost him nothing...but didn't lift a finger when assisting you might have made his own position more difficult,' she retorted. 'That is not what I call "affection" or "loyalty". One deserves better from one's family.'

Like watching a stable mongrel run out to bite a pure-bred hunting dog twice its size, Max couldn't quite get his mind around the audacity of little Caro Denby nipping at the mighty Earl of Swynford with her disapproval.

'You intend to offer me better,' he asked, bemused.

Looking up at him, her face still fierce, she said, 'Of course. I told you I would when you agreed to wed me. I just promised it again before God and those witnesses.'

'My little warrior,' he said. But her unexpected loyalty penetrated deep within him, soothing a place still raw and aching. He'd thought to protect and defend her from his father; he'd never expected *her* to defend *him*.

'I know you must still want his approval; he is your father, after all. But you are no longer a puppet dancing as he pulls the strings, forced to settle for whatever he decrees. You have wealth of your own, a patron in Colonel Brandon who is independent of his influence. You can meet him on *your* terms now.'

He'd never before considered it, but she was right. The idea of being truly out of his father's shadow was…liberating. 'You really are ferocious,' he said, half-amused, half-serious. 'Remind me never to cross you.'

Her fierceness vanished in a grin. 'That's probably wise. I suppose I am passionate about those things I believe in.'

'Like your horses.'

'And your future. But I can't disapprove of the earl completely. If he *had* supported you as he should, you wouldn't have been exiled and at Barton Abbey to rescue me.'

'I've become more thankful by the hour that I was.'

As the coach bowled along, a gallery of the ladies he'd squired on one occasion or another suddenly ran through Max's mind. All had been practically quivering with eagerness when he introduced them to the earl, echoing his father's opinions, anxious to win his favour. His bride not only had made no such effort, she'd practically tweaked his father's nose.

Because the mighty earl had not stooped to stand by him.

Max shook his head anew. He'd known from the moment they'd met that Caro was unique; how she continued to surprise him!

Having traversed the short distance between parish church and his cousin's house, the coach halted and a footman ran up to let down the steps.

Caro took a deep breath. 'Well, here we are. I hope Lady Gilford spoke the truth when she promised there would be only a few close family and friends at the reception.'

'If you can face down my father,' Max said as the footman helped her out, 'you can face down anyone.'

She gave him a rueful smile. 'I'm better at facing people down when I'm angry. Unless your family and friends incite my hostility by criticising you or the quality of the Denby Stud, I'd rather avoid conversation. I communicate much better with horses.'

'Tell them to neigh,' he suggested, eliciting a giggle as he led her in.

Chapter Fifteen

Caro paused uncertainly beside Max on the threshold of Lady Gilford's reception room as the butler announced the bride and groom, to the applause of the assembled guests. Lady Gilford had told the truth; probably not more than thirty people stood within a spacious room that could have easily had many more.

Their hostess immediately took Caro's arm and led them along, introducing friends and relations. Caro tried to do her part, nodding, smiling, dredging up names to match faces from her vague memories of her brief London Season. She didn't want to embarrass her hostess or Max by appearing to be the gauche, country bumpkin she truly was.

She even managed to do tolerably well, she thought, when meeting again Max's mother and his aunt, Mrs Grace Ransleigh, two ladies who had little reason to like her.

Hiding whatever chagrin she must be feeling to find her splendid son married to a woman so lacking in all the society graces, Lady Swynford congratulated her and pronounced her charming. The hostess of Barton Abbey, whose house party she'd marred with scandal and whose private rooms she'd invaded, was equally forbearing when she begged that lady's forgiveness.

'I may have initially resented your actions, but your insistence on revealing the truth about you and Max won my gratitude in a moment,' Mrs Ransleigh told her. 'I'm delighted to wish you both very happy.'

Thinking guiltily how disappointed both his mother and aunt would be if they knew the true terms of the bargain she'd made with Max, she said, 'I hope to make him so.'

Mrs Ransleigh gave her a shrewd glance. 'I think he's luckier than he knows.'

'Indeed I am,' Max agreed, reclaiming her arm, which set little shivers vibrating deep within her. 'I can't wait to discover just how much,' he added in a murmur meant for her ears only, accompanying the words with a look that whispered of warm sheets and intimate caresses.

The vibrations magnified, making her hands and lips tremble as a surge of both desire and panic washed through her. Her cheeks heating, she mumbled an incoherent reply to Mrs Ransleigh.

Turning away from Max, who continued chatting with his mother, she found herself face to face with Alastair Ransleigh.

After all the good will and compliments, his sardonic expression was a reviving slap, for which she uttered a silent thanks. Seductive innuendo confounded her, but the patent disapproval on his face she could deal with.

'Mr Ransleigh,' she acknowledged him with a curtsy. 'I'm sure Max is happy you journeyed to London to celebrate with him.'

'But you are not?' he shot back.

Shrugging, she raised her chin. 'Whether or not you approve of my wedding him is a circumstance over which I have no control. I could assure you I meant the best for your cousin, but only time will prove the truth of that.'

He inclined his head. 'A clever response and correct on

both counts, *Mrs Ransleigh*. I must warn you, there are four of us who have guarded each other's backs since we were children. Play my cousin false, and you will have not just me, but three other Ransleighs to deal with.'

Caro laughed. 'Do you think to frighten me? I realise your opinion of ladies is very low, Mr Ransleigh, but not all women are cut from the same cloth. Just as appearances in Vienna are not proof your cousin bears any blame in the attempt made on Lord Wellington.'

'We agree on one point, then,' Alastair replied.

At that moment, Max turned back to her and discovered Alastair's presence. After exchanging greetings, the two cousins shared a few moments of handshaking and hearty, man-to-man congratulations.

Watching them, Caro had to smile. Their deep mutual affection was so obvious that, knowing Alastair Ransleigh's sad history, she supposed she could forgive him his suspicions.

But it had been a long, exhausting week; so weary was Caro that she silently rejoiced as the guests paid their respects to their hostess and began drifting out. For a short, cowardly moment, she wished she could go back upstairs to the chamber she'd shared last night with Eugenia and listen to her stepsister's eager chatter until they both fell asleep.

But she'd made a bargain and it was now time to begin fulfilling it. Instead of sleeping upstairs, she'd spend the night in a suite at the Pultney Hotel…with her new husband.

She swallowed hard. Max had shown her nothing but kindness, had suffered scandal on her behalf, had been the instrument of saving her beloved horses. He'd given her much; now she must respond by doing the hardest thing that had ever been required of her: placing control of herself and her body in his hands.

She wasn't going to do it trembling like a coward.

So she nodded with an appearance of cool self-possession

as they took their leave of the party. Tried not to flinch when Max took her arm, too acutely conscious of his presence beside her to make any sense of the thanks he offered Lady Gilford.

Then they were out of the door, down the steps and he was handing her into the hackney. As he climbed in after her, she tried to think of some polite and amusing topic of conversation. But the courage necessary to keep herself from trembling sapped all the strength she had left, leaving her mind an utter blank.

Embarrassed, she hoped her nervousness was not as apparent to Max as it was to her. But since she jumped every time he touched her and he was not a stupid man, she figured miserably that he was probably only too aware of it.

When his voice came out of the darkness, she braced herself for some reproof about her timidity. Instead, he said, 'I must admit, in all the rush to finish up the details necessary for the wedding, I've not thought much beyond today. We could take a bridal trip, if you like. I'm ashamed to admit, I have no idea where you might wish to go. Do the wonders of ancient Rome appeal to you? The mountains of Switzerland?'

Seizing on that safe topic, she said, 'Have you visited them?'

'Rome, yes, and some other parts of Europe during my travels to and from Vienna.'

'What did you find most interesting about Rome?'

Fortunately, he'd found the city fascinating and was quite willing to describe it. Caro needed only to insert an enquiry here and there to prompt him to elaborate on his observations.

After a few minutes during which nothing more was required of her than to listen, Max said, 'But enough of my travels. Would you like to visit the city?'

'Perhaps some day. For now, I wish to return to Denby Lodge as soon as possible. As you may recall, the winter sale takes place—'

Before she could finish her remarks, the carriage braked and slowed to a halt. Max hopped out and waited by the steps for her to alight. A mix of dread and anticipation accelerating her heartbeat, she put a cold hand on his arm and followed him into the hotel.

Chapter Sixteen

Acutely conscious of the powerful, virile man beside her, Caro responded with mechanical civility to the manager's greeting. Her nerves tightened as if turned upon a vice with each step up the stairway as a servant led the way and ushered them into an elegantly appointed sitting room. In her super-sensitised ears, the soft snick of the door as he exited echoed as if he'd slammed it.

Numbly Caro noted the trunk Dulcie had packed for her sitting inside the adjoining dressing room. Opposite that, beyond a partially opened door, was a bedchamber dominated by an enormous, four-poster bed.

Images danced through her mind…Max's warm, strong hands stroking her skin as he removed her gown…his hard lean body, naked in the candlelight.

A wash of heat coursed through her. Jerking her gaze away from the bed, she tried to shut the thoughts out of her mind.

She turned to find Max, with an amused smile that said it must not have been his first request, asking if she'd like a glass of wine.

Seizing upon anything that might calm her nerves, Caro accepted gratefully. Beneath the anxiety, eddies of excitement were building. Her body whispered its hope that tonight

Max would ignore their bargain and claim his marital rights. Lead her into the bedchamber, press her against the softness of the mattress, caress and kiss her as he removed her gown and bared his own body to her touch and admiration.

Her hands tingled at the thought of running the pads of her fingers over his arms, his legs, the flat nipples of his chest.

In another part of her brain, a near-panicked awareness shouted she must avoid that outcome at all costs…or she was lost.

Hoping he would make that decision soon and remove her from this agony of speculation, she walked to the sofa and perched on the edge, her back to the bedchamber door.

He brought her the wine and took a seat beside her.

'Before we arrived, you were saying you wished to go home?'

'Y-yes,' she said distractedly. Heavens, how was she to think when he sat so close beside her she could feel the heat emanating from his body, his soft exhales of breath?

'As you may remember,' she forced herself to begin again, 'the winter sale will take place in less than a month. There's much work that must be done.'

'I can well imagine.'

She looked down, unwilling to meet his gaze as she continued, 'It's not…necessary that you come to Denby, too. You've lived all your life in a hectic political household, took part as diplomats from every nation met to decide the future of Europe, then fought against Napoleon at Waterloo in the greatest army ever assembled. I wouldn't expect you to be content rattling about a horse farm in Kent.'

Even as she uttered the words, she felt a completely illogical pang of regret. She'd come to hope they might pursue the friendship begun these last few days, she suddenly realised. In the moments when his imposing physical presence was not setting her nerve endings afire and turning her mind to mush, she'd enjoyed his companionship. Life without his intoxicating presence would seem somehow…tamer, less vital and exciting.

'Would you miss me if I don't accompany you?' he murmured. Before she could decide how to reply, he distracted her by placing one warm, strong hand on the back of her neck.

Though she jumped at first contact, she soon found the gentle massage of his fingers on the tightly corded muscles wonderfully soothing. Oh, how she wanted to lean in and give herself up to the pleasure of his touch!

Soon, she might have to give up everything…perhaps even her very life. The tension retightening, she leaned away from his hand.

'I will miss you,' she answered honestly. 'But I gave you my pledge not to interfere in your life and I meant it.'

'I see. I could escort you home, at least. Unless…you don't want me to meet your neighbours?'

That question was so absurd she had to laugh. 'Nonsense—I shall be proud to introduce you in the neighbourhood!' Envisioning the probable reaction, she added with a grin, 'I'm sure many in the county will be astonished to discover that mannish scapegrace Caro Denby, who could scarcely make it to church with her skirts unmuddied and her gloves clean, managed to land an earl's son. I'm afraid there are several matrons whose opinions of my running the stud matched Lord Woodbury's.'

'In my guise as the elevated son of an earl, would you like me to snub them?'

'I think you'd find them difficult to snub! Even the prospect of having to be pleasant to me wouldn't be distasteful enough to discourage those with marriageable daughters from seizing the opportunity to have their girls flirt with you, so they may claim acquaintance with your family when they go to London.'

To her dismay, at the prospect of having the lovely, blue-eyed Misses Deversham or the curvaceous brunette Miss Cecelia Woodard make eyes at Max, she felt a sharp pang of what could only be jealousy.

The ambitious mothers of local maidens were not the only ladies who would be happy to claim Max's acquaintance in London. Now that he once again had the promise of high position, all sorts of women would be throwing out lures, hoping to entice a handsome earl's son with a conveniently absent wife.

Was letting him go a mistake?

She shook her head. This was ridiculous. Max was not hers to hold. Even if he cared for her, under the terms of the bargain they'd made, she had promised him the freedom to pursue any women he wanted.

She looked up from that disagreeable fact to find him watching her, a slight smile on his face. 'If I can't discourage them from flirting with a snub,' he murmured, that heated, caressing tone in his voice again, 'then I shall just have to play the besotted bridegroom.'

Her mouth dried and panic jockeyed with attraction in the pit of her stomach. She stared at him, unable to tear her eyes from the intensity of his gaze, feeling the looming presence of the wide bed in the room behind them as if it were branded upon her shoulders.

The moment of surrender or resistance was imminent, the knowledge of its nearness pulsing a warning in her blood.

Her body craved surrender with every rapid heartbeat. Her mind, grimly conscious of the danger of the Curse, screamed at her to resist.

Sure she would go mad, pulled between two such diametrically opposing demands, a sudden, frantic desire to put off the decision filled her. She opened her lips, but her brain had gone blank and she could think of nothing else to delay the moment any further.

Would he take her now? In the next few minutes, she would finally find out.

Chapter Seventeen

Torn between wanting him to bed her and dreading that he would, when Max took Caro's hand again, she jumped.

Instead of tightening his grip and leading her into the bedchamber, Max released her. 'Caro, Caro,' he murmured. 'I'm sure you know all about encounters between a stallion and a mare, which don't appear very pleasant.'

She felt her face heat, but better to address the matter head-on, as it were. 'Not for the mare, at any rate.'

'I'm not so sure she doesn't enjoy it, but I'll bow to your superior knowledge of the equine species. I don't suppose you have any experience about mating of the human kind?'

'None,' she admitted. 'I thought gentlemen didn't want brides who had such experience.'

'That may be true, but it does create a drawback. You have nothing but my assurance that coupling between a man and a woman is nothing like what you've observed. It can be gentle, tender, cherishing.'

She nodded, every image his words conjured up stringing her already taut nerves tighter. Oh, how she wanted to experience it! If only she dared let him touch her, boldly and unafraid of the consequences. Still torn in opposing directions, she wished desperately he would make the decision for her and get on with it.

Distracted by those chaotic thoughts, when he touched a thumb to her cheek and stroked it, again she flinched.

He shook his head and chuckled. 'That's what I thought. Relax, sweeting. I promise I will never hurt you. You believe that, don't you, Caro?'

To her dismay, a tear pooled at the corner of her eye, then ran down to wet his thumb. She was acting as dithering and missish as the sheltered *ton* maidens she despised, she thought, disgusted with herself, the battle between his powerful attraction and her need to resist it making her uncharacteristically indecisive.

Before now, she'd always made up her mind quickly and acted upon it. But until now, she'd never imagined there could be something that appealed to her so powerfully that she was tempted to risk the Curse.

He'd just given her a perfect opportunity to tell him about it, she realised. Why not reveal the true reason for her fear and reluctance?

She was about to confess it…until she remembered Lady Denby's advice. Even the stepmother devoted to her wellbeing discounted the seriousness of the Curse. Max, who had no experience at all with childbirth, would probably dismiss her concern as laughable.

Or, even worse, pity her cowardice.

Lady Denby was doubtless right about the other, too. Max might not have yet expressed a desire for a son, but, eventually, he would want one. They both knew the promise she'd extracted from him not to consummate their marriage was unenforceable. The best she could hope for would be to delay that consummation long enough to achieve for the stud what her father had dreamed, before Max's desire for a son led to its probable result.

'Caro!' he called softly, telling her that she'd been silent too long, debating how best to answer his question. 'You can't truly believe I would hurt you!'

'No, no, of course not.'

'Good,' he said, relief in his tone. 'Then believe this, too. I respect you and care for you. Yes, I also desire you, as a lovely woman who is much more attractive than she knows. But regardless of my rights as your husband, I will never force intimacy upon you. Never take from you anything you are not willing to give, that you do not hunger for as fiercely as I do.'

Oh, if only she did not hunger for it so fiercely, she thought, suppressing a sigh. 'I understand. And thank you.'

'A kiss to seal the bargain, then?'

Caro eyed Max uncertainly. Was a kiss simply a kiss, or a prelude to more? But he'd just said he wouldn't force her. And surely she was sensible enough to resist letting a simple kiss turn into something else.

Besides, she had burned to kiss him since that interrupted moment in the solicitor's office. Why not stop worrying about what might happen next and simply enjoy claiming what she'd been denied?

Giddy anticipation thrumming through her, she gave in to the force that, since their first meeting in the conservatory at Barton Abbey, had impelled her towards him. 'A kiss,' she agreed.

She angled her chin up and closed her eyes, waiting, a breathless excitement feathering through her veins. Through closed lids, she could sense his face descending toward hers, feel the warmth of his breath on her cheek. Anticipation coiled tighter and tighter within her, impatience mounting to at last feel the brush of his mouth against hers.

But after a moment, when he had moved no further, she opened her eyes and looked up at him, puzzled.

He was gazing at her intently, the energy emanating from

the molten blue of his eyes like the crackle in the air before a lightning strike. 'I promised never to take from you, Caro,' he murmured. 'To give you only what you desire. So...show me what you want.'

Somewhat dismayed, she stared back at him. She'd never kissed a man in her life besides Harry and that hardly counted. They'd both been twelve when he surprised her by bussing her on the lips. She'd punched him afterwards.

Max had probably kissed dozens of women. Maybe hundreds.

Struggling with that daunting observation, her cheeks heating with embarrassment and thwarted desire, she said, 'I don't know...what to do.'

She feared he'd laugh at that humiliating confession, but instead he smiled. 'Don't think, just feel. Do what you want.'

What did she want? To touch him. The thick, wavy dark hair that always brushed his forehead. The smooth skin of his forehead and cheeks, the chin that in the late evening showed a dark shadow of stubble.

Uncertain, tentative, she reached up and ran her hand through his hair, to find it thick, luxurious, silky-coarse. Its soft slide against her fingers was arousing, making her want more. Emboldened, she traced the faint lines of his forehead, brushed a fingertip across his eyebrows, drew her nails lightly across the stubble of his chin. Traced her thumb across the surface of his lips, the skin firm, but softer than she expected.

He'd watched her expectantly as she explored his face, but as she traced her finger across his lips, his eyes drifted shut. 'Yes,' he murmured against her finger. 'Yes.'

Suddenly, she wanted to know if the stubble that clicked against her nails would sound the same, brushed against her teeth. Urging his head down, she leaned up and opened her lips, raking her teeth across his chin, catching the taste of him on her tongue.

Heat and pleasure jolted through her. She added tongue to teeth, her finger twining in his hair as she licked and nibbled the short, wiry stubble that carried the taste and scent of male and shaving soap.

A sharp imperative began thrumming in her blood. Though she'd not yet had her fill of his chin and the strong underside of his jaw begged to be explored, she simply had to taste his mouth.

Rather than joining her lips to his, at first she licked them, tracing them from corner to crest to corner. A deep groan sounded, echoing in her chest—his or hers, she wasn't certain.

Fevered impatience building tighter within her, she licked his lips again, then pressed hers against their wet surface. But that didn't seem to be close enough, deep enough. Her tongue teased at the corners of his mouth and, before she could realise what she wanted, he opened for her.

She slid her tongue inside to discover a new world of wonder. Another wave of shocked, fevered excitement swept through her as her tongue collided with his.

And then his hands came up to cradle her face, gentle but urgent, and he was kissing her back. The rasp of his hot, wet tongue as he stroked it back and forth, back and forth against hers sent a heated excitement pulsing to the very core of her.

Her whole body seemed to be throbbing, melting. Her breasts felt heavy, turgid, the nipples tingling, while warmth and wetness pooled between her thighs.

He teased her with his tongue, tracing the edge of hers, then withdrawing, while, frantic, she pursued his. When he suddenly clamped his lips around her tongue, sucking it deep into his mouth, the pleasure crested until she thought she might faint.

Her breath came in short, fevered pants and she couldn't seem to draw in enough air. A sharp need built in her, driving her towards something she didn't recognize, but wanted desperately. Her nails biting into his back, she clung to him, kissing him urgently, suckling his tongue and lips, trying to get closer, deeper, as if she might penetrate to the very core of him.

And then he broke the kiss, pushing her away before tucking her under his chin and holding her close. Against her ear, she could feel the hammering of his heart, the rapid rise and fall of his chest as he drew in breaths as ragged as hers.

'Well,' he said unsteadily a few moments later, 'that was certainly worth the bargain.'

Her mind was still so fuzzy, she could barely understand his words, much less produce a reply. While she fumbled, trying to recover, he pushed away and slid to the far side of the sofa.

Was that his hardness she saw, straining against his trouser front? A sudden desire filled her to touch him.

Before she could act upon the urge, he said, 'With all you've had to do these last few weeks, you must be exhausted. If we're to leave for Denby Lodge early tomorrow, you must rest. Take the bed; I'll be quite comfortable on the couch here in the sitting room.'

Bringing her hands to his lips, he kissed each fingertip, stirring the fire still not banked within her. 'Rest well, dear wife. I shall see you in the morning.'

So…he didn't mean to claim her. An incoherent protest formed in her still-foggy brain. Suppressing it, her aroused nerves sparking and sizzling with frustrated need, she nodded blankly, struggled to her feet and stumbled into the bedchamber.

Only to return to the sitting room a moment later. 'I'm sorry, but since it was our wedding night, I…I told Dulcie I wouldn't be needing her. I can't unfasten the bodice of this gown without assistance. If you wouldn't mind…?'

'Of course.'

She turned her back to him, still in that half-aroused state where relief that he would not be bedding her battled with frustration.

Her sensitised nerves felt every small tug and touch of his fingers as he loosened the ties of her gown, then the laces of her stays. There were too many layers of clothing, she thought, yearning for just one touch of his hands against her bare skin.

Then, when she thought he'd complete the process without it, he smoothed his hands from the nape of her neck to the edge of her bodice, loosened the material of gown, stays and shift, and pulled it away from her skin. As if he, too, could not end the night without making a small beginning on exploring her body, he slipped his fingers under the loosened garments and slowly stroked the flesh beneath.

She froze, closing her eyes, every bit of awareness focused upon the delicious friction between the slightly rough pads of his fingers and her bare skin. Oh, that he might continue stroking her, working from the back of her gown to the front, where his questing fingers might explore the swell of her breasts, discover the nipples peaked and aching!

For a few thrilling moments, it seemed he might, as he caressed his fingers slowly from the back of the gown around to her shoulders. But he halted there, thumbs resting on her bared collarbones as he pulled her against him and nestled his chin in her hair.

After cradling her a moment, he released her and stepped away. 'I'd better stop now,' he said, his voice sounding strained. 'Can you manage from here?'

'Y-yes, I think so,' she stuttered.

'Goodnight, then. Sleep well.'

He gave her a little push towards the bedchamber, then closed the door behind her.

In a gradually fading sensual haze, she removed her gown, shift and stays, drew on the night rail and climbed into the mammoth bed. The chill of the linens against her body finally extinguished the last of her fevered tension.

'Sleep well,' Max had advised. As Caro pondered the power of her response to him this night, she wasn't sure she'd be able to sleep at all.

Even now, thinking about kissing him brought her senses simmering back to life. When she reviewed her behaviour since arriving at the hotel, she had to suppress an hysterical laugh. After dithering in a missish quandary between desire and dismay, she'd fallen into his hands like a ripe fruit after one simple kiss.

She'd been right to fear the potent effect he had on her. They'd been wed barely half a day, and if he'd made any move to join her in the big bed she'd not have repulsed him. Indeed, before stumbling into the room, she'd come very close to inviting him.

It didn't do any good to remind herself that though he liked her, he wasn't in love with her; that she'd given him full freedom to pursue other women, a freedom he would almost certainly exercise at some point.

She still wanted him and burned for his touch.

Even reminding herself that giving in to the craving he elicited so easily would surely lead to her conceiving a child and testing the power of the Curse didn't lessen his hold over her—at least, not while he was touching her.

And he was so clever, drat him. If he'd cajoled or tried to coerce her, it would have been much easier to resist him. Instead, he'd promised never to hurt her...and let her desires set the pace of their intimacy.

She remembered the thrill of exploring his face, his lips, the wicked taste of his mouth, and groaned. At this rate, she was going to be dragging him to bed within a week of their return to Denby.

The danger was not just his physical appeal, devastating though that was. Their outings together this week as they prepared for the wedding had shown him to be not just kind and thoughtful, but clever, insightful and amusing. She *liked* being with him and could all too easily imagine coming to depend on his presence. Missing him when he went away, as he surely must.

She didn't want to end up like her cousin Elizabeth, pining away for the husband who'd beguiled and then abandoned her. Not that Max would treat her so shabbily, but it would never do to let herself grow too fond of a man who would probably never see her as more than a pleasant companion.

Sighing, she punched the pillow and turned over. There was still so much work left to achieve the dreams she and her father had had for the stud. War had put a temporary end to negotiations with the Italian owners from whom they had purchased Arabians in the past, but with matters on the Continent stabilising after the final defeat and exile of Napoleon, she could renew the correspondence. Visit Ireland to choose the necessary mares, then begin the complicated and delicate process of breeding the right dams to the correct sires and cross-breeding the offspring into the bloodlines they'd already established.

By that point, the stud would be established enough to turn over to another manager, if necessary. Her father had estimated it would take several years to reach that stage.

How was she going to resist Max long enough?

Despite her need to resolve that dilemma, the exhaustion of the last few weeks began to gather her in its grip. But before sleep pulled her under, she concluded her best hope was to allow Max to escort her to Denby Lodge and introduce him to the neighbourhood, as he seemed to want. Then, before her senses triumphed over good sense, she must persuade him to leave.

Chapter Eighteen

Three weeks later, Max stood at the rails of a paddock at Denby Lodge, watching Caro work with a young gelding. Though he came here every day, he didn't think he'd ever tire of observing the expertise and finesse with which she coaxed, enticed and commanded the young animal to do as she bid.

As soon as she had finished working the gelding, they were to take their daily ride, during which she showed him around the estate and he encouraged her to talk about her horses. Having spent most of his boyhood away at school, he was discovering he genuinely enjoyed the simple routines of country life and learning how she had helped Sir Martin establish the stud.

She stretched a hand out, coaxing the horse—a movement that pulled the fabric of her jacket taut enough to outline her breasts. His breath hitched and his body tightened.

He'd always thought her lovely, even in the breeches and boots, which, with a semi-defiant glance at him, she'd resumed wearing after arriving home. But here on her own land, among the horses she loved, she positively glowed with determination and purpose.

She was driving him crazy. A lithe, unconsciously sensual grace filled her every move. The enthusiasm and passion with which she attacked every aspect of her work, which brought a becoming flush to her face and a dynamic energy to her actions, kept him continually aroused. So far, he hadn't broken his promise to take only what she was willing to give, but keeping it was about to kill him.

Just thinking about that kiss on their wedding night made his pulse jump and his member harden. He'd suspected from the first that she possessed a highly passionate nature; he'd been looking forward to awakening it. But all the passion he could wish for had been present in her very first kiss which, making up in ingenuity and enthusiasm what it lacked in expertise, had nearly brought him to his knees with frustrated desire.

After closing the door to her bedchamber on their wedding night, he'd damn near had to warn her to lock it, fearing he might lose the battle to keep himself from slipping in later. Caressing her, while she was compliant and drowsy with sleep, into the acquiescence he sensed waited just below the surface.

With so promising a beginning, he'd hoped that after returning home to her beloved stables and familiar routine, she might come to him within a day or so. But though he believed she no longer feared him, he still hadn't managed to beguile her into crossing that final barrier and inviting him to her bed.

And so, although he had initially intended to remain at Denby Lodge only long enough to see her settled and meet her friends and neighbours, he found himself lingering, hoping each day might bring the moment when she finally gave herself up to the passion that always simmered between them. How he longed to show her the richness and joy physical union could add to the growing friendship they already shared!

She seemed more relaxed and approachable on their daily rides, sometimes giving him kisses or permitting touches she shied away from at the manor. Innocent that she was, perhaps she believed the possibility of being discovered by some farmer or woodsman and the lack of a proper bed kept her safer from seduction.

His lips curved in a grin. He'd love to demonstrate what could be accomplished with the aid of a saddle blanket under the concealing canopy of an accommodating stand of oak.

Maybe today?

At that moment, a groom trotted over to her. After turning the gelding's reins over to him, Caro walked to the fence.

'I'm sorry to have kept you waiting,' she said with an apologetic smile as she climbed over the rails to join him. 'I'm making such rapid progress now with Sherehadeen, I'm afraid I lose track of time.'

'I enjoy watching you. It's a true gift, the knack you have for working with horses.'

She shrugged. 'It's more experience than gift,' she replied modestly—which Max didn't believe for an instant. 'Anyone could do so, with the proper training.'

'Maybe you could show me, then.'

Surprise widened her eyes. 'It's such a slow process, I didn't think you would be interested. But if you'd like to learn, I'd be happy to show you.'

'I would like it,' he said, catching up her hand and kissing her fingers. *How I wish I might learn the right touch to use with you*, he thought, watching her eyelashes flicker briefly, as if savouring the contact. How he burned to make her feel more intensely, so intensely she'd be propelled beyond caution into a passion that would not be denied.

'Where are we to ride today?' he asked as he gave her a leg up, letting his hands linger as long as he dared.

'Another place that's very special to me. I used to visit there almost daily, but I…I haven't been back for a while.'

'Then it shall be special to me, too.'

She raised her eyebrows, as if she didn't trust his words. But though he'd never been above making pretty speeches to gratify a lady, he found he didn't even attempt to flatter Caro. She was so straightforward herself, it seemed…dishonest, somehow, to offer her Spanish coin. Somewhat to his own surprise, he found that whatever avowals of interest, support or affection he offered were absolutely sincere.

As they walked the horses side by side, Caro said, 'I did appreciate your treating me as "special" at Squire Johnson's dinner party last night. In fact, I must commend you for playing "the devoted husband" on all our neighbourhood visits with the same perfection you bring to the role of "haughty earl's son".' She chuckled. 'Thereby astounding several matrons who were certain you could never have seen anything appealing about Caro Denby beyond her enormous dowry.'

He found himself irritated with her. 'That's not true, Caro, and you know it. Why do you so underrate your many excellent qualities?'

'Oh, I don't underrate my talents. But you must allow even Stepmama despaired of me and she holds me in great affection! The skills I do have are not those generally possessed by females or esteemed by such arbiters of behaviour as Lady Winston and Mrs Johnson. Who were both astounded, I'm sure, when you repulsed Lady Millicent's attempts to partner you at cards.'

'With my bride garbed in a gown as lovely as that golden dress you wore last night, why would I wish to look at anyone else?'

'Perhaps because she was so intent on trying to seduce you?'

Max groaned, feeling almost…guilty that Caro had noticed the widow's none-too-subtle efforts. He'd been saddled with Lady Millicent, the highest-ranking female in the neighbourhood, as a dinner partner, and she'd taken every opportunity during the meal to brush his elbow, touch his hand or bend low over the table to give him a good view of her assets.

'Was it that obvious?'

'Probably. To me, anyway.'

'In my younger days, I might have found her attentions flattering.' *And in his frustration right after Waterloo, he might have taken her up on her offer.* 'But though she's handsome enough, I thought her casting out lures right under the nose of my wife to be quite distasteful. I didn't wish to cause ill feeling in the neighbourhood, but I had a difficult time rebuffing her advances with even a show of courtesy.'

Caro looked down at her hands on the reins. 'I'm glad you rebuffed her,' she said gruffly, 'even though I have no right to ask it.'

'You have every right, Caro. You're my wife. It would be shockingly bad conduct for me to embarrass you in front of your neighbours by loping off like a hound on a scent after a woman whose pedigree is far more elevated than her morals.' He grinned. 'I far prefer loping off after you.'

She looked back up, her eyes mischievous. 'Should I interpret that as a challenge?'

'Do you want it to be?'

'Very well, race you to the fence at the end of the meadow.'

Before the last of her words reached his ear, she'd kicked her mount to a gallop. He set off after her, loving the rush of wind in his face, the thrill of the chase surging in his blood.

It had been like this since their wedding night, she leading him, he pursuing. Like every day and night since, she reached the end of meadow just ahead of him. But soon, they would reach it together, he vowed.

He was about to applaud her victory, but as they rounded the crest of a small hill near a stone-walled enclosure, she suddenly dismounted, her face solemn. Above the wall, its edges draped by the forlorn, still-leafless branches of a rambling rose, he saw the tops of several gravestones.

Her gaze already focused on the graveyard, she paced slowly forwards. Unwilling to break the silence, Max reined in and jumped down, walking beside her to the gate, where they turned the horses free to graze. He followed her to a pair of marble tombstones whose carvings read Sir Martin Denby, dead the previous year, and Lady Denby, beloved wife, deceased some twenty-five years previous.

When Caro knelt by her father's gravestone, he went to his knees beside her. To his surprise, she reached over to take his hand. He wrapped it tightly in his own.

'I used to come here often when I was a girl,' she said softly. 'Mama died giving birth to me, so I always wondered what she'd been like. A portrait of her hung in Papa's room, but he never visited her here. Not until after his death did I understand why. Riding the farm, working with the horses, sometimes it seems like he's just away on a trip, maybe in Ireland looking at breeding stock. But coming here, seeing the date on that stone, I can't escape the fact that he is really gone.'

Tears tracked down her cheeks. Knowing how rarely she wept, sadness filled him for her grief. 'I'm so sorry, Caro. Lady Denby told me how close you were. Losing him must have been so difficult.'

'Stepmama is wonderful, but we're as different as…as these old boots and a pair of satin slippers. Papa and I understood each other, knew what the other was thinking and feeling without a need for words. He was…everything to me. Father. Teacher. Adviser. Friend.'

She looked over at him. 'This is the first time I've been able to bring myself to visit since…since he joined Mama here. Thank you for coming with me.'

He raised the hand she'd given him and kissed it. 'You're not alone any more, Caro. You have me now.'

Two new tears welled up, sheening her eyes. 'Do I?'

She did, he thought, suddenly recognising that truth. He'd pledged his faith to her the day they had exchanged their wedding vows, but after sharing her life every day for almost a month, he felt that commitment to her on some deeper level. Before he could assure her of that, she rose and turned to walk out.

As he followed, she asked, 'Were you ever close to your father? Even if you were not, it must have been difficult to face his disapproval.'

Mention of his father called up that familiar acid blend of anger, bitterness, pain and regret. 'Yes, it's hard to accept he considers me a disappointment when, my whole life it seems, I wanted only to earn his attention and approval. I was the second son, not the heir, not the one who received whatever interest he could spare from his public life.'

Remembering, Max smiled faintly. 'I used to wait for his occasional visits at home or school with as much fear and anticipation as if he were the king himself. When I left the army, I was thrilled and honoured that my contribution in the diplomatic corps might assist his work in the Lords. But after Vienna, when I became the subject of rumour and speculation he considered damaging to his efforts, I was banished.'

'What…what did happen in Vienna?' When he looked up sharply, she said, 'I don't mean to pry! But I cannot believe you would do anything dishonourable.'

Warmth filled him at her avowal. 'Thank you. Even without knowing the circumstances, you've shown more faith in me than my father.'

She smiled. 'We've already established his conduct left much to be desired. But you needn't tell me if you don't wish to.'

'I don't mind.' Somewhat to his surprise, he realised that was the truth. He'd fobbed off the curious who'd enquired after he'd been sent home, sharing the facts only with Alastair and his aunt, but he knew Caro would listen carefully and return an honest opinion, rather than mouth useless platitudes.

Leaning against the stone wall, watching their mounts grazing in the distance, he said, 'Going to Vienna as aide-de-camp to Lord Wellington was a great opportunity. Even beyond the chance to assist a great man and do some small bit for my country, it was fascinating to be part of such a brilliant assembly of statesmen and diplomats.'

'I can well imagine!'

'Shortly after we arrived, I made the acquaintance of Madame Lefevre, widowed cousin of one of the French diplomats, whom she served as a sort of housekeeper and hostess. Many of the delegates, after Napoleon's devastation of Europe, despised the French and would have nothing to do with them. But I had to sympathise with the difficult task faced by Prince Talleyrand and his staff, trying to keep the country they loved from being dismembered and punished after all those years of war.'

She nodded. 'As we would wish to safeguard our beloved land.'

'Exactly. At any rate, unlike most of the females present, Madame preferred not to call attention to herself. At the many social events, she kept apart, observing rather than participating. It was that aloofness, as much as her beauty, that first caught my eye and, on a whim, I asked her to dance. Impressed by the keenness of her observations, I sought her out at other functions and we struck up a friendship. Unlike nearly every other woman I'd been associated with—until you—she demanded very little from me.'

Caro made a rueful grimace. 'No, *I* only demanded that you marry me.'

A demand to which he was daily becoming more reconciled, he thought, smiling at her. 'Like you, she never sought compliments or presents or commanded my slavish attention. Quite the contrary—she always appreciated even the most trifling assistance. I soon noticed, however, that she often had bruises on her wrists, sometimes even on her face. When she finally admitted her cousin abused her, I was outraged, but there was nothing I could do about it; despite the rumours later, she was never my mistress, nor had I any legal pretext to intervene on her behalf. Frustrated that I could not improve her circumstances, I did what little I could. She never asked more of me.'

Max laughed bitterly. 'Or so I thought. In the months since Vienna, I've gone over every action and conversation. I truly cannot recall her ever expressing any political opinions. Perhaps she was no more than an unwilling pawn, forced by her cousin's threats of violence to participate in the plot. But the plan worked masterfully; in using her as bait, someone must have known I might resist seduction, but I would never refuse to assist a lady in distress.'

He sighed, gazing sightlessly into the distance as he continued, 'The night of the incident, she sent an urgent note summoning me from the room where I waited to accompany Lord Wellington to an important meeting. After asking my help on a small matter, she deliberately delayed my return; meanwhile, a hired gunman burst into the room where Wellington awaited me and fired at him. Thank the Lord, he escaped unharmed. Madame Lefevre and her cousin disappeared from Vienna that same night.'

'I've combed my memory, trying to find some sign, some indication I'd missed, that a plot was afoot...' He shook his head. 'I just don't recall any. But if I had not allowed myself to be lured into assisting her, the conspirators could not have found such an ideal opportunity to attack England's most skilful general.'

'You can't know that for sure,' Caro objected. 'Had that opportunity not occurred, Wellington's enemies would have searched out others. No one of sense could fault you for responding with chivalry and compassion to what appeared to be a lady's unfortunate circumstances! Did the authorities not pursue Madame and her cousin?'

'I'm not sure. My relationship with her was well known enough that I was…detained that same night, while an inquiry was launched into my involvement. Otherwise, I would have set off to look for her immediately.'

She must have noticed the constraint in his voice. 'You were…confined?' she asked.

He grimaced. 'Not in prison. Just transferred to rooms far from Lord Wellington's and forced to remain there. Under guard. Watched over,' he added, feeling his face flush at the words, 'by soldiers of the unit I'd lately led in battle.'

'How awful for you,' Caro said softly, compassion in her eyes. 'But surely no one believed *you* would have had anything to do with an attack on your commander!'

'Before any official determination could be made, Napoleon escaped from Elba. The Congress quickly adjourned and the principals scurried home to their respective capitals. Then came Waterloo and here we are now.'

'Is there nothing else you can do to finally clear your name?'

'The Foreign Office implied that, with the whole matter having been overcome by events, it wasn't worth attempting. However, Colonel Brandon, my former commander who's now searching for a new post for me, believes that if I could locate Madame Lefevre and obtain testimony corroborating my behaviour during the affair, it would be quite helpful.'

'Then you must go to Vienna,' Caro said. 'Surely the truth will absolve you.'

'Thank you,' he said quietly, glad to have had his intuition confirmed. Somehow, he'd known she would believe in him and urge him to seek vindication. 'I'm inclined to go to Vienna after leaving Denby, while Colonel Brandon explores his connections. Though I'm not certain, even if I can find Madame and compel her to testify, that it will change my father's opinion.'

'Oh, Max, I'm so sorry,' she said, reaching over to run a finger down his cheek.

He caught her hand and held it there, thrilling to her touch.

'The earl may be a great man in the affairs of the nation,' she continued, 'but he isn't half the father Sir Martin, simple country squire, was to me. Though I shall *try* to keep my disapproval to myself when I meet your father again, I cannot help feeling he is a selfish, foolish man to carelessly throw away his son's affection.'

Once again, the idea of Caro Denby utterly unimpressed with the man whose voice still rang in the halls of Parliament and whose approval was sought by most of his peers made Max smile. 'You did make your opinion rather clear at the wedding. I was quaking in my boots, waiting for him to deliver one of his famous set-downs. As one who's received quite a few, I assure you, he can deliver a jobation that will rattle the teeth in your head.'

Caroline merely sniffed. 'He could try. I shouldn't have chastised him, I know. Since I certainly don't wish to make matters worse between you, I shall attempt to be more conciliating in future.'

'My sweet defender,' he murmured, squeezing her fingers.

'Your defender, yes. You have me, too, now, you know.'

Max felt an odd little pang in his chest at that avowal. She would stand by him, care about him, support him…as none but his fellow Rogues ever had.

It seemed that she didn't find him valuable only as Max-the-earl's-son or Max-the-rising-diplomat or even Max-the-soldier. Simply being Max was enough. A strong surge of tenderness and gratitude tightened his chest.

Uncomfortable with the intensity of the emotion, he pushed it away and turned his mind instead to enticing sensual connotation of her words.

Oh, how he wanted to have her! Under his intense gaze, she blushed and looked away, telling him she'd just realised the double meaning of her words. But in this instance, her protective assumptions about the countryside were correct; he could hardly seduce her with the shades of her parents looking on.

At that moment, a sudden gust of wind nearly sailed the hat off his head and a large cold drop of rain lashed his cheek.

'The weather is looking to turn,' he said, gazing up at the scudding dark clouds. 'We'd better head back.'

'Thank you for coming with me. I knew I must return some time, but I'd been dreading it. Having you here made it…better. Not so lonely.'

To his surprise, he realised that for much of his life, despite the accolades of the sycophants and admirers who'd always wanted something from him, except when in the company of the Rogues, he'd been lonely, too. Until now.

'I'm glad,' he said and led her back to the horses.

He had returned to the house, while, despite the rain that began to fall steadily, Caro headed back to the paddock to work, telling him she'd see him at dinner. Max wandered to the library, thinking to choose a book. Instead, he found himself staring out of the window, thinking about Caro.

He recalled their conversation at the graveyard today. He'd

never shared with anyone the conflicting feelings he felt for his father. He'd never before realised how alone he'd often felt in the midst of his own family. Perhaps it was because being with Caro felt so different. Where she was, he felt a sense of warmth, affection and serenity, as if he...belonged.

A stab of unease rose at that conclusion. It would be vastly deflating for Magnificent Max to fall in love with a female who, thus far, gave little evidence that his hopes of fascinating *her* would ever be realised.

Maybe he ought to give up both that and his attempts at seduction—for the present, at least—and head to Vienna. The longer he waited, the less likely he'd find any trace of Madame Lefevre.

He'd not yet decided what he meant to do when Caro burst into the library, excitement shining in her dark eyes. 'I've just received a letter from Mr Wentworth! It seems the breeder in Italy to whom Papa wrote long ago, hoping to obtain another of his excellent Arabians, actually received his offer! Even better, he accepted Papa's terms.'

'That's wonderful news,' Max said, pleased for her. She'd just been telling him of her father's plans to introduce new Arabians into the stud's bloodlines. 'How soon will you be able to get the horse?'

'Almost immediately, it turns out. Signor Aliante had to wait for cessation of hostilities on the Continent to transport the animal, but, Mr Wentworth writes, the stallion has just arrived in London. Mr Wentworth is having him sent down to Denby; he should arrive in a few days. Papa would be so proud! This is the first step toward achieving everything he wanted the stud to become!'

Max smiled, charmed by her enthusiasm and the look of pure happiness on her face. 'We should celebrate, then.'

'We should! I'll have Manners see if there is any champagne in the cellar.'

Max stepped over to give her a hug, but she waved him off. 'Don't; I'm all over mud. I shall see you soon at dinner!'

When they met later in the dining room, the vision Caro presented was worthy of celebration. Her auburn hair was arranged in a delightful tumble of curls and the flattering gown she wore showed her magnificent bosom to full advantage.

She was unusually animated throughout dinner, plying him with questions about the army, everyday life on campaign and his impressions of Spain and Portugal. Normally as soon as they finished eating, she left the table, giving him a hurried excuse for a kiss before going—alas, alone—to bed so she might rise at dawn to begin her workday in the stables.

But this night, she stayed at the table, as if as reluctant as he to end the splendid camaraderie of the evening. She laughed as he told her about the night of pouring rain when he'd bivouacked in a Portuguese stable, wrapped up in his cloak on a thick layer of hay. And been awakened repeatedly through the night by the cows attempting to eat his mattress.

Eyes glowing, she touched his hand, let her fingers linger on his arm. She seemed more relaxed—and less guarded—than at any time since the kiss on their wedding night. All his instincts telling him capitulation was near, Max exerted himself to be at his most charming, teasing her, trying everything he knew to beguile and entice her.

Finally, noticing the long-suffering look on the face of the footmen standing at his post by the sideboard, Max said, 'Shall we withdraw and let Joseph clear the table?'

Caro glanced at the mantel clock and straightened with a start. 'Heavens, it's much later than I realised! Excuse me, Joseph, for keeping you well past the time you should be putting your feet up.'

'Thank you, mistress,' the footman responded. 'Shall I have Mr Manners bring the tea tray to the study?'

'No, it's too late for tea. Tell the kitchen staff to bank the fires and go to bed.'

As the footman bowed himself out, Max claimed the decanter and led her to the study. 'Shall we finish the last of the wine? It will help you sleep.'

'It's been such a marvellous day!' With a slow grin as she sank on to the sofa, she gave him a naughty look that sent heat all the way down to his toes. 'Maybe I don't want to sleep.'

Max tried to tell himself not to read too much into that statement. But a wild hope blazed through him, like lightning in advance of a storm.

Seating himself close beside her, breathing in her enticing scent, a sharp desire filled him to bend down and cover with kisses that delectable swathe of bare skin from her throat to the tops of her breasts. He ought to put up his glass and take himself off to bed before he lost control and broke his promise, but he couldn't bring himself to end this enchanted spell of an evening.

'We should go to bed now, I suppose,' Caro said as she drained her glass. From beneath her lashes, she gave him a look that was part enticement, part hesitation.

Beguiled by her loveliness, hard and nearly mad with repressed desire, Max found it increasingly difficult to hear the little voice urging caution. 'Let me escort you up.'

His heart leapt and his member stiffened further when she replied, 'That would be…lovely.'

She offered her arm. Trying to restrain the excitement racing through him, he took it and walked her out, thinking she must surely be able to hear the thundering beat of his heart.

A few moments later, they reached her room. After he

opened the door and walked her inside, his heart seemed to stop altogether.

Would she invite him to stay…or bid him goodnight?

Chapter Nineteen

Standing inside her bedchamber door, Caro smiled back at Max. It *had* been an excellent day, the best she could remember since Papa's death.

She had all the horses for this year's sale, including the gelding she'd been working today, nearly ready. With Max's steady presence beside her, she'd finally had the courage to visit the graveyard and acknowledge that Papa was truly gone. She'd never stop grieving for him, but today, she'd finally allowed herself to lay him to rest.

Best of all, the Arabian stallion, the animal her father had considered the key to bringing the stud's bloodstock to a new level of quality, would be arriving any day.

Max had been the perfect companion, seeming to understand how much the achievement of Papa's goals meant to her. In truth, he'd encouraged her almost since their first meeting to talk about her horses and her plans for stud. And he'd even finally told her something of his own life, his difficulties with his father, his hopes of clearing his name.

Tonight, she would put out of mind the truth that the partnership that buoyed her today could only be temporary, for Max must soon leave, either to Vienna, or back to his life in London.

'Thank you for a wonderful day. A wonderful evening.'

'I'm so glad you'll soon begin realising your father's dream, Caro.'

Wishing she dared ask him to stay, she waited for him to bid her goodnight. Instead, his intent gaze locked on her face, he lingered.

She wanted him to linger. To admit the truth, she burned for another kiss like the one they'd shared on their wedding night.

There would be very few more nights when he would be near enough to kiss. If she were careful, maybe she could chance allowing herself something more intimate than the quick peck on the cheek that had been all she'd dared offer him since they returned to Denby.

Her heart commencing to beat a rapid tattoo against her ribs, she said, 'Won't you kiss me goodnight before you go?'

'With pleasure, my lovely wife,' he said, his deep voice sending a thrill of anticipation through her.

The kiss was delightful—a long, unhurried brush of his lips against hers, ending with a sweep of his tongue across their sensitive surface.

Excitement shot to every nerve, tingling in her nipples, pulsing between her thighs. Without quite intending to, she found herself kissing him back, deepening the pressure of her lips on his. She wasn't sure whether she opened to him or he to her, but suddenly their tongues were tangling, twining, licking, sucking.

She pulled his head down, wrapped her arms around him, plumbed his mouth with her tongue until she was breathless and dizzy. Until her breasts felt swollen and aching for his touch. As she arched her neck, he trailed tiny kisses from her mouth over her chin, down her neck, to the top of her low-cut bodice, then licked the skin beneath the gown's edge.

Suddenly, more than she'd ever wanted anything, she

wanted to have the gown and stays removed and feel his mouth against her bared skin.

Papa was gone; she'd never get him back. But the man who'd helped her accept that loss was vital and alive beside her. Before he left her, too, fiercely grateful and pulsing with need, she simply must have a touch and taste of him.

Ignoring the little voice shouting of danger, she caught his chin and tipped it up to face her.

'I want you to unlace me.'

'Whatever my lady wishes,' he replied, the hard glitter of desire in his eyes making her pulse leap.

Don't think, he'd told her on their wedding night. *Do what you feel.*

Insistent, driven, shutting her mind to everything but the sensations he aroused in her, she directed his hands to the tapes of her gown, the ribbons of her stays. Kissing him still, she let him loosen and pull them away, then guided his head down to her bared breasts.

She cried out at the first touch of his tongue on their sensitive surface, marvellous, exquisite, beyond anything she could have imagined. She threw her head back, gasping, as with fingers and tongue, he explored each breast, from the plump fullness beneath around to the top and finally, thrillingly, suckling the hardened nipples.

Heat and need consumed her. She pulled at his shirt, clawing at the cravat as he unwound it and tossed it aside. Jerking the shirt open, she slid her hands inside, her fingers seeking his nipples as his mouth laved, caressed and pleasured hers.

Emboldened by an urgent imperative that would not be denied, she slid her hands down his chest to his trouser flap and plucked open the straining buttons. His manhood sprang forth and she filled her hands with it, wrenching a cry from him.

While he suckled her, gasping, she fingered his length, from the hot, velvety tip to the coarse sacs beneath. Without realising how she'd got there, she felt the edge of the bed behind her. Her wobbly knees gave way and she sank back upon it.

Max tugged off her skirts while she kicked at them to help him, until she was clad only in the thin linen chemise. His eyes were a fierce blue in the candlelight that played over his powerful shoulders, his chest rising and falling rapidly in time to his ragged breathing. She leaned forwards to yank down his breeches, then paused to admire him, jutting proudly erect before her. He groaned and shuddered when she grasped him again and traced his length, then laid her cheek against it. 'Beautiful,' she murmured, 'Beautiful.'

With a growl, he kicked off his breeches and pulled her up against the pillows. Kissing her, he smoothed his hands down the thin fabric still covering her belly, then dragged the linen upwards and parted her legs to his view, his fingers tracing the most intimate part of her as he gazed at her. 'Beautiful,' he murmured in return.

When he touched the small nub at her centre, intense sensation rocketed outwards, making her cry out and leap beneath his hand. Murmuring, caressing her again and again while she thrashed her head against the pillows and the intensity built and built and built. His fingers dipped within her wet passage, massaging her in a maddening, delectable, slow liquid slide, in and then out again.

Suddenly she simply had to have him there, the firm hard length of him filling the place his fingers were stroking. With an incoherent murmur, she urged him above her, widened her legs and guided him to that pulsing, aching, spot.

She let out a sob of relief as he entered her, then stiffened with a little gasp at the stretching, tearing pain. Immediately he stilled, soothing her with kisses until her body relaxed and the pulsing within her began again, impelling her to thrust her hips and pull him deeper.

But holding himself above her, his elbows locked and arms corded with effort, only slowly did he increase the penetration. Wanting him deeper, wanting *something* she craved desperately, but which seemed to dance just beyond reach, she thrust up to meet him as he drove downwards, until she felt him fully encased within her.

He began to increase the rhythm now, faster and faster, seeming as driven as she. Suddenly she reached the precipice and sailed over, while starbursts of delicious sensation exploded within her.

Gasping, spent, she sagged back against the pillows, head whirling from wine and sensation. Murmuring her name, Max cried out. Moments later, he collapsed beside her and drew her close, cradling her against his chest.

Smiling, sated, satisfied, Caro fell asleep.

The warm tickle of a sunbeam on his face woke Max the following morning. As his mind rose slowly to consciousness, he reflected that he must have drunk more wine than he'd thought to have slept so late, when memories of the previous night came flooding back.

Grinning, he stretched languorously, an expansive feeling of contentment filling him. He'd always suspected Caro would be deeply passionate. The reality had proved better than his imaginings.

He couldn't wait to test that fact again. Though judging by the sun, the morning was rather far advanced, maybe he could do so even now.

But as he prepared to rise, he realised he was not in the bedchamber he'd occupied since coming to Denby Lodge, but in hers. The linens on the bed beside him were cold. Where had she gone?

Knowing his Caro, she'd probably tiptoed out at dawn, leaving him to sleep while she went off to work with her horses. With only a few weeks remaining before her sale, he advised his disappointed body, he'd probably not be able to lure her back to bed again this morning.

Would she meet him boldly this morning or blush to face him in the light of day, after giving herself wholly and urgently into his hands? Handling him in return. A hot flush of desire rushed through him as he recalled how she'd stroked him, fitted him to her, linked her legs behind his back to urge him deeper.

Despite her midnight display of passion, by daylight she'd probably be shy, he predicted. Suddenly he couldn't wait to discover which Caro he'd meet today, the practical, pragmatic horsewoman in her breeches and boots, or the wicked siren who'd stroked him in her bed.

Pulling on enough clothing to be decent, he jogged back to his chamber, changed into fresh attire and headed downstairs. Stopping in the breakfast room for some nourishment, he learned from Manners that the mistress had eaten early and gone to the stables. Tossing down his last sip of ale, he gave the butler a broad wink that had the servant hastily biting his lip to keep from smiling as Max walked out.

Max chuckled. The fact that the mistress had slept with her husband last night would be all over the manor by now.

As he neared the barns, Max picked up his pace. From a distance, he could just make out Caro standing by the fence of the first paddock, where she'd been working the gelding on a lunge line yesterday.

Joy, effervescent as the bubbles in last night's champagne, rose in his chest. He couldn't wait to see her, kiss her again. Though he'd been forced to enter this marriage, the reality of it was turning out to be better than he'd ever dared hope. With the passionate relationship he'd needed to seal his satisfaction with the bargain finally developing, he couldn't help but congratulate himself.

After spending every day with Caro for nearly a month, he found her as interesting, intelligent and amusing as he had the day she'd propositioned him for the first time in the greenhouse at Barton Abbey. He'd come to admire her expertise with horses and appreciate the firm grasp of business affairs that allowed her to run the stud with such efficiency. The scope of her interests and depth of her knowledge of the world, on display each evening as they talked over dinner and tea, continued to surprise and delight him.

To have ended up wedding a lady who combined the straightforward demeanor of a man with the passionate response of a vixen was a stroke of good fortune. To have found all that in a lovely woman who was also a substantial heiress made him the luckiest man in England.

All that remained to make his life complete would be to find Madame Lefevre and have her testimony clear his name.

Her back to him as she spoke with the head trainer, Caro didn't see him approach. After pausing until the conversation had concluded and the groom turned away, Max seized her by the shoulders, twirled her around and pulled her into his arms, then leaned down to place a kiss on her forehead.

'How is my lovely wife this morning?'

'Max!' she protested, her face colouring.

Shy, just as he'd predicted, Max thought, grinning.

'Walk with me?' he asked, his hands resting on her shoulders. 'I wish you'd awakened me before you left. I would have liked to demonstrate my appreciation for last night in a most *tangible* way.'

His fingertips first warned him that something was wrong, as he felt her shoulders stiffen under his touch. But his giddy mind still hadn't quite accepted the fact as she pulled free.

'I'm glad you were…satisfied.'

Her cool tone and averted face were so shockingly different from the joyous, passionate woman he'd made love to just a few hours ago, he felt her withdrawal as sharply as a slap. His delight and anticipation swiftly faded.

As he searched her averted face, trying to figure out what had happened, the happiness he'd felt upon waking this morning leached away, as water held in the hand seeps through clenched fingers.

'What is it, Caro? What's happened?'

'There's nothing wrong,' she said quickly, even as she took another step back, as if she couldn't tolerate his nearness. Avoiding his gaze, she added, 'I'm just...tense, with the sale so close upon us and so much left to do.'

He wouldn't let her retreat. Catching her chin, he forced it up, so she had to look him in the eye. 'Don't go all missish on me! Where's the straightforward woman I married? *Something* is distressing you. Why not just tell me what it is?'

To his dismay, her forehead creased and her lips began to tremble, while tears gathered at the corners of her eyes.

'Come on, Caro,' he coaxed, her reaction sparking real concern in him now. 'You know I don't bite.' Trying to distract her, he put a bit of wickedness in his smile as he added, 'At least, not so that it hurts.'

'It may hurt more than you can possibly imagine.'

Before he could ask her what she meant, she gave him a short nod. 'You're right; I have to tell you. Let's walk.'

A shock of alarmed disbelief ripped through him when he went to take her elbow—and she brushed his hand away.

Crossing her arms protectively in front of her chest, she said, 'You know how strongly I resisted getting married. Though it's true that I never wanted to wed anyone but Harry, there was another reason for my resistance. An even more serious one.'

While he listened in disbelief, she briefly told him about a condition which had afflicted nearly every female of her mother's family, a condition that had resulted in those women dying in childbed with their first child.

'Obviously, I know nothing of childbirth other than that it can be dangerous for the mother. But…you are saying there is some sort of—of flaw of the body that afflicts all women of your blood?'

She smiled without humour. 'I call it "the Curse".'

He shook his head. 'You truly believe in this? Isn't it more probable it is just unhappy coincidence?'

She hugged herself more tightly. 'Lady Denby said you'd probably think that. She doesn't believe it either. But I do. I've seen it. Not in my own mother's case, of course, but with my cousins. Four of them, dying as young women in birthing their first child.'

While he struggled to wrap his mind around those facts, she finally looked up at him. 'So you see, I haven't been trying to tease or bedevil you. As drawn as I am to you—and you cannot help but have noticed how much—I was…afraid,' she finished, two tears tracking down her cheeks. 'Afraid of what might happen, if I let you make love to me.'

Knowing how difficult it must have been for his strong, fierce Caro to admit that, appalled by what he'd just heard, Max could think of nothing to say.

'I thought, since you could have any woman you fancied, maybe you wouldn't desire me. I thought I could resist you. But last night…I wanted you more than my next breath. And it was wonderful beyond anything I could have imagined! But this morning, all I could see in the dull orange of the rising sun was the face of my cousin Anne as she died at dawn, holding my hand. And blood, everywhere blood.'

'Oh, Caro,' he murmured, and pulled her into his arms. This time, she did not resist.

For a long moment, he simply held her, her muffled sobs

resonating against his chest, while disbelief, horror and concern for her chased each other around his head.

Finally, she calmed and pushed away. He let her go.

'Why didn't you tell me this before we were wed?' he asked, anger beginning to merge into his tangle of emotions. 'Don't you think I had a right to know that ours could never be a normal marriage, without—without putting your life at risk?'

'I did tell you I wanted a marriage in name only,' she reminded him. 'And you did agree…though we both knew such a condition was not enforceable.' She shrugged. 'I didn't wish to show myself to be the coward I am. Besides, it is *my* risk.'

'Devil take it, Caro, I'm not such a monster as to heedlessly put your life in danger to satisfy my own lust!'

'What's done is done,' Caro said. 'I'm afraid you are saddled with me now. After last night, I shall just have to accept the risk. There are compensations, after all.' She gave him a wan smile. 'I shall no longer have to try to resist you.'

Even knowing the danger he placed her in, having to resist her would be difficult for *him* as well. A few moments ago, despite being shocked and appalled by what she'd revealed, just the feel of her breasts pressed against his chest, her flat belly rubbing against him, had been enough to make his member stir. Knowing the power of passion, he realised how insidiously his body could lure him into ignoring the risk.

Like standing near a burning building as fire consumed it, he felt falling around him the charred bits of this morning's illusion that with Caro, the marriage he hadn't wanted could turn into a close, fulfilling union.

Once again, not her fault. She *had* asked for a marriage of convenience. One like his parents'. Only he, arrogant bastard that he was, had thought to turn it into something more.

'Maybe it would be best if I made sure we both resisted temptation,' he said at last. 'I'm not sure I really believe in this "Curse" of yours, but it's enough that you do. Damn it, Caro, I don't want you risking your life. And frankly, I have even less desire to be a father than I did to be a husband. Heaven help me, with the example I had, what would I know about fathering?'

She flinched and he realised his reminder about his reluctance to wed must have hurt. But right now, hurting too, he couldn't make himself utter words of comfort.

'Why don't I leave for Vienna, as I've long planned? You've got your horses to train and the sale coming up; I'm sure you don't need me here complicating your work.'

'Distracting me,' she amended, making him feel a tad better. But then, taking an unsteady breath, she nodded her assent. 'Yes, that would probably be best. I've a thousand things to do and you will want to get on with your life.'

On with his life…leaving behind the inconvenience of a wife who cringed at his touch. How easily, Max thought, sorrow twisting like a knife in his gut, Caro seemed able to dismiss him.

Whereas, after their month together, *he* was now linked by affection as well as law to a wife he could not bed. Anger flared hotter. Once again, he was trapped in an impossible situation.

Maybe he could at least right the one in Vienna.

'Very well. I'll make arrangements to leave immediately. Today, if possible.'

She nodded vigorously. 'That would be best. As I shall be very busy all day, I may not be able to see you off, so I'll bid you farewell now. Good luck, Max. I hope you find the evidence you need.'

She stepped towards him, kissed his cheek briefly and stepped back. He made no attempt this time to pull her into his arms.

'Goodbye, Max. May you have a safe and successful journey.'

At that, she turned away and set off at a near-run towards the barn, as if she couldn't escape his presence quickly enough.

Max stood and watched her retreat, the idyll of their country life retreating with her. Joy had already drained away; now even his anger dissolved, leaving in its place a sense of loss that wounded him more sorely than he could have ever anticipated.

If his being gone was what she wanted, he'd oblige. He had a deal of experience in being sent away, too.

Turning on his heel, wildly contradictory emotions churning in his chest, Max set off for the house.

From the safety of the barn, Caro watched Max walk away. She pressed her lips together, her nails biting into the stable rail as she resisted the temptation to run after him, ask at least for a parting kiss to remember him by.

Ask him to stay.

But he'd been angry as well as appalled when he walked off. Would he ever kiss her again? Would she even see him again?

A throb of emotion made up of strong relief and a deep agony pulsed through her. The tears she'd been suppressing began to drip down her cheeks as she gave in to the memories warring within her.

She'd awakened in his arms, filled with a bone-deep peace and sense of wicked delight as she remembered each delicious kiss, touch and caress from the night before. She'd snuggled closer, trying to decide whether to awaken his quiescent member with strokes and kisses, or begin at his toes and explore every inch of his strong, perfect body.

Until her muzzy, sleep-dulled brain had cleared enough

for her to realise the full implications of what she'd permitted—nay, *encouraged*—Max to do. Dismay and horror rushed through her, bringing her fully awake in an instant.

He'd only spilled his seed within her once. Perhaps she hadn't conceived…yet.

But despite her dismay, merely thinking about him buried deep inside her body, moving within her, setting off such exquisite and powerful sensations, sent a rush of arousal through her.

Loving him had been quite simply the most marvellous, incredible, amazingly powerful experience of her life. Even knowing the danger, thinking about it reignited within her the desire to entice him to love her again and again and again. Aware now of its potential for delight, her body hungered for his caress, eager to repeat the journey towards that precipice, wanting to reach it with him and soar over together into ecstasy.

Watching him disappear around the bend leading to the house, fighting to keep herself from trying to recall him, she now understood why her mother and aunt and cousins had been willing to risk the Curse. It had little to do with a wife's duty to bear a son and everything to do with the euphoria of completion and the sense of union with another human soul that forged a bond even deeper than the one she'd shared with her father.

Could she let him go?

After her father's years of preparation, with the arrival of the Arabian, the dream of having the stud fulfil its full promise was within reach. The horse would be here within days. All that remained then would be to visit the breeders in Ireland for suitable mares and the last step of the crossbreeding process could begin.

Papa had estimated several years would be required to evaluate the foals and determine the final, best mix. But if she had at least one full year, she might get the process far enough under way that, if necessary, she could turn it over to someone else. With the stud books kept carefully and with continuous consultation, Newman might be able to carry on the programme without her.

If she worked diligently all that time, perhaps, when all was in place, she could seek out her husband. Ask to start over. Accept the risk of the Curse in exchange for the joy of being fully his wife.

If he would take her back. She tried to put out of her mind all the legions of beautiful, talented, enticing women waiting to amuse, seduce and pleasure a man like Max Ransleigh. Women she'd promised him complete freedom to enjoy.

What a fool she'd been, giving her blessing to that! Doubly foolish, for she'd let herself become attached to Max Ransleigh.

He didn't belong to her. Since it was inevitable that he return to his world, better for her that he leave now.

That bitter truth burning in her gut, she turned away from the door and forced her mind back to the horses. She'd work here until late tonight, hoping he completed his preparations and left today. She wasn't sure she could stand another scene like the one they'd just played.

Another painful stab of emotion seared her chest, shaking loose a few more tears. Angrily she swiped them from her cheeks. She'd felt bereft when Harry first left to go to university, too. But eventually the rhythm of life on the farm, bearing her along its stream of endlessly repeated tasks, had soothed the ache.

It would again.

But somehow, the prospect of accomplishing Papa's dream no longer filled her with the same thrill as before.

Chapter Twenty

Nearly two months later, Max waited impatiently in an anteroom of the British Ambassador's suite in Vienna. After a month of travelling by horse, carriage and mail coach from one inn or boarding house or manor to another, he was tired, gritty and not happy to be kept waiting by the men whose subtle condemnation had propelled him into the position he was in today.

As the door swung open, Max looked up to see Lord Bannerman, the undersecretary to the ambassador, walking in. Immediately Max's spirits rose; Bannerman was a gifted and discerning diplomat whose talents he had come to appreciate during his days on Wellington's staff. Thank heavens this time the embassy had seen fit to send in someone of authority, rather than the clerk who'd met him when he arrived in Vienna six weeks ago.

'Ransleigh, good to see you again,' Lord Bannerman said, shaking Max's hand. 'I understand congratulations are in order? You're recently married, I hear, and to a considerable heiress.'

'I am and thank you,' Max replied, an ache tightening his chest. Long, weary days of travel and fruitless searching had helped him avoid pondering the unresolved matter of what to do about Caro and their marriage…most of the time. But it remained ever just outside his thoughts, a lingering wound that refused to heal.

'Jennings told me he'd given you as much information as we had on Madame Lefevre. Were you able to turn up anything more?'

'No,' Max said, a month of frustration in his voice. 'What Jennings gave me was damned little. If I may be frank, my lord, I don't think the Foreign Office has much interest in my turning up anything.'

Bannerman smiled. 'You have to admit, Ransleigh, the whole situation was awkward. An attempt on Wellington's life, you claiming one of Prince Talleyrand's own aides was involved, Bonaparte's escape from Elba, every delegation in turmoil. Talleyrand insisting he had no knowledge of any plot and offended by the accusation that someone on his staff would stoop to assassination, neither one of the principals available for questioning… I'm afraid no one is very interested in dredging up that old problem.'

'Except me, whose reputation and career were tarnished.'

'Which was most unfortunate,' Bannerman said, genuine regret in his voice. 'You're a man of great talent, Ransleigh. You would have made a fine diplomat.'

A shock ran through Max. Through all the weeks of tiresome and ultimately futile investigation, he'd stubbornly kept alive the hope that he might somehow find vindication. But in the finality of Lord Bannerman's tones, he realised the trail had gone cold and the only authority with the reach to rake up the ashes had no intention of doing so.

He might truly never be able to clear his name.

Before he accepted that, he'd make Bannerman spell it out completely. 'So, as far as the Foreign Office is concerned, that's an end to it? That's why I was fobbed off with a mere clerk when I arrived and sent tromping through half the post-ing towns of Austria and Italy?'

Bannerman shrugged…and suddenly Max understood why the highly ranked Bannerman had been dispatched to interview him this time. 'Ah, now I see. The ambassador wanted you to find out if I *had* uncovered new evidence, then evaluate anything I might have discovered, so it could be suppressed if the Foreign Office deemed that prudent.'

'Yes,' Bannerman replied without apology. 'Very astute, Ransleigh. You truly would have made a superior diplomat.'

'No chance of that now, when I'm being officially pre-vented from clearing my name,' Max retorted bitterly.

Bannerman shrugged. 'Which means you must be destined to play some other role. I do understand your eagerness to wipe that blemish from your record. But, speaking as friend now, I strongly advise you to proceed no further with this. Prince Talleyrand has proved himself very helpful in restor-ing King Louis to his throne in France. The Foreign Office would find it most indelicate for someone to try to prove evidence of Bonapartist plotting amongst the prince's staff, perhaps upsetting the new balance we are trying to achieve.'

'So my good name is to be sacrificed in the cause of main-taining that balance.'

'Talleyrand holds the key to delivering France. We'll not do anything to undermine him. While you were fighting at Waterloo, would you not have sacrificed your life to keep Hougoumont from falling to the French, perhaps giving Napoleon the victory and unleashing a whole new wave of conquest upon the Continent? Of course you would have,' Bannerman answered for him. 'What is happening now in France may not involve cannons firing, but the outcome is no less important.'

Swallowing hard, Max nodded. 'You are right; one man's

reputation is not more valuable than the peace of Europe. So I'm wasting my time here.'

'A visit to a city as lovely as Vienna could never be considered a waste,' Bannerman returned blandly.

For a year, Max had been driven by the burning need for vindication. Pain and despair twisted in his chest as that hope died.

He'd never be seen as redeemed by his father. Never regain the trust of Wellington.

'I assure you, the Foreign Office does appreciate what you are sacrificing. I understand Colonel Brandon is looking for a War Department posting for you? We'll certainly assist in whatever way we can.'

'Thank you for that. And for your candour.'

'The business of diplomacy sometimes involves compromises we wish we didn't have to make. Good luck, Ransleigh. Best wishes to your bride.'

Max shook the hand Bannerman offered and, his spirits as weary as his body, walked from the room. As he passed the clerk manning the desk just inside the embassy entrance, the functionary called out, 'Mr Ransleigh! I have a letter for you.'

Only a few people knew he'd gone to Vienna. Since Alastair, the former poet, now seldom put pen to paper, the missive was most likely from his mother or aunt, Max thought. Thanking the clerk, Max took the letter.

With a shock of surprise, he noted the address was written in a feminine hand he didn't recognise. Might it be from Caro?

The unhappy terms upon which they'd parted had remained a hard, indigestible lump in his gut since that morning by the paddock at Denby Lodge.

After his departure, he'd deliberately thrust the problem from his mind, so that over the intervening weeks, he'd resolved none of those emotions. But now he found himself hoping it *was* Caro who had written—and was eager to see what she might have to say.

Restraining his impatience until he reached the privacy of his hotel suite several streets away, he unsealed the letter and rapidly scanned the lines.

My dear Max, I've directed this letter to the embassy, knowing they most likely will be able to pass it along to you. The sale at Denby went quite well, all the horses being placed with suitable owners and a number of new clients leaving preliminary orders for next year.

Immediately after the sale, she continued, her tone friendly, conversational, as if they'd never parted so bitter and abruptly, *I departed for Ireland, where I'm now visiting breeders with whom my father always worked. There are several very promising mares; after making my final choices tomorrow, I'll be travelling back to Denby.'*

He turned the note over. The words that met his eyes there sent such a shock through him, he sat upright in his chair.

I must apologize for the abrupt and hasty manner in which we parted. I hope, in time, you will forgive me for not revealing everything about my condition before we were wed, and we can start anew. I remain your affectionate wife, Caro.

Max re-read the last paragraph three times, the phrase 'I hope…we can start anew' resonating deep within him. He shook his head and sighed. The truth was, despite his anger and frustration the day they'd parted, he'd missed her. After barely a month of marriage, she'd inveigled her way into his consciousness and his everyday life so quietly but effectively that for these two months apart, he felt some vital element was missing, even as he tried to convince himself there wasn't.

With Caro around, almost every day had brought some new insight, some perspective he'd never envisioned, born out of a life experience so different from his own. Some new bit of knowledge about horses or breeding, or a clever flash of humour that delighted him.

She was different from any woman he'd ever spent time with. He found her at once maddening, intriguing, impossible...and enchanting. As he read the letter one more time, the hard lump of anger began to soften and melt away. In its place grew an eagerness to see her again and heal the breach between them.

He let her image, which had been dancing at the edges of his mind the whole time they'd been apart, play again on the centre stage of his mind. Caro, in boots and breeches, coaxing the gelding on a lunge line, or putting one of the sale horses through his steps. Sitting at the dining table, tickling his mind with her observations while her bared shoulders and handsome bosom tantalised his senses. Caro, in those ridiculous spectacles and hideous dress, the first day he'd met her at Barton Abbey.

An expansive sense of hope rose in him, filling in the cold despair left by the wreckage of his quest to find Madame Lefevre. Lord Bannerman was correct; if vindication was not to be had in Vienna, his future must lie elsewhere. And his wife would play a part in it.

He was re-reading the letter when a knock sounded on the door. The hotel servant delegated to serve as his valet appeared, announcing, 'A lady calling on you, sir.' He held out an engraved card.

Max didn't need the raised eyebrows of the servant to know a 'lady' would never visit a gentleman at his hotel. Glancing at the card, he noted the caller was Juliana von Stenhoff, a very expensive courtesan with whom he'd had an on-again, off-again liaison throughout the months of Congress last year.

'Did the lady give her direction?'

'She's waiting in the lobby, sir, and asked if it would be convenient for you to receive her now.'

Whatever did Juliana want with him? Curious, he said, 'Send her up, then.'

Though he'd not spent much time in the city itself, he was not surprised that Juliana had discovered he was back; she was impeccably well connected to the upper echelon of official Vienna. Doubtless, she also knew *why* he'd returned.

Perhaps Juliana, like Lord Bannerman, wanted to discover if he'd had any success. Max flattered himself that she'd developed an affection for him during their relationship and had been distressed by the disastrous end of his mission in Vienna.

Too bad he would not be able to tell her he'd found a way to rectify that finale.

A few moments later, Madame von Stenhoff swept into the room in a cloud of expensive perfume.

'Max! It's wonderful to see you again!' she exclaimed, offering him her powdered cheek to kiss before settling in the chair he showed her to. 'I'd heard you'd come back to Vienna. I called earlier, but was told you'd gone off into the countryside.'

'Yes, I've done a good bit of travelling.'

'Trying to find the Lefevre woman?'

'Yes. And frankly, having no luck. Bannerman at the Embassy just advised me to give up the search altogether. It's in the past and all those officially involved want to keep it that way.'

'I'm so sorry! I'd offer to corroborate your story, asserting that, being otherwise occupied by *me*, you couldn't have been bewitched by the French widow. But I'm afraid that wouldn't serve.' She laughed—a tinkling, musical sound that suddenly seemed studied and artificial to Max's ear. 'You men are such awful creatures! None of you would believe that possessing one mistress would stop a man from attempting to entice another.'

Letting that comment pass, Max said, 'I do appreciate your willingness to help.'

'I've always been willing to help…you.' She laid a soft white hand on his arm. 'I'm very fond of you, Max. I've missed you. Perhaps, now that you're back, we could…rekindle old memories?'

Gently he removed her hand from his sleeve. 'There's a small impediment. I have a wife now.'

She shrugged. 'Back in England—and running a horse farm, of all things, I hear! Quite wealthy, though. A clever match, under the circumstances. One that certainly doesn't create any impediments for me.'

The truth was, the fact that he was now married would not be considered an impediment by most of his peers. Nor had he entered marriage promising fidelity. Indeed, the wife in question had already given him permission to indulge himself.

As he knew well, Juliana von Stenhoff was quite a delicious indulgence.

But the fact that Caro had stood by him, believing in him to the point of confronting his father, made taking advantage of that permission smack too much of a betrayal he couldn't stomach. Despite the fact that, unless he was willing to put her at dire risk, they could never again be intimate. No matter how much his frustrated body clamoured for release and his mind whispered there was no harm in it, as Caro would never even know.

But *he* would. Nonsensical or not, tempted though he was by Juliana's sophisticated loveliness, he just couldn't do it.

'I'm afraid this business of having a wife does make a difference to me,' he said, catching up her fingers and giving them a brief kiss before releasing them. 'I appreciate your visit. But you should probably leave now.'

She stared at him for a moment in disbelief. 'Then everything we shared meant nothing to you?'

'Like the Congress itself, momentous and exciting as it was, now it's…over.'

Juliana made a moue of distaste. 'Well, if that's how you wish to look at it… I've never had to beg and don't intend to start now. Enjoy your time in Vienna, Max…alone.'

She rose in a swish of skirts. He could tell she was angry, not really understanding his reluctance to play the game as it had always been played in their world. As he himself had once played it.

Max couldn't blame her. He didn't fully understand what had changed in him either.

As she reached the doorway, she paused to look back over her shoulder. 'She must be special…this wife who runs a horse farm.'

A vision of Caro filled his mind: dark eyes glowing with concentration, auburn hair copper in the sun, as she soothed and gentled and guided a new foal. Spangled by candlelight, stroking and caressing and arousing him.

'She is,' he murmured.

'May she lead you a merry chase!'

Max laughed ruefully. 'She already has.'

Watching the slender, impeccably groomed, seductively dressed figure of the courtesan retreating through his doorway, Max thought that she could hardly be more different from his wife in dress, appearance, background and manner. Yet both women possessed a deep sensuality, cultivated and calculated in Julianna, natural, genuine, unstudied in Caro.

He felt a wave of longing for his wife, her presence, her conversation, her touch. He wanted her back in his life.

Besides, even if full intimacy was denied them, there were any number of other ways to pleasure her—and for her to pleasure him—that would bring them satisfaction without any risk of her conceiving a child.

Suddenly, he couldn't wait to teach her.

Nothing further could be done in Vienna, hard as it still was to concede that fact. Time to accept that and move on.

He probably ought to travel by way of London and call on Colonel Brandon. But then, as soon as possible, he would go back to Denby Lodge.

Caro was a challenge he'd yet to master. But if in spite of her permission, he was giving up all other women—and it appeared he was—he'd better go home and figure her out.

Chapter Twenty-One

Back at Denby Lodge, Caro stood by the barn door, supervising the installing of the new mares brought back from Ireland. The horses had made the transit in very good condition; she could begin working with them tomorrow.

She sighed, fighting fatigue and a vague depression. The day Max left, she'd felt relief that she'd no longer have to struggle with the impossible task of trying to resist him. But once he was gone, she'd missed him terribly. Missed his stimulating conversation over dinner, the interest he showed in the stud and his encouragement to realise her goals; missed their rides around the estate, during which she'd been acquainting him with the fields and woods she loved so deeply.

With her newly awakened senses clamouring for satisfaction, she drove herself hard each day so she might fall into bed too exhausted to yearn for his touch.

And there was something more. At first, she tried to tell herself her abrupt swings of mood and sudden desire to burst into tears were simply nervousness about the sale, even though, under her father's supervision, she'd conducted such sales many times. But by the time she finished her travels in Ireland, she could no longer deny that something more had changed than simply the loss of Max's presence.

For the last month, she'd awakened every morning with her stomach in turmoil, frequently finding herself forced to cast up her accounts before even rising from her bed. The smell and taste of food remained vaguely nauseating; she tired far too easily and her breasts had grown swollen and tender.

Then, for the second consecutive month, she'd missed her courses that were usually regular enough to set a clock by. Much as she tried to resist the conclusion, she knew she must be with child.

After the first flurry of panic, she'd come to a calm acceptance. Unfair as it seemed to have succumbed after only one interlude, if she had conceived, no amount of wishing otherwise could undo the condition. Instead, knowing the time she had left to work the stud might be even more limited than she'd imagined, she'd pledged to devote all her flagging energy and effort towards training horses for next year's sale and beginning the breeding process with her new acquisitions.

She'd written to Max from Ireland, once she'd been fairly sure about her condition. She'd debated telling him her suspicions, but ended by not doing so. If he chose to come back to Denby, she'd tell him then, but she didn't want the fact that she might be carrying his heir to force his hand, if he preferred not to return.

Sadness whispered through her. She could hardly blame him if he didn't come back. She'd already given him her blessing to conduct a life apart from her, in the London that was as dear and familiar to him as the barns and fields of Denby Lodge were to her.

Why should he visit a horse farm, when he had important work in the city…and his cares could be eased by some beautiful Cyprian skilled in the arts of pleasing a man?

She'd thought surely when she returned from Ireland, she

would be able to shake off her melancholy, that beginning to work the new horses would revive her energy and enthusiasm.

But for the first time in memory, returning to Denby Lodge hadn't filled her with excitement and unmuted joy. Instead, as she rode about the estate today, she'd found herself thinking about Max.

The wide sweep of meadow by the river reminded her of the day they'd picnicked there, him regaling her with stories about incidents from the Congress of Vienna. Reining in near the dense wood across from the manor brought back the afternoon they'd stopped there, walking the horses while she answered his questions about managing timber. In her desire to show him all her favourite places, she'd somehow managed to imprint his presence all over Denby land.

Now, everywhere she looked, she saw Max.

Perhaps it was because she carried his child. Now that she'd got beyond her initial terror, she was fiercely protective of the baby. Max Ransleigh was like the prince who visits the peasant girl in a fable: fascinating, exciting, larger than life, but a figure who would touch her life only briefly. All-too-ordinary horseman's daughter Caro Denby would never hold him here with her agricultural pursuits, but if she survived the birth of his child, she would have something of him to treasure always.

She put a protective hand over the slight round of her belly. And if he did, for some reason, return?

She couldn't expect him ever to spend much time at Denby, especially since he'd emphatically stated he had no desire to be a father. Sorrow filled her at all he had missed, having so distant a relationship with his own sire. Oh, that he might discover through their child the depth and richness of the love she'd known with her father!

But if he should come back, she'd made up her mind that, for as long as he remained at Denby, she would cast aside all inhibitions and do everything in her power to seduce him as often as possible. She'd revel in exploring the potent desire that drew them together, until he left for London again or her thickening body made her no longer attractive to him.

If he came back… Sighing, she released the rail and walked towards the groom who held out the new mare's lead.

Two weeks later, Caro was schooling one of the new mares in the paddock when she noticed someone at the bend of the lane walking toward the stables from the direction of the manor. Concentrating on her task, at first she paid little attention, until a familiar *something* about the stance and gait of the approaching figure seized her attention.

It couldn't be…yet she was almost certain the man walking down her lane was Max.

Disbelief turned to surprise and then an upsurge of excitement as the gentleman drew nearer and she identified him with certainty.

Why he had returned, she had no idea, but, dropping the mare's lead, she ran to the fence and scrambled through it. 'Max!' she cried, sprinting toward him. 'Is it really you?'

'Did you miss me, then?' he asked, studying her face as he halted before her.

Too happy to dissemble, she said, 'More than I ever believed possible.'

'Good,' he said, grinning. 'Why don't you show me how much?'

Caro threw her arms around his neck and pulled his face down, her lips assaulting his with two months of pent-up hunger. He opened to her, kissing her back just as fervently, until they were both breathless.

Finally, Max broke the kiss. 'Now, that's what I call a welcome! But I'm all-over dirt from riding; let me get back to the house and make myself presentable. Perhaps we could have tea? There's so much we have to discuss.'

'I should like that. Just give me some time to turn over the rest of today's training to Newman.'

'Shall I meet you in the salon in an hour?'

'Yes, an hour.'

He kissed the tip of her nose. 'I'll see you again soon, then.'

Her heart thudding in her chest with anticipation, Caro watched him walk with long, confident strides back down the lane to the manor, unwilling to let go of the sight of him until the curve of the lane took him from view. Joy filled her heart and mind to overflowing, washing away, at least for the present, all the fears, disappointments and worries that had plagued her.

He had come back. Whatever happened after, she would have him for tea and dinner and through the night.

Recognising the immensity of the joy and gratitude suffusing her at seeing him again, she finally had to admit another truth she'd long suspected, but had avoided acknowledging. Despite her counsel and caution and knowledge of the dire consequences, she'd fallen in love with her husband.

Just as it was too late to avoid the power of the Curse, there was little she could do now to protect her heart. Though she knew he was fond of her, he would probably never return the intensity of the affection she felt for him. But though he might not love her, she was certain she could seduce him into making love to her.

For however long he remained at Denby, she intended to fully enjoy his presence…and his touch.

Calling out for Newman, she hurried into the barn.

After reviewing the training schedule in record time, Caro raced back to her chamber and had Dulcie help her into her most attractive gown, scandalising the maid by leaving off her undergarments. One good thing about increasing, she thought as she regarded her reflection critically in the glass—her breasts looked even more voluptuous than usual.

She hoped he wouldn't be able to take his eyes off them.

When the maid finally finished, she nearly ran down the stairs to the parlour. She slipped quietly in, feasting her eyes upon Max, who stood facing the hearth. 'Hello again, Max,' she said, walking toward him. 'Welcome home.'

'Hello, Caro,' he said, and pivoted to face her. To her satisfaction, after greeting her, his eyes dropped immediately to her neckline. The thought of his eyes—and soon, his lips—lingering there made her nipples tighten and sent a spiral of desire through her. *My dear Max*, she thought, excited anticipation filling her, *you're about to get a welcome I hope you will never forget.*

Caro was even lovelier than he remembered, Max thought as his wife poured tea. She wore that gown of soft green he liked so much—not the least because it showed off her figure to perfection. Indeed, that taunting glimpse of her full breasts in that scandalously low-cut gown—he must remember to have her order a dozen more just like it—had his mouth watering and his whole body throbbing with desire.

He tried to summon enough wit to ask her about the sale and her trip to Ireland, and to respond to her questions about Vienna. But having not availed himself of the delights offered there, all he could think of was how long he would have to wait before he could coax Caro up to bed and begin leading her down all the many paths to delight.

'How goes Colonel Brandon's quest to find you a post?' she asked as she handed him a cup. 'I imagine you talked with him in London before returning here.'

'Actually, I didn't stop in London,' he replied, seating himself beside her on the sofa. *After two months away, he'd been too impatient to see Caro again.* 'Now that the sale has concluded, I thought perhaps I could wait for news here.'

'Of course you can, as long as you like.' She looked down at her teacup, her cheeks colouring. 'I'm…so sorry about what happened before you left. As I told you in my letter—'

'Apology accepted, Caro. You don't need to explain. I would have preferred knowing the whole truth at the beginning, but there was no deception; you made your preferences plain from the first. I was the one who wilfully misunderstood.'

She looked up, a film of tears in her eyes. 'I should have made myself tell you the whole. After I had not I…I wasn't sure you'd ever forgive me enough to come back.'

'I had to come back. I missed my wife.'

She smiled tremulously. 'You did?'

'Yes. You did say you missed me, too, didn't you?'

Nodding, she put down her cup. 'And promised to show you how much. Shall I do so again?' she asked, a hot glow in her eyes that sent an answering blaze of heat through him.

'By all means,' he replied, setting aside his own cup, his fingers trembling with eagerness.

She put her hands on his shoulders and kissed him again, then placed little nibbling bites over his chin and lips.

He responded avidly, opening his mouth to her. Another blast of desire roared through him when he felt her hands under his coat, tugging at the buttons of his waistcoat, scratching aside the linen of his shirt to find bare skin beneath. With her fingertips, she kneaded and massaged the muscles of his chest, all the while licking his lips, sucking and nipping at his tongue.

Dizzy, his pulse hammering in his temples, Max could scarcely catch his breath. Though he finally broke the kiss, he clamped his hands over hers to trap them under his shirt, craving the feel of them against his bare skin. 'I love the way

you welcome me, dear wife,' he said unsteadily, 'but if you
don't stop, I won't be able to wait until dinner, much less tonight, without trying to woo you into bed.'

'I don't want to wait, either,' she said, taking his hands
and moving them down to her breasts. 'Touch me, please.
Oh, I've burned for your touch!'

'And I've burned to touch you,' he murmured. With Caro
so eager—and himself beyond eager—the idea of waiting
hours, through dinner and conversation and the tea tray, was
simply unacceptable. But he didn't wish to ruin what was
promising to be a spectacular reunion by having some footman or housemaid stumble into the parlour and discover her
sitting on his lap with her bosom bared and her skirts about
her waist.

Mind made up, he leapt up from the couch.

'Where are you going?' Caro gasped, dismay on her face.

'Nowhere, sweeting,' he said, smiling at her distress. 'And
neither are you.' Striding over to the hearth, he snatched the
key from its place on the mantel, swiftly locked the door and
returned to the sofa. Dropping the key beside his cup, he said,
'And where were we, wife?'

'Ah, my clever husband,' she said, raising her smoky gaze
to his. 'We were right—' she placed his hands over her breasts
'—*here*.'

'I love *here*,' he murmured before leaning to take her
mouth hungrily while he cupped her breasts and rubbed his
thumbs over the prominent nipples. With a little cry, she
yanked down her bodice and suddenly his hands were filled
with warm, bare flesh. She must have left off both chemise
and stays, he realised, before turning his attention to laving
and sucking first one nipple, then the other.

While he suckled her, she moved her hands in a sensuous
slide down his bare chest. When the constriction at his trouser front suddenly eased, he realised she was unbuttoning

the flap. He felt cool air as she freed him; an instant later, the coolness was replaced by the warmth of her hand. His member leapt and he cried out as she gripped him lightly, stroked him, rubbed her thumb over the tip.

'Not yet, or I'll never last,' he gasped. Gently plucking her hands away, he said, 'First, let me show you how much I like being back.'

'I give myself into your hands,' she said, angling her head back upon the sofa cushions and arching her back, displaying her bare breasts to him. 'What of these, my lord?' She guided his hands under their ripe fullness. 'Do you like these?'

'I love them.'

'Then show me…with a kiss.'

Eagerly Max leaned forwards, cupping and caressing one breast, his thumb working the nipple, while he sucked the other into his mouth.

He felt her nails bite into the skin of his back, through his shirt. 'Ah, I like that, too,' she panted.

His mouth still at her breasts, he reached down with one hand, tugged up her skirts and slid his fingers beneath them. Grasping her leg, while he suckled her, he smoothed and caressed the back of her knee, the satin expanse of one thigh.

Moaning, she let her legs fall apart, giving him the access he needed. While he lightly nipped first one nipple, then the other, he slowly moved his hand higher, to the velvety inside of her thighs. Teasing the tight curls apart, finding her moist and ready, he rubbed the nub at their centre.

She gasped and bucked against his hand. Soothing her with a murmur, he pressed her back against the cushions and stroked her again, matching the rhythm of his fingers to that of his tongue against her nipple. Her breath sobbing in and out, she began moving her hips against his ministering hand.

He followed her frantic motions, increasing the pace. Her breathing turned to short panting gasps, her nails cutting into the flesh of his neck. He slid one finger, then another, into her slick depths while massaging the tender nub above with his thumb. Seconds later, she reached her peak and came apart in his hands.

For a few moments, she lay limp against the cushions. Then she opened dazed eyes and smiled at him.

'That was amazing.'

He felt like a strutting peacock, full of self-satisfied masculine pride at the compliment. 'Thank you. I found it rather amazing, too.'

'Did you? But I do think it was unfair of me to find pleasure, while you had none.'

'Watching you is a pleasure.'

'I should like to return the favour…if you will let me. Though I'm not perfectly sure just what to do, I expect you can guide me.' She reached to slide a finger down his still-rigid length.

Gasping as pleasure pulsed through him, he caught her hand. 'I think you have a natural talent.'

'And does that…not please you?' she asked, her tone anxious.

He wondered if she'd been told that wives were to lie still during their husbands' efforts, enduring with silent decorum. 'It pleases me immensely.'

'Good. I was never brought up to behave like a decorous lady. And with you, I fear I can't make myself behave like a lady at all. So won't you let me please you…more?' Extracting her fingers from his restraining hand, once again she traced his length.

His manhood leapt beneath her stroking fingers and he gasped for breath. He'd wanted only to give her a taste of passion, intending to wait for the privacy of a bedchamber and the lazy uninterrupted hours of the night to show her more.

But the exquisite feel of her stroking him, the idea of her

exploring his body not in the dimness of a candle's faint glow, but boldly, in the full light of day where he could see her every expression, was so enormously arousing he couldn't make himself tell her to stop.

'Do you like that?' she asked softly.

'Yes,' he said on a groan.

'Good,' she said and kissed him. And as he had done for her, in rhythm to the stroking of her tongue within his mouth, she slid her hand up and down his length, fondling the taut sides and creamy tip, until he shattered in her hands as she had shattered in his.

After a few moments, when strength returned to his boneless arms, he gathered her close. For a long quiet moment, they simply held each other.

With her head cradled on his chest, listening to the sigh of her breathing as it steadied, Max felt a surge of new hope for the success of their union.

Finally, he moved her back to arm's length. 'I'm afraid we must now tidy ourselves and prepare for dinner before the household is scandalised.'

'Why should they be? We're respectably married, and you've been gone a long time. A *very* long time.'

Max thought of the many occasions when his father had been gone for months. But he couldn't imagine his reserved mother or the rigidly formal earl enacting a scene at Swynford Court such as the one they'd just played out in this parlour, no matter how long his father had been absent.

While he smiled at the very notion, Caro said, 'I suppose we must tidy up. I'm afraid I've quite ruined your neckcloth.'

'To say nothing of the silk of your bodice and skirts.'

'I'll order a tub. Will you come and help me bathe?'

Despite their recent activity and his fatigue, desire stirred in him again. Was she inviting him to what he thought she was inviting him? Even if just to watch, he was ready.

'I wouldn't miss it.'

With a sigh, she levered away from him. She gave his spent member a loving stroke before doing up his trouser flap. While he in turn tried to restore her ruined bodice, she helped him tuck in his shirt and button his waistcoat.

'There. We're not quite respectable,' she said, 'but at least we are clothed.' She linked her hand in his. 'Walk with me, won't you? It's shameless of me, I suppose, but I can't get enough of touching you. Does that displease you?'

'Not a bit. I can't get enough of touching you.'

They had repaired to their separate chambers while water was fetched. A few minutes later, she responded to his knock, bidding him to enter. He found her wrapped in a dressing gown, standing beside a steaming tub.

'I was waiting for you to help me in.' She surveyed his coat and breeches with a frown. 'But you're not ready.'

'Did you plan to wash me, too?'

'If you like.'

He imagined warm, wet silky skin, with her touching him all over. Hardening immediately, he said, 'I should like it very much.'

'Let me act as your valet, then.'

And so she did…nearly driving him mad in the process. After peeling off his coat and waistcoat she took her time removing the remaining clothing, rubbing and stroking each new area of skin uncovered. His wrists and forearms, biceps and shoulders, chest and flat nipples that puckered under her touch as she removed his shirt. She pulled his breeches down over his bottom, opened her dressing gown and wrapped it around the two of them, hugging him close, rubbing her belly against his erection and the soft rounds of her breasts against his chest.

After pulling his head down for an urgent kiss, she said, 'We must climb in before the water gets too cold.'

He helped her in and followed, sinking into the blessed heat. But before she could turn to face him, he lifted her to sit on his lap, facing away from him. Pulling her against him, he kissed and licked her neck, cupping her breasts to hold her against him in the gentle ebb and flow of the water.

He found it delicious, exciting, and soon they were both panting with arousal. He lifted her, guided himself between her legs and anchored her against him with one hand cupping her mound, the other parting her curls to caress the little nub.

'Please,' she gasped. 'This time, I want to feel you inside me.'

'No, sweeting, we don't need to take the risk. I can show you other ways to pleasure that will not endanger you.'

In one swift motion, she levered herself off his lap, turned to straddle him and, before he realised what she was doing, thrust down hard, taking him deep within. He cried out as a wave of heated sensation engulfed him—the warmth of her body, her scent, the hot sweet tightness of her passage embracing him, rocking against him in the semi-weightlessness of the water. Taking his hand, she touched it to where their bodies joined.

'See,' she gasped. 'Is this not…better still?'

In the tiny part of his brain not overwhelmed with sensation, he knew he should push away and withdraw. But then she kissed him, her tongue ravishing his mouth as she wrapped her legs around his back and thrust against him again and again, rocking into him with the ebb and flow of the heated water.

And then there was nothing but wetness and heat and ever-higher waves of sensation as the tension built and built until all he could do was kiss her back and clutch her to him and ride out the pleasure. Finally, she cried out and writhed against him while he pulsed and emptied himself deep within her.

She sank back against him limply. Cradling her to his chest, he leaned back against the side of the tub, resting his head on the edge, his soul filled with a deep sense of peace.

He *had* come home, he realised. There was nowhere else he'd rather be than right here, a wonderfully passionate Caro naked in his arms, his member sheathed in her.

But no…he should not be sheathed in her! Conscious thought returning in a rush, he sat up straight. 'Caro, sweeting, we mustn't do this. I didn't come back to place you at risk, but to—'

'Hush,' she said, putting a finger to his lips. 'You don't have to worry about that any more.'

His nascent guilt subsiding, he relaxed back into the tub. 'You've discovered the Curse is an illusion?'

'No, I still believe it. But there's no longer any reason for me to fear intimacy because…because I'm already with child.'

His sleepy languor dispelling as effectively as if the bath-water had suddenly turned to ice, he cried, 'With child! Caro, are you sure?'

'Almost positive. I have all the signs and I've twice missed my courses.'

Consternation displaced the sense of peace and well-being. 'Devil take it, Caro, what are we to do?'

'Nothing. There's nothing that can be done now. Except, I hope, more of this.' She rocked against him.

Despite his dismay, a pulse of sensation throbbed through him, stiffening his member. Before he could form some response, she pressed a long soft kiss on his lips.

'My dear Max, what happens now is in God's hands. But if something untoward should transpire—'

'Don't even think it!' he interrupted.

'—then I should like to know that I had tasted all the sweetness life can offer. And nothing I have ever tasted is sweeter than this. Did you not find it wonderful, too?'

'Yes,' he affirmed. 'It is indeed wonderful. But, Caro, shouldn't you see a doctor? Let me take you to London with me when I go to meet with Colonel Brandon. Surely there's a specialist there who could examine you and determine—'

'No, Max. My cousin Anne consulted the best physician in London. He checked her carefully, laughed at her fears and told her there was absolutely nothing wrong with her. But there is some good news in all this; those few who do not succumb to the Curse seem to have no difficulty with subsequent births.'

A *frisson* of hope lightened the weight of guilt and apprehension. 'That is good news. We shall just assume that you will fall in that group.' *And so he would maintain, to ease her fears, if nothing else.*

She nodded. 'I'm not going to spend the next few months looking over my shoulder for the Grim Reaper, but savouring every bit of enjoyment life has to offer. Won't you help me?'

What else could he do, but try to make these next months happy for her? Though he would never have knowingly put her at risk, if he had not called up every charm and trick he knew to seduce her that long-ago night at Denby, she might have resisted him…and not now be facing this test. 'Of course.'

'And, Max…I know you have no desire to be a father. I'll try to make sure that the child isn't a burden to you.'

Another little shock zinged him. In his concern for Caro's health, it hadn't really registered that, at the end of it all, he would be a father. He could hardly think of anyone less suited, he thought, his dismay and apprehension deepening.

Those emotions must have been writ clear on his face, for Caro laughed softly. 'It won't be as bad as all that. The farm is a wonderful place for a child to grow up. Don't worry; on your visits, he will only be presented to you when he's on his best behaviour, his face freshly washed and his nankeens clean.'

Her eyes glowed as she spoke about the child…his *son*. 'You are happy about the prospect?'

'I love it,' she said simply.

He wished he could avow some excitement of his own… but his tongue seemed stuck to his teeth. He realised it probably hurt Caro that he was unable to respond with enthusiasm about the child she now seemed eager to bear, but he'd never dissembled to her.

He'd concentrate on handling one challenge at a time. While he tried to dredge up some anticipation for being a father, he'd work to keep Caro's spirits cheerful…and try to persuade her to see that London physician.

Suddenly he was conscious of how cold the bathwater had become. 'Come, we'd better get you out before you catch a chill.'

She let him help her out. After they'd both wrapped up in thick robes, she said, her tone wistful, 'Could I ask a favour?'

Ignoring a stab of alarm, he said, 'What would my lady have of me?'

'Sleep in my bed tonight. Let me touch you, taste you… everywhere.'

Max blew out a relieved breath. 'Willingly. Though I suppose we must dress and dine first.'

'I'll order a tray. I want to dine with you clad only in your dressing gown, knowing there is nothing beneath it but skin, every inch of which you are going to allow me to explore.'

Amazingly, he felt desire rising again at the thought of Caro touching him, tasting him.

'Then I am at your service.'

So, wrapped in dressing gowns—he imagining as eagerly as Caro her dining with nothing but bare skin beneath the soft covering of her robe—they huddled together on the sofa in her sitting room. Once the food arrived, Max discovered he was starving and fell upon the cold ham, cheese, biscuits and ale with enthusiasm.

They talked of the investigation in Vienna, the success of Caro's sale at Denby Lodge, the pedigrees of the new mares she'd just purchased and the prospects for the foaling season to come.

Finally, replete, he took Caro's hand and kissed the fingertips. 'Now, my dear wife, to bed.'

'Finished at last, my lord glutton?' she teased. 'I hope your appetite for other pleasures is equally robust.'

'I shall be delighted to demonstrate just how insatiable I can be,' he promised.

'Good.' Taking his hand, she led him through the door into the bedchamber. Slipping beside him on the bed, she guided him back against the pillows and tugged his robe open. 'Now, it is *my* turn to gorge myself.'

And she did, beginning at his toes, stroking, nipping, suckling and tasting, in a long slow assault that had him breathing hard by the time she reached his ankles and gasping by the time she reached his knees. His fingers clutched the linens as she worked his thighs, parting them, stroking, kneading them with her fingers. His aching member jutted up proudly when she reached it, his body already dewed in perspiration at the thought of what she might do there.

She rubbed her face against him, wrapped his hardness in the silk of her hair up to the smooth tip, then traced the tiny opening with her fingertip and her tongue, caressing the sacs beneath with a silken brush of strands, before taking him in her mouth.

His hands splayed on the bed, his back arched, he moaned and cried out as she explored him, tasted him, devoured him. Just when he felt he couldn't hold on another second, she climbed up and straddled him, thrust him deep inside and rode him, her beautiful full breasts jutting above him.

Afterward, he pulled up the bed linens and wrapped her in his arms, too full of awe to speak. What a wonder she was, shy yet brazen, calm and patient with her horses, yet sensual and demanding. Intelligent, inquisitive, thoughtful, an expert in her realm, though she focused on pursuits unlike those of any woman he'd ever known.

Uniquely Caro. *His* Caro.

Max woke several times in the night, to find Caro touching him—her lips to his, or her hands tracing the muscles of his chest, or her fingers exploring the contours of his manhood, nuzzling his chest as it swelled at her caress. He showed her how he could pleasure her as she lay on her side with him behind her, stroking into her while her tender nub and breasts lay open to his touch. In the dark of early morning, he kissed her from sleep and cradled her beneath him, her legs wrapped around his back as he thrust deep and hard, driving her into the softness of the mattress.

Finally, one last time as dawn began to light the sky, he insisted it was his turn to taste and explore her. He began at her temples, licking and sampling, moving down to her chin, the hollow of her throat, the tender skin beneath her ears. While he kissed her, he slid his hand down to cup her mound, parted her moist folds to caress the plump nub within, slipped a finger inside and back out, massaging mound and nub and passage. Continuing his gentle efforts there, while she gasped and murmured, he moved lower to lick her shoulders, her collarbone, her elbows, her wrists. After tasting her breasts again, he proceeded to her belly, nibbling on her hip bones, licking the deep recess of her belly button until she shattered against his fingers.

Giving her a few moments for her ragged breath to steady,

he set off again, this time to the silk of her inner thigh. He revelled in the warmth and scent of her, his goal almost within reach. Finally finding what he craved, he circled her nub with his tongue, suckled it, raked his teeth over it.

By now, she was gasping and straining against him, but he refused to hurry. Wanting to inflame her by gradual degrees, he slowed the rhythm as he licked and stroked her passage, intoxicated by the taste of her, almost painfully aroused by the thought of being embraced within her heat as she reached her climax.

But before he could tease her over the edge, she pushed at his shoulders, urging him back. 'Go with me,' she pleaded.

Drawing himself up, he entered her as she wrapped her legs around him to hold him deep. For sweet exquisite moments, they moved together, one flesh, one purpose, one goal. At last, she cried out, her hands gripping his shoulders, as his seed burst within her.

Exhausted now, they lay spent in each other's arms and slept.

It was nearly noon when they finally woke. Looking out of the window at the full daylight, Caro groaned. 'I must do some work, I fear. Though with you here, I wish never to leave my bed!'

'It will still be here later…and so will I,' he assured her.

To his delight, she asked him shyly if he'd like to accompany her to the stables. He quickly agreed, marvelling how she could be so reticent about that when she seemed not at all embarrassed to descend the stairs with him at nearly noon and demand a plate of bread and cheese from servants who must know what they'd been doing abed all those hours.

Content to stand at the rail and observe Caro's expertise, he found the routine of training as fascinating as ever. When he complimented her on her skill in soothing the skittish young mare she'd been working, she said, 'It's easy, really. You just have to observe what she's telling you with her neck and ears and haunches, and move at her pace. Would you like to try?'

'I'm a rank novice,' he replied. 'I don't want to make a mistake and set back her training.'

'You won't. Horses are very forgiving, if they sense you mean them well. I'll show you what to do.'

And so he proceeded to the centre of the paddock, where she taught him how to hold the lead rein, how much pressure to apply from it to the mare's halter, what verbal commands to use.

Then she had him stand behind her, his hands on the reins along with hers, while he tested and mastered the touch. After several circuits around the ring, she removed her hands, letting him do it on his own.

The mare continued to circle on command, just as she had for Caro.

'Excellent,' she told him. 'See, you do have the touch.'

He felt a glow of pride at her praise, even though, with her standing before him, her warm round bottom rubbing against his legs, he was finding it increasingly difficult to concentrate on technique.

Finally he abandoned the attempt altogether, dropping the reins and wrapping her in his arms. Murmuring, she leaned into him and pulled one of his hands down to cup her breeches.

Amused and tantalised by her boldness, he caressed her, his member leaping when she shivered under his touch. Whirling her around, he gave her an open-mouthed kiss, his heart exulting.

Who could have imagined he would find Venus in an old pair of breeches and her father's worn riding boots? The angle of her cheekbones, the contour of her lips, the sleek curve of her hips and roundness of bosom; the scent of her hair and skin, the taste of her mouth; everything about her intoxicated him. He wanted to inhale and devour and savour.

Breaking free with a mischievous glance, she snatched up the lead rein. 'We'll set her free in the meadow and take the tack back to the barn.'

After turning the mare loose, they walked inside to hang up the reins, leads and halter. Caro looked up at him, her eyes heavy-lidded.

'What are you thinking about?' she asked.

'Bed,' he answered promptly. 'Or tea, like yesterday's.'

'Beds are very nice,' she agreed. 'But I've always loved the scent of the barn…all that sweet, fresh hay, forked into mounds as soft as a feather mattress.' Slowly she wet her lower lip with the tip of her tongue.

His body responded instantly. He couldn't banish the threat of what might happen in seven months. But he would willingly give her all the pleasure she wished for now.

'Soft as a feather mattress?' he repeated, pulling her into the nearest box stall, empty now that all the horses had been loosed in the pastures. Turning to face him, she plucked open the buttons of jacket and blouse and bared her breasts. 'Are you thinking of these?' she murmured.

With an incoherent growl, he bent and drew one taut nipple into his mouth, raking it with his teeth, while she arched her neck, gasping. Her fingers fumbled for the buttons of his trouser flap, wrenched them open, found him hard and eager.

His breathing grew ragged and his pulse accelerated as she stroked him while he suckled her. Finally, lifting his head to kiss her lips urgently, he half-walked, half-stumbled with her to the mound of hay in the corner of the box. After pulling off her boots, he settled himself into the fragrant cushion. With hands now trembling with eagerness, he pulled down her breeches while she unbuttoned his trouser flap, then lifted her to straddle him and guided her on to his lap. They both gasped as his hot, hard member touched her moist folds. Seizing his shoulders, she kissed him and thrust down hard, taking him deep.

His breath coming fast and hard, he cradled her soft bottom, pulling her tightly against him as he moved slowly within her. Whimpering, she tried to speed the pace, but he wouldn't let her, maintaining instead a steady, barely quickening rhythm that soon had her crying out with every thrust, until she spasmed around him and he followed her over the brink.

For a few moments, Max lay back, lazy and replete, twining her braids around the fingers of one hand while he trailed the fingers of the other over her breasts, admiring their voluptuous fullness, the nipples cherry-red from his teeth and tongue.

'You continue to amaze me,' he murmured.

'I can't seem to help myself. It's no wonder full knowledge of lovemaking is kept from maidens. If they knew it could be like this, there would never be another virgin bride.'

'It isn't always like this.'

'Isn't it?'

'Well, it's always good. But not…amazing, wonderful. You make it so, Caro.'

She smiled, her expression tender. 'No, I'm quite sure it is you who make it so. Thank you, Max. I never expected to know such happiness. I…thank you.' She kissed him gently.

Just then, Max heard the murmur of voices and the sharp strike of hoofs on the stone floor. 'We'd better get presentable, lest we scandalise the grooms as we have the household staff.'

Grinning, he pulled her up. Kissing and touching delaying their efforts, she managed to button his trouser flap and tuck in his shirt while he retrieved her boots and helped her into her breeches. Hand in hand, nodding to the grooms as they passed them, they walked out of barn.

Max stood in the sunlight, breathing deeply of the soft country air, his senses replete, his mind filled with a sense of peace more profound than he could ever remember experiencing in London or back at Swynford Court.

Here there was no autocratic father to please, no hunting for a suitable position. Only his deeply sensual, straightforward Caro and days filled with the rhythm of challenging work. He had the odd thought that he could almost believe he would be content to stay here for ever, pleasuring and watching over Caro and her horses.

'What next, my fair taskmaster?' he asked, pulling a stray bit of straw from her hair.

Smiling, Caro had opened her kiss-swollen lips to answer, when suddenly her eyes widened at something she must have seen behind him. A look of incredulous delight lifting her face, she cried, 'Harry!'

By the time Max recalled the identity of the person with that name, his wife had run over to throw herself into the arms of the man she'd told him she'd always intended to marry.

Chapter Twenty-Two

A jolt going through him, Max watched as a tall blond man in the uniform of the 33rd Foot caught his wife and swung her around before setting her back on the ground. 'Caro! It's so good to see you again!'

'When did you get back?' she demanded. 'Why didn't you write you were coming?'

Dropping a kiss on her hands before releasing them, the officer stepped back. His smile fading to a frown, he gave Max a hostile glance.

'There wasn't time,' he replied, turning his attention back to Caro. 'When I got your letter, I talked the colonel into letting me come back to take care of some battalion business he was going to entrust to another officer.'

'My letter?' she echoed, looking puzzled.

'The one you wrote telling me that Woodbury had convinced the other trustees to sell the stud. You sounded so desperate, I thought I'd best get back here with all speed. I feared I'd find you distraught, maybe with the horses already gone. Instead,' he said, his tone turning frosty as he inspected her, 'you look like you've just been trysting in the barn. With him?' He transferred his disapproving gaze to Max.

Caro's cheeks flamed a guilty red, turning the lieutenant's

expression even grimmer. But before Max could intervene to tell the man a thing or two, Caro said, 'I have a lot to explain. But first, let me introduce you. Max, as I imagine you have guessed, this is Lieutenant Harry Tremaine, my oldest and dearest friend. Harry, this is Max Ransleigh.'

After the two exchanged stiff bows, Harry said, 'Earl of Swynford's son, aren't you? On a buying trip for him, I expect? Let me wish you well before you depart.'

'Please, Harry…' Caro protested. 'With your permission, Max, I'd like to tell Harry what…has happened since I first discovered Woodbury meant to sell the stud. We'll rejoin you in the house a bit later.'

'Why do you ask for *his* leave?' Tremaine demanded.

'Because he's my husband, Harry,' she said quietly. 'Did you not know?'

The stunned shock on Tremaine's face announced quite clearly that he had not. 'Husband!' he echoed. 'No, I hadn't any idea. What the deuce has been going on?'

'It's…complicated,' she allowed, giving him a strained smile. 'With your leave, Max?'

He would have preferred to order the man off the property. Everything about Lieutenant Harry Tremaine made him bristle with outrage, from the proprietary manner in which he looked at Caro to the way he strutted about the paddock with an unconscious air of authority, as if he had every right to be at Denby Lodge, monopolising its mistress.

Still, though he'd much rather challenge Tremaine to a bout of fisticuffs, Max bowed to Caro's wishes. He supposed her 'oldest friend' did deserve to receive an explanation of the radical change in Caro's life—without an outsider listening in. 'I shall see you later,' he said grudgingly. 'Not much later, though,' he added in a warning tone.

'Thank you,' she said simply. 'Come along to the paddock, Harry. While we talk, you can see the new mares I have just purchased.'

Max walked back towards the manor as his wife led the interloper into the paddock, trying to master the anger, resentment and, yes, jealousy nipping at him.

So this was the man she loved, the one she'd always thought to marry. He hadn't much worried about Lieutenant Harry Tremaine while the soldier was halfway around the world.

Now that he was back in England, was Max playing the fool, letting his wife speak to her old lover in private?

After the last two days, Caro ought to be sated. But she'd shown herself to possess an incredibly sensual appetite.

Might she try satisfying it with Tremaine?

Stop it, he ordered himself. This way lay madness. Caro had made him a solemn promise before God and he knew down to his bones she meant to keep it. He'd talk to her about Tremaine when she came back to the manor, but he'd not insult her honour by going back to fetch her.

He reached the house, went to the library and poured himself a large glass of wine. He only hoped their talk would be of short duration.

Meanwhile, at the paddock, Caro distracted Harry for a short time as, with a true horseman's interest, he inspected the new mares. Soon enough, though, he completed his appraisal and turned back to her.

'Married!' he exclaimed. 'How is that possible?'

'I think I'm offended. It's not *impossible* someone would want to marry me,' she said, trying to lighten Harry's thundercloud expression.

'You know what I meant,' he said impatiently. 'The marriage is final, then? You can't get out of it?'

'No. We wed in church, before God and witnesses. It's fully binding.'

'Why Ransleigh? I didn't even know you were acquainted with the man.'

Omitting that she'd originally requested Max to ruin her, Caro briefly summarised what had happened at Barton Abbey, her refusal of Max's first offer, then the desperation over the sale of the stud that led her to reconsider. Harry listened in grim silence.

'I'm sorry, Harry, if you feel…betrayed,' she said when she'd finished the account, 'but truly, it was the only alternative—'

'I understand,' he interrupted. 'I don't like it, but I understand. As soon slay you where you stand as take away the stud. Damn Woodbury! I just wish I had been here, so you could have turned to me. Or that India wasn't so damned far away, that I could have returned here before it was too late.'

'I wish you'd been here, too. But you weren't. And that's an end to it.'

'An end…to us?' He shook his head disbelievingly. 'I can hardly imagine such a thing. I've never even considered marrying anyone else.'

Caro felt tears welling in her eyes. From the moment she'd decided to marry Max, she'd dreaded having to eventually face Harry and explain why she'd all but jilted him. She'd thought then that he would write her before returning from India, so she'd have time to prepare for the difficult reunion.

Groping to find the right words, she said, 'I never had either, until circumstances forced me into it. But if I had to marry someone else, I'm glad it was Max. You'll like him, Harry; he's a good man—kind, intelligent, sympathetic.' *Whose touch drives me wild*, but she didn't need to tell Harry that. 'Most importantly, he understands how I feel about my horses and supports my continuing to work with them, much as Papa did.'

'You must give me leave not to like him…now that he possesses all I've ever wanted.'

Caro felt another jolt of sadness and stiffened, fighting it. She couldn't weaken; she owed Max more than that. 'No. But some day you'll find someone else worthy of you. Probably a lady better suited than me to be your wife.'

'Forgive me if, at the moment, I don't find your prediction very comforting,' Harry said bitterly.

The pain and sadness of her best and oldest friend slicing her to the quick, Caro wished she could find something more soothing to say. But even in her distress, a subtle awareness distanced her from his pain.

Deep within her glowed the memory of Max's kiss, his fierce possession, the shared passion that bound her to him and made them one. Much as she might regret Harry's heartache and the fact that there could never be a future between them, she belonged to Max now.

'I expect not. I had weeks to reconcile myself; being hit with the news all in an instant, it will take time for you to accept it.'

'Or to persuade you to run away with me.'

She smiled. 'I couldn't and you know it, or you'd never have said such a thing. Well, that's the whole of it. We'd best go back now.'

'I suppose. I wouldn't want your *husband* to get jealous.'

Caro laughed. 'I sincerely doubt he would. But staying out here tête-à-tête is bound to cause gossip. And—' the sudden realisation sent a pang of regret through her '—now that I'm married, I suppose you mustn't run tame here any more.'

She looked up to find Harry watching her, his face bleak. 'On the voyage back, I thought of all the changes I might find when I arrived. The stud sold, the horses scattered. You sunk into despair and depression. Never once did I dream I might have to give up the dearest friendship of my life.'

Not until this moment had it struck her that marrying Max inevitably meant the death of her closeness with Harry. Max could become an even better friend, a little voice said. She pushed aside that probably vain hope.

'I'd never thought it, either. But there's no use repining over facts that cannot be changed. We can only face the situation with honour, and go forwards.'

As she turned to walk towards the manor, Harry grabbed her shoulder. 'Just once more, I want to hold you like you were still to be mine,' he said. Before she could think to resist, he pulled her roughly into his arms and kissed her.

At the shock of his lips brushing hers, she slammed her hands into his chest, shoving him away.

'Last time you tried that, I planted you a facer!' she cried angrily. 'I ought to do so again.'

'I'd deserve it, I suppose. But despite that lapse, I am a man of honour. I'll not cross the line again.'

Reading the sincerity in his eyes, Caro knew he meant it. 'Let us try to salvage something of friendship, then. Come in with me. I'd like you to become better acquainted with Max.'

Harry shook his head. 'I couldn't greet Ransleigh now with any appearance of courtesy. Perhaps later, before I return to India. I'll send a note first…so you can ask your *husband* for permission to receive me.'

She nodded. 'That would be helpful.'

'Helpful. Devil take it!' He closed his eyes, obviously trying to take in the enormous implications of her marriage. 'Goodbye for now, then,' he said when he opened them, his face now shuttered. 'My sincerest wishes for your continued health and happiness.'

'Goodbye, Harry. Give my best to your family.'

He bowed, then walked back to the stable to retrieve his

mount. A moment later, she watched him ride by on the trail through the woods leading back to his father's manor. A chapter in her life now closed for ever.

Sighing, she trudged towards the house. She must get back and reassure Max. Not that she thought he would truly be jealous, but it must be disconcerting to watch one's wife fling herself into the arms of the man she'd once proclaimed she meant to marry. Even though said wife had vowed she'd given up all ties to her former lover and pledged her loyalty to him.

She wondered how long Max would stay…if she could entice him to linger. Sighing, she shook her head at her own idiocy. Two nights and days of delicious lovemaking and she was falling further than ever under the spell of her dynamic, sensual, compelling husband.

She probably ought to urge him to return to London… before she grew to long for his company even more keenly.

The thought struck her then, and unconsciously her hand strayed to her lips. She'd been shocked by Harry's unexpected kiss, filled by an immediate sense, on a level deeper than reason or honour, that having him touch her was *wrong*. Beyond that sensation, though, she'd felt…nothing. No stirrings of desire, no immediate tingle of sensual arousal like that which suffused her whenever Max touched her.

Apparently she now belonged to Max even more completely than she'd known.

Despite that truth, forcing her oldest friend to ride away from the wreckage of their friendship left an aching pain in her breast, as decades of fond memories clashed with honour and commitment, splintering into sabre-sharp shards within her heart.

Her emotions in turmoil, slowly she walked back to the manor.

Where her husband waited.

Chapter Twenty-Three

Max paused in pacing the library to pour himself another glass of brandy. He glanced up at the steadily ticking mantel clock, then out the window again. How long could a simple talk take?

He had to clutch the glass and take another gulp, trying to resist the almost overwhelming urge to pace back to the stables and put his hands in a stranglehold grip around the neck about which his wife had recently clasped her arms. A furious, irrational rage boiled in him at the mere thought of the possessive look Tremaine had cast at Caro, a rage made even more inexplicable since, if he considered the situation rationally, he didn't really doubt that his wife would do nothing more than explain to her childhood friend the tangled trail of events leading to their marriage.

Tremaine had been genuinely shocked to discover Caro wed. Max tried to force himself to dredge up some sympathy for the unhappiness and chagrin her old friend must be feeling.

He wasn't having any luck.

The intensity of his instinctive response to Tremaine and his inability to reason it away disturbed Max. He'd vied for female attention before, and though admittedly he'd seldom had to yield a woman he wanted to another, he'd never experienced anything like this fierce, primal sense of ownership, this desire to maim and destroy any man who dared touch *his* lady. This must be what jealousy felt like and he didn't much enjoy the emotion.

But then he'd never been married before, nor entered into any relationship with a woman meant to last longer than an affair.

For the first time, he began to understand the ferocity of the pain and rage that had driven his cousin Alastair after he'd lost the woman he'd loved.

Not, of course, that he loved Caro like that, he assured himself. He'd told her from the very beginning that he expected fidelity in a wife, though at the time he hadn't dreamt how strongly even a hint of attention from another man would affect him.

He was still wrestling with this unprecedented tangle of emotions when a knock sounded at the door. His spirits leapt, but instead of Caro, the butler stood at the threshold, offering him a letter newly arrived from the post.

Recognising Colonel Brandon's hand, he broke the seal and scanned it. The colonel wrote that he'd found a promising post in the War Department and wished Max to return to London and consult with him about it.

An honourable position where he might do some good, the Colonel described it. What he'd sought ever since returning from Waterloo appeared now within his grasp.

He should leave immediately. But pleased as he was at the prospect of employment, he felt a curious reluctance to leave Denby Lodge. Max didn't want to look too closely at how much Lieutenant Harry Tremaine's unexpected return played in that hesitation.

Before he could examine the matter further, the door opened again and this time Caro herself walked in.

She gave him a tentative smile. Immensely happy to see her in a way he could not explain, Max walked over to kiss her forehead. 'Lieutenant Tremaine is not joining us?'

'No. He's not yet been back to see his family.'

Guiltily aware of how delighted he was she'd returned alone, Max said, 'I hope the interview wasn't too painful.'

'I hope you're not angry I wished to see him alone. But I did feel I owed Harry an explanation.'

'No, I'm not angry.' As long as explanations were all she gave Tremaine, he was satisfied.

'Being totally unprepared to see him, I'm afraid I greeted him with...rather too much enthusiasm, for which I apologise. I'd completely forgotten that I'd written to him the night I returned from the solicitor's office, before I thought of coming to you. Elizabeth's father still franks her letters; one of the servants must have put it into the post.'

'How did he take the explanation?'

'He...wasn't happy, but he's a man of honour, as you are. In any event, I made you a promise of loyalty and fidelity before we were married. I fully intend to keep it. That and my...affection belong to you now.'

He'd known as much, but having her reaffirm it eased the turmoil of emotions churning within him. Reassured on that front, he recalled the colonel's letter.

Holding it up, he said, 'I've just heard from Colonel Brandon. I must return to London to consult with him. Why not come with me? You could see a physician, buy whatever you need...'

Smiling, she shook her head. 'I've already told you there is nothing a physician can do for me. And I have everything I need. It's sweet of you to be concerned, but with the new mares just arrived and the stallion to work, plus all the training to supervise, I must stay here, where I belong. Doing the work that marrying you, dear Max, allowed me to continue.'

A brief shadow flitted across her face. 'With luck, work I can bring to completion before time runs out. But enough of that.'

Max frowned, her words reviving his worry over her health. He still wasn't sure he really accepted the reality of the Curse, but he didn't want to take any chances with Caro's life. 'Are you sure you should continue working the stud?'

'I'm feeling quite well…except for first thing in the morning. And though I suppose after several more months, I may have to give up riding, for the moment I am fine.'

'Can I not coax you to at least consult a physician here, if you will not travel to London? It would make me feel easier.'

Giving him a look of resignation that said she was just humouring him, she replied, 'I suppose I could, if it would ease your mind.'

'It would. Being responsible for your condition, I want to take every possible precaution.'

With a little sigh, she looked away. 'Yes, you would feel responsible, I suppose. Though you shouldn't.'

He caught her hand and kissed it. 'There will really be a child? I confess, I find it hard to accept the truth of that.'

'Sometimes I have trouble believing it, too, even as I feel my body changing.'

An unprecedented sense of awe and tenderness filling him, he gathered her into his arms. She came willingly, laying her head against his chest. For a long moment he held her there, her cheek against the steady beat of his heart while he nestled his chin into the sweet fragrance of her hair. He found he didn't want to let her go.

He wished she'd agree to accompany him to London, but it was only reasonable that she'd want to stay at Denby, training her horses and working with the new breeding stock.

'Do you…think you will return to Denby before the birth?' she asked.

'Of course! In fact, I'll probably return here immediately after I consult with the colonel. I'm going to try to convince you to come to London for your lying-in, where there will be physicians and midwives to attend you.'

'We have those in the country, too, you know,' she said with a chuckle. 'After all the horses I've helped birth, I probably know as much about the process as any midwife. When the time arrives, Lady Denby will come to assist me. I hope to give you a healthy son.'

'Right now, I'm more concerned with having a healthy wife. You are…' He hesitated, his tongue trying to form other words before he made it say, 'Very dear to me, Caro.'

She leaned up to kiss him. It started as a soft slow brush of her mouth against his, but then, as if she just couldn't resist the temptation, suddenly she teased his lips apart and slid her tongue into his mouth.

A rush of desire flooding him, he kissed her back with equal hunger, moving his hands down to cup her bottom and fit her against his arousal.

After a moment, with a sigh, she pulled away. 'Would that we could "take tea" again now, my naughty husband! But there are tasks I must finish before nightfall.'

Stepping away from him, she licked one finger and painted the moisture over his lips. 'Until later, my dear Max,' she promised, chuckling as she danced away from the hand he tried to snag her with before she could exit the room.

Max smiled as he watched her go. He hoped she never stopped surprising him. His disappointment with the outcome of the investigation in Vienna and this afternoon's jealousy of Harry Tremaine faded as an effervescent feeling of hope and well-being buoyed his spirits.

He'd have new, fulfilling work, a tantalising, amorous

Caro for his wife…and, with any luck, a healthy child. With Caro's help, he might even work out how to be a better father than his own.

In London ten days later, Max sat once more in Colonel Brandon's study as his mentor poured some refreshment. He couldn't help recalling that the last time he'd shared a brandy with the colonel here, he'd returned to his rooms to find a frantic Caro, imploring him with a new proposition he hadn't been able to refuse.

Thank heavens he hadn't! He smiled, recalling their last night together before he set out for London. She'd certainly proven her affection, in so many delectable ways that he'd been doubly reluctant to leave for London without her. Indeed, he told her outright that she was spoiling him; he simply couldn't get enough of her.

With a naughty smile, she'd replied that she couldn't get enough of him and tilted her hips to take him deeper.

She'd thought he was teasing, but the words had held more truth even than he wanted to admit. He'd had affairs with women much more practised than Caro; it was her utter lack of artifice that so mesmerised him. He found her uninhibited joy and considerable inventiveness endlessly arousing.

'Here's a brandy to toast the business,' the Colonel said, pulling him from sensual reverie. 'First, congratulations on marrying your heiress. Your wedding, and the earl's blessing on it, helped speed the business of finding a suitable post.'

'What does this posting involve?'

'Logistics and procurement. Requires a man with a talent for organisation, a good head for figures and the ability to, shall we say, persuade sometimes recalcitrant suppliers to deliver contracted goods on time and as specified.'

'I'd work out of London?'

'For the most part, though you would need to visit the suppliers and army units upon occasion. If you accept it, would your bride join you here?'

'Probably not. She's a country girl at heart and very devoted to her farm and her horses.'

'Aye, I'd heard as much.'

Recalling the pains Caro had taken to present an unflattering picture of herself to the *ton*, Max could only imagine what the Colonel had heard. 'You should probably discount anything that's been said about her. She's clever, intelligent... and utterly bewitching.'

'All April-and-May with you, is it?' The colonel chuckled, slapping him on the back. 'I'd heard 'twas a match of convenience, so I'm happy to learn 'tis more than that.'

At the colonel's words, Max suddenly realised that, some time between his first visit to the colonel's lodgings several months ago and tonight, their relationship *had* become more. Just how much more, he wasn't quite sure. 'How soon would you need my answer?'

'Take your time. There's no one else of your ability and lineage who'd be better for the job, so I can persuade the head of department to wait on your answer.'

'I would like to talk it over with my wife. She's increasing, and I don't like leaving her alone.'

'That's wonderful news! Here's to the safe delivery of an heir!'

That being a toast to which Max could drink with enthusiasm, he raised his glass to the colonel. Though he remained for a time longer, chatting with his former commander about the activities of other acquaintances from their regiment, with the business concluded, he found himself eager to be off.

It hadn't been mere politeness when he'd told the colonel he was impatient to return to Caro. Even if the Curse were an illusion, he wanted to be there, so she wouldn't have to carry alone the burden of worrying over it.

If he did accept the colonel's post—and it seemed so ideal, there was no reason he shouldn't—he probably would have to assume it before Caro reached her time. All the more reason to try to persuade her to come to London to deliver the child.

Maybe he could also talk her into having some competent female stay with her at Denby Lodge after his departure. Lady Denby would be occupied with her daughter's Season until summer, but perhaps her cousin Elizabeth might agree?

He didn't intend for the person holding her hand in his absence to be Lieutenant Harry Tremaine. Surely the man would need to return to India before Max had to take up his posting in London.

Perhaps, before he returned to Kent, he'd pay a quick visit to Caro's cousin Elizabeth. And while he was there, he could ask her about the Curse.

Chapter Twenty-Four

Half an hour later, Max knocked on the door of Lady Elizabeth Russell's town house in Laura Place. Learning from the butler who admitted him that his mistress was at home, Max told him to tell her he wished to consult with her about her cousin, Caroline Denby.

After showing him to a parlour and pouring him wine, the servant departed to fetch his mistress. A short time later, Lady Elizabeth entered the room.

'Good evening, Mr Ransleigh. What a pleasure to see you again! Did Caro accompany you to London?'

'No, I'm afraid I couldn't persuade her to leave Denby Lodge. She's just taken delivery of a new Arabian stallion and several mares from Ireland.'

Elizabeth laughed. 'Then I doubt you'll get her to budge from the stables before next spring. All is...well with her, I trust?'

'She is in excellent health at present. I'd like to ensure that she stays that way. Which is why, although I have not yet consulted her about this, I wished to speak with you.'

Elizabeth's smile faded. 'Is something wrong?' Her eyes widening with alarm, she cried, 'Sweet Heaven, please tell me that she's not with child!'

Until that moment, Max hadn't been sure he really credited the existence of the Curse. But as he watched the colour drain from Lady Elizabeth's face, the anxiety that he'd been suppressing since Caro had first told him about her pregnancy boiled to the surface.

Consternation drying his mouth and speeding his pulse, he said, 'She believes she is. So maybe you'd better tell me everything you know about the Curse. How can I help her through it?'

Elizabeth shook her head, tears welling in her eyes. 'I don't know that there is anything you can do.'

Frustration sharpening his tone, he snapped, 'So she seems to believe, but there must be *something*. Does it spring from some weakness of the body? Will she lose the child before term?'

'No, it's not until after the birth that the difficulties begin. Bleeding. Fever. Death. It happened that way with her mother, aunt, cousins—nearly every female on her mother's side for the last two generations. When we were little, we used to joke about it…until it claimed cousin after cousin.'

Max had wanted to believe the deaths were coincidence, illusion, tales told to frighten young brides. But this much loss seemed far more than random coincidence.

'The physicians can do nothing to prevent it?'

'Apparently not. Our cousin Anne consulted every prominent practitioner. She was examined several times and each doctor pronounced her perfectly normal. But when her term came, she died anyway, just like the others. Whatever flaw causes this, it must be deep within the body.'

Max's mind raced while he tried to think of something else that might be done to counter the threat. But if physicians could do nothing…

'Is she…in good spirits?' Elizabeth asked.

'She was distressed when she first told me about it, before I went to Vienna.' After what Elizabeth had just revealed, Max wished even more fervently that she'd first told him about it before he'd seduced her, rather than after. 'Since my return, she's seemed quite unconcerned.'

Elizabeth shook her head. 'That's so like Caro. Knowing that if she is with child and nothing can be done, there is no point worrying about it. No wonder, with new horses arrived, she won't leave Denby! She must be desperate to push the training along as quickly as possible in case—' She broke, flushing. 'What can I do to help?'

'I've been offered a posting in the War Department. If I accept it, I may have to leave Denby Lodge before Caro reaches her time. I'll return for the birth, of course, but I shouldn't wish to leave her alone in the interim and Lady Denby will be occupied with her daughter until the end of the Season.'

Elizabeth nodded. 'I'm expecting my grandmother from Ireland for a visit, but I could bring her with me. Just let me know when you'd like me to come to Denby.'

'Thank you.' He grinned ruefully. 'Caro will probably have my head for washing for finding her a companion without consulting her wishes first, but I would feel better if she were not alone these next few months.'

'Of course. You…care about her, don't you?'

'Very much.'

Elizabeth smiled. 'Then go back to her. And tell her I'll be praying for you both.'

Little more than a day later, Caro was about to hand over to the head trainer the lead line of a young horse she was breaking to saddle when the familiar gait of a tall man approaching the paddock made her heart skip a beat.

'Max?' she cried, tossing the reins to Newman and pacing over to the fence. 'I didn't expect you back so soon!'

Delight lightening her spirits and a smoky sexual awareness firing her blood, she reached for the top rail, hungry for the first touch of him.

'Hello, Caro,' he called as he approached.

He looked dusty and tired, as if he'd been travelling swiftly and hard, she thought as she climbed the rails. He held out his hands to steady her as she clambered down the other side.

Then gathered her into his arms. 'I missed you, sweeting.'

Pulling his head down, she kissed him fiercely. With a groan, he wrapped her in his arms and kissed her back just as fiercely.

Some time later, regretfully, she broke the kiss. 'Shall I walk you to the manor? You can tell me everything Colonel Brandon said.'

'Do you have time now? I don't want to interrupt your training.'

Normally, she would be annoyed to have her routine disturbed…but this was Max and she'd missed him acutely. 'Yes, I'm ready to take a break…to see you.'

Linking her arm in his, she said, 'What did you learn about the posting? Do you think you'll accept it?'

'It involves the purchase and shipment of supplies to army units. And I'm inclined to take it. Are you sure you couldn't consider coming to London with me? I'd feel much easier knowing you were nearby, with all the superior resources of the city—the best physicians, midwives, aides, close at hand.'

She shook her head. 'As I told you before, we have doctors here. And I have my work, as you will have yours.'

Much as she hated to ask it, best that she know straight away how much time she had left with him. Trying to keep her tone casual, she said, 'When must you return to London?'

'No particular time. The colonel said he would hold the position until I'm ready to take it. I thought to stay at Denby with you for a while, perhaps until your stepsister finishes her Season and Lady Denby returns.'

'But 'tis only January and she probably won't return until May or June at the earliest.'

'I happened to speak with your cousin. Lady Elizabeth. If I must leave earlier than that, she mentioned she might be able to come for a visit. I don't like to think of you here alone.' He shook his head and sighed. 'I wish there were something more I could do to protect you.'

'There's nothing,' she said, reaching up to stroke his face. 'But as I told you earlier, the handful of Mama's female relations who didn't perish after birthing their first child seemed to go on to bear others without problem. So don't be burying me yet.'

He snaked out a hand to still her lips. 'Don't even joke about that! Perhaps I'll stay until May or June, then. If you'll have me.'

'Then let us enjoy each other to the fullest until May or June…or until I'm too large and cumbersome to be desirable.'

'You will always be desirable to me.'

'That sounds most promising,' she said, a thrill going through her at the welcome news that she might be able to seduce him again and again, right up to the end.

But even as she rejoiced in the news, a little voice warned that the longer he stayed, the more impossible it would be to keep her heart from shattering when he left. But she couldn't make herself lie and tell him she'd prefer him not to remain.

Instead, she said, 'If you will stay for a while, could I ask you a favour?'

'Of course.'

'Would you mind having me show you the stud books and operating records for the farm? Acquaint you with the horses we have and which stage of training they are in, introduce you to the trainers? So if…anything should happen to me, you'd be more knowledgeable about the stud and better able to decide whether you would want to keep it or sell it off.'

He stopped abruptly and turned to cup her face in his hands. 'I would love to learn more about the Denby operations. But not for that reason. You are going to survive and thrive, Caro, and so is our child. I won't accept anything else.'

Once again her heart did that little flip, and for a moment, she considered confessing her love for him. Might he have come to love her in return?

If fondness was all he could muster in response, such a declaration would likely just make him feel uncomfortable, especially since it seemed he felt guilty about getting her with child. Unwilling to spoil the warm intimacy of the moment, she pushed the question from her mind.

'My sweet Max,' she said instead, 'the outcome isn't in your hands, you know. But I do like having you here. I was so lonely after Papa died, some of my joy in being at Denby was lost. You've restored it to me.'

'I'm glad. Strange as it seems, you've made me feel more at home at Denby in the short time I've spent here than I ever did growing up at Swynford Court or in Papa's vast house on Grosvenor Square. Thank you for that.'

He leaned down to kiss her, softly and gently this time. She closed her eyes, savouring his touch. She would savour every moment with him, she thought fiercely. Since she could not know how many—or how few—there might be.

Chapter Twenty-Five

Approaching six months later, Max leaned against the paddock rail, watching Caro work with the young colt on the lead line, coaxing him to follow. Though heavy with child, she still moved gracefully, he thought with affection, watching her smooth, economical gestures.

'The colt looks better today.'

'Yes, he's getting used to my touch. It also helps that he's finally decided the leaves blowing in the trees and the grasses tapping against the railings aren't a danger to him.'

'I wish I could convince you to stop working the lead line.'

'Really, Max, you worry too much. I've already agreed not to ride any more and train only the smallest colts.'

'Even colts are large and powerful enough to do you an injury,' he countered, concern for her sharpening his tone. 'They may be smaller than two-year-olds, but like Balthazaar here, more skittish and less predictable.'

'Skittish, yes, but none of my horses are unpredictable, if one is alert to their signals. It's my own fault if I fail to heed what he means when he stretches his neck or pricks up his ears.'

Concerned about the danger or not, after months of watching Caro with her horses, he still marvelled at her deft touch and the almost mystical way she seemed able to communicate with the steeds, from foals to four-year-olds fully trained and ready for sale.

'If you don't like my working with Balthazaar, why don't you take him?' she said, breaking in on his thoughts.

'Gladly, if it will get you on the rail and me in the ring.'

As she'd taught him, he walked slowly to the centre where she was working the colt, careful to let the horse see him and accept his presence, not taking over the reins until the animal continued his circuit at a steady pace.

For the next half-hour, while Caro watched, Max eased the horse through a series of patterns, exerting more and more pressure as he taught the animal to accept his commands to advance, stand, move right and left. So absorbed had he become in this slow but exacting process, he was surprised when Newman, the head trainer, appeared at the rail.

'I'll take him in now, Mr Ransleigh. Well done, by the way. You're looking to become almost as good a trainer as Miss Caro.'

'Thank you, Newman,' Max replied, a swell of pride and satisfaction lifting his spirits at the man's rare words of praise. 'Still, it seems to take me so long.'

'As long as is necessary, sir. You heed that old horseman's motto: "If you think things are going too slow, go slower." But you've got a real touch; the beasties respond to you.'

'You do have a deft touch,' Caro said, joining him at the rail as Newman led away the colt.

Max's pleasure deepened. Caro was as sparing with her praise as Newman. Growing up an earl's privileged son, for much of his life he'd had fulsome praises heaped upon him, whether or not his performance merited it. He prized Caro's honesty; one never had to question whether her compliments were genuine.

'If I earn your approval, I'm doubly pleased.'

'It's all trust and patience, Max. This isn't a battlefield,' she said, gesturing towards the training paddock, 'with a winner and a loser. Either both win, or both lose.'

'Like in a marriage?'

'Exactly,' she said, then made a face at him as he snagged her elbow, pulling her down before she could clamber up the rails. 'We'll go through the gate, if you please.'

'Honestly, you're fussier than a brood hen with its chicks,' she protested.

'If I were truly fussy, I'd order you to stay in the house.'

'Where I'd go mad within a week, cooped up with nothing useful to do. Besides, if you *ordered* me to remain, I'd feel nearly honour-bound to climb out of a window.'

'Perhaps I'd just order you to stay in my bed.'

Her eyes danced. 'Now, that's a command I might feel inclined to obey.'

Leaning down, he gave her another kiss, his hands cradling the heavy round of her belly. He'd thought, living with her day after day, their passion would mute, or that as her body grew bigger with child, her appetite for the sensual would decline.

But neither had happened. As her expanding belly limited certain romantic encounters, she thought of new and unexpected ways to pleasure him. He found her body, ripe with his growing child, irresistibly erotic.

'You've made great strides as a trainer,' she told him as he walked her out of the gate. 'Not that I should be surprised, since you apply to that endeavour the same intensity of concentration you employed when memorising the blood lines of the stud and the system used to keep the estate books. Though I must admit, I never really expected you to stay long enough to learn it so well.'

'Why should I not stay?'

'After spending your life at court, in the halls of Parliament, and engaged in great battles, I thought you would find living on a small farm deep in the countryside far too boring.'

'I admit, I once thought that might be true. I've come to enjoy being a part of the rhythm of life on a great agricultural property, involving myself in activities I barely noticed when I lived at Swynford Court. There's a deep satisfaction in coaxing horses to follow my lead, as I used to coax men. I think I've come to love it at Denby almost as much as you do.'

'I'm rather surprised, though, that Colonel Brandon hasn't been urging you to take up your position.'

'I've stayed this long, I might as well remain until after the child comes.'

'Truly?' she asked, surprised.

'Truly.'

'I admit, I will feel…easier, knowing you won't be leaving.'

He would too, Max thought. After months with the potential of the Curse simmering at the back of his mind, he was too concerned for her welfare to tolerate the chance of being away when her time came, only if all he could do to help was encourage her. And he truly had found a measure of peace and contentment, working the stud with her, as profound as it was unexpected.

In fact, he was beginning to wonder if he really wanted to accept Colonel Brandon's post at all…particularly as it meant he would have to leave Caro and his child for months at a time.

Suddenly Caro gasped, jerking him from his thoughts. 'Oh, that was a sharp one!' she said, putting a hand to her belly.

'What is it?' Max asked, immediately concerned.

'A contraction, that's all. Mrs Drewry, the housekeeper,

says it's quite common to have these pains off and on as I near my time.'

'Are you sure? Maybe we ought to summon the midwife.'

'Just like a brood hen—' she teased before stopping in mid-sentence. Pain contorting her face, she began breathing rapidly.

'Let me carry you to the house,' Max said, his concern deepening.

'I don't need to be carried,' she said fretfully.

'Take my arm, then. We're sending for the midwife.'

Before she could reply, another pain hit her. She latched on to Max's arm, her fingers biting into his flesh. To his further alarm, she made no further protest about calling the midwife.

Ten hours later, the contractions had not abated. Rather, they had grown steadily stronger and more frequent. The midwife had arrived to assist; Dulcie and the housekeeper scurried in and out with hot water, candles, spiced possets and lavender-scented cloths to mop Caro's sweat-drenched face.

Max alternately paced the room and sat by her side, wishing there was more he could do than rub her back and hold her hands through the worst of the contractions. Looking down at his wrists ruefully, he realised he was going to have bruises.

But as the night wore on towards morning, her suffering intensifying without the labour seeming to progress, the midwife began to exchange worried glances with the housekeeper. The relatively trouble-free months of Caro's pregnancy had lulled Max into an increasing confidence that the uproar over the Curse was just a myth, but at the growing concern on the midwife's face and the deep groans of misery Caro was not able to suppress, he was beginning to lose faith in that theory.

After one particularly painful bout, when Caro lost the

struggle to keep herself from screaming, the midwife examined her, then removed her hands, shaking her head.

'What's wrong?' Max demanded.

'The babe's turned. Most come head first, which is easiest, but I can feel the babe's feet. It's much harder to birth one backwards.'

'Whatever is keeping the damned doctor?' Max barked, looking over at Dulcie, whom he'd charged to dispatch one of the grooms to bring back the local physician.

'I'll check again, master,' Dulcie said, hurrying out.

Caro's eyes, which she'd closed to rest between pains, flickered open. 'Baby...is turned?'

'Yes, missus, I fear so,' the midwife said.

She nodded absently, her face pale, her hair damp with sweat, dark circles of fatigue beneath her eyes. 'Happens... like that sometimes...with horses. Must turn baby.'

'I expect the doctor will try that, when he arrives,' the midwife said.

'Don't wait. Do it now.'

'Mistress, I'm not sure I want to try that.'

'Must. Can't...go on much longer.'

Icy shards of panic sliced through Max's veins. If Caro, who never gave up on anything, felt she couldn't bear much more, things were very bad indeed.

'Do you know what to do?' he asked the midwife.

'Aye, sir, but 'tis difficult. And will be very painful for your lady wife.'

'If you can't get it to turn, the baby is going to kill her,' Max said harshly, putting his worst fear into words for the first time. 'I'll hold her. You turn the child.'

'Oh, sir, I be not sure I want to—'

'Do it,' Caro said again, not opening her eyes. 'Mrs Thorgood, you...know what to do. Do it now.'

The midwife took a deep breath. 'Hold her still as you can, sir.'

Murmuring encouragement, Max slipped his arms around Caro's shoulders, leaning her back against his chest. At his nod, the midwife went to work.

With a wail, Caro bucked in his arms. Ignoring her agony, the midwife pushed and pulled at her belly, while Caro writhed in his arms. Nausea rose in Max's throat, but he choked it down. If Caro could endure this, so could he.

Finally, with a cry of triumph, Mrs Thorgood said, 'Look ye, sir, the babe be turning!'

Max wasn't sure exactly what he was seeing, but the contours of Caro's belly shifted, as if a leviathan inside was flexing and stretching. A few moments later, the midwife said, 'Babe's crowning! Hold on, missis, won't be much longer now!'

The rest of the birth seemed to happen all in a rush. What seemed a very short time later, the midwife had eased the slippery body free, wiped its mouth, given it a slap on the bottom, and as Max heard his child's first cry, wrapped it in soft flannel and handed it to him. 'It's a fine son you've got, Mr Ransleigh.'

Exhausted himself, Max sat back, looking with wonder at the miniature face peering resentfully up at him from within the flannel folds. 'It seems my son isn't any happier about his passage into this world than his mama.'

Despite his light words, Max's heartbeat sped and a sense of awe and humility filled him as he looked at the miracle in his arms. He reached over to grasp Caro's limp hand.

'We have a son, Caro. It's over now, sweeting.'

'Not quite,' the midwife said. 'There's the afterbirth to come.'

Before Max could ask what that meant, Caro groaned. Suddenly the sheets beneath her turned red, as if a swift crimson tide had flooded the shore.

'What's happening now?' he demanded.

The midwife's face blanched. 'She's bleeding, poor lamb. Oh, if it weren't the same thing what killed her poor mama!'

Max had seen blood on the battlefield, severed limbs, men missing arms, hands, bodies missing heads. But this was *Caro*, and a fear he'd never felt when facing the enemy's guns flooded him as the stain on the linen grew wider and wider.

'Can't you stop it? Stanch it somehow?'

'It comes from within her, sir, where the cord attaches. It'll stop on its own…if it does.'

Before the blood loss kills her, his mind filled in the unspoken words.

'What can we do, then?'

'Pray,' the midwife said.

So, tucking her cold hand in his, Max prayed. Surely she'd not suffered all the agonies of birth to slip from him now. He pleaded, bargained, begged the Almighty, promising to do whatever the Lord directed, if only he would spare Caro's life.

She seemed so still, her pale face waxy. But suddenly he realised the red stain was not getting any larger.

'It's stopped,' he whispered to the midwife. 'Is she safe now?'

'Depends on how much blood she lost. And whether fever sets in.'

Max stifled a curse. Each time he thought all the perils had ended, another presented itself. The midwife and Dulcie tried to talk him into leaving the room, bathing and changing out of his stable-grimed clothing, taking some dinner, but Max couldn't bring himself to leave her side. He felt the wholly illogical but none the less overwhelming conviction that if he left the room, he'd lose her for ever.

So he choked down some soup the housekeeper insisted

on bringing him and, as the long hours of the night crept towards morning, he dozed fitfully.

Max came fully awake just before dawn…when he realised the cold hand he'd been holding was now burning hot.

He called for the midwife, who touched her forehead and roused the maid to send for cool water. He was bathing her hands and face with sponges dipped in cool water when at last the doctor arrived.

'Thank heavens you're finally here,' Max cried, overwhelmingly relieved to have someone with medical expertise to buttress his ignorance.

Quickly the midwife related to the doctor what had transpired. After checking the baby and pronouncing him healthy, Dr Sawyer came back to Caro's bed.

'The fever's not breaking,' he observed. 'I should bleed her.'

It was the common medical practice, Max knew. 'But she's already lost so much blood,' he protested.

'Bleeding is the only thing that will remove adverse humours from the body,' the doctor said. 'It may seem harsh, but better harsh remedies than to lose your wife, eh? If you'll move aside, sir, I'll get started.'

Panicked indecision, worsened by fatigue, distress and the horror of having to stand by impotently while Caro suffered, held him motionless, stubbornly clinging to her hand. He was no medical expert…but on some subconscious level, he felt beyond doubt that bleeding Caro now would kill her.

'I can't let you,' he said at last. 'She's too weak.'

'She's too weak to support the contagion in her blood. If I don't remove some of it, I assure you, she *will* die.'

'I can't let you,' he replied desperately.

'You wish to go against my considered medical opinion, Mr Ransleigh?' When Max nodded, the doctor said, 'Then there is nothing else I can do for her. But know this, sir; if the worst happens, her death is on your hands.'

Considerably affronted, the doctor gathered his tools and left the room. Max stared down at Caro, tossing her head restlessly on the pillow.

Had he just condemned her to die? Would she die anyway, no matter what anyone did?

Max had commanded men in battle, ordered troops into positions that had resulted in the death and maiming of many men. But never had he given an order that might have more dire consequences than this one.

His back ached, the stubble on his cheeks itched and he was tired beyond comprehension. But as dawn moved into daylight, he waved away again any suggestion that he leave Caro to the midwife's care and sleep.

He would see her face when she woke…or watch her breathe her last.

He'd thought he'd felt helpless after Vienna, when control over his future had been wrenched from his hands. He'd thought he'd reached the depths of despair after his father had repudiated him and Wellington had refused to have anything further to do with him. But never had he felt as despairing and helpless as he did sitting by Caro's bed, his numb hands bathing her face as Mrs Drewry and Dulcie changed tepid water for fresh.

Unable to bear the thought that he might never talk with her again, he said, 'Newman told Dulcie that Sultan is pacing his stall. It seems he knows you are ill and is concerned for you. He wants his favourite rider back again. The grooms are putting the two-year-olds on lunge lines today and half the four-year-olds began dressage; you should see Scheherazade high-stepping, as if he were born to the knack! But I'll need your help with the colts who aren't yet saddle-broken; I still don't know how to do that. Your son is waiting to become acquainted, too. You do know you have a son, don't you?'

She lay still and silent now. His vision blurring with unshed tears, Max continued, 'He'll need you to sit him on his first pony, teach him to train his horse and read its moods, as his mother can. Caro, you can't l-leave me yet. There's too much left for us to share.'

On and on he talked, as if he could hold her to life by the power of his voice. That slight figure on the bed, now shivering with fever, now burning his fingers with her heat, had been the sole focus of his life for nearly six months now. Every day, she'd come to fascinate him more than she had the first time he'd met her, in that preposterous gown and those ridiculous glasses.

She'd touched his soul as profoundly as she'd pleasured his body. He couldn't envision a future without her. As soon as she was out of danger, he'd write to Colonel Brandon, turning down the post. What need had he to puff himself off with a high government position, trying to persuade his father or anyone else he was important?

He belonged at Denby Lodge with Caro…whose opinion of him was the only one that mattered.

Why had he not realised until this day, when he might lose her for ever, how much he'd come to love her?

Finally, some time after noon, exhaustion claimed him. Slumped over her bed, he fell asleep, his head resting beside hers on the pillow.

It was dark when he woke, the room illumined by a single lamp. He sat up with a start, rubbing sleep from his bleary eyes. Then he clasped Caro's hand.

Which was clammy—cold now, where it had been hot before. His gaze shot to her pale face and colourless lips, the eyelashes collapsed limply against her waxen cheeks.

Alarmed, he squeezed the hand he still held. Then, while he looked on with a relief so deep he thought he might pass out from the force of it, she stirred and opened her eyes.

'Max,' she whispered, a tiny bit of colour returning to her face. 'You stayed.'

'Every minute.'

'I was so tired and I hurt so badly. It felt like I was wandering in a fog, uncertain which way to go. Your voice brought me back.'

Gently, as if she might shatter at a touch, he wrapped his arms around her. 'I was so afraid I was going to lose you.'

She gave him a glimmer of a smile. 'I thought if I died, you could have my money and still marry the woman you wanted. You may be stuck with me now.'

He put his fingers over her lips. 'I don't want any other woman. I don't want any other wife. Only you, Caro. Only the outrageous, passionate, unconventional woman who's turned my whole life upside down.'

Weakly she squeezed his fingers. 'I'm so glad. In fact, over the last few weeks I decided that, if all went well, I didn't want to live the rest of my life apart from you. I've already turned much of the work of the stud over to Newman. I could turn over the rest and go with you to London. If…if you want me.'

Max sucked in a breath, shocked by the enormity of what she was offering him. 'You would give up the stud?'

'Since Papa's death, all I wanted was to realise his dream. But now I have a dream I want even more. To be your wife.'

Humbled, Max kissed her limp hands. 'I love you, Caro Ransleigh. But you needn't make such a sacrifice. I'd like to stay here and run the farm with you, building the stud's bloodlines…and watching our son grow.'

'What of Colonel Brandon's post?'

'I suppose I've known it for some time, but after last night, the truth became perfectly clear. Someone else can have Brandon's post. You and Denby and our new babe are my world now. I don't ever want to leave it again. Do you think you could teach me how to be a proper father, as you've taught me so much else? Could you love me and share Denby with me?'

'Foolish Max,' she murmured. 'Couldn't you tell? I've loved you almost from the first, though I fought accepting it for months. You won't need me to teach you about fatherhood; from the gentleness and patience you show the horses, I know you'll be a wonderful father to our baby. But I must insist that the terms of our bargain change. I withdraw my permission for you to dally with any lady you fancy. I'm a selfish, greedy woman, who wants to keep all your passion for herself. And if you're ever tempted to stray, I warn you, I'm a crack shot.'

Max grinned. 'I don't doubt it. Shall we begin again?'

He dropped to one knee. 'Caro Denby, will you marry me and be my wife, my one and only love, never to be parted, for the rest of our lives?'

Joy lit her weary eyes. 'Now that, my sweet Max, is a bargain I can accept with my whole heart.'

* * * * *

REQUEST YOUR FREE BOOKS!

HARLEQUIN® HISTORICAL:
Where love is timeless

2 FREE NOVELS PLUS 2 **FREE GIFTS!**

YES! Please send me 2 FREE Harlequin® Historical novels and my 2 FREE gifts (gifts are worth about $10). After receiving them, if I don't wish to receive any more books, I can return the shipping statement marked "cancel." If I don't cancel, I will receive 6 brand-new novels every month and be billed just $5.19 per book in the U.S. or $5.74 per book in Canada. That's a savings of at least 17% off the cover price! It's quite a bargain! Shipping and handling is just 50¢ per book in the U.S. and 75¢ per book in Canada.* I understand that accepting the 2 free books and gifts places me under no obligation to buy anything. I can always return a shipment and cancel at any time. Even if I never buy another book, the two free books and gifts are mine to keep forever.

246/349 HDN FVQK

Name	(PLEASE PRINT)	
Address		Apt. #
City	State/Prov.	Zip/Postal Code

Signature (if under 18, a parent or guardian must sign)

Mail to the **Harlequin® Reader Service:**
IN U.S.A.: P.O. Box 1867, Buffalo, NY 14240-1867
IN CANADA: P.O. Box 609, Fort Erie, Ontario L2A 5X3

Want to try two free books from another line?
Call 1-800-873-8635 or visit www.ReaderService.com.

* Terms and prices subject to change without notice. Prices do not include applicable taxes. Sales tax applicable in N.Y. Canadian residents will be charged applicable taxes. Offer not valid in Quebec. This offer is limited to one order per household. Not valid for current subscribers to Harlequin Historical books. All orders subject to credit approval. Credit or debit balances in a customer's account(s) may be offset by any other outstanding balance owed by or to the customer. Please allow 4 to 6 weeks for delivery. Offer available while quantities last.

Your Privacy—The Harlequin® Reader Service is committed to protecting your privacy. Our Privacy Policy is available online at www.ReaderService.com or upon request from the Harlequin Reader Service.

We make a portion of our mailing list available to reputable third parties that offer products we believe may interest you. If you prefer that we not exchange your name with third parties, or if you wish to clarify or modify your communication preferences, please visit us at www.ReaderService.com/consumerchoice or write to us at Harlequin Reader Service Preference Service, P.O. Box 9062, Buffalo, NY 14269. Include your complete name and address.

HH13

Read on for an exciting excerpt of
THE DISSOLUTE DUKE
by Sophia James

"I saved the best proposal of all for your ears only."

A streak of cold dread snaked downward. "You want a divorce, no doubt?"

At that he laughed, the sound engulfing her.

"Not a divorce, my lady wife, but an heir, and as you are the only woman who can legitimately give me one, the duty is all yours."

She almost tripped at his words and he held her closer, waiting until balance was regained.

Shock gave her the courage to reply. "Then you have a problem indeed, because I am the last woman in the world who would ever willingly grace your bed again." Disappointment and anger vibrated in her retort as strains of Strauss soared around them, the chandeliers throwing a soft pallor across colorful dresses resplendent in the room. The privilege of the Ton so easily on show.

Scandal had its own face, too!

It came in the way his fingers held her to the dance even as she tried to pull away and in the quiet caress of his skin over hers.

Memory shattered sense and the salon dimmed into nothingness; the feel of his hands upon her nakedness, the smell of brandy and deceit and a wedding quick and harrowing in that small chapel.

Even the minister had not met her eye as he said the

words "To have and to hold from this day forward…"

Taylen Ellesmere had stayed less than a few hours.

Her husband. A different and harder man from the one who had left her and was now back for a legitimate heir.

"If there wasn't a male left in Christendom save for you, I still would not…"

He broke over her anger.

"I will gift you the sole use of the Alderworth London town house on the birth of our first son and pay you a stipend that will keep you independently wealthy in fine style."

Blackmail and bribery now.

"And if the child is a girl?"

"Then I will dissolve all contracts and allow you what I offer regardless. I would not tie you to such a bargain forever should you in good faith produce only a female Ellesmere."

She frowned, barely believing the words she was hearing. "There are other women here who would jump at your offer, Your Grace, if you obtained a divorce and remarried."

"I know."

"Then why?"

"Salvation." He gave no other explanation as he smiled at her, the deep dimple in his right cheek caught in the light. So very beautiful.

Lucinda felt the muscles inside her clench.

Look for
THE DISSOLUTE DUKE
by Sophia James, available next month from
Harlequin® Historical!

CAPTIVE OF THE CLAN

To regain control of his fractured clan Robert Matheson must take Lilidh MacLerie hostage as a bargaining tool. But Lilidh is no ordinary captive. She's the woman he once loved—and rejected!

Rob's touch is etched permanently into her memory and, unaware that he was forced to repudiate their love, Lilidh has never forgotten the man who broke her heart all those years ago. Now, looking into the eyes of her captor, she no longer recognizes this fearsome leader. She should be afraid—there's no telling what he will do. But something about him both excites and unnerves her in equal measure....

Look for

At The Highlander's Mercy

(Book 2 of The MacLerie Clan) by Terri Brisbin in April 2013.

Available wherever books are sold.

HARLEQUIN® HISTORICAL:
Where love is timeless

BEAUTY IS IN THE EYE OF THE BEHOLDER

Considered the plain, *clever* one in her family, Lady Cressida
Armstrong knows her father has given up on her ever marrying.
But who needs a husband when science is the only thing to set
Cressie's pulse racing?

Disillusioned artist Giovanni di Matteo is setting the *ton* abuzz
with his expertly executed portraits. Once, his art was inspired;
now it's only technique. Until he meets Cressie….

Challenging, intelligent and yet insecure, Cressie is the
one whose face and body he dreams of capturing on canvas.
In the enclosed, intimate world of his studio, Giovanni
rediscovers his passion as he awakens hers.

Look for
The Beauty Within
by Marguerite Kaye in May 2013.

Available wherever books are sold.

www.Harlequin.com

HH29738

Get Your
Coventry Romances
Home Subscription NOW

And Get These
4 Best-Selling Novels
FREE:

LACEY
by Claudette Williams

THE ROMANTIC WIDOW
by Mollie Chappell

HELENE
by Leonora Blythe

THE HEARTBREAK TRIANGLE
by Nora Hampton

A Home Subscription! It's the easiest and most convenient way to get every one of the exciting Coventry Romance Novels! ...And you get 4 of them FREE!

You pay nothing extra for this convenience: there are no additional charges...you don't even pay for postage! Fill out and send us the handy coupon now. and we'll send you 4 exciting Coventry Romance novels absolutely FREE!

SEND NO MONEY, GET THESE
FOUR BOOKS FREE!

MAIL THIS COUPON TODAY TO:
COVENTRY HOME SUBSCRIPTION SERVICE
6 COMMERCIAL STREET
HICKSVILLE, NEW YORK 11801

YES, please start a Coventry Romance Home Subscription in my name. and send me FREE and without obligation to buy. my 4 Coventry Romances. If you do not hear from me after I have examined my 4 FREE books. please send me the 6 new Coventry Romances each month as soon as they come off the presses. I understand that I will be billed only $9.00 for all 6 books. There are no shipping and handling nor any other hidden charges. There is no minimum number of monthly purchases that I have to make. In fact. I can cancel my subscription at any time. The first 4 FREE books are mine to keep as a gift. even if I do not buy any additional books.

For added convenience. your monthly subscription may be charged automatically to your credit card.

☐ Master Charge **42101**   ☐ Visa **42101**

Credit Card # _____

Expiration Date _____

Name _____
(Please Print)

Address _____

City _____ State _____ Zip _____

Signature _____

☐ Bill Me Direct Each Month **40105**

Publisher reserves the right to substitute alternate FREE books. Sales tax collected where required by law. Offer valid for new members only.
Allow 3-4 weeks for delivery. Prices subject to change without notice.

A Keeper
For Lord Linford

Margaret SeBastian

FAWCETT COVENTRY • NEW YORK

A KEEPER FOR LORD LINFORD

Published by Fawcett Coventry Books, CBS Educational and Professional Publishing, a division of CBS Inc.

ISBN: 0-449-50271-6

Printed in the United States of America

First Fawcett Coventry printing: February 1982

10   9   8   7   6   5   4   3   2   1

A Keeper
For Lord Linford

1

Lake Winandermere is, like its name, a long and peaceful body of water—or it was until the Londoners, prevented by the wars from attending the usual watering places upon the Continent, discovered that Winandermere and its sister waters offered a beauty and peace that had become rather rare in the Midlands and the Southern Counties. It was early days in the nineteenth century and the Lake District was beginning to feel the brunt of an invasion of tourists, such as it had never experienced before.

The tempo of life about the lakes was accelerating; those who could serve the needs of the visitors prospered, and they accepted the changes that tourism brought with it. As a signal of the change, Winandermere Water had been rechristened, without benefit of ceremony, Lake Windermere. The old name had proved too much of a mouthful for the impatient, ever-pressed Londoners.

Still, for all that the essential peace of the scene that Windermere provided the viewer on its shores was not to any great extent diminished, and this day had been tranquil and beautiful. It *had* been, but in one small corner of its ten-mile length, just off Bowness, a small tempest broke out as the sun beamed in its descending glory upon a day that had been one of its best efforts, ever.

The mirror surface of Windermere was being ruffled near its central shore by a lady rising from its depths in a manner completely unlike the Botticelli's Venus. For one thing, she was not truly rising but rather splashing her way to shore; and for another, she was fully clothed and as fully drenched. Water was dripping from her sodden clothing, and her raven ringlets were ringlets no longer but stringy wisps that plastered themselves about her face and shoulders, defeating her attempts to brush them out of her eyes.

It was just as well because her eyes were filled with stormy rage so that her glances must have withered to obliteration the two smiling ladies, standing on the shore, witnesses to her plight.

Miss Ancilla Gordon, wet to the bone and in a poor humor for pleasantries, merely glared at Miss Darcy, her friend, safe and dry, looking as though she were fresh out of a bandbox.

"It is rather late in the day for bathing, don't you think, Ancilla?" remarked Caroline Darcy.

Lady Diana, the other friend, who was sporting a dainty parasol, gave it a twirl and stamped a tiny foot. "Ancilla, whatever *happened?* Shall we go for assistance? Is Lord Linford in any danger? It is an awfully large boat."

In as much dignity as her moist condition would allow, Ancilla drew herself up for a moment and replied: "I have no wish to discuss it. As for his lordship, the gentleman is in need of a keeper! He can sink or swim and I should not turn a hair! Will you just look at what that bubblehead has done to me? I am sure that every last bit of my clothing is in utter ruin! And my hair! I shall be hours at unsnarling it—"

At that moment, a chubby, smallish gentleman came bustling out to them, a look of great anxiety upon his countenance. He was wringing his hands as he gave vent to a despairing cry: "Oh, my heavens! You did not leave my lord to fend for himself! I say, someone call the watch—or whatever they have got here! We cannot have my lord drown! No, indeed!"

"I assure you, Mr. Symonds, if anyone is in need of succor it is myself and not your perishing lord!"

"Perishing?!!" screamed the cleric. "Heaven forbid!"

"Mr. Symonds, there is nothing to fly up into the trees in it! I am sure his lordship will manage to rescue the boat with his usual grace. As you were his tutor, I should think you would have gone to the pains of instructing Lord Linford in the proper use of oars," admonished Ancilla, scathingly. "Will you just look upon your late student's handiwork!"

But Mr. Symonds had not remained to listen. He carried his handwringing to the edge of the water and pranced about offering little cries of encouragement to Lord Linford.

His lordship was floundering about, eight or so yards out in the water, with an overturned little rowboat that seemed to have a mind to enjoy itself in deeper waters.

Lord Linford paused in his exertions and with a silly

grin on his face, called out: "Have no fear, Miss Gordon, I shall have this beast under control in a moment!" Then, in a lower tone that could still be plainly heard by the onlookers, he exclaimed: "Symonds, you blithering fool! Come out to me and give me a hand with this or I shall be all night at it!"

"Oh, but, my lord, it is so very *wet* where you are!" Mr. Symonds complained, and proceeded to dance a little jig in sympathy.

Ancilla had turned about even as she had made up her mind to retire to the carriage, which awaited them on the road. She paused and regarded the struggling young man and his dithery companion.

With a sigh, she explained to Lady Diana and Caroline: "I might as well go to his rescue. The good Lord knows that I cannot get any wetter than I am. Oh, what a bungling fool that man is!"

She went back into the water even though her friends tried to dissuade her. The water was to her shoulders as she came up to Lord Linford and the dreadful little boat.

"Oh, I say, Miss Gordon, you really ought not to have come out. I am getting it turned about you see—"

"Oh, hush! Here! There is no manner of use in turning it about! Do you push from where you are, and I shall tug from the front of it. That is all that is necessary, your lordship."

"But, of course! Now why could not I have thought of that?"

"I am sure you could have—eventually; but it gets rather chilly out here by the wee hours of the morning, and Mr. Symonds is about to have kittens upon the shore in the sight of all if you should happen to miss your dinner, I am sure. Now, are you ready? I have had enough of bathing in Windermere for the day if you have not."

The fact that the weather had been perfectly marvelous made the day only that much more beastly for Ancilla. It had never been her idea to show Lord Linford about, it had been at her mother's insistence. His lordship was the son of a friend of a friend, and he had been sent up to the Lakes on a repairing lease.

It was her opinion that what ailed the Viscount no manner of physician could cure. The man was a mass of awkward absurdities in all that he essayed, and that he needed a keeper was self-evident from the start. The Reverend Mr. Symonds had been represented as the Viscount's companion, but she had a clearer estimate of the relationship. Since his lordship was too old to have a governor for guidance and there was nothing tutorial about Mr. Symonds, the best that could be said for the latter was that he was acting as bear-leader to the Viscount. Such a one as was the Viscount had every *need* of a bear-leader, except that she did not think that Mr. Symonds was at all competent. Though he was something more graceful than his charge, he was not a whit more intelligent.

She was very much relieved, therefore, that after moments of confusion and indecision, Lord Linford's wet clothing convinced him to go off to his own lodgings to change and not to foist his company further upon her and her friends. As it was, Ancilla could have wished that she did not have to enjoy her friends' company either, for she felt all bedraggled and not at all charming. But, as both young ladies were the guests of her mother, she had no choice and had to sit fighting off a chill while her ears were belabored by the chatter of Lady Diana and Caroline.

They were "positively dying to know what had occurred." As Caroline put it: "It was as though you had been wiped off the face of the earth, my dear! What did he do to cause an upset?"

"I assure you it was nothing at all unusual," replied Ancilla wearily. "Lord Linford is not at all adept with oars. You see, one dropped from his grasp and he reached over for it—unwisely, to say the least. Now, I pray you will allow me some peace until I have had a chance to change into dry clothes. This afternoon's adventure has been most upsetting."

"Oh, indeed! How very *witty* of you," exclaimed Lady Diana. "Upsetting! *Upsetting!* Oh, how I admire that you can be so funny at a time like this! *Upsetting!*"

Caroline and Ancilla exchanged weary glances, the latter being thankful that they were almost arrived at Storr, where the Gordons had rented a villa with a charming view of Windermere Water.

Lady Gordon's calm reception of her bedraggled daughter could have easily led one to believe that immersions in Windermere Water, fully clothed, were a common occurrence. She merely suggested that Ancilla repair to her room and change, and she invited Diana and Caroline to come sit with her and tell her of the day's doings.

But Diana was in all haste to consult with a mirror. She had taken her lovely complexion out under the country sun for hours and had no great faith that her parasol had preserved it from Nature's touch. She begged to be excused and withdrew.

Caroline would have loved to chat with Lady Gordon, but she, too, needed to bring her appearance in order. Furthermore, she did not think that anything further regarding the mystery of Ancilla's aquatic adventure would be revealed until that young lady was present too.

Lady Gordon had no objection to her guests retiring, for she was bursting with anxiety and curiosity to learn what had occurred to have put her daughter into such a state of distress. As soon as the young ladies had disappeared up the stairs, she arose and proceeded to her daughter's chamber.

Ancilla was out of her wet clothing and was being briskly toweled by her maid. The chill of the waters had paled her features and, now, some of her natural color was being restored. She looked up as her mother came in and remarked, sourly: "Mama, that was no favor you did me. The Right Honorable Viscount Linford is a fumble-footed, fumble-witted ass. Did you see in what condition I was upon my return?"

"Now, now, child, you do not appear to have taken any harm from your experience. I surmised that you were out on the lake with him and that you managed to fall into the water. It could have had dreadfully serious consequences, I admit, but you have come through it all, all right, so I do not see that there is any call for melodramatics. What I do not understand is how it comes about that neither Diana nor Caroline was in the least discomposed. It is never like you to be so clumsy as to fall into the water and get yourself thoroughly drenched from head to foot. Surely, you are at least as nimble as they."

"Oh, they were not in the boat with him—"

"You did not go out alone in a boat with a strange gentleman, I hope!" exclaimed her ladyship, her face tight with disapproval.

"I could wish I had not, considering the outcome— but I did not see anything exceptional in it. He gave all the appearance of a mild-mannered gentleman. I did not know that his mildness derived from a stupidity and an awkwardness second to none. The boat was rather snug for more than two and it was just for a bit of a jaunt out upon the waters and back to shore. We were each to take a turn with him. No, I do not see that there was anything exceptional in it."

"I suppose not, if that was the way of it—but why do you insist that Lord Linford is such a poor specimen? I have it from excellent sources that he is positively brilliant. Do you know that, despite his youth, he is a Fellow of the Royal Society?"

"An artist?"

"No, my dear, that is the *Academy*. *He* is some sort of a philosopher, something like Sir Isaac Newton, I believe—a *natural* philosopher, I suppose. They tell me that he was a disciple of Mr. Henry Cavendish."

"Not the queer fish who resided in Clapham Common, surely?"

"Ancilla, I wish you would not express yourself in such common language. Mr. Cavendish was not a 'queer fish.' He was quite the authority on pneumatics, I understand."

Ancilla shrugged. "That is certainly an odd topic to become an authority upon. I have not the vaguest idea what it pertains to."

"Well, neither do I, but I am told it is of the first importance to Natural Philosophy and Mr. Cavendish has been recognized for his contributions since ever we either of us were born. That he should have devoted any of his time to a gentleman as young as Lord Linford says a great deal for his lordship."

"I should say it says very little for either Mr. Cavendish or the Royal Society. The Viscount is a bore and quite the most unhandy fellow it has been my misfortune to know. I am sure that Mr. Cavendish had more need of him than I do, and I wish he would go back to London before I am put to the trouble of entertaining him again. From the look in your eye, Mama, I suspect that you have plans in that direction, do you not?"

"Child, a viscount is nothing to sneeze at, I assure you. It is not as though your father were alive to see to such matters, and I have been out of the swim of London society for too long to be able to be of much use in that regard, you see."

"No, I do not see. What regard do you have reference to?"

Lady Gordon looked uncomfortable. "Really, Ancilla, you try my patience! I should not have to explain every detail to you. You are quite old enough to realize that time is passing and you do not have any gentleman calling upon you. Now, it seems to me that a viscount would make you a most unexceptional husband. I am sure that I could never hope to find you anyone so eligible."

Ancilla laughed. "Then I bid you try, Mama. I have an idea that anyone you can find will be more suited to me than the Viscount Linford. If he is so brilliant, he hides the quality well."

"Oh, but do give the fellow a chance! It was your first meeting and it is very unwise to base your opinions upon a mischance that would never happen again. For all you know, you may have acted unwisely and thus precipitated yourself into the water. It could have happened that way, you know."

"Yes, it could have happened that way, but it did not. The man is in need of a keeper and I am forced to believe that that horrid Mr. Symonds is his companion for that very reason."

"Now, there you go again, jumping to all manner of

unreasonable conclusions. Mr. Symonds is nothing of the sort. He accompanies the Viscount for a very good reason."

Lady Gordon by this time had taken a seat. She nodded her head authoritatively as she made her statement.

Ancilla, who was now being helped into fresh clothing by her maid, stared at her mother, expectantly. For a moment there was silence.

"Mama, you are not going to leave it at that, I pray. What is this very good reason?"

"I am sure that I do not know, but I am equally sure that it is nothing to do with a keeper. The very idea!"

Ancilla shrugged. "I suggest that we leave the eminent Viscount to his Mr. Symonds."

"My love, the matter is not to be dismissed so lightly. Just think what a triumph if, upon our return to London, you were to be announced as promised to a viscount. I should be delirious with delight."

"And so should I were it any viscount but Linford. Mama, you talk as though we were in exile. We only came out to the Lakes so that you could have time to regain your composure and allow the period of mourning to expire. There is naught to say that we cannot return to London without the least degree of shame attending it."

"You talk like a child, full of exaggeration! Ancilla, the Viscount is a neighbor and, I hope, a friend. He is bound to pay us a visit—and do not forget that our guests are every bit as eligible as you. It would be a crime against nature if you were to allow them to gain his lordship's interest right under your very nose and under your very own roof. What would people say?"

"They would say that my taste is unexceptional— nor do I think that, after today's stupid calamity, either

Diana or Caroline would be interested in his lordship. They have as much aversion to being drowned as I do."

"Fiddlesticks! They cannot help but see an opportunity and leap at the chance. You may mark my words but you will regret your inaction when either Diana or Caroline marches down the aisle with Viscount Linford on her arm. I tell you, the gentleman is a catch!"

"Mama, there is no need to carry on so! I shall marry whom I please and when I please. The Viscount is *not* numbered amongst the possibilities."

"Well, I should like to know who is! It is criminal of me to take you out of London when you are at your prime. I'll wager that you would have had a dozen offers before the season was at an end. I know that I shall regret it all the rest of my days. You were not *meant* to be a spinster forever."

Ancilla laughed. "And I do not intend to remain one. Considering that I am not yet twenty, I do not think that I needs must accept the first gentleman who offers. There is time."

Her change of attire was completed and she turned to get a glimpse of herself in the pier glass. Satisfied, she turned to Lady Gordon and went on: "Besides, this was our very first meeting. Mama, you are making too much of it. If my guess is correct, Lord Linford is bound to be a slow top with all the rest of his failings. *If* he should ever think to make an offer—heaven forbid!— it will be years hence, I assure you. Come! Enough! We have our guests to entertain."

2

Master Joseph Pringle, proprietor of the White Lion, the foremost of the two inns situated in Bowness, was exceedingly proud of his establishment. It boasted one of the finest views of Winandermere, which could be had by any of his guests from the grand porch that had been constructed especially to preserve and present the view for and to his custom. Having taken advantage of this natural vista, his charges were in accordance, with the result that his clientele was of the upper strata of society as a general rule.

Master Pringle might have been characterized as a generous man, for he never stinted in his concern for the comfort of his lodgers. Then again, it might have been that he hoped to make the lightening of their purses as pleasurable as was possible. In any event, were it the scenery or were it the management of the White Lion, in season its guest list always boasted of distinguished visitors to the Lakes. Viscount Linford was just such a visitor and had a suite of chambers to himself and his companion, the Reverend Mr. Symonds.

There was a great deal of clucking when his lordship appeared in the common room, his clothes a mass of damp wrinkles, accompanied by Mr. Symonds, whose face was wrinkled, too, in exaggerated consternation for his lordship's plight.

But for all the expressions of dismay and shouted orders, Lord Linford might have stood for hours amidst the confusion if he had not brushed his way through the innkeeper, his staff of maids, and the skittery Mr. Symonds and made his way to the door of his chambers. There he turned about and summarily dismissed all but his companion, entered his room and, with a gesture of annoyance, ordered Mr. Symonds to shut the door and allow no one to disturb them until called.

Lord Linford's mood of irritation did not fall away as he stripped himself of his wet things, and it left Mr. Symonds at a loss as to how to begin a conversation. He opened his mouth to make some remark, but closed it abruptly when the Viscount placed a lumped-up, sodden pair of trousers in his hands. In all the time since his lordship had suffered his immersion, this was the first instance that Mr. Symonds had come into contact with wetness, and it had a most unsettling effect upon him. He let out a little shriek and dropped the garments, making a face. The bundle fell with a splashing sound, throwing off random drops as it hit the floor. Some of those drops landed on Mr. Symonds' boots, causing him to hop about in a vain attempt to avoid them. When he saw that his boots were bedewed, his face lit with horror as he exclaimed: "Heavens, I am all wet! I shall take my death from exposure!"

"Symonds, do not be an ass! Sit down and be still!" growled the Viscount. "If I had not proved myself to be a thorough ass myself this day, I should sack you on the spot!"

"Oh, dear!" murmured Mr. Symonds, growing very small as he hurried to seat himself as far away from the Viscount as the space in the chamber would allow.

"You pretend to gentility; then how could you have stood by and allowed the lady to come back into the water?" demanded Lord Linford. "It was bad enough that I lost the oar and upset the craft. The last thing I could have wished was to be ordered about by a lady when I was perfectly capable of handling the business. Why, dash it all, did you not come to my aid, instead?"

"But, my lord, you were all wet and she was all wet. What profit was there if I should have got all wet into the bargain? In any case, it was not at all ladylike for Miss Gordon to have ventured forth into the lake again and put you to shame. As you say, it was not at all necessary, for you were perfectly capable of handling the business without aid from anyone."

His lordship glared at him. "You should have stopped her! By not doing so, you made a cake of yourself, just as I had already managed to do for my own self. We are, the pair of us, spectacles of ineffectuality, and I shudder to think how this incident will be bruited about the Lakes. I should not be surprised if it follows us to London. My reputation for being a fiddlehead will certainly be enlarged upon."

"Oh, my lord, you are making too much of it! It is nothing of the sort! You, a Fellow of the Royal Society, to be up in the boughs over such insignificant nonsense, is quite out of order, I do assure you. Actually, it was all the fault of Miss Gordon, as you will plainly see if you give it a moment's thought. It was she who made of the business a disgrace."

"Ah, then you do admit that there was something exceptional about the business! Here, take these wet underthings and do something with them," he ended, carelessly tossing them at Mr. Symonds.

The gentleman was quite unprepared to receive the damp linens, and never had a chance to dodge. They wound up in a sodden pile on his lap. He stared down at them with an expression of misery and asked, in a small voice: "But what am I to do with them?"

In exasperation, Lord Linford exclaimed: "Symonds, a green valet would be of more use to me at this moment than you with all your erudition. Do *something* with them! Get one of the maids to see them dried and mangled back into shape—and if that cannot be accomplished, dispose of them. I pray the former for I am not sure that I have brought enough attire to withstand another such baptism."

"My lord, I shall do what you wish, but I would point out that my purpose in accompanying you to this district was to provide enlightened conversation. I do not pretend to be a valet—and now, I am sure that you have done for *my* clothing. See, my midriff is thoroughly wetted!"

"Cease your whining and make yourself useful, Symonds. I do not recall that we have had much conversation since we arrived, enlightened or otherwise."

Mr. Symonds rang for a maid, who promptly responded at the door. He did not dare to open it more than was sufficient to pass out his coat and his lordship's clothes, because Lord Linford was standing about clothed only in freshly donned unmentionables. Then, seething with indignation, he came back into the chamber and addressed the Viscount.

"My lord, despite the fact that I am indebted to you for my living, I must speak."

He stood rigidly at attention and waited for his lordship to acknowledge his statement.

"Ah, now we shall have some of this enlightened conversation, methinks! Say on, reverend sir!"

"Truly, my lord, this is no laughing matter, and I could wish you would adopt a more sober attitude."

"Do get on with it!"

"I respectfully wish to point out to your lordship that the only remarks you have made to me from the time we set out for the Lakes were upon a topic which I, as man of the cloth, could in no way respond to."

"What the devil are you getting at?"

"You appear to have a fixation, my lord, on a particular topic that has no place in gentle society."

His lordship began to chuckle, and Mr. Symonds' face began to stiffen.

"Females!" exclaimed Lord Linford.

"The Sex!" amended Mr. Symonds.

"My dear Mr. Symonds, I suggest that you have not learned all your lessons. You are wed and I am not. I have spent all of my life, closeted with books and Cavendish's apparatuses, and to the extent that I had become morbid beyond bearing. It was not just a change of scenery that was recommended to me, but a change of company as well. You will recall it was with Sir Samuel Harring I consulted, an enlightened and expert physician if ever there was one. I did not think that I could go on a repairing lease into a solitude that would have only heightened my discomfort, and that is why I engaged you to accompany me. I told you then, and I tell you now, I am in a mood for a bit of a frolic and whatever follows. So, if females are on my mind, there is a very good reason for it. I suggest that you put aside your missishness and give me the benefit of your advice and experience—and frankly, too, or we shall have nothing to converse upon."

"But, my lord, as a man of the cloth—"

"As a man of the cloth, it is your duty!"

"Dear, dear, I am exceedingly embarrassed—"

"Stab me if I see why you should be!"

"There are the conventions, you know—"

"Hang the conventions! There is you and there is me. If you are to be of the least value to me, we shall talk together upon any topic under the sun. Symonds, I am beginning to believe that I overvalued your erudition. It is one thing to discuss pneumatics with me, but it is more needful that you are able and willing to discuss *people* with me. Now help me on with this coat!"

With a great sigh of resignation, the Reverend Mr. Symonds assisted his lord into his coat.

Although the Villa at Storr was constructed on an ample plan, the comforts of Londoners had not been consulted so that the ladies were put to some inconvenience, having to adjust themselves to smallish rooms and poorly equipped kitchens. But, though the staff of locals knew nothing finer, a reasonable semblance of comfort was achieved. Dinner parties were well managed if with little style, and the lack of pinneatness was suffered for the rustic air it lent to the accommodations.

Ancilla had achieved with the change of attire her sense of humor, and had dismissed from serious consideration the episode and its cause. Now, the ladies were all gathered in the drawing room, from whose great windows their eyes could feast upon Winandermere's beauty, while dinner was being prepared.

"...Of course, I shall ignore the event," Ancilla was saying. "As his lordship will continue to be a neighbor for some time, I imagine, it stands to reason that I shall not be able to ignore *him,* but that is not to say that I expect to take much delight in his company should we happen to be thrown together. Nonetheless, I *do not expect to find myself together with him in any sort of watercraft ever again!*" she ended, laughing.

Lady Diana's face was quite intense as she banged her fist into her lap in time with her remarks: "Oh, Ancilla, that is *kind* in you! It is so *considerate* in you to overlook the *peril* his lordship placed you in! Truly, *I* do not *know* how you can be so *magnanimous!* I am sure that *I* should positively *die* from embarrassment were it to have happened to *me!*"

Said Caroline: "There is no need for embarrassment, Diana. If anyone ought to be embarrassed, it is his lordship. On the other hand, it would be too severe to condemn Lord Linford for what may not have been his fault after all. Speaking for myself, I should not be the least embarrassed to engage his lordship in friendly conversation when next we meet."

Ancilla looked bored, but Diana had a very tense expression on her face. She nodded emphatically and said: "Yes, you are quite right, Caroline. It is too *harsh* a punishment to *visit* upon his lordship. *I,* for *one,* will *not* be the *least* embarrassed to speak with him."

Ancilla laughed. "I hardly think that any of this is your concern. I never thought to be embarrassed in his lordship's presence and merely pray that I shall be spared his company in the future. The figure he cuts is something less than dashing."

Remarked Caroline: "Well, of course, I would not go

so far as to hold Lord Linford up as a paragon of grace, but one must take into account the gentleman *is* a viscount and ought to be allowed some departure from the usual."

"Ah, yes!" exclaimed Diana. "That is a very good point you make! And what is more, Lord Linford, although he is a bit thinner than he ought to be, is not altogether unhandsome."

"Yes, and there is the further consideration, my dears," rejoined Ancilla in a superior tone. "It so happens that his lordship is the most eligible gentleman at the Lake at the present time. That is nothing to be lightly overlooked."

Caroline appeared to be annoyed. "Truly, Ancilla, just because you cannot get along with him is no reason to look down upon those who can. Very well, his lordship *is* the most eligible gentleman about. Surely *that* is not a reason to cut him dead."

"My dears, my dears," intervened Lady Gordon, "we shall be at dinner soon and this conversation is not likely to encourage one's appetite. I suggest we leave Viscount Linford for another time and devote ourselves to a topic more in keeping with the peaceful contemplation of the beauty that resides just outside of our windows. Ah, if one could but capture the vista and carry it back to London with one!"

A maid came into the drawing room to announce a visitor. Lady Gordon took up the card and read it.

"It is a Captain Wildish. Now who can he be, and to come calling at such an inconvenient hour? I do not think I ought to receive the gentleman. If he wishes, he can call upon us in the morning, a more proper time."

"Oh, I do not think so, my lady," said Diana. "Captain Wildish is staying at Ambleside and that *is* a distance. Besides, I have heard tell of him and he is a most *courteous* person, with *entrée* to all the *best* people."

"Oh, truly, Lady Gordon, I do think we ought to receive the gentleman," said Caroline. "Heaven knows it has been rather deadly here at Storr for lack of friends, and Ancilla's *unfortunate* experience with the only gentleman within a stone's throw is bound to limit our acquaintanceship even more than before, considering that she will not forgive the Viscount. I say that we ought to have Captain Wildish in."

"But it so near the dinner hour, children!" protested Lady Gordon.

"Oh, but we can put it back a *little* time!," exclaimed Diana. "It is really quite *simple!*"

Rather reluctantly, her ladyship gave her permission and the maid went to fetch the caller.

He came into the room and his presence filled the chamber. His teeth flashed in a charming smile of greeting as he presented himself to her ladyship, bowing with a graceful flourish of his arms. He was dressed in accordance with the strict dictates of the style that Beau Brummell had devised, his linen gleaming against the contrast of the dark coat and trousers he was wearing. His boots were freshly blackened and brushed to a high polish. Not a speck of dust marred the perfection of his attire. It was obvious that he had come in a carriage. His appearance was too natty to have allowed of his having ridden.

Ancilla was very pleasantly impressed with his appearance. That last gentleman had fitted his clothes as poorly as he had fitted his oars and so Captain Wildish was a refreshing sight by comparision.

The ladies were very much interested to hear the Captain's reasons for this late visit and gave him their attention once the introductions had been made. It was obvious that Captain Wildish was a man who expected to gain everyone's attention and he was not in the least bashful to address them.

"Ah, ladies, I must apologize for coming upon you at this late hour, but I had no choice. It was less than an hour ago that I heard the news of the catastrophe in the lake. I happened to be visiting with some friends, just beyond Bowness—Windermere in fact—when it came to our ears. As soon as I could make myself presentable, I set out to call upon you, to offer my sympathy and my assistance in the event that were needed. It is criminal that they should permit all manner of incompetents to take boats out upon the lake and thereby imperil the welfare, nay the lives, of innocent companions. Oh, how I have prayed that nothing worse than a wetting was suffered! I pray you will take pity upon me and inform me at once of the worst! Is the lady who was the miscreant's victim reposing in her chamber—alive and well, the Lord permit?"

It was a brave figure he made as he stood before them, his hand thrust into his waistcoat à la Napoleon, fearful of the dreadful news that might be imparted but bravely standing to it, refusing to be daunted by the worst.

Diana stared at him, her heart in her eyes, her hands clasped together at her breast.

Caroline was sitting back in her chair regarding the Captain out of speculative eyes, and Lady Gordon had a hand to her lips while she gazed wide-eyed with surprise at the gentleman.

Ancilla was overcome by an odd feeling of guilt that somehow she ought to be at Death's door for the Captain's benefit and it so tickled her that, like her mother, she, too, had a hand to her lips; but it was to hide an irrepressible smile.

The silence in the room was become awkward and Captain Wildish began to look with appeal at first one of the ladies and then another, awaiting some word in response to his remarkable declaration. The air of great confidence that had attended his entrance showed signs of wilting and Ancilla took pity on him.

"Dear Captain Wildish, I pray you will not be too disappointed when I inform you that your great concern is not warranted. As you can see, I have suffered naught from my bath in the lake and am quite fit. Nevertheless, I wish you to know that I am touched by your concern for one whom you never numbered amongst your acquaintances until this moment."

The Captain's look of concern quickly dissolved into his sparkling smile. "My dear Miss Gordon, I may breath again! You cannot know with what relief I gaze upon your lovely features in the happy knowledge that my worries were all for naught! I am delighted, Miss Gordon. I am ecstatic, Miss Gordon! And I am humble, Miss Gordon, that you will accept me as a friend!"

If Captain Wildish had been a friend of some standing with her, Ancilla could not have helped but be touched by his tone and its expression. But considering that this was her first sight of him, the quiver in his voice, the caressing quality of his tones gave her the impression that she was witnessing a play actor delivering his lines. She was completely untouched but somewhat amused by the gentleman's oratory and she replied: "Indeed, Captain Wildish, you make too much of it. I am pleased to make your acquaintance and pray that I may never be the subject of such concern, as you have shown, in the future."

"With all my heart, Miss Gordon, I say amen to that."

"Oh, Captain Wildish, I am *thrilled* to have been *here* to see how *deeply* concerned you are for your fellow being!" exclaimed Diana. "It is not too much to say that the *world* would be a *better* place if in it there were *more* gentleman like *you*, sir!"

"Ah, my lady, it is very high praise that you offer and I do not feel worthy of it—but I have no choice than to accept the plaudits of so lovely a creature. It would be less than gallant of me not to do so."

"And I pray, Captain Wildish," put in Caroline, "that your gallantry will not be overextended if you managed to allow us to see more of you. I admit that Storr is something far from the center of things. Is it any better at Ambleside?"

"Oh, my dear Miss Darcy, but of course it is! You have a most delightful place here at Storr. In fact, as a longtime visitor to the Lake Country, I can tell you that the Curwin Villa is the choice place to stay on Windermere; but as far as becoming acquainted with all the marvelous people about the Lakes, one must go to Ambleside. There can be no question, my dear Miss Darcy, and I should think that you ladies would make it your business to come up to Ambleside to lend it the glorious loveliness of your beauty. I should be delighted to carry you there myself—but, alas, I have but a small curricle with but room for one or two others than myself. But, perhaps, I can arrange something in that regard. Lady Gordon, if you have no objection, I should be pleased to hire a carriage for the day that you wish to go to Ambleside. There will be an Assembly Tuesday next. They are delightful affairs and it pains me to even think that you and your daughter and company should miss any one of them."

"Ah, yes, Captain Wildish, it is a thought and I thank you for your offer. I pray you will allow me to think on it," replied Lady Gordon without any marked enthusiasm.

Just then, there was heard the tinkle of a tiny bell. Captain Wildish, who had been staring benignly down upon Ancilla as he toyed with an eyeglass, quickly turned about, and once again his countenance registered deep anguish.

"Dear, dear Lady Gordon, how can I apologize to you for having taken up so much of your time?" he asked, holding his arms out to her in a gesture of defenselessness. "I have never—and I swear it—I have never seen time pass so swiftly! Your charm and grace, that of the lovely ladies who presently surround me on every side—why, no man—no, not a one—could spare a moment of his attention for the passing hour, and so I must plead guilty to intrusion. I beg you will forgive me! I shall depart at once and leave you to your dinner. I have but six miles to go for my own and shall be thinking of this delightful visit every step of the way."

Lady Gordon would have rather encouraged him on his way but etiquette demanded that she make some gesture of hospitality.

"But of course, Captain Wildish, we would not think to let you depart until you sat yourself down and joined us at table for dinner."

Captain Wildish bowed deeply. "Again, fair ladies, I would refuse but gallantry, perhaps excessive in my case and therefore a fault, will not permit it. I accept, my lady, and with all my heart. Truly, you have been as gracious to me, a stranger, as was Lady de La Warr, in whose illustrious family, I make a claim, a very humble and distant claim, mind you, of membership. Are you at all acquainted with Lady de La Warr, Lady Gordon?"

"No, but I have heard of the de La Warrs, of course, although I have never had the pleasure of making an acquaintance of any of that family."

"Oh, then it will be my great delight to see that you do, my lady. You will find Lady de La Warr as gracious as she is charming and I am sure that you will find a great many things to talk about. Ah, I see one of your servants has opened the dining room doors. Ladies, my pleasure!"

But for the fact that Caroline asked an occasional question or two, conversation at dinner was a veritable monologue. Captain Wildish felt it incumbent upon himself to discourse at length upon his family connections. Caroline spared none of the others when she managed to press him upon some detail in his recounting of his various visits to the de La Warr family seat, Buckhurst Park, Withyham, Sussex.

Under Caroline's persistent interrogation, it turned out that Captain Wildish's claim to a family connection with the de La Warrs was owing to the fact that his mother was a distant cousin to the lady Sackville who had married the present Earl. It struck Ancilla as being a deal less in importance than the Captain was intent upon having them believe.

Lady Gordon had been debating with herself as to the propriety of them entertaining a stranger, and a man. Although she was pleased to learn that Captain Wildish was connected to the de La Warrs, she could have hoped that it had not been so faint. But, up in this land for holidays, there was a distinct lessening of formality, due in part to the fact that so many residents were not permanent. The Captain, if somewhat over-solicitous in his manners, still carried himself in his conversation and in his deportment before them in a most unexceptional way. There were some few of her neighbors in London whose manners would not stand comparison to the Captain's.

When the meal came to an end, the Captain declined to be left alone with a bottle and a cigar and joined the ladies in the drawing room. There, he proceeded to satisfy his curiosity over the details of Ancilla's mishap.

He began by inquiring: "I say, Miss Gordon, I do not believe I heard you mention the chap's name who pitched you overboard this afternoon. May I ask who he was? Someone new to the area, perhaps?"

"Yes, Captain Wildish. Lord Linford came up to the Lakes but a few days ago and my lady mother was able to introduce us to the gentleman by reason of a mutual acquaintance in London. But I do protest, sir. His lordship never did anything to me at all. It was a case of leaning a bit too far over in attempting to recover an oar, you see. Clumsy perhaps, but hardly premeditated."

"Lord Linford. I say, that does have a familiar ring to it! Now, let me see. . . ." He paused as though in deep thought. "Would he be a rather tall chap, never in what I should call the best attire, nor would I describe him as the most graceful of men. Now would he be something like?"

Ancilla smiled. "Something like, indeed! Do you know the Viscount well?"

"Oh, no," the Captain hastened to deny. "I am happy to say I have no connection with the fellow. He was pointed out to me when I stopped at the inn in Bowness. Had I the least idea that it was he who had caused you such distress, Miss Gordon, I should have had a word to say to him, you may rest assured."

"Really, I am glad that you did not, Captain Wildish. I am beginning to think too much has been said about the affair already."

"Ah, but that is kind of you to think so, my dear— But I should not like you to go away from these beautiful lakes with poor opinions of them. Not everyone is so cloddish with the oars as this Viscount Linford appears to be. I should welcome the opportunity to show you how truly inspiring, how truly beautiful, Lake Windermere can be from a small boat. You would not have a thing to worry about, I assure you. I have been on the Lakes in season for many a year and have never had a spill."

"It is so very considerate of you, Captain Wildish, to put yourself to the trouble, and I am sure that some day I shall take you up on it. In the meantime, do you happen to know anything about that odd little Mr. Symonds who trails the Viscount about?"

"Oh, Symonds? But of course, he...." The Captain stopped in midsentence and a shrewd look came into his eyes for an instant. It was there, and then it was gone so quickly that Ancilla could not be sure.

The Captain appeared to have recovered from whatever impediment of recollection he had suffered and went on: "Oh, no, not that one. There is another Symonds I was thinking on. No, I know naught about the Viscount and his companions—but, pray, has this mischance affected your feelings toward his lordship? I should think it would."

Ancilla laughed lightly. "I do not see why it should. I felt nothing for the gentleman before we went out in the boat and so there was naught to change in the way of my feelings for him. I do not think he is in my style of friend, but then that may be *his* good fortune."

"Then you are not much taken with titles, Miss Gordon?"

"I do not despise them, if that is what you are getting at. You seem to have a power of respect for them, Captain, or you would not be so proud of your connection with the Earl de La Warr, I am thinking."

34

The Captain laughed. "But of course, there is nothing disgraceful about titles; however I put my faith in blood, Miss Gordon, and I do it before titles. The de La Warrs and the Sackvilles are a type of the finest blood England can boast. That is why I am proud of my connection. Now, I am sure that anyone as lovely as you, Miss Gordon, must be of such fine stock as would be unexceptional in any circle."

"I pray that you are right, Captain Wildish, but I cannot be so sure. The branch of the Gordon clan my father could trace his ancestry to was not noted for much and came away from Scotland so long ago that only the name remains as reminder of our ancient forebears. I fear, Captain, that we are but undistinguished members of an undistinguished family. My late father was a gentleman who managed to leave a respectable estate by dint of industry, sir, but that is all one can say for him. In my opinion, that is sufficient."

Captain Wildish was not sensible of having been put down and went on to exclaim: "Excellent, Miss Gordon! It would not have been the thing for your late father to have left you penniless. I salute your late father, Miss Gordon, and I respect your late father. Allow me to say that if there is any way I can be of assistance to you or your lady mother, you must never hesitate to call upon me. Not for an instant must you hesitate, Miss Gordon, or I shall feel that I have gained no advantage with you."

There was an ebullience to his manner that left Ancilla breathless and wishing that he would devote himself to the others. She smiled sweetly and thanked him once again for his consideration moving, as she did so, to bring him before the other ladies.

Lady Gordon, suppressing a yawn, remarked upon how pleasant it had been to have his company to dinner.

Captain Wildish took the hint and immediately began an encomium upon the gracious hospitality he had received, ending with a promise to call again. Then he took his leave and departed.

The ladies were rather fatigued and it could be that Lady Gordon spoke for them all when she commented, as the door closed behind him: "I should prefer that his next call would not be so close to the dinner hour."

3

Viscount Linford was preparing to go out the following morning. He had some idea of repairing to Storrs to make his apologies all over again to Miss Gordon and also to her mother. Mr. Symonds was moving about the room, putting it in order, chirping his disapproval at the manner in which his lordship threw things about. It was nothing unusual in the reverend gentleman and his twitters made no impression on the Viscount.

Lord Linford was standing before a mirror, a most dissatisfied expression on his face as he fumbled with his neckcloth which although unsoiled, because of a lack of stiffening, refused to shape itself in any stylish way.

There was a knock on the door and Mr. Symonds opened it, welcoming the visitor.

"Good day to you, Ivo," his lordship tossed over his shoulder as he made a pass with his neckcloth. "You are up and about rather early this day, I see."

Captain Wildish, whose attire quite put the Viscount's in the shade, laughed heartily. "Indeed, Andrew, I knew I should find you at your everlasting struggles to come up with the fashion of the times, and thought to find some amusement in it."

"Confound you, man! Come and give me a hand with it or I shall never leave this room this day."

"Ah, have you got an engagement, my lord?" inquired the Captain, unceremoniously pushing Mr. Symonds out of his path as he stepped over to join Lord Linford at his toilet.

He turned the Viscount away from the glass and began to fiddle with the recalcitrant neckcloth. He could see at a glance what the trouble was.

"This is not a proper cloth! There is no starch in it! Who does your laundry?"

"I have not the vaguest idea. I leave such matters up to Symonds," replied Lord Linford with a shrug.

"Then I suggest you sack him out of hand and engage yourself a decent valet. Symonds, from his appearance, does not strike me as being the least use to you."

Mr. Symonds bristled. "Captain Wildish, I'll have you know I am a man of the cloth and never made any pretense of knowing the first thing about the vanities of the world."

"Aye, a man of the cloth—but never of the *neck-cloth!*" rejoined the Captain, laughing heartily at his own witticism.

His lordship smiled and said: "Ivo, leave Symonds

be. He is a good man and I need him about to make the sort of conversation that pleases me."

"Indeed. How dull!" said Captain Wildish, looking Symonds up and down as though he were some sort of insect. "Andrew, I never shall understand your attraction for all that trivia in which you indulge when there are so many more interesting things for a chap to think on."

"I cannot imagine anything more interesting than the way in which a seemingly homogeneous gas, such as our air, can be separated into phlogistic and antiphlogistic moieties—"

Captain Wildish's hands fell away from about Lord Linford's neck as he raised them in horror and exclaimed: "Heaven preserve me from such talk! Linford, I haven't the vaguest idea of what you are saying and, frankly, I am not at all inclined to hear your explanation. I am sure that I should be incredibly bored with it!"

Lord Linford laughed. "Precisely. And so it is with most people, but Symonds understands the business enough for me to discuss with him my ideas on the subject. Henry bequeathed me a bit of a puzzler to work on while I took this holiday."

"That would be Cavendish, the late recluse, I take it."

"I prefer to think of him as having been England's foremost natural philosopher of the times, my dear Ivo."

"Have it as you will. I did not come to speak with you about your petty interests, but to tell you that, as far as the Gordons and company, you are persona non grata with them for your idiocy of yesterday. Instead of playing about with gases, it seems to me that you would be better advised to take up the study of water—

lakewater in general and the proper handling of small boats in particular."

Captain Wildish's hands had come up to his lordship's neck again, but they were brushed aside as the Viscount tore the offending neckcloth from his neck and stared at his friend.

"Is that truly a fact, old man? How do you come to know?"

There was an air of mockery in the Captain's manner as he replied: "I am not one to waste my time when there are so many beauties just waiting for the proper sort to pay them attention. I called at their villa late in the day, late enough to force them to invite me into dinner with them, and proceeded to make an apology for all the clumsy louts in the world."

"You, sir, are an unprincipled dog!" stated Lord Linford with no great sign of emotion.

"Yes," laughed Captain Wildish, "it makes things so much easier, too."

"Ivo, I think you have gone too far. I need no one to disparage me, I manage quite well by myself upon that score—"

"Oh, I am not so unprincipled as that, my lord. I did not mention you by name. As a matter of fact, I pretended no acquaintance with you at all, so you see I was not taking *you* down particularly."

"My, how awfully, bloody kind of you," sneered his lordship. "Now, what the devil am I to do? I had intended to get over to Storr this morning and try to mend matters, but I suppose, with your usual aplomb, you have sunk me deeper than I did myself. Pray, what is the attraction, old boy?"

Wildish looked at his nails and shrugged. "I am rather tired of going about the country, having to dine upon my experiences and meet my expenses with petty sums obtained from doting females. Now, down at Storrs are a bevy of beauties, and if I do not miss my guess, the least of them quite worthy of my station in life. I must surmise further that they are well endowed in the pecuniary sense as well, and each could easily afford the moderate expenses my mode of living entails."

"I must say you are frank and altogether a fast worker. By any chance have you got your eye on a particular one of them?"

"Now, that was a problem to me, old friend, but I was able to meet it with my usual ingenuity, as you shall hear.

"Lady Diana would be the most brilliant catch for a chap in my circumstances. In that company, residing at Curwin's Villa, she has got to be quite the wealthiest. Yes, as I think back, I should estimate her costume as having set her papa back a cool three hundred and fifty guineas. Furthermore, she struck me as having one or two apartments to let, so I should not have the least trouble in gaining a handsome allowance from her, especially if her parent is no brighter than his daughter. But, it strikes me as flying a bit high. I should have a devil of a time paying court to her with my forever light pockets.

"Miss Caroline Darcy, on the other hand, is too sharp for her own good and certainly mine. You ought to have heard the catechism she put me through."

"I should have been very entertained, indeed," interjected Lord Linford.

Captain Wildish grinned. "Never you mind, my friend, I had my wits about me and she did not get all that much out of me. As a matter of fact, I took the opportunity to improve their opinions of me even as I was making my choice amongst 'em."

"So I am left to conclude that you have set your sights upon Miss Gordon, am I?"

"Ah, yes, Andrew, I have always had the greatest respect for your talents in the mental department. Once again, you have managed to hit the nail on the head. Ancilla Gordon is precisely my type of female, not too bright, quite docile—you ought to have seen how she swallowed everything I had to say about incompetents endangering the safety of companions in small boats—"

"Thank you, my dearest friend, for the compliment. Perhaps I can repay it some day."

Captain Wildish laughed, goodnaturedly. "I dare say—but it may well take a hundred years, my lord."

Lord Linford turned back to the mirror, made some desperate twists of the neckcloth as he exclaimed: "There! And there! And there! Now, stay put, you bloody rag!"

He turned to present himself to Wildish, asking: "I think that is the best anyone can do with the beastly thing! What do you think of it?"

"I think that it will do for you, considering the state of the rest of your attire. I say, Andrew, why do you not see to a proper tailor and a proper valet? Heaven knows you can afford the best. Actually, there are times when I am ashamed to be seen in your company. I have to go about explaining that you are the eminent Linford, disciple of Cavendish, before people can be at ease with you. If Brummell were back in England, I think he would drum you right out of the rolls of acceptable gentlemen!"

"Bah! I have more important things to attend to than haberdashery. Yes, I think it will do," he ended, patting at his throat. "At least it feels comfortable."

"What, pray, has comfort to do with fashion?"

42

"I do not know and I do not care—but about Miss Gordon: I wish you would set your sights in a different direction."

Captain Wildish stared at Lord Linford as though he could not believe his ears.

"Eh, what's this? I say, Andrew, has the soft and lovely Ancilla managed to penetrate to that flinty heart of yours? Why, if I thought that you had any chance with the lady, I should step aside with the utmost alacrity. But you have got to face the fact, old man, that you are definitely not in Miss Gordon's good books. I do not see how you can even begin to think so, after the dousing you served her yesterday."

"One can always make sincere amends."

"Can one though? My dear Linford, why do you not stick to your vapors and airs. About women, you know not a thing. No, my friend, I can not see allowing Ancilla to go to waste. If I were to step aside in your favor, I should only be affording an opportunity to some sharper to take her away from the both of us. Better she be mine. She certainly will never be yours. You have done the business with her to a turn and upon your very first encounter."

His lordship was not very satisfied. His face mirrored the fact as he donned his coat.

"I do not suppose that I could make it clear to you I have no intention in Miss Gordon's direction except that of restoring a modicum of cordiality between us. You are an ass if you think that upon my first encounter with a female, I fall head over heels in love with her. I just disagree with you that Miss Gordon is your sort and, out of a spirit of gallantry towards her, would spare her the annoyance of your attention."

Captain Wildish's face reddened. He blew out his

cheeks. "Stab me, but you do not mince words with a fellow, do you?"

"Why ought I? We are friends, are we not, and I am but stating the facts of the matter as they appear to me," pontificated his lordship.

"B'gad, you are talking as though it were some one of your philosophical laws of nature! May I point out to you, sir, that we are not speaking of pneumatics now, but of the facts of everyday living? In fact, I shall prove just how wrong you are! My attentions are annoying to the fair sex, are they? Oh, if only you would agree to a wager, I should make my fortune—but as I shall be in the way to making it anyway, you may consider your challenge accepted. I shall prove to you that not only can I have my way with any female I choose, but I shall marry whom I choose as well."

His lordship's nose tilted upward slightly. "I do not recognize any sort of wager or any sort of challenge. I simply warn you that I shall never permit you to disgrace Miss Gordon."

"I never said a word about disgracing her!" retorted Captain Wildish, angrily.

"If she were to marry you, it would be a disgrace for her."

"Lord or no lord, friend or no friend, Andrew, you cannot expect me to swallow such an insult."

"I do not see what you can do about it, Ivo."

"I can bloody well call you out, I can!"

Completely unperturbed, his lordship shook his head: "No, that would be a violation of His Majesty's laws. Duelling is quite illegal, you know."

"It hardly matters! Duels are being fought all the time! If you refuse my challenge, I shall horsewhip you and label you coward!" retorted Captain Wildish, his anger mounting.

44

"That would not be wise, my friend. I am not averse to brawling with you if that should prove necessary but weapons are out."

For a moment, the Captain stood gasping for breath. "What!" he exclaimed, "You would pit yourself against me, with your fists who have been a sportsman all of my life?"

His lordship cocked his head and studied his friend. "I have studied the art of pugilism and, although we are well matched for weight, I am taller and have a reach of arm much beyond yours. I suspect that you can deliver the more powerful blow, but I should cut you to ribbons before you found the opportunity. So, as I was saying, I beg you will not set your cap for Miss Gordon. For the bath I gave her, I think I owe her at least that."

Captain Wildish shook his head in disbelief. He stared at his friend and began to chuckle. "You know, Andrew, I am inclined to believe that you just might be able to take my measure with fisticuffs, but that has nothing to say to the business with Miss Gordon. You may do your damndest to interfere in that quarter, I do not mind one bit. Nonetheless, I should warn you that you have bitten off more than you can chew if you think *you* can begin with her. I shall take special care to encourage her in her low opinion of you. Your word will be worth next to nothing against mine."

"Ivo, this is a poor sort of conversation at this hour of the day and between friends such as we have been to each other, but I shall not be dissuaded from at least making the attempt to snuff your business with Miss Gordon. Now, let us leave this matter and speak of other things."

Captain Wildish shrugged and said: "That leaves us

very little more to say, I am thinking. Now, I have business to see to. When shall we meet?"

"As I, too, have matters to see to. We shall meet when Fate allows."

The Captain nodded and departed.

"My lord," said Mr. Symonds, "Captain Wildish is quite correct. You ought not to have anything further to do with Miss Gordon. Aside from the fact of the embarrassing business with the boat, the lady is definitely not the sort of female to make you a proper viscountess."

"So you have decided to act the counselor to me, have you? I suggest that you are wasting your time. I have not said that I am interested in Miss Gordon beyond the demands of friendship, and Wildish's most unreasonable position with regard to the lady appears to stem from the same delusion that you suffer from."

"But you have never expressed an interest of the least sort in any other female in all the time I have known you. In fact, Miss Gordon is the very first of whom you have addressed yourself in anything resembling cordiality, my lord."

"What has that to say to anything? Circumstances brought us together and I did what was proper and said what was proper."

"That is a mild manner of describing the capsizing of a boat, my lord."

His lordship grinned. "Devil take you, Symonds! You know what I mean. Miss Gordon appears to me to be a nice sort. Until the catastrophe, I think we were having a pleasant time together. I know that *I* was."

"There! You see that you were affected by her! My lord, for a gentleman who has had very little experience of the Sex, I caution you to go carefully. Especially with Miss Gordon. She is not at all ladylike!"

"You are not making any sense! You were not with her and I was. What do you know of her that I do not?"

"Did you not see how brazenly she went back into the lake and waded out to you? That was never a female's place. Why, I do believe that she would have tried to bring the boat in all by herself if there was no one about to help her! Truly, a shocking spectacle, my lord. I cannot picture *your* viscountess forgetting her station to such an extent."

There was a wry smile upon his lordship's face as he replied: "I will admit that she did try to take over the helm, as it were, when she got out to me. But that is hardly anything to hold against the lady. What were *you* doing all that time to assist me?"

"Oh, you cannot expect me, a man of the cloth, to have so forgotten the dignity of *my* station as to have put my appearance before the world in a poor light. If there had been but time, I should have gone to the boat tender for assistance; but Miss Gordon was back into the lake, making an exhibit of herself—and not to your advantage, my lord—before there was a chance. Now, I put it to you, my lord—"

"No! I put it to you, Symonds, that you do not know what you are talking about! Perhaps I do not know anything about the ladies, but I strongly suspect that my ignorance in this instance is tenfold worthier than your missishness. I mean to say, the situation may have looked desperate to the lady and so she did what she believed necessary. On the other hand, you did absolutely nothing but looked on so that you could find trivial points to carp on. By God, even Wildish's remarks are worthier than yours! Now, I intend to see

Miss Gordon and there's an end to it! I assure you there is not a viscountess in my eye!"

"Oh dear! Oh dear!" sighed Mr. Symonds, dramatically.

His lordship, who was now on the point of leaving, turned and asked: "Now, what is the matter?"

"Ah, my lord, it was just a poor thought. It is nothing."

"You have all the appearance of a man whose existence is about to end. Something is the matter."

"I am sure you will not heed what I have to say, my lord."

"I quite agree, yet I would hear what is on your liver in any event."

"Then it is simply this. I beg your pardon if I insist that, by reason of my age and my vocation, I know something more about these matters than you, my lord—"

"Oh, for heaven's sake! Are you a barrister preparing to state your case? Spit it out, man!"

"My lord, you will agree that Miss Gordon is a most attractive female—I might even put it that she has a certain claim to beauty."

"I am relieved to learn that there is nothing at fault with your eyesight—but what you have said can apply equally to all of the ladies in Curwin's Villa, not excluding Lady Gordon herself."

"Yes, but none of the other ladies had so taken your notice as has Miss Gordon. That is why what I have to say concerns her and only her."

"I assumed as much hours ago."

"You say that you are not much affected by the lady—but you do not truly know this. Only time will tell. Considering her various charms and your vulnerability to them, I am forced to conclude that you will

48

ultimately wed the lady. I am only a humble curate, dependent solely upon yourself for my living. After you have wed, what shall become of me? Your wife will insist upon your assigning the living to another, some relation of hers—"

Lord Linford burst into laughter. "So that is what this is all about? Out of respect for your collar, I shall not call you idiot; merely imbecile. How you can manage to make such an impossibility a cause for worry, I do not comprehend. If anything, it is early days indeed for such concern; but if it will relieve your anxiety upon the score, I shall make it a part of the marriage articles that you shall not only be the cleric to officiate at our nuptials, but your tenure shall be sacrosanct from the grasping relations of my wife."

Mr. Symonds' eye lit up with happiness and he clasped his hands before him, exclaiming "Oh, my lord, I should be forever grateful!"

His lordship laughed again, exclaimed, "Oh, but you *are* an imbecile!" and stalked out of the room.

4

Caroline dropped into her lap the copy of *Ackerman's Repository* she had been perusing, sighed and stared out the sitting-room window at the vista of blue Windermere. There was a slight breeze rippling the clear waters in interesting little patches that slowly changed their form as she gazed.

"I do not know why I am looking at the latest fashions. It only makes me long for London and all the engagements I could be enjoying," she complained.

Lady Diana, the only other person in the room, replied: "Then I do not see why we did not go out with Lady Gordon and Ancilla. It would have been *better* than having to sit about doing *nothing* here in Storrs. *I* should have *liked* to go up to Ambleside and do some shopping. It was so very *kind* of Captain Wildish to have *offered*," she declared—as usual her fists were clenched in her lap and beat time with her remarks.

"Then *why* in heaven's *name*, did you not speak *up*, my dear?" retorted Caroline.

"Simply because it was *perfectly* obvious his *little* carriage could barely permit of his *taking* Ancilla and her mother up with *him!*"

"Lady Gordon has both carriage and coachman, darling! It would have been the easiest thing for us to have followed behind."

"Well, I did not think of *that!* Since you had, it was your *place* to have *suggested* it!"

Caroline responded: "Truly, my lady, if you had a wish to go, you ought to have said so. I had no desire to accompany them. The ride would have been such a bore. For some reason, which I fail to fathom, Captain Wildish seems to be taken with Ancilla—or Lady Gordon! I am sure I do not know which."

Diana smiled. "I am sure you are not *serious*—not about Lady Gordon, surely."

Caroline shrugged. "One never knows about that sort. If I were Ancilla, I should take with a huge grain of salt anything that Captain Wildish says to me."

"Oh, but I do think that you are *jealous!*" exclaimed Diana, bouncing a bit in her seat. "*I* envy Ancilla, for it begins to appear that she has got an *admirer*. We have been at Storrs almost an *entire week* and I cannot say that we have found very much to do but *stare* at a lake. Whatever *you* may think of Captain Wildish, he *does* offer a bit of excitement compared to what *we* have been experiencing."

"I shall not gainsay you, but it does not make me feel very well pleased with the gentleman that he did not think to arrive in a vehicle sufficient to carry us all. I think he did it a-purpose to have Ancilla to himself."

"Oh, that is *nonsense!* Lady Gordon is along with them. I do not see how *that* can forward his plans."

"He has got to start somewhere, does he not? It is but a first step. I'll warrant you, one way or another, he will arrange a further meeting, perhaps at the Assembly—"

Diana scoffed: "How can he even *begin!* Ancilla is our *hostess,* and it would be very *inconsiderate* of her to go off to an Assembly, leaving us to *languish* in the villa."

Caroline replied: "I venture to say that I have a little more confidence in the good Captain's cleverness than do you—and that is why I believe it will all turn out for the best. Naturally, he will have to arrange for an entertainment that will include us all. Yes, I do not think it makes any difference with whom Captain Wildish elects to begin."

"But he has such a *small* carriage!" protested Diana.

In exasperation Caroline turned her gaze to the window. Something she saw made her start.

"Oh, I say! But that will not be any objection at all. Lord Linford's carriage will be more than adequate—"

"The Viscount? I do not see what *he* has to do with anything."

"Just leave matters in my hands and you shall. If I do not miss my guess, it is that very gentleman who is about to make a call upon us. I am sure it is his carriage coming up the drive, this very instant."

Diana made a face. "Oh, not *him!* Why, he it was who almost *drowned* poor Ancilla. Have you forgotten so *soon?*"

"Diana, you are a little idiot! It was not you he tried.

to drown but Ancilla. In any case, I was never sure that it was all his fault, and I would hear his side of the story. Look you, we are here at the Lakes and there does not appear to be much chance of our meeting with anyone better than Wildish and Linford—and that is still one gentleman short for the three of us. If you have no liking for his lordship, it is quite all right with me, for I have never cared to share an escort."

"Caroline, what*ever* are *you* suggesting?!!" exclaimed Diana, her fists beating down upon her lap, as she leaned forward, tensed to hear what Caroline had to say.

"It is a dim prospect we share of having a gentleman to take us about. I am suggesting that we be very nice to Lord Linford so that we may have his company for the time we have got to spend at Storrs."

"But I have never had to do anything like that before!" wailed Diana. "I have always had a gentleman to myself!"

"This is not London, my pet, and there do not appear to be enough gentlemen to go 'round—unless, of course, the prospect of sharing Lord Linford's company is so distasteful to you. Then I shall have him all to myself."

"I think you take too much upon yourself! I do not see why I cannot gain his lordship's interest for my own while I am here."

Caroline stood up and brought a hand up to pat her hair as she looked down upon her ladyship. "My dear, I am perfectly willing to enter the lists against you for his lordship, if that is how you wish to proceed." She dropped her hand and came over to Diana. "But my thought was a deal less selfish than yours. If Ancilla succeeds with the Captain and we succeed with the Viscount, it will be a deal easier for us to go about, three ladies with two escorts, than if we were to squabble for his lordship. Only Ancilla would profit by it, not either of us—and then, who can say but we might find other gentlemen to pay attention to us? Certainly it will never happen unless we find a way of meeting them. I, for one, am not particularly interested in either Captain Wildish or Lord Linford. I merely wish to get about, to find some semblance of diversion."

"Caroline, *I* am not at *all* sure I understand you, and I certainly do *not* approve—but it makes no difference at this stage because I hear his lordship at the door. I wonder how he can dare to show his face *here!*"

"Well, I am not about to sit still and wait for the maids to answer," declared Caroline. "If the Viscount's company is all we may be blessed with, I am bound to make certain of it. Will you join me?"

"Caroline, it is not fitting that we ought—"

"Oh, go to blazes, my dear! One can never be sure of what tack a servant will take."

She rushed from the room, and Diana gave a little flirt of her head before she began to primp for the possible appearance of his lordship.

Caroline returned leading Lord Linford by the hand.

"You know Lady Diana, my lord?" she said by way of introduction.

Lord Linford stated that he had that pleasure and seated himself at Caroline's invitation.

She said: "Poor Lord Linford called with the expectation of speaking to Ancilla. I had to tell him that she was gone out with Lady Gordon and Captain Wildish. Is that not unfortunate?"

"Oh, indeed. Very unfortunate, my lord, but I am sure that they will be returning shortly. Why do you not wait for them? I pray that we can make your stay pleasant."

"I am sure that you could, Lady Diana, and I am gratified that you should be willing to take the trouble after the cake I made of myself. I came expressly to make apologies to Miss Gordon for the ordeal I put her through and to thank her for coming to my assistance. It was very brave of her, I thought."

"Yes," agreed Caroline. "Ancilla is not one to stand upon appearances. Something more forward than most, not that I would hold it against her. I am sure you do not, my lord."

"Of course I do not, Miss Darcy, although I must say her action had me worried for a moment. It was all I could do at the time to manage the capsized boat, you see—but it all turned out for the best, I am happy to say—at least, it was no worse for her action, I mean to say."

"Yes, indeed," said Diana quickly. "But, my lord, how do you *manage* to amuse yourself here at the *Lakes?* I was just thinking that it is so *dismal*, sitting about all day with *nothing* to occupy one's self."

"Oh, I say, if I could be of service to you ladies in any way, I should be most happy to oblige you. I came, hoping that Miss Gordon would join me for a spin—if Lady Gordon would permit it—but that was purely to be an effort to recoup my standing with her. I should not mind at all to place my carriage and myself at your disposal. Do you think Lady Gordon would have any reservations if I were to take you about? Of course, I should never think of keeping you out late."

"Oh dear, *I* am not at all *sure*, you see—" began Diana.

Caroline interrupted and declared, flatly: "I am sure that her ladyship would make no objection whatsoever. It was she who introduced you to us, Lord Linford— and it is not as though there were but one of us. Yes,

I am sure it would be unexceptional and I should like to join you."

"Yes, of course, Caroline, you are quite right. I am sure *I* should have thought of it, too," said Diana, with a brilliant smile at her lordship.

The ladies went out to get light wraps to keep the dust off, and Lord Linford went over to the window and gazed out at the lake.

5

Ambleside, in Grasmere parish, with a population but five score short of a thousand, was a bustling market town, set on the northern extremity of Windermere Water. It boasted a weekly market and a woolen mill, but most of all it was the center of attraction for most of the tourists to the Lakes.

The Gordon ladies were much impressed at how very busy the little town was and both of them remarked at the different modes of speech that could be heard. It was very much like London in the respect that the Yorkshire dialect and the Scottish dialect could be heard in counterpoint to, say, the Cockney. Only, in Ambleside there was more than a sprinkling of French and Italian, which attested to the attraction of the Lakes for tourists from the Continent.

The shops, by comparision to the West End and High Holborn were quite tiny but the proprietors were never so high in the instep and seemed anxious that their customers departed their premises pleased, even if they had not found the particular goods to satisfy them—which was more often than not the case. Nonetheless, both Lady Gordon and Ancilla enjoyed their perambulations about Ambleside, and Captain Wildish proved himself a considerate escort and a knowledgeable guide.

By the time they were done with the place and on the road back to Storrs, both ladies were delightfully fatigued and happy to enjoy the passing scene. Since the Captain had made it a very pleasant little excursion for them, when he came to suggest that they accompany him to the next Assembly at Ambleside, out of sheer gratitude, Ancilla endorsed her mother's consent.

This acceptance of his invitation so encouraged the good Captain that he went off into a long discourse, the subject of which was the eminence of the de La Warrs. Ancilla quickly regretted her impulse and prayed that this failing of the Captain's would not intrude itself upon their attendance at the Assembly.

When they arrived back at the Villa, they were received by Diana and Carol who had with them Lord Linford.

Despite Ancilla's stated conviction to the contrary, the sight of his lordship contributed to a feeling of discomfort. Although she refused to admit to embarrassment, the slight added color that came to her cheeks might have been taken for the fact if anyone had noticed. But, at the moment, the conversation that was developing between the two gentlemen held everyone's attention.

"Ah, the Viscount Linford, is it?" declared Captain Wildish, holding out his hand. "Now that I see you, my lord, I am sure that we have met previously."

Rather drily, Lord Linford replied: "I am sure we have, sir. In fact, I am amazed to find you in the midst of such refined company, Captain. I compliment you upon the improvement of your taste."

There was a nasty ring to the Captain's laughter as he replied: "The Viscount will have his little joke, I see. I am sure that he mistakes me for another of his acquaintances. It is not to be wondered at after he has suffered so from his recent, unlooked-for immersion in Windermere."

Before the Viscount could reply, he quickly turned to Ancilla and said: "Oh, I do beg your pardon, Miss Gordon! Not for anything would I have freshened your pain by recalling that distressing episode. I do humbly beg your pardon, not only for myself but for his lordship's maladroitness, as well."

Caught completely unprepared, the Viscount exclaimed: "Oh, I say, Ivo, that is most unfair of you! I am certainly sufficiently competent to make my own apologies! Miss Gordon, this so-called friend of mine—yes, I have known him for ages—is playing at games with me. I pray that you will not take his remark to mean that I had no intention of making an apology to you for the dreadful mishap of yesterday—"

Ancilla was not amused and had had quite enough. "Lord Linford, I do assure you that not another word is necessary. You did not do anything on purpose. It was merely an unfortunate happenstance, and I think that the less said, the better."

Lord Linford was listening to her intently. When she had done, he drew forth a silken handkerchief and mopped at his brow, saying: "Thank you, Miss Gordon!

I am in your debt for the consideration and forgiveness you show me."

Ancilla, seeing how deeply disturbed he was, could not repress a feeling of pity for him. He seemed to be so incapable of maintaining his poise in what was at best a mildly embarrassing circumstance. At some cost to herself, she changed the subject.

"The worthy Captain has invited Mama and myself to the next Assembly. Is that not nice of him?"

Oddly enough, there appeared to be a look of guilt or apprehension on the Viscount's countenance. He opened his mouth to say something but Diana was before him.

"Oh, how *lovely!* Then we can all go *together!*" she declared happily.

Now it was the Captain's turn to look bewildered. "I say, how jolly!" he said, weakly.

"Yes, isn't it though!" replied Caroline. "His lordship invited the both of us, Diana and myself, to the very same function."

"Oh, I s-say!" stammered his lordship. "It was not quite like that at all!"

Immediately Caroline turned a hard stare upon him, color mounting up into her cheeks. Very coldly, she demanded: "My lord, if I have misunderstood you, I pray you will make yourself clear at once."

His lordship took a step forward and raised a hand in a gesture that he never completed, for he snatched it back and put it behind him as he said, with a shake of his head: "Oh, I do assure you, Miss Darcy, I never meant to contradict you. If that is what you thought, I do apologize for giving you that impression. No, what I meant to say was merely that—well, not *merely,* please understand—but the invitation was intended to include Miss Gordon and Lady Gordon as well, you see. Of course I was delighted that you accepted, that is that Lady Diana and yourself did, but I had hoped— that is, I had intended for the other ladies to go with us...."

His voice died away as the effort to explain further became impossible. Again his handkerchief was applied to mop at his brow.

And again Ancilla experienced a surge of pity. He certainly was in desperate need of a keeper, she thought, if he could not even manage a conversation as simple as this. She brought his agony to an end by replying: "Indeed, my lord Viscount, it was very sweet of you. Please be assured that we would have accepted your gracious invitation had we not already agreed to attend with Captain Wildish. But, do you not think the arrangements would be much simplified if we all of us went together? I am sure that the Captain would not mind, would you, Captain Wildish?"

"Uh—Oh, no! No, not at all, I should be quite pleased to—"

"Excellent! Then you shall all be my guests at the Assembly," declared Lord Linford, beaming, his eyes filled with a look of gratitude as he gazed at Ancilla.

Ancilla smiled back at him, thinking that he was like a puppy who might have licked her hand for her having patted him on his head.

She remarked the Captain out of the corner of her eye and noted that he was not as happy as he had been. He was rather quiet and there was a thoughtful expression on his face. It made her wonder what there was between the two gentlemen. From the start of the conversation, it was the Captain who was on the offensive. Now that she had taken a turn in it, Lord Linford was obviously the winner of whatever contest there had been, and it could be easily read in the contrasting expressions on the respective gentlemen's faces.

Rather strange, she thought. There did not seem to be any great thing at stake to warrant this bit of confusion, and she was set to wondering if that was how Lord Linford always affected people. She knew *she* was confused. And as she glanced about the room to study the looks on the faces of her mother and her two companions, there could be no doubt but that they were just as confused as she.

6

Perhaps the greatest claim to fame the Salutation Hotel could make was the mention made of it by Mr. Wordsworth in his *Guide to the Lake District* which had recently been reissued, without the drawings of the Reverend Mr. Wilinson. Ancilla was not taken with the appearance of the structure and wondered how such a poor little excuse of a hotel could boast of having an Assembly Room.

She did not think the hotel to be so much larger than most of the taverns they had passed along the way up to the Lakes and presumed that the two Assembly rooms of Almack's in London encompassed more space than did the entire Salutation Hotel. She was sure that this local Assembly would prove a disappointment. There could never be enough patrons to make for an interesting dance card, and she was relieved that between the three of them, the ladies could lay claim to two escorts. Her feelings were shared by Diana and Caroline as became clear from the snatches of whispered conversation that passed between them.

Once within the drab stone edifice, they quickly revised their opinions. There was an Assembly room of sorts and, if it was not so much larger than the drawing room back at the Villa, it was packed with a mass of humanity far denser than anything the Villa had ever experienced. This in itself was nothing to be downcast about. A goodly crush always made for a merry time; however, in this case, the female population of the Salutation Hotel was far in excess of the male and, as most of them were young ladies of an age with Ancilla and her guests, the prospects of a comfortably enjoyable evening drained quickly away.

Captain Wildish's popularity was quickly attested to when he became surrounded almost immediately upon his appearance within the room. Obviously he was known to all and liked immensely. One might almost have said adored from the way the ladies gathered about him, pressing aside Lady Gordon and the three girls.

The Captain, much to his credit, showed no surprise at this enthusiastic reception and began, at once, to pencil in his name upon any and all of the cards that were thrust at him.

"How incredibly crass!" exclaimed Diana disdainfully disapproving the scene. "I cannot imagine what it is they see in him to cause all *that* much frenzy!"

"If you will but look about you, my lady, you will see at once that there is a dearth of gentlemen about, eligible or otherwise. If we are to dance at all, I strongly suggest we follow suit, or we shall be sitting next the wall for the entire evening," Caroline pointed out.

Lord Linford, who was also witnessing Captain Wildish's reception, turned to Ancilla.

"Miss Gordon, it would be my great pleasure if you will grant me a dance with you."

Ancilla had been about to follow Diana and Caroline into the fray. A furtive glance in her mother's direction showed her that Lady Gordon was deep in an exchange of greetings with some of her acquaintances, and she was tempted to pretend not to have heard his lordship.

It was very evident that the Captain was a partner to be desired and she had no wish to lose any advantage. What was more, she could hear the orchestra running through some of the newly introduced waltzes and never doubted but the Captain was most proficient in their performance. As for Lord Linford, he was not the sort to be up-to-the-nines at anything that was of importance, she was sure.

Above all other considerations, the waltz was not a nice dance, and it was looked down upon in all the best circles of London society. Obviously, what could not be danced in London was of no concern in Ambleside. In fact, since all of the visitors were Londoners as far as one could tell, it might appear that this great distance from London was being taken as a license to execute the scandalous figure. Just think of it! The gentleman had to place his arm about his partner as they skipped about the floor in time to those rousing measures of Weber, Beethoven and Schubert from the Continent. So very naughty but utterly thrilling! All the young ladies had, in secret and amongst themselves, learned the step and some, some very few and daring ones, had actually danced a few measures with gentlemen—but, of course, *never* in public.

Here at Ambleside, far from the harsh vigil of the Patronesses of Almack's, there was a chance to dance as she had never danced before. She just had to get the Captain's name down upon her dance card!

But, alas, she had paused, and that was significant acknowledgement that she had heard his lordship's request. Reluctantly, she turned about and handed her card to him.

The time it took for Lord Linford to write "Andrew" in one of the spaces on her dainty pasteboard card quite did away with her chance to approach Captain Wildish. Not that there would have been much of an opportunity to have reached him through the crush of his admirers. Resignedly, she stayed to chat with the Viscount who appeared to take it as a great favor from her. Out of the corner of her eye, she observed the triumphant smile on Caroline's lips as she showed her card to a pouting Diana. Ancilla prayed that Caroline would spare her that gesture.

As she gave her attention to Lord Linford, she was not happy with him. She did not begrudge him the dance, it was the fact that she had got *him* for partner when she might have had the Captain.

Upon any other occasion, she assured herself, dancing with Captain Wildish would never have amounted to any great thing; but this evening in Ambleside, the privilege appeared to be the only thing sought by all the young ladies. Caroline had managed to garner him for a dance and Ancilla needs must be satisfied with a string of undistinguished partners of whom Viscount Linford must prove the least satisfactory. She could just imagine what a poor dancer he must be, and her feelings regarding him were more than a little colored by his blundering into her path here, and, in a sense, that day on the lake. That he had managed to attend the Assembly all by himself, from under the guardianship of that poor excuse, Mr. Symonds, was indeed a wonder, she thought, disdainfully.

The first two dances were the usual set pieces and, as her partners were known to her only as they had been introduced by themselves, a practice that was frowned on in cosmopolitan polite society, there was very little cause for remarks with them before and after the dances. It was the third dance that stirred a pang of envy in her breast, for it was to be a waltz. It in no way diminished her pain to see Caroline wafted out onto the floor, practically in the arms of Captain Wildish, the both of them laughing with glee. Her partner for this piece was a blond youth of insipid complexion whose manner was perfectly matched to it. There was no spirit to his movements and whatever address he might have possessed was completely dissipated by the necessity of his having to place his arm about her. If a fish could dance, Ancilla thought, it could do better than could Mr. Simpkins. She avoided looking in Caroline's direction and put a great smile on her lips as she went gliding about the floor with little assistance from Mr. Simpkins, who was beginning to perspire profusely.

Ancilla did not find the dance at all pleasant and placed the responsibility for its dullness upon Mr. Simpkins. Although she never gave voice to her opinion, Mr. Simpkins appeared to sense it, which added a deal to his discomfort. By the end of the piece, they were both glad the ordeal had come to an end. Mr. Simpkins managed to thank Ancilla for a delightful dance in hurried accents, mopping at his brow with a great white handkerchief while he did so. As soon as he felt he had said all that was proper to the occasion, he bowed and quickly departed. Ancilla's attention had already been drawn to the gleaming expressions of enjoyment on the faces of Caroline and Captain Wildish. For them, it had been a positive pleasure, for herself a dismal experience.

A tall figure approached. She quickly fumbled for her dance card, her heart filled with dismay. Yes, it was Lord Linford's turn to dance with her!

It was going to take a very special effort for her to be civil to the gentleman. He was becoming a symbol to her of all that could go wrong when things should be festive. As she donned the smile that was expected of her, she gave herself small cheer by thinking that it was good the waltz was over and done with before she had to trust herself in the arms of a clumsy fool. She would consider herself the most fortunate of females if the very next number on the program proved to be a set piece. The figures of the dance would remove her quickly from his lordship's vicinity and they would pass each other but infrequently during the performance. In the small time that they had to execute a figure together, the chances of his disgracing them both with some new awkwardness would be quite slim.

"Indeed, my lord, you are prompt," she remarked as he came up to her. "You cannot have liked your recent partner to have torn yourself away so quickly."

He smiled. "You are quick to notice, Miss Gordon. As a matter of fact, the young lady—whose name I do not recall—was more than a passable dancer. The trouble was that my mind was upon you. I did not think that you were enjoying yourself with that young limb who, I may remark, departed your company as swiftly."

Color mounted in Ancilla's cheeks as she thought:

70

The tactless oaf! With her lips parted in a cold smile, she replied: "Then, my lord, if I was so obvious, perhaps you will suggest that I go to the gentleman and apologize."

"Oh, I say, Miss Gordon, I was not suggesting anything of the sort. Nor do I think that anymore be said upon the subject. If anything, he showed a deal more unease with the dancing than did you—"

"Lord Linford, you are being something uncomplimentary to me, I must say. If you have taken a dislike to me, I will be more than pleased to relieve you of your promise to dance," she said, raising her wrist from which the dance card dangled, and continuing in dramatic tones: "Here! I give you leave to strike your name from my card."

He frowned. "I do not seem to be making myself very clear to you, Miss Gordon, and offer an apology. But that is not at all my feelings—but, of course, if *that* is what *you* wish me to do, I shall take my leave of you on the instant."

"I do assure you, my lord, it is not what I wish," she replied coolly. "It was merely that the tenor of your remarks led me to believe it was *your* wish."

"No, not at all! I do assure you, Miss Gordon, my remarks were never intended in any way to be critical, to say nothing of insulting. My word, Miss Gordon, I am devastated to think that you would entertain any such notion of me."

"Then perhaps I ought to apologize to you, my lord," she replied with a warmer smile, "for that is what I was doing."

He smiled, too, looking something relieved to have gotten over a sticky passage and answered: "It is your privilege to think of me in any way you please, Miss Gordon, but I must inform you, I have no such freedom.

71

I find you altogether charming and would never think of you upon any but the highest terms."

Ancilla, her feelings now unruffled, nodded and smiled at him.

He glanced at the orchestra and said: "I see that our fellows are not about to begin again for a bit. I pray you will be pleased to come sit with me and chat."

There was little Ancilla could answer to that. She glanced at the orchestra, too, Yes, the musicians were chatting together and imbibing some refreshment from mugs. It would be yet awhile before they took up their instruments again, she had to agree.

"Yes, my lord."

He led her over to some chairs and they sat down. He smiled at her and she smiled at him, both of them with an expectant air. But, as nothing in the way of conversation was forthcoming from him, Ancilla, rather than sitting idly together like a pair of grinning idiots, began to rack her brain for something to say.

"Lord Linford—" she finally began, only to be interrupted.

"My dear Miss Gordon, I should take it as a special favor if you would condescend to address me as Andrew."

Ancilla, considering how she felt about him, thought he was being a little forward, but she began over. There seemed to be no choice.

"Ah yes, Andrew. As I was about to say—"

"And I would pray that you would extend the same privilege to me, Miss Gordon."

Since he was intent upon coming so far, Ancilla again could do naught but grant him the favor.

"But of course, Andrew—"

"Thank you, Ancilla! I am so very pleased to be upon a first-name basis with you, my dear. I—"

Ancilla had no idea what he was about to say, but, lest it were to be something in the way of compliments, which she had no wish to encourage from him, she broke in: "I do not see Mr. Symonds about, Andrew. Did he not wish to come to the Assembly?"

"Oh no; Symonds is not one for these earthly entertainments, as he puts it. I strongly suspect that the true reason is his wife."

"His wife? Is she along with you, too?"

"No, she is back in London where they reside. I tell you it was something of a chore to drag him away from her so that he might accompany me upon this holiday."

"Does he love her so? How terribly romantic! I did not think he could cut so dashing a figure."

Lord Linford laughed. "Symonds, dashing? Not by far! He has not a notion of the meaning of the term! No, not at all! He was more than willing to leave London with me. It was Mrs. Symonds who made the difficulty, you see."

"In what way, may I ask?"

"She is bound to preserve his reputation at any cost—"

"But he is a man of the cloth, I thought. Surely, his avocation must always speak well of him, Andrew."

"Unfortunately, Mrs. Symonds is not so sure. Oh, she is sure of the cloth but not of the gentleman. She does not trust Symonds out of her sight. Not only is she fearful that he will fall before temptation, but that he will be forever tempted, at any appreciable distance from her matronly side. Having an acquaintance with the lady, I can well believe it but for the fact that Symonds, himself, is not what you would call a chaser of skirts. On the contrary, in that regard, I do not think there is a more frightened fellow upon the face of this earth. Again, knowing his better half as well as I do,

73

I cannot blame him. In his case, his marriage vow was for him more in the nature of an affliction than a blessing," he ended with a laugh.

There was disapproval in Ancilla's tone as she retorted: "I do not think it is nice in you to say so, Andrew."

He sighed. "I suppose not, but the fellow can get on one's nerves, you know. He is, in fine, missishness personified. I am beginning to regret that I ever thought to bring him along."

"For how much longer will you be staying at the Lakes?"

"How long shall *you* be staying, Ancilla?"

"Pray do not concoct some Banbury tale that my being here has something to say to *your* being here, Andrew."

"Is such a notion so distasteful to you, Ancilla?" he asked, and stared intently at her.

She laughed uncertainly and replied: "A most flattering sentiment, dear sir, but hardly to be taken seriously."

He smiled. "Yes, I dare say there is not sufficient evidence to support the hypothesis; but then, when one studies matters philosophical, one must be patient, must one not?"

"I am sure I do not understand a word you are saying, my lord—Oh heavens, another waltz! One is a thrill, but two is something daring, I should think."

"Rather than shock you, my dear, I shall not press you for the dance. Perhaps—"

"Oh, I have no objection, my lord, if you do not. It is just that in London the dance is not at all respectable, you know. I am sure that out here, it hardly matters. It will be my pleasure, my lord."

Lord Linford looked discomfited. "Then I regret hav-

74

ing to disappoint you, Ancilla. I am not familiar with the steps. Allow me to find another partner for you."

Ancilla almost gave her approval but the thought struck her that gracious as Andrew's offer appeared to her, it might look like something disagreeable to strangers to the situation. It could be taken for a fact that Andrew was passing her off to someone else. It did not sit well with her.

"Er—no, Andrew. I have no objection to sitting out the dance with you."

"You know, my dear, it pleases me well. I had thought that you may have had some reservations about me, especially after I spilled us both out of the boat. I am glad to see that we may yet be friends."

Ancilla smiled, even as she regretted not having taken him up on his offer of another partner. She did not think that they had all that much to talk about.

Andrew cleared his throat and continued to stare at Ancilla while the couples on the floor went skipping up and down in time to the music.

"Yes?" said Ancilla, wishing desperately that he would say something to which she could respond. She was feeling very uncomfortable at being the subject of his silent scrutiny.

"Eh, what? Oh, I—er—I did not say anything," he said, half-apologetically.

"Oh, I thought you did," replied Ancilla, feeling quite silly.

At that moment, like a refreshing breeze, Captain Wildish, his teeth flashing in a great smile, came striding up to them with a hail.

"Andrew, for shame! Ah, Miss Gordon, my apologies for his lordship. Andrew, how can you sit here like a lump in the company of this beautiful lady and all that blood-tingling music just begging to be danced to?"

"Ah, Wildish, what are you doing here? Where is your partner?" answered Andrew.

"Fate has been unkind to the little lady, but I think she begins to smile upon me, my lord. She had the misfortune to sprain her ankle, and I left her with her relations. By your leave, my lord, I would ask Miss Gordon to join me on the floor. This dance should not be wasted."

Ancilla did not wait for Andrew's response but rose to her feet immediately.

"Captain, I should be delighted."

The Captain took possession of her arm, and, just before he began to lead her onto the floor, he exclaimed: "Hah!"

They left Andrew looking very unhappy. He had only half-risen from his seat before they were off, whirling away down the floor.

7

The senior serving woman at the Villa, who performed the duties of butler and housekeeper for the Gordons, took it upon herself to arrange for coffee to be served in the drawing room after Miss Gordon and Miss Darcy wandered off in that direction without more than a glance about the dining room. Her action was not in consideration of her mistresses but rather to minimize her own exertions on this morning after the Assembly.

Her decision proved to be well taken, for Lady Diana came into the dining room, a half-hour later, inquired after the others and went off to the drawing room, too.

Perhaps twenty minutes later, Lady Gordon made her appearance. She came into the dining room, inspected the preparations for breakfast, nodded absent-mindedly and inquired: "Have any of the girls come down yet?"

Upon being informed that the young ladies were gathered in the drawing room, Lady Gordon nodded and said: "I have no wish for anything this morning. Serve coffee in the drawing room."

She turned and went out.

Upon entering the drawing room, her ladyship was pleasantly surprised to find that her wishes had already been carried out, but her thoughts did not linger upon it. She had something else on her mind.

As she took her seat, she said: "I am so pleased that we are all together this morning, for I have got something to discuss with you. I pray you all had a pleasant time at the Assembly?"

Ancilla and Caroline nodded in response to her inquiry, but Diana shook her head and exclaimed: "It was a most *odious* time! It was eminently unfair, I *must* say!"

Lady Gordon turned to her and said: "Dear, dear, I am sorry to hear it. Whatever was wrong, Diana?"

"It was such an *awful* crush and the people had *no* regard for precedence, to say *nothing* of decorum. I know that Captain Wildish was *dying* to dance with me, but, because of the way people behaved, he *never* got the chance! Really, it was a most *despicable* affair!"

She turned to Ancilla and demanded: "*You* know how it was, Ancilla! While *some* people thought *nothing* of thrusting themselves forward in the most *brazen* way—" she turned to glare at Caroline—"others, with *proper* breeding, could only stand by, *petrified* with shock at the *indecency* of the proceedings."

Said Ancilla: "I am sorry you failed to dance with whomever you wished, but I ought to inform you, my dear, that Captain Wildish did come for me—and at a time when I was being bored to distraction—"

"Now, ladies, that—or rather, whom—is the matter I wish to discuss," Lady Gordon intervened. "You all must realize that we are females alone and in a strange place. Fortunately, I have friends all over England and Westmoreland but that is no exception to the case.

"Whilst you young ladies were flinging yourselves about the dance floor in a most execrable fashion, I took the pains to make acquaintances and to learn something more about this gentleman who appears to have quite taken your fancy. Diana, you have nothing to reproach yourself with for having failed to gain the Captain's attention—"

"I did *not* fail—!"

"Never you mind, my lady, the sport is not worth the candle, as they say—and I have particular reference to Captain Wildish. The man is a ne'er-do-well and has a reputation, foully tainted. Ancilla, I pray you are listening attentively? I have no wish to entertain that gentleman further."

Ancilla smiled and said: "Oh, Mama, you have naught to fear. The Captain is a superb dancer, but that is as far as my interest in him extends. However, despite what you may have learned about him, I do not see that we needs must forgo his company. He is a pleasant jackanapes. Knowing that and allowing ourselves to be entertained by him is nothing exceptional. Do you not agree with me, Caroline?"

"I do *not!*" Diana cut in, defiantly. "I *always* thought that Wildish was no *better* than he *should* be, and I *must* agree with my lady. Captain Wildish is not *fit* company for *any* of us."

"Rubbish, Diana!" exclaimed Caroline. "The fellow

is quite charming and I see no harm in him. *I* know myself to be more than a match for such as he."

"*Who* does not?" retorted Diana, quickly. "I just do not think it is at all *proper* to be *seen* with him!"

"I am sure it is no worse to be seen with Captain Wildish than it is to be seen dancing the waltz!" put in Caroline.

"That is precisely the point I was coming to," said Lady Gordon, somewhat agitated. "The waltz is bad enough by itself, and so is the Captain, by himself; but the two of them together are most unseemly, and I am happy beyond belief that it occurred here in Westmoreland rather than in London. Ancilla, if word of last night's business were to reach the ears of any of the Patronesses of Almack's, I am sure you would lose all chance of their notice. They will not tolerate such bad behavior. It is much too fast. A voucher for Almack's must be the devout wish of every lady, young or otherwise!"

Ancilla did not look concerned as she replied: "Oh, bother the thing!" Replied her ladyship: "Regardless of what you say, Miss Gordon, I tell you I do not want to see that man here ever again. There is a bad odor to him, and he cannot be up to any good."

"I do not see how you can say so, Mama. He is the bosom beau of Viscount Linford, and whilst I pity him for that privilege, yet it must speak well of him. The Viscount may be a sad specimen but he is quite acceptable, you must admit."

"I admit nothing, my dear. I heard it from the Captain's very own lips. He has but a slight acquaintanceship with his lordship."

"I regret to have to contradict you, *ma mère,* but I have it upon the authority of the Viscount himself. In the course of a conversation with him, last night, I learned the Captain and he were schoolchums together at Eton. Wildish has known better times, obviously, and, from what I gather, his connections have served him in good stead. His connection with Lord Linford is certainly not the least of them."

"Is that a fact? Then perhaps, he is not so bad," said Lady Gordon. "Oh, but I just do not know! If you had but heard all that was being said of him last night!"

"I am sure it means nothing," replied Ancilla, very superiorly. "People will talk nonsense when they have nothing else on their minds. I do not say the Captain is a prime specimen. Not at all! But that is not to say his company must pollute those he chooses to associate with. Lord Linford looks none the worse for claiming him friend—although I wish some of the Captain's charm would rub off on him and make him something more interesting. Actually, the only objection I have to Captain Wildish's company is that we are bound to suffer the attentions of Lord Linford along with it."

"Well, my dears, I am of two minds at the moment and shall have to give the matter thought. I should be devastated if your associating with the likes of Captain Wildish were to reflect poorly upon your reputations. A lady's good name is her most precious possession, you know."

A carriage was heard in the lane and, as it came to a stop, Diana quickly rose from her seat and went to the window.

"I *perceive* we are about to have a caller and *who* do you think it is?"

"The Captain!" exclaimed Ancilla and Caroline together.

"Oh dear, so soon?" feebly protested Lady Gordon.

"No! It is the Viscount's diminutive *shadow!*" cried Diana gleefully at their having missed their guess.

There was a groan from Ancilla. "Oh, say it is not he! He is every bit as bad as his master. We are in for a very dull morning, methinks."

"Ancilla, that is not a very proper attitude for a young lady to adopt with regard to a respectable man of the cloth. I pray you will remember I brought you up better than that."

"I have all the respect for Mr. Symonds. It is just that he is a most dreadful little bore. Truly, I do not see how two such dull individuals can get along together so famously."

"That will be quite enough, my dear. The gentleman will be in to see us shortly. Do sit up, child. You give me an ache just to see you!"

Mr. Symonds came into the room, smiling bashfully and bowing twice to each lady.

"Your ladyship, you must know how much pleasure it gives me to undertake this little task for his lordship, Viscount Linford, my patron. Of course, you will understand that it is *not* in the normal course of my duties that I come to you."

He laughed insipidly and proceeded. "But, when one is in strange country, one never knows when one will be called upon to do that which he would, in the usual course of things, never condescend to. But then, his lordship, Viscount Linford, my patron, is of a very commanding aspect, and one has not the wish to disappoint his lordship in any way, if you see what I mean."

The ladies exchanged puzzled glances, and Lady Gordon replied: "Mr. Symonds, will you not be seated? Perhaps you would like to have a sip of coffee or a bun or something? I am sure we are all pleased to receive you, but must protest at any hint of condescension on our part. I am sure we do not intend it."

Mr. Symonds plumped his small rotund form into a

chair and gratefully accepted a coffee cup and saucer, taking a generous bite of a sweet bun that accompanied them. He sipped and munched for a bit, but as soon as he was able to swallow, he gasped a little and then exclaimed: "My, that was very good. You cannot know how fortunate you are that you have fare from your own kitchen. Alas, we have been away from our dear hearths, the Viscount and I, for more than a week and in all that time, not one mouthful have we had as sweet as this." He ended with a gesture of his bitten-through bun.

"Ah yes, how thoughtless of us! We must invite his lordship to dine with us in the not too distant future. How much longer does Lord Linford expect to remain at the Lakes, Mr. Symonds?"

"My dear Lady Gordon, truly, I wish I knew. His lordship does not have any plans for the future that I know of. But this brings me to the point we were just discussing. Of course, I was not aware of the least condescension in your manner to me. By condescension, I was referring to this little duty that his lordship requested of me. As I was saying, I do it out of the deep affection that I hold his lordship in, but I should never consider condescending so far for any other, I do assure you."

Again the ladies exchanged puzzled glances.

Said Ancilla: "Worthy sir, I fear you are not making yourself clear. Have you come to us to complain of his lordship's treatment of you?"

"Good heavens, no!" exclaimed Mr. Symonds, holding up his hands in shock. "Oh, if that is what you believe, I pray you will never breathe a word of your suspicion to my Lord Viscount, for it is categorically untrue. I could not hold his lordship in greater affection than if he were my own dear relation. No, indeed! On the contrary, I was only trying to tell you that, as a man of the cloth, the fact that I am stooping so low as to deliver a message for his lordship, is due solely to the fact that I do hold the gentleman in such high regard."

"A message? What message?" demanded Lady Gordon.

Unfortunately, at that moment, Mr. Symonds had elected to make another ferocious assault upon the bun and was in the midst of washing it down with a swallow of coffee. He attempted to interrupt the process, but his response was rather muffled by the glutinous mixture of bun and coffee occupying his mouth. In his confusion, he breathed when he ought to have swallowed with the result that a tiny geyser of coffee issued forth with his garbled words and he was seized with a paroxysm of coughing.

For the moment the ladies were too startled to do anything more than regard the gentleman with shock. Then Ancilla got up and went over to him, inquiring if there was aught they could do for him.

He attempted to reply but managed only a wheeze. The coughing continued, somewhat abated, and Mr. Symonds was now in sufficient control of himself to wave Ancilla away with one hand while he brought out a handkerchief with the other and covered his face with it.

Ancilla sat down again and they waited for Mr. Symonds to completely regain his powers of conversation. In due course, he did achieve it and, with tears blinking from his overstrained eyes, he proceeded to make profuse apologies for the spectacle he had just made of himself.

Ancilla was inclined to agree that the reverend gentleman had made everyone uncomfortable. What particularly annoyed her was that it should have happened just when the Viscount's bear-leader—she could not help thinking of him in that fashion—just when he was about to impart information concerning this mysterious errand he was performing for Lord Linford.

After all apologies were made, Mr. Symonds appeared to be confused, for he reached for his hat and was upon the verge of departing.

"What of your errand, Mr. Symonds?" asked Ancilla before he could start saying his farewells.

"My errand? Ah, yes, my errand! Oh, Miss Gordon, I am so glad that you saw fit to remind me. I had clean forgot what I was about. Really, it is quite horrid when one is attacked by a fit of coughing. I do assure you I am in perfect health, although I deem it necessary now to have the doctor call. Do you not think it is wise?"

"I am sure it is, but before you go, it would ease our curiosity to know more about this errand of yours."

"Ah, yes, the errand! Miss Gordon, I—er—of course, I address you, your ladyship, as well. In fact, I am sure I speak to all of you ladies. Now, what was I saying?"

"The errand, Mr. Symonds!" said Caroline, impatiently.

"Oh, yes, that of course. The thing of it is that as a man of the cloth, I do not make it a habit, performing what some may term menial tasks—"

"My dear Mr. Symonds," intervened Lady Gordon, "I am sure we all quite understand that this errand of yours was in no way demeaning to your high standing in your calling. Now, pray just what was it in aid of?"

"Why, it was in aid of my lord, of course. The gentleman requested me to come to you with a message."

Said Caroline, in a pedantic tone: "And so you have come, Mr. Symonds. We are all of us willing to attest to the fact that you have come to us with a message;

but what we cannot attest to in any fashion is the content of the message."

"Oh, but you shall, as soon as I divulge my lord's instructions to me."

"So there were instructions, were there?" persisted Caroline.

"But, of course, Miss Darcy. I just this moment informed you of that fact."

"Indeed you did, Mr. Symonds. You did so inform us, but you never got on with it. Will you please do so now?"

"Well, it was all so very simple. I assured my lord that it was not a task beyond his own excellent powers. Nonetheless, he persisted and so I have come."

"You have come, Mr. Symonds, but you have yet to speak, Mr. Symonds. I am quite in agreement with you. I have no doubt but that a schoolboy could have carried out this errand in a better fashion; yes, even his lordship. You have managed with the greatest difficulty, methinks, to have informed us of a message, but the message itself seems to be nowhere near to its delivery despite your efforts."

"Miss Darcy, I do believe that you are toying with me," said Mr. Symonds, looking affronted

"Then I apologize to you, Mr. Symonds, for I would never think to affront you lest I never hear what the message is."

Mr. Symonds took her remarks as a complete apology and nodded to her. He then went on, "My lady, my patron, my lord Viscount Linford, extends his compliments and begs you will accept his offer to take all of you out for an airing this afternoon. He has engaged the finest coach in the neighborhood—in fact, it is being lent to him by the Earl of Thanet and there is none more wealthy than he in all of Westmoreland."

Having finished his little speech, Mr. Symonds folded his hands and awaited a reply.

Ancilla racked her mind for an excuse to decline the invitation but her mother responded without hesitation. "Mr. Symonds, please inform Lord Linford that we shall be delighted to accept his gracious invitation. We shall be looking forward to his arrival here at the Villa."

Mr. Symonds now had recourse to his handkerchief. There was an air of relief about the manner in which he mopped at his forehead.

He got up and bowed, saying: "It will be my sincere pleasure to so inform his lordship."

Soon he was gone and the ladies were able to talk amongst themselves.

"I do declare!" exclaimed Lady Gordon. "Why, if that is not the strangest man I have ever known. What a fuss to make about so simple an errand!"

"But why did you think it necessary to accept for all of us, Mama?" asked Ancilla. "It is just another instance of Lord Linford's lack of presence, to send so inept a courier. I do not see why we have got to be at his lordship's beck and call. Why can he not find other folk to afford him entertainment?"

"Really, Ancilla, *I* was under the impression that his lordship was offering *us* entertainment rather than the *other* way about," put in Diana. "I do not see what *you* are taking exception to. I should think that a *drive* in one of Lord Thanet's *coaches* is very *much* to be desired. Why, we might even be *tendered* an invitation to *dine* with the Earl."

Caroline nodded and said: "Truly, Ancilla, it is not as though we had any great choice of company. I should think that we would be wise to make the best of Lord

Linford's company. Heaven knows that there was a lack of fine specimens at the Assembly."

"There is always Captain Wildish," said Ancilla.

"Ancilla, I am not all that assured of the Captain's—" began Lady Gordon, only to be interrupted by a maid. "Yes, what is it?"

She was informed that the Captain was inquiring if he might come in for a visit with the ladies.

Her ladyship sighed. "Oh well, as long as he has come out, I do not see how we can refuse. What is the hour?"

The maid informed her that it was some minutes past one, which caused her to remark: "I suspect that we shall have a guest for our collation this afternoon. I suspect, too, that the Captain chooses his time well."

Captain Wildish was a definite change after Mr. Symonds and even Lady Gordon had to admit that it was a pleasure to entertain him.

He inquired after each lady's health, with due respect for precedence, beginning with Lady Gordon, proceeding to Diana and leaving Caroline for last.

The look of intent interest on his countenance as he hearkened to the noncommittal responses of the ladies would have been most convincing if even one of the ladies had any indisposition to report. Ancilla marveled that he could display such gravity in the face of such excellent spirits and good health and fervently wished that they had some alternate for company beyond him and the worthy Viscount.

But Captain Wildish had come with a purpose and he soon delivered himself of an offer to take the ladies out for a drive about the Lakes.

Since Lord Linford's invitation had already been

accepted, Lady Gordon was forced to decline and did so, explaining that he had been forestalled by Lord Linford.

The Captain flashed a grin and remarked: "How very generous of Linford! I am sure you will have a splendid time with him. As for myself, I shall merely reserve my invitations to you for a more appropriate time. But I should never rest so long as I was not sure that Linford was sufficiently acquainted with the roads. By your leave, I shall invite myself along just to make sure that we do not get lost—and that we all of us have a pleasant time of it."

Once again Lady Gordon was taken aback by the brashness of the fellow and could not think of a thing to say.

Caroline, however, saw the Captain as precisely the right ingredient for what must otherwise have proven a dull afternoon. She declared: "It will be quite all right I am sure, Captain. Why not! The more the merrier, I say."

Diana was looking very troubled. "I do not mean to say that it is *not* perfectly splendid, Captain Wildish, that you have decided to come along with us; but as Caroline says, the more the merrier. I think that there ought to be someone else. It cannot be all that comfortable when there are so few gentlemen and so many ladies together."

"The lady speaks—and I listen!" declared the Captain, taking up a gallant posture. "I have in my acquaintance any number of gentlemen who would be only too happy to accompany us. But say the word and I shall summon a horde!"

Said Lady Gordon: "I believe one other gentleman

will be quite sufficient, Captain Wildish—providing, of course, our host for the afternoon has no objection."

"Oh, you can leave Linford to me. I can wind the fellow about my little finger. Think no more upon it. It is as good as done."

8

"**No, Symonds,** you are *not* to accompany me this afternoon. It seems to me you would do well to spend your time with the Rector of St. Martin's. Your presence this afternoon would act as a damper upon the occasion."

"I pray you will forgive me, my lord, if I persist in expressing my devout wish to accompany you upon this excursion. I have an appointment to speak with the Reverend Mr. Robison another time. I think it is more important, in fact, it is my duty, my lord, to accompany you."

"That is putting it a bit strong. Your duty is to your flock—"

Mr. Symonds' cheeks turned pink as he interrupted. "I beg your pardon, my lord, but, although you are quite my superior in rank and station, still I am some years your senior and engaged in a profession whose main concern is the spiritual welfare of all people; aye, even those who condescend to me. Nor, my lord, is it your place to remind me of where my duty lies. In this case, although it would be my choice to spend an interesting afternoon with Mr. Robison, it is incumbent upon me as your curate and as your companion in your travels to afford you the benefit of my advice, and that whether it is sought or not!"

Lord Linford smiled down at the little man. "I admire your spirit, worthy reverend. Still, I do not see what there is about this outing that concerns you."

"It is you, yourself, my lord. Despite the fact that you are of an age when most gentlemen have had more than a taste of the world and its vanities, you, sir, are only upon the threshold. I am concerned that, without guidance from a sober authority, you will be laid by the heels and fall to temptation. That, my lord, is why I must sacrifice my interest for yours. I pray you will allow me to accompany you."

"I am touched that you are so concerned for me, and I believe it is sincere. The trouble is that it is misdirected. It is not as though I were about to afford myself some low form of amusement. I am going out with Lady Gordon, her daughter and her guests. Pray, what do you find exceptional in it?"

"Oh, I assure you, my lord, I have no objection to your company. What I do have reservations about is your manner of comporting yourself. I do believe that you will ask one of the ladies for her hand in marriage before ever you are aware of what you are doing. You have no experience in these matters, you know."

Lord Linford laughed. "Oh, Symonds, you are a prize, and a constant source of amusement to me. I think you take your association with me too seriously. Believe me, there are many more people in need of your sage counsel than are in this room at present. I bid you go to them. If this outing I contemplate does not prove a bore to you, it still will prove a trial, not only to you but to the others as well. An outing at the Lakes is in no way improved by having a man of the cloth along. No, although I have a deal of affection for you, my dear sir, this is a time when your absence will afford me greater pleasure by far than your presence."

Mr. Symonds bowed his head in defeat. He said: "My lord, you will admit I saw my duty and I tried to do it?"

"Quite."

"Then I am satisfied. My lord, I wish you a pleasant afternoon."

"Thank you, Symonds. I wish you an interesting one."

Mr. Symonds nodded and departed, leaving his lordship to continue with his preparations.

9

Lord Linford was feeling quite satisfied with himself as the coach, which he had so cleverly borrowed from Lord Thanet, complete with coachman and footmen, rolled ponderously up the drive to the Curwin Villa. Although he was by nature reserved, especially with the opposite sex, he had no modesty where his powers of thought were called into play. He knew Wildish for being a fast buck with winning ways, but he did not give him much credit for cleverness. It was all well and good for Wildish to have issued his challenge, his conceit in his personal charm being so obvious, but his lordship was inclined to believe that when it came down to scratch, as it were, their respective mental endowments would count for all. Precisely what *all* amounted to, he did not try to fathom. He was satisfied that he had a wish to continue with Ancilla Gordon's company, and the business with Wildish was bound to make the prospect so much more amusing.

Actually, he was quite willing to credit his station with having given him entrée to Lord Thanet; still, it was his own cleverness that had given him to think of the coach, a most comfortable vehicle as it turned out. One that Wildish could never match in the district, he was sure, especially as his friend never had anything to speak of in his pockets.

Yes, Wildish was extending himself beyond his means when he thought to engage himself against the resources of Viscount Linford.

It was no wonder that the Viscount looked startled and more than a little annoyed when, upon being conducted into the Gordons' drawing room, he found more company than he had expected.

He was greeted by a cocky grin from Captain Wildish as the latter presented a Mr. Selkirk, a total stranger to him, with the remark that Mr. Selkirk had kindly consented to join them in their outing.

His lordship made a cool acknowledgement and turned to glance at Ancilla. There was a strange look in his eye.

Ancilla had been studying him, puzzled at the lack of congeniality in his response, and, as there seemed to her to be a question in his glance which she could not fathom, raised an eyebrow and nodded to him.

His lordship sighed and announced that he had a coach, capable of accommodating all in comfort if they would be pleased to start and stood back, quite unhappy.

Ancilla was dissatisfied that she had understood Andrew's glance correctly and arose and went over to him. But, at that moment, Mr. Selkirk had engaged

Diana in conversation with an eye to making sure she would be his companion on the trip and Captain Wildish had started for Ancilla, a similar purpose in his mind.

When the latter saw Ancilla, apparently making her choice, his poise did not desert him for an instant. There was not the slightest hesitation in his stride as he ended up with Caroline instead.

When Ancilla appreciated what had happened it was already too late, and she berated herself for a fool. Now, she was bound to spend the trip with his lordship, a fate she had been determined to avoid, and the idea of speaking to Andrew about his look of disappointment passed completely from her mind.

Out in the drive, an impasse quickly developed. The Thanet coach was an impressive specimen of the coach-builder's art. It was in an excellent state of preservation, gleaming from fresh varnish and redolent with the smell of freshly tanned leather, and looked extremely capable of transporting its riders in high comfort. What it did lack, however, was the capacity to hold seven passengers. Actually, it was a broad-beamed old-fashioned design. If it had been of recent vintage, four would have been as many as it would have had room for. Speed, and therefore lightness dictated modern design, but on the rough, illkept roads of Cumberland and Westmoreland, speed was out of the question.

Captain Wildish proceeded immediately to hand Lady Gordon into the carriage.

"Wildish, it is my privilege to do the duty. Please stand aside," said Lord Andrew.

The Captain laughed and stepped back. "As you are our host for this afternoon, I must comply, but you will admit it is rather unworthy of you to insist upon it."

"I assure you there is some method in my madness. You see, we have got seven and there are but six seats. I do not suppose you thought about that."

"Oh, I say!" exclaimed Captain Wildish, his contemptuous smile vanishing.

The Viscount turned to the ladies and said: "There is no need to concern yourselves, ladies. Your comfort will be seen to."

He gestured to Mr. Selkirk to stand aside with the Captain and helped Lady Gordon into the carriage. He waited to see how she would arrange herself before he resumed.

Her ladyship sat herself down in the center of the rear squab, facing forward.

His lordship turned immediately to Lady Diana and directed her to seat herself alongside of Lady Gordon. After helping her up, he did the same for Caroline. Then he assisted Ancilla to the forward squab, by the window, and sat himself down beside her.

"Now there is but one seat for the two of you, gentlemen. I am sure you can imagine the depth of my regret that Lord Thanet was so niggardly with the seating, but you will admit that it is beyond my power to make any more room available within."

Mr. Selkirk looked daggers at Captain Wildish and said: "I have never ridden outside, and I do not intend to begin at this late stage."

With that he stalked over to his horse, mounted and rode away down the drive.

"My apologies, Wildish, but I never expected so large a party," said Lord Linford, grinning at the discomfited Captain.

For a moment, Captain Wildish glared at the Viscount. Then, thinking better of it, he let out a bark of laughter and said: "Of course, my lord. Selkirk's loss is my gain."

He walked around to the other side of the coach, entered it, and sat down alongside of his lordship.

The viscount called out to Lord Thanet's coachman and the coach began to move.

Ancilla found Andrew's behavior quite bewildering. She had had it upon the tip of her tongue to suggest that the Gordons' carriage be brought out and the party travel in two vehicles. Not escaping from her calculations was the possibility that she might find the opportunity to travel separately from his lordship. But, there was such an intensity about his lordship's manner as he went about seating everyone, that she had not dared. Then, too, there was this strange air of triumph that wreathed Andrew's features as they started out and quite the opposite expression on Captain Wildish's face that she was quite sure she had missed something important in the exchange between them.

Indeed, both gentlemen appeared to be acting rather strangely, she thought, as she sat back and looked out of the window.

There was nothing interesting to see. They were on the road to Ambleside with which she was now quite familiar. If the road-builders, whoever they had been, had only thought to have built the road upon the banks of Windermere, the view could have been one of magnificent beauty, but they had laid it out sufficiently inshore so that estates, together with small hills and many trees were almost always between them and the lake view. Only an occasional glimpse of Windermere could be caught when the road wandered closer to the shore and the trees thinned out.

She was aware that Andrew was looking at her, and not entering into conversation with the other passengers. Captain Wildish, seated on the other side of Andrew, was talking with Diana, seated across from him, whereas her mother was engaged in talk with Caroline, beside her. Ancilla began to feel uncomfortable. The least she could do was to speak with their host, since he did not appear to be at his ease and, furthermore, she suspected that it was herself that he wished to speak with. As she had her head turned from him, he required the brashness of a Captain Wildish to gain her attention—and that he most certainly lacked.

She turned about and smiled. "To what place are you taking us, Andrew?"

He smiled back at her and replied: "If the poets can be trusted, to the most beautiful of all the lakes, my dear—and there is one spot in particular. Fortunately, it is rather conveniently located, so that we shall not have to scramble across country to get to it."

"I do not understand. You have been to it, this place?"

"No, but I have seen an engraving of it and, if the artist has done his subject justice, it ought to be quite a picturesque setting. It is, perhaps, a bit far for a day's excursion, but I think the view will be worth it."

"Why are you so mysterious? What is this place?"

"Have you been to Ullswater?"

Ancilla shook her head. "No, we have not taken much advantage of the district. But then we have not been here all that long."

"Then you cannot know anything of the region about Ullswater."

Ancilla shook her head. "But I have heard that it is quite a beautiful water."

"Yes, that is what I have been told."

"Oh, then you have not been there either?"

"No. Like you I have not been here all that long—"

"I see. Then it was recommended to you, is that it?"

"Not exactly. Before I came out I studied the area. I have a most excellent set of volumes on English and Welsh topography—oh, it took the longest time before the subscription was completed. As a matter of fact, I was rather young when it began, some eighteen volumes produced over a span of years, extending from the first year of this century to 1815, but two years ago. The thing is that in the volume which treats of Cumberland, there is an exquisite engraving of Airey Force, just before Gowbarrow Park—an estate of the Duke of Norfolk—it was a place I wished to visit—but not by myself, you see."

"I take it as a compliment—for my mother and my friends—that you invited us to join with you, Andrew; but it puzzles me that you did not go off with Mr. Symonds, your er—companion."

"Oh, I could never bear it with Symonds along. He is of the old school and sees a lesson in every stone and blade of grass, never the beauty of Creation. It is odd, that. In none of the old church writings did any of the scribes include some appreciation of their surroundings. You may read till your eyes ache in the Venerable Bede, but you will never find that the old cleric has a word to say of the beauties of the places he has seen—and I should imagine that all of England must have been much more beautiful in his day, so untouched by the hand of modern man."

For a moment, Andrew was lost. He turned to Ancilla and asked: "Now, how the devil did I ever get onto that tack?"

"Oh, I do not mind at all. What you are saying is

101

most interesting," Ancilla said, hurriedly. For a moment, as he had warmed to his subject, his cloak of reserve had dropped from between them.

"Do you really? Then perhaps you will find Airey Force worth your while."

"I am sure I shall. I have been disappointed by the inaccessibility of Windermere's beauty from the road, and thus far it is the only lake we have had an opportunity of observing."

"Yes, but once we are past Ambleside, there will be more to see. I have been up to Kirkstone Pass and the view from there is quite good—that is, when the mists will permit."

Ancilla was now quite interested to continue the talk, but Andrew seemed to have run out of things to say and had turned to look out the window as they passed through Ambleside and found the road to Ullswater.

She sensed that he was anxious about something, for he kept trying to peer forwards and upwards, not at all at ease with himself.

Finally, he put his head out the window and called up to the coachman: "Blinker, how is it ahead?"

Back came the reply: "Not easy, your lordship! The pass be thick with cloud!"

Even as he spoke, the sun dimmed and the carriage began to climb into patches of thin mist. Andrew swore under his breath and sat back in his seat, a dark frown on his face.

None of this had been lost by Captain Wildish, who now remarked: "Andrew, old boy, the weather gods do not smile upon you this day. Where are you taking us?"

"It will be all right in the end, Ivo," he replied, looking anxiously about him, to see how his other guests were responding. "I have heard that heavy mists constantly fill Kirkstone Pass. It will be quite all right once we are down to Broad-Water—"

Remarked Caroline: "If that is the lake I believe you have reference to, my lord, it is called Brothers' Water, I have been told. There is a grisly tale of two brothers having been lost in it—"

"Oh, is that a fact, Miss Darcy?" said Andrew, unhappily. "In any case, I am sure that we shall be free of the mists once we have descended so far."

And, in fact, the mists did remain behind in the pass as they began to descend into the Vale of Ullswater; but, by the time they had completed the passage over Kirkstone crest, the sun had quite deserted the day, leaving everything the eye could see in a somber mood. The same dullness could be seen in the Viscount's glum expression.

"Not a very propitious day for an excursion, Andrew, what?" commented Captain Wildish. "Ah, but do not despair, for the fair company more than makes up for the loss of the day."

Andrew turned to Ancilla and said: "My dear, I was so very sure that this would be a perfect day. I never counted on Westmoreland weather being so fickle."

Ancilla could understand Andrew's disappointment, but he was looking so despondently at her she had to say something to put his mind at rest.

"I am sure it but adds to the beauty of the place. It is not as if it were a raging storm without. See how the colors glow in the subdued light."

"Thank you, Ancilla. It is kind of you to say so. It was just that I wished this to be a merry little trip, you see. Instead, we have a day that is anything but joyful in aspect."

"Oh, Andrew, I think you put too much upon it. It

is only an outing and nothing more. Hardly a business to get one's wind up, you will agree."

He nodded, unsmilingly. "Yes, nothing of the least importance, I am sure," he replied, and Ancilla thought she detected a bitter note in his voice.

Lord Linford's expression was such as to put a damper on the party for the rest of the journey to Patterdale Hall where the party was entertained by Mr. John Mounsey, Esq. whose ancestor, by reason of wit and a strong and accurate bow, discouraged a band of moss-troopers on a raid down from Scotland. He was now enjoying the unofficial title of king of Patterdale which, for generations, had been accorded to the descendants of the Mounsey, and proved a jovial host.

During the course of the light repast, he regaled them with the exploits of the Mounseys, which deeds appeared to comprise the only noteworthy history of the district.

On the point of departure, Mr. Mounsey, who had pretty well monopolized the conversation throughout the visit, took it upon himself, to deliver a discourse upon the qualities of his district.

"My Lord Viscount and ladies and gentleman, as you have heard me tell, I have spent all of my existence in Patterdale, which name, by the way, comes to us from St. Patrick to whom our chapel was dedicated in days of yore. Yes, well, as I was saying, I have spent all of my days in the district and am pleased to see the great number of pilgrims come into the Vale to enjoy the sights of nature. I do not set myself up as an authority of the beauties of the sights of nature, but I am a fair-minded man, and, if that is what they wish to see, I say: Welcome to Ullswater and feast your eyes if that is what pleases you.

"For myself, I need none of these vistas that the poets

make so much of. It is a good land and there are good people in it, and that is all I need or desire. However, do not let anything that I say dissuade you from proceeding on to the Lake. Ullswater may not be the size of Winandermere, but Mr. Wordsworth has written reams of verse about it and that is good enough for me.

"My Lord Viscount, it was a pleasure to receive you and your gracious company and if ever you are a mind to bend a rod with me on the lake, it will be my sincere pleasure to have you as my guest. There is skelly and char and the finest trout in all of England to be had for a length of line and a fly, my word on it!"

Mr. Mounsey then saw them mounted into their coach, commented upon its striking resemblance to that of Lord Thanet's and laughed heartily upon being informed it was one and the same. He then proceeded to catechize the coachman as to the location of Airey Force. When he was satisfied that the man was quite up to reaching it, he bid all the guests a fond farewell.

"A charming gentleman! Truly a charming gentleman," remarked Lady Gordon.

"Ah yes, my lady," said Captain Wildish. "Mr. Mounsey, despite his being filled to overflowing with the pitiable history of the place and his ancestors, was a most diverting fellow. Something long in the wind, however—so unlike our host. I say, Andrew, has the cat got your tongue?"

"Ivo, if I have something to say, I shall say it, but unlike others I know, I say nothing when I have nothing to say."

"No need to snap a chap's head off. I was merely thinking that your luck with the weather is not unlike your skill with a boat. Look at the sky! I'll wager it will be a dampish trip back to Bowness this afternoon."

Said Ancilla: "Captain, you make it sound as though it is precisely what you wish."

"I beg your pardon, Miss Gordon, if I have given you that notion. It is the very last thing I could wish. I would never hope for such a poor ending to Lord Linford's little treat. But I will admit to wondering why his lordship chose this direction to travel. Had we gone west to Coniston Water, I'll lay a bob to a shilling, we should have found a brightly shining sun."

"Be that as it may," said Andrew, "it was a place of beauty I had it in mind to show you. I am filled with despair that the sun has not shown its willingness to cooperate."

Ancilla had noted how the Captain had smirked at her when he had mentioned boating and she resented it. She it was who had suffered from that episode, not he. It seemed to her that the Captain had no ingrained right to make a remark that ought to have been reserved to her, and as she had no wish to exhume the incident, he ought to have had even less.

"Captain Wildish, you continue with remarks that mislead me into believing that they are not well intended. I say that, as his lordship could not possibly control the vagaries of the weather, we ought not put the blame of it at his doorstep. Speaking for myself, I am quite pleased to be along and am looking forward to this sight of great beauty he has promised us."

"Oh my dear, dear Miss Gordon, how you will persist in misunderstanding me!" exclaimed the Captain, managing a smile and a look of hurt at the same time. "I, too, would not have missed this excursion for anything. In fact, I am honored that Lord Linford suffered me to come along with all of you—"

"The word is well chosen, Ivo," interjected Andrew.

"Might I suggest a change of topic? I fear you are boring the ladies."

"Oh, I say, Andrew, if I am provoking you, you have only to tell me to be still—"

"Be still!"

The very directness of the command caught the Captain quite unprepared. He remained with his mouth open, staring at the Viscount. Then he snorted, blew out his cheeks and stared sullenly out the window.

But now Caroline came to his rescue. "Oh la! Captain, you must not take Lord Linford at his very word. He was only funning, I am sure. Actually, I think your point is well taken. The day has turned dismal and I am almost prepared to suggest that we turn about and put off this Airey Force for another, more pleasant time."

"Well, *I* do not *agree!*" said Diana. "We have come so far, it would be a complete waste to turn about now. *Besides,* upon another day, especially a more *pleasant* one, there may be more *intriguing* things to do than to visit with a madman king and go to see a waterfall."

Ancilla did not have the heart to look at Andrew. Her imagination was quite up to the task of picturing the hurt and disappointment in his face. She did not understand why this trip should have loomed so importantly in his life, but it was obvious that Wildish did and was intent upon destroying any hope of its being pleasant. With the weather as his confederate and, now, her two friends being beastly, thoughtlessly or otherwise, Andrew could have no doubt that his choice of diversion was not going off well at all.

She was only thinking of how badly he must suffer if the trip were now to continue. For his sake, as well as those of the others, she turned to him, placing a hand upon his arm and said: "Andrew, all things considered, the day does not bode well. If it should storm before we get back to Bowness, it will have been one thing after another. Perhaps we ought to turn back at this point, even select another way home, to vary the scenery."

The look he conferred upon her told her immediately that her suggestion was not well received. Andrew's face did not change its expression as he replied: "Quite so, Miss Gordon. I shall see to it at once."

He called to the coachman to stop. Even before the coach had ceased to roll, he opened the door and slipped out. Quckly he shut it and swung himself up to the box alongside the driver. The coach began to back and wheel, finally got itself turned about and headed back the way it had come.

There was silence in the coach as everyone stared at Ancilla, whose cheeks had grown quite red.

"Ancilla, that was not at all genteel in you," admonished Lady Gordon. "You have rebuked his lordship and I do not think the gentleman will join us again. Whatever was in your mind to speak to him so?"

Captain Wildish was not smiling as he offered: "Truly, ladies, it is nothing to grieve yourselves over. Miss Gordon, it is as I have been trying to say to you, but you would misunderstand. The Viscount is something of an odd fish. You must not take it to heart if he thinks he has got something to crab about. I know the fellow and it is ever the same with him."

Ancilla was feeling bad enough to have inflicted damage to Andrew's feelings when that had been furthest from her intentions. Wildish's comment was particularly annoying to her. In fact, she was more than willing to blame him for the way things had turned out.

"I marvel, Captain, at how well you do know the

Viscount—and how soon. At first, you did not lay claim to any great acquaintance with his lordship."

The Captain pursed his lips in thought before he answered. Then his face brightened and he said: "Ah yes, but that was only because I wished to spare you the unpleasantness of the gentleman's temper, such as we have witnessed this day."

"Indeed, it was very kind of you, sir. I noted the degree of delicacy with which you tried to placate him this afternoon."

Captain Wildish smiled. "Yes, but despite my best efforts, it proved quite hopeless. In a way, I feel that I must bear some responsibility for allowing Linford to vent his pettiness upon you all. Tomorrow, I should like to invite you—"

He paused as his mind raced to determine how he was to achieve the wherewithal to accomplish the proposal he had in mind.

"Er—perhaps the day after tomorrow—for this day has proved rather fatiguing to us all—we can go for a drive that will prove a deal more pleasant. I pride myself upon my knowledge of the Lakes and their beauties, and can promise you something better than Linford essayed."

Diana's fists clenched in her lap as she firmly stated: "*I* do not care to join you, sir. Although I hold no brief for Lord Linford's *conduct,* I find *your* treatment of his lordship quite *shocking.* I think *all* of you ought to be ashamed of yourselves, especially *you,* Ancilla. Lord Linford was trying to be gracious, and if the weather turned out to be dismal, the fact cannot be a matter to *his* discredit."

"Oh, I say!" Captain Wildish responded weakly before her onslaught.

Said Ancilla: "I do not see that you have any call to

single *me* out. It was quite obvious that the day was ruined, thanks to the Captain's charming disparagement of his lordship's plans. I merely thought to bring this ruinous excursion to an end before it turned disastrous. I fear his lordship misunderstood my purpose as did you all."

"Indeed, Ancilla, it was not very well done of you," declared Lady Gordon. "His lordship took it unkindly, and I fear that it served to put him out with us. In short, you succeeded in achieving whatever it was that the good Captain has been at worrying his lordship ever since we commenced this little journey."

"But, Mama—"

"Ancilla, I have no wish to discuss this point with you at this moment. It is you, Captain, to whom I would address my remarks. From your behavior this afternoon, I cannot imagine how you can call yourself friend to Lord Linford. It is possible the gentleman is suffering from a bout of brain fever but that is no excuse for our harshness with him. All things considered, I do not see any advantage to our prolonging our sojourn at the Lakes and shall begin to make plans to return to London at once. This day has been a trial to everyone and I have no wish to witness a repetition of it."

"Oh, I say, my lady, it is not—"

"Oh, but Lady Gordon, it is too soon!" protested Caroline. "I am sure we shall find other, more suitable company here. There is nothing doing at this time of year in London."

"Children, my mind is made up. I do not know what Lord Linford's version of this poor excuse for a drive will be, but it will not serve any good purpose for word of it to get about the City and we not there to present our side of the affair."

There was a bleak expression on the Captain's face

as he said: "Am I to understand that my presence is distasteful to you?"

"Captain Wildish, it is my opinion that wé give some thought to that point. Our removal to London will provide us with the opportunity to do just that. I suggest that, when you are in the City, you call upon us. We shall have come to a conclusion about you by then."

"That is being rather blunt, my lady."

"As, at the moment I am quite out of patience with you, sir; my daughter, sir; and his lordship, I can only say, sir, it is most unfortunate that we must continue to share this coach for the ride back to Bowness."

It was a rare mood her ladyship was in and the girls thought it wiser to refrain from further comment. Captain Wildish, for his part, found his position awkward, especially as his estimate of her ladyship's character was in need of drastic revision. Great discretion, rather than great charm, was called for.

With as sober a mien as he could maintain, he replied: "My lady, I deeply regret anything the least offensive you have found in my manner. As for restoring your good opinion of me, I pray that you will allow me that opportunity when I come to call upon you in London. You may rely upon it, but I shall journey to London for that purpose and that purpose alone."

Her ladyship nodded and said nothing more. It was quite obvious that there was nothing more to be said and a pall of silence descended upon the occupants of the coach.

10

Mr. Symonds was supping on a bit of porridge in his chamber when there came a knock upon his door, followed by: "Symonds, are you there?"

His spoon dropped into his bowl as he hastened from the table and scurried to the door.

"My lord!" he exclaimed. "You are back so soon!"

"Am I?" snarled Lord Linford, coming into the room. "I see that you are eating your supper so it cannot be so very soon."

"Oh that is just a bit of food to supplement a rather sparse collation Mrs. Robison served. Oh, my lord, you cannot imagine the poverty of the clergy hereabouts! I mean to say, they have to manage on so very little, I cannot begin to imagine how they keep body and soul together."

"Is that a fact?" replied his lordship, showing no sign of interest, and pulling a chair out from the little table upon which Mr. Symonds' bowl rested.

He sat down and said: "Go on with your meal. I have no wish to disturb you."

"I am not in the least disturbed, my lord. In fact, I am quite done with it. I pray your visit to Ullswater was pleasant? But I am sure it was. I have heard so much of the beauties of the place.

"My own little business with the Robisons proved quite interesting. The gentleman's knowledge of the Scriptures is unexceptional but he knows nothing of natural philosophy and will have nothing to do with it. He *is* rather unworldly, considers prying into nature's secrets a violation of God's privacy. Truly, my lord, I was aghast at the very idea. I fear that we parted upon something less than the best of terms. It was no manner of use to discuss pneumatics with him."

Lord Linford chuckled. "It is such a new and novel field for a cleric, I do not wonder at it, Symonds. But I thought that you would find your own callings a common ground for discussion."

"Oh, we did, my lord, we did, but even there, I found it most difficult to follow him. You see, when he speaks of flocks and shepherds, he is not speaking figuratively at all. So when I said that I was the shepherd of my flock, he was immediately interested to know about the quality of their fleece—which I took as a reference to their affluence—and when he began to query me about how they were bred, I was shocked to the core until I comprehended it was my farm stock he meant. I tell you, my lord, it made for a little embarrassment. Indeed it did!"

Lord Linford laughed and remarked: "It might not be a bad idea if you and he were to exchange livings.

He sounds as though he is in need of some town bronzing whereas you, my reverend friend, may have had too much."

"Oh, my lord, I pray you are not serious!" exclaimed Mr. Symonds, growing pale.

"No, of course, I am not. Well, as far as I am concerned, I have quite had my fill of the Lakes and intend to return to London forthwith."

"I am delighted to hear it," said Mr. Symonds, beaming. "I take it that the particular vista you were seeking out was something of a disappointment?"

"Ha! Disappointment, indeed! We never got to see the place. It turns out that I gravely misjudged Miss Gordon. I do believe that she has quite thrown herself away upon Wildish."

Mr. Symonds' face fell. He had been standing all this while, his napkin tucked under his chin. Now, he slowly sank into a chair and conferred a look of commiseration upon Lord Linford. "Oh dear, oh dear," he said, sadly, shaking his head, "and now you are heartbroken. My lord, 't is a pity, but there is a bright side to the business. I never thought the lady was for you and so—"

"What are you bleating about? Why, in heaven's name, should my heart be in the least affected?" demanded his lordship, angrily.

Mr. Symonds blinked and said, rather hesitantly: "But you did say that you were interested in the lady—and you did say that you had no wish to see her thrown away upon Wildish. Now, it has turned out precisely in a way you could never wish. I do not think it is beyond reason that you should be sadly disappointed in the lady."

"Of course, I am disappointed in the lady, your worthiness, but it is not for *my* heart's sake, only for hers! I know Wildish and he is not the sort for her."

"I should think that is best left to the *lady's* judgement, my lord."

"Bah, you are being waspish, now! What can she know of so scurvy a knave?"

"But you are speaking of a friend of yours. It astounds me that you should even number him amongst your acquaintances if that is the case."

"It has nothing to do with it. He is a charming fellow and we get along well enough. It is just that he has turned a serious eye to seeking out his advantage, and I did not think that Miss Gordon ought to be his victim."

"Then it was your duty to have warned her," said Mr. Symonds, sternly.

"I do not think I would have been thanked for my pains. Surely you understand how people are. Tell them *not* to do thus and so, and that is precisely what they *will* do. No, I thought to gain the young lady's interest, her affectionate interest, I might say, thereby interposing myself between Wildish and her."

Mr. Symonds shook his head in wonderment. "My lord, that was your only interest in the young lady?"

"Of course! What, did you think it was, a passion I had for her?"

"As a matter of fact, that is precisely what I thought, and I was unhappy about it. You will recall, I clearly stated my position. She was not an appropriate female for a man of your parts—"

"Yes, I heard your nonsense, and it was as wide of the mark then as it is now. That was not my purpose at all in this."

"A bit of knight-errantry on your part, my lord?"

"You need not look down your nose at me—but that is, more or less, descriptive of my motive. The thing of it is she can see no wrong in him and so I have stepped out of it."

"My Lord Viscount, you have only known the lady a matter of a few days. How can you take it upon yourself to meddle in her affairs? How can you expect her to put up with it?"

"I was *not* meddling. In fact, I never breathed a word to her about what was between Wildish and myself," snapped Lord Linford.

"Then who informed her of your meddl—er—I beg your pardon—your interest, may I ask?"

"Symonds, you have got it all wrong. It never came to that. Unless Wildish has seen fit to inform her now, she has no idea of anything at all. It was strictly between Wildish and myself. No, I cannot believe that he would have had anything to say to her on it. After all, the chap is a gentleman."

Mr. Symonds glanced down at his hands, turned them over and back, then reached to his ear and tugged at it.

"If I understand anything at all, my lord, it is that we are about to return to London for the reason that Miss Gordon will have Wildish; but this is no disappointment to you at all. If that is so, why must you return to London? Much as I should like to see the City again, you were sent out to the Lake District for a change of air and for diversion, my lord. What precisely does a Miss Gordon, or any other female, have to say to it?"

"Not a blessed thing! I have had my change of air and for diversion, there has been the Viscount Linford making a chronic ass of himself before the world. What the Gordons think of me is only too plain to be missed. They will support even a fribble like Wildish against me in the most minor matters."

"The Gordons will? Miss Gordon?" queried Symonds, his eyebrows on high.

"Bah, all of them!"

"Then it goes to prove what I have been saying. Any female who, for even an instant, can prefer Captain Wildish to you, my lord, is not worthy of your consideration. Still, I do not see that as a reason for departing the district. There are other lakes about. If you wish to avoid further concourse with the Gordons and with Wildish, I would suggest Derwent Water, by Keswick. It is not so great a body as are Winandermere or Ullswater, but many think it quite up to the latter for beauty of scene. Mr. Robison remarked to me that he was greatly puzzled why so many visitors to the lakes preferred Ullswater along with Mr. Wordsworth. Although there is grandeur and dignity to Ullswater and, of course, there is beauty there, too, Mr. Robison feels, along with Mrs. Gaskell that Derwent Water has much the greater proportion of beauty. Those are her very words—I say, my lord, are you listening to me?"

There was a blank look in Lord Linford's eyes. He asked: "Wordsworth? Gaskell? I am sure that I am not acquainted with these people. Are they friends of yours?"

"Heavens, no! They are a gentleman and a lady of letters. Mr. Wordsworth is one of the leading poets of the day and Mrs. Gaskell is an authoress given to writing works of a superior quality, even though they are but novels—"

"So they would have us stay at Keswick instead of Windermere. I do not think so. It is all the same to me. If only Cavendish were still about; he knew a great deal about a great many things—"

"With all due respect to the Honorable Henry Cavendish, my lord, the man was a recluse and could not have had *first*-hand knowledge of anything outside of his precious laboratory and library. These people have been to the Lakes and seen with their own eyes all of the beauty that is to be had for the looking. In fact, Mr. Wordsworth is a native of the district and maintains a residence at Grasmere, a few miles beyond Ambleside."

"No."

"No, my lord?"

"I have no wish to linger. So long as I remain in the district, there is always the possibility of meeting with Miss Gordon. The prospect displeases me."

"I am beginning to wonder at what it was she said to you that you should have taken such a violent dislike to the lady."

"Oh, it was nothing she said—well, not exactly so. Perhaps I had better tell you what did take place."

"Yes, for I am very puzzled. I hold no brief for Miss Gordon, but I never took her for an ill-mannered female."

"Oh, I do not mean to imply that there was rudeness or insult in her manner. Nothing of the sort. It was that a time came for her to make a choice between Wildish and myself, and she made it easily enough."

"A choice between you two gentlemen? My lord, do you know what you are saying? Out of the blue, you made an offer. This, I can well believe, for you are unworldly beyond belief, but that Captain Wildish should be making an offer, too, boggles the mind. He is too polished for that—but that is not my point. It is you, my lord, who are in need of a keeper until you have learned how to go about in polite society!"

There was a grin of surprise on his lordship's face as he declared: "I must say, Symonds, I have never heard you discuss anything in such spirit. But, my friend, you are quite out in your conclusions. For some odd reason, you have got your mind on marriage and that, I do assure you, is the very last thing on *my* mind. No, it was not anything like what you suspect. It was the weather, dash it, the bloody weather that did my effort at altruism in. I mean to say it was never so bad as to call for all those snide remarks from Wildish, not that I did not hold up my end in the exchange, mind you. Nor was the weather at all as threatening as he made out. Miss Gordon has eyes to see with and there was no storm raging or about to break. All that was evident were the clouds hiding the sun, and that was never any excuse to turn back from an excursion I had gone to great lengths to plan. You know how I made a visit to Lord Thanet and, through his offices, was enabled to arrange a stopover at Mounsey's—and there was the excellent carriage his lordship lent to me. I mean to say these things, all for the comfort of my guests, required not a little trouble to effectuate.

"But, my dear Symonds, do you think that any of them cared a whit for the effort I put out? Do you think any one of them took into account the thought I expended for their entertainment and convenience? Do you think for one moment that Miss Gordon would have taken the trouble to compare myself and what I had accomplished with Wildish's mere tagging along? No! Not a bit! And what is more, she had the nerve to invite the blackguard along on *my* outing! I tell you, it is not fair. Here am I going to all this trouble and there is Wildish, smirking about as though *he* had anything to say to it!"

"My lord, my lord, restrain your passion! There is no call for such choler as you are venting. It is nothing so serious! But, my lord, from what you have told me, in all fairness to Miss Gordon, I do not see how she comes into it. It is Wildish you are displeased with."

"Where are your ears, man?" demanded Lord Linford, striding up and down the room. "Do you not see how she it was who turned the trick upon me?"

Mr. Symonds shook his head and said: "No, I do not. It has all been Wildish thus far."

"Oh," said Lord Linford, brought up short. "I dare say I did not come to the point as yet. Well, when it could be seen that the sun had departed for the day, there was all manner of remarks anent the poor weather, Wildish leading the chorus until Miss Gordon demanded that we turn right about and put off the trip to Airey Force for another time. You can imagine how I felt. Here was this lovely lady I had every intention of delivering from Wildish's fell clutches, and with a word, she had rendered my entire purpose futile. I could see the look of triumph in Wildish's eyes as I acceded to my lady's wish. Bah, if I never lay eyes on either of them for a hundred years it will be too soon!"

There was a look of disgust upon Mr. Symonds' countenance as he sat quietly for a moment. Then, with a sigh, he said: "My Lord Viscount, I do declare that I must agree with you—"

"How could you not!?"

Unperturbed the little cleric went on: "—And prepare immediately for our departure. You know so very little of the world and its ways, you will be better off in London in your own study. Although I am a man of God and would have been shocked to the core at my ever recommending more worldliness in a person, for you, my lord, it is the only remedy. How you will manage to get it, immersed in philosophical transactions with like-minded recluses, I know not, but I shall pray that the Almighty in His infinite wisdom will find a way for you."

There was a pained expression on Lord Linford's face.

"I must say you have an odd way of coming to some agreement with me, but so long as you agree that we ought to leave this place, I'll not debate the matter. With regard to my studies, I am in no great hurry to resume them. There are other efforts that hold fascination for me. I read about it in the transactions of the Royal Society. We shall return to London by way of Windsor, spending a day or two at Slough. I would pay a call upon the Royal Astronomer."

Mr. Symonds leaped up from his seat with a clap of hands. "Excellent, my lord! It should prove a most interesting visit, I am sure. Do you think that Mr. Herschel will permit us to peek through that great glass he has constructed?"

His lordship smiled. "I certainly hope he will allow it. I should like to have a good look at the telescope. Perhaps I shall order one constructed for myself and raise my sights to the stars!"

11

"Ancilla, my dear, I must tell you that I am rather disappointed in Caroline—and, as I come to think about it, I am something displeased with Diana—but that is not to say that I am at all pleased with you, my daughter. In fact, I am sure that you have gained my deepest displeasure of the three of you."

Mother and daughter were seated together in a little sitting room to the rear of the Villa. Their two guests were off in another part of the house, allowing them the rare privilege of being private with one another.

Ancilla, a little smile on her lips, knitted her brow and replied: "Just as I am sure I did nought willfully to displease you, I am sure that neither Diana nor Caroline did so, either. Pray, tell me wherein I have caused you any displeasure."

"Oh, I do not claim that you went out of your way to be unpleasant, not any of you, but the fact remains you behaved abysmally towards Lord Linford yesterday. The poor man was at a loss for words at your lack of appreciation."

"But, Mama, it was *his* behavior that prevented me from making it clear to him!" she protested. "Actually, it was quite rude of him to have withdrawn himself from the coach at the very moment I wished to explain things."

"And what, may I ask, was there to explain? It sounded to me as though our friend, Wildish, had managed to make everyone miserable with his graceless comments on the weather. Not one of you ladies took the trouble of putting him down."

"Mama, I was about to do something of that nature but I was not given the opportunity—and there was you, my lady. I do not recall that you had a word to say—"

"Now that will be quite enough, child. You are being impertinent, you know. It would have been beneath my dignity to have entered into an exchange with the Captain. It was for any of you ladies to have made your wishes plain—which, incidentally, you, my dear, made frightfully clear. In short, you did, in effect, give your approval to Captain Wildish's suggestion that we turn back—"

"But, Mama, I was about to explain to the Viscount that we could do it all another time! Some time when the weather was more promising, even the very next day. I did not wish us to appear unappreciative of his efforts to entertain us—"

"But that is precisely what you managed to accomplish. I am sure that Lord Linford has had quite enough of us and it is hardly likely we shall see him call at the Villa again."

"Yes, I know that, and it is quite upsetting to me. He completely misunderstood me, and I am at my wits' end trying to find a way to clear up the matter. I do admit that neither Diana nor Caroline was the least help yesterday, and as for Captain Wildish, I think you gave him all he deserved—but, do you not think it would have been better to have reprimanded him before the Viscount, instead of waiting until his lordship had exiled himself up to the box?"

"Well, my dear, it was as you say. There was never a chance. Lord Linford escaped us before we could do the least bit to let him know where our preferences lay. The man is rather difficult to deal with, I am beginning to believe."

Ancilla laughed sourly. "It is never news to me, Mama. I should say that his lordship is an original in the worst sense of the word. Perhaps he was embarrassed by what had occurred, but that was no reason for him to have passed it on to me. Can you imagine how I felt when he turned from me, without a word, and removed himself? At the worst I had not said anything that Captain Wildish had not said, and he did not turn from him. Truly, I wonder what goes on in the gentleman's mind that makes him behave so oddly."

"Do you think it is catching? I mean to say that everyone knows Mr. Henry Cavendish, brilliant though he was, was not altogether there in his upper story, so it should come as no surprise that his protegé, Lord Linford, suffers from the same complaint. Perhaps it is better that we do not have anything more to do with the gentleman. It is too late in life for me to be taken for an original, I am sure."

Ancilla laughed. "Oh, that would be an old wives'

tale, Mama! Whatever he has got, I am sure it is not catching. After all, there is Mr. Symonds, who spends a great deal of time with the Viscount and he is a reverend gentleman."

"Far be it from me to criticize a reverend gentleman, my dear, but that Mr. Symonds does not strike me as something less than an oddity himself. Yes, I am sure that whatever his lordship has got, it is catching, and we shall do well to avoid his company in the future."

"I assure you, Mama, I have not the least objection to doing without the august presence of the Viscount Linford, but not for the reason *you* give. I shall not say the man is a bore, but he most certainly is a trial. Yes, I think we ought to give it all up and return to London. Both Diana and Caroline are dissatisfied with the Lakes, and for lack of decent company, I must admit, I am, too."

At that point Diana and Caroline sauntered into the room.

Lady Gordon and Ancilla both looked up with smiles of greeting, and Diana came rushing forward, exclaiming breathlessly: "Lady Gordon, we *must* speak with *you!* It is of the *utmost* importance!"

"Yes, my child, what is it?"

"Caroline and I have been talking about what we ought to do—"

Here, Caroline broke in: "Diana, I thought we had agreed that I should speak for the both of us!"

Diana turned about and retorted: "*I* did not agree to *any* thing of the *sort!* I am *sure I* can speak for *myself!* Now, my lady, as I was about to say—"

"*Diana!!* I strongly urge you to let me speak. *You* will spoil everything because you do not think before you speak. You are far too impulsive!"

"Really, Caroline, I am quite sure that *I* can speak

126

as well as *any*body on earth! Just because you believe *you* are smarter than *I* am is no reason—"

"Now, now, ladies! That will be quite enough! *I* have something to say to the both of *you*—" interrupted Lady Gordon, sharply.

Diana did not let her finish but said: "Oh, in *that* case, my lady, I should not dare to interrupt you."

"Of course, my dear," said Lady Gordon, nodding and smiling, "but I am quite willing to allow you to precede me. Now, what was it you wished to say, Diana?"

"I am *sure* that since *Caroline* is *dying* to speak, we ought to *let* her do so."

"I really do not care which of you chooses to speak so long as one of you does so. Caroline?"

"My lady, thank you. It is simply that after yesterday's calamity, brought upon us by the awkwardness of Lord Linford, there are no friends left to us in this neighborhood. It was no fault of Captain Wildish that Patterdale was suffering such poor weather. Yet, because of some imagined slight to Lord Linford on his part, we are to be denied the gentleman's company. I, myself, do not appreciate what the one thing has to do with the other—"

"*Yes*, my lady," said Diana. "Truly it was *bad* of you to have dismissed Captain Wildish as you did. He is a perfectly *harmless* gentleman, whose only *concern* was for our pleasure in the day. Lord Linford, on the other hand, turned quite as nasty as the *weather,* and you did not have all *that* much to say to *him!*"

"I regret, my dears, that you did not truly understand the circumstance," responded Lady Gordon. "Ancilla did, you know, and I am sure that she does not see the Captain as blameless in the unpleasantness that ensued. Nonetheless, I quite agree with you. Lord Linford proved himself no prize host."

"I do not see what you have to blame in Captain Wildish—" Diana began to protest when Caroline cut her off.

"Diana, will you cease to belabor the point! Lady Gordon must, as she agrees with us in principle, come to our conclusion. Do you not see that there is no point in pursuing the business of the gentleman? We can now proceed to our suggestion."

"Of *course!* Lady Gordon, we wish to *return* to London!"

Caroline's voice was caustic as she remarked: "Indeed, that was marvelously tactful of you, Diana."

She turned to Lady Gordon, quickly, before Diana could retort, and said: "My lady, it was what all of this was leading up to. The fact remains that outside of the Viscount and the Captain, we are without friends in our own style. It is rather silly, don't you think, to be going about the Lakes all by ourselves when in London, we might have our choice of the best in company? Unless, of course, you have further business in the district, I should like to suggest our immediate departure."

"Then we are all of one mind, I should say," replied her ladyship.

"But *we,* Caroline and I have no wish to stay on! I want—"

"Diana, can you not understand the simplest thing? Her ladyship agrees with us, and we are going back to London," put in Caroline, impatiently. "Is that not so, Lady Gordon?"

"Quite," she replied, with a sigh. "Of course, you realize there will be all manner of inquiry as to why we have returned so early, and I must caution you to refrain from saying anything to add to our embarrassment—or to that of the gentlemen in the case. Before we left, I informed the world of our holiday, and so we had better have some good reason for our earlier-than-planned return."

"*I* do not see why *we* have got to *lie* to save Lord Linford's reputation," said Diana with a pout. "I think the *world* should be told about *him*."

"My dear Diana," spoke up Ancilla, "whatever you may tell the world, it will always see two sides of the situation and it is safe to wager that the version they will adopt will be the least complimentary to any of us. No, my lady mother is right. I would strongly advise that we say merely the weather was not as salubrious as we thought it would be—"

"And pray *how* do you suppose Lord Linford will report *his* version of the affair?"

"I would sooner trust to Lord Linford's remarks on the occasion than I would to Captain Wildish's. His lordship does not strike me as being a vindictive sort. I am not so sure about the Captain."

"If that is how you feel about his lordship now, it was obviously a different tale when we were beyond Patterdale, yesterday," said Caroline. "Have you forgotten so soon how you took the Captain's part against Lord Linford?"

"No, I have not forgotten a thing, my dear. If his lordship had but stayed a moment longer, I could have made myself clear. But he did not and a misunderstanding arose. I had been about to say that, in light of the weather, calling it off for that day would have been wise, but I never intended he should have been given to understand that we are all of us dissatisfied with him, as the dear Captain implied."

"But we *were* displeased!" interjected Diana. "His lordship must have *feathers* for brains for even *conceiving* the idea of taking us out for a drive on such a *poor* day."

"That is utter nonsense!" retorted Ancilla. "If you will recall, all was well until we started to descend from Kirkstone. It is hardly to be expected that Lord Linford is a weather prophet. Certainly, Wildish is not. He had naught to say until the weather turned bad. Truly, it was not at all fair of him."

Said Caroline: "Ancilla, the Viscount boasts of having a knowledge of pneumatics and that has to do with vapors and airs. Is not weather a phenomenon dependent entirely upon the vagaries of vapors and airs? I think so, and it gives me to think that Lord Linford is not as brilliant as everyone believes."

"Oh, Caroline, you cannot believe what you are saying. Farmers and husbandmen can predict what the weather will be. It is hardly to be expected of a gentleman. It is perfectly clear to me that whatever it is that Lord Linford deals with, he does so in some library or other, and it has nothing to do with anything so mundane as whether the day will be bright or dull."

"Never in all of my days have I been forced to listen to such utter nonsense as all of you are speaking!" exclaimed Lady Gordon. "Yes, I do not think the Lakes will serve to entertain us, much less contribute to your common sense. I do not care what any of you has to say to it, I am surrendering the lease to Mr. Curwin and removing us back to London at the first opportunity. Perhaps, some day, you will, all of you finally reach that stage of age and breeding when you will appreciate a visit to the Lake Country. For the present, I deem it quite hopeless. Diana, Caroline, I pray you will write to your parents and inform them of your imminent return."

This time it was Lord Linford who sought out Captain Wildish. He found him taking his ease in a small

130

chamber, just off the servants' quarters of the White Lion.

Upon being admitted into the chamber, he came brusquely in, ignoring Wildish's hearty greeting.

"You base villain, you! How do you dare to grin at me, a sign of friendly affection wreathing your countenance, all false!"

"I might ask how dare you come to call upon me, after the damage you did to me in the eyes of our lady-friends, my lord. Oh come now, Andrew, as we have both overreached ourselves, there is nought to do but to find our interests somewhere else, and with the hope that they are each distinctly different and apart from each other."

"As is usual with you, your words make no sense. Do you deny that you did your utmost to cast a pall upon the drive and so rally the ladies that they insisted they be returned forthwith?"

"I had no need to cast any pall at all. The weather took care of that! All that I did, Andrew, and I pray you will take the trouble to recall it, was to say the perfectly obvious. The weather was threatening a downpour and we had not even got to your perishing waterfall. The ladies, being bright and intelligent, did no more than agree to the obvious, and it was you, my friend, who managed to make a mountain where not even a molehill had existed before."

The Captain settled himself down in an easy chair and beckoned the Viscount to be seated, too. He was chuckling as he said: "I warned you I was out to gain my way with Miss Gordon, and you took up the challenge—"

"That gave you no right to make a fool of me!" exclaimed Lord Linford, accepting a chair. "It was never as bad as you insisted upon making it out to be. To prove my point, it never did rain; no, not even a thin drizzle!"

The Captain shook his head in good-humored exasperation as he picked up a decanter and poured out gin into two tumblers. "I beg your indulgence, my lord, but my pockets are not as heavy as yours, and even this libation of mother's ruin is strictly on tick—my own, of course.

"Which brings me to the reason I am so glad to see you. I have managed to run up quite an account here, at the White Lion. As ever, I have not the faintest hope of settling it. Can you see your way to lending me twenty guineas? I would not stick at accepting a pound or two more, I assure you."

"Whatever the game you are playing, my dear Wildish, the rules are odd to say the least. You have gone to the greatest trouble to ruin my standing with the ladies of Curwin's Villa and now you expect me to support you, financially, in your base purposes towards Miss Gordon. I should say not!"

"Dash it all, you owe it to me! Ruin you, do you say? Ruin me, rather! You brought your downfall upon yourself by your odd humor of betaking yourself out of the carriage and up to the box for the rest of the trip—and left me to bear the accusations of having stepped on your toes, poor thing! Now I have got all of my work to do over again. I have been placed on a probation of sorts until the ladies can be brought 'round again to receive me in London—"

"London? What are you saying? You have been invited to call upon them in London. Then they have departed—and not a word of it to me?"

"If they have, I have not heard of it either, so do cool yourself down a bit and tell me what you think of the gin."

"The gin is not a fit drink between gentlemen! Now, what the devil is this you were telling me?"

"There you have it, and it is the best I can afford—which is putting it rather strongly, for I swear I *cannot* afford it at all. Just peek at my slate over the bar and you will see I speak the truth. Why, our host was most unpleasant when I ordered up this last bottle—"

"Oh, will I never get any sense out of you!? Here is forty pounds! Now, continue with what you were saying. If, as you say, you are in their black books, how can you have been given an invitation to call upon them in London—and what, precisely, does it all mean?"

"They did not like my manner towards you, my lord Simpleton, which is not to say that they were enamored by *your* manner to them. It would appear that I did myself as much damage in their eyes as I achieved against you. So, we, neither of us have gained any advantage—and I thank you for your generosity, my lord. If you like, I shall call up our miserable landlord and demand the finest in his cellar. It pains me to see one so fine as you, my friend, reduced to swilling gin."

"Indeed, I suffer for you, but I am more interested to learn of your situation with Miss Gordon than I care about gin. What damage did you do?"

"It is as I said. I am not sure of the way in which Miss Gordon responded, but Lady Gordon dusted me rather thoroughly, gave me to understand I was a bounder even if she did not put it that precisely—"

The grim look upon the Viscount's face relaxed and he nodded, approvingly. "I should have had more faith in you, old boy. There never was a need for me to worry. Your true colors are easily seen. I am very relieved to hear it."

"Oh, I pray you will not be too easy on that score! I have not done with the Gordons. For one thing, there is something of a fortune there and Miss Gordon is a prime 'un."

"Yes, but she has marked you well and I am encouraged to believe you will get nowhere with her."

"Far be it from me to disturb your fool's paradise, but I think I shall. In any event, it will be vastly entertaining to try to press my suit with her."

His lordship's eyes opened wide. "Then you are serious in this business? That is a change!"

"Andrew, I am always serious. Other gentlemen who are perennially down-at-the-heels, as I am, go to the gaming tables to find their next meal; others rely upon their powers of narration to dine around, spreading all that is juicy in the way of gossip; but my way is pleasanter, I assure you. I am always serious in my dealings with the Sex, to gain my living for the moment—or for my lifetime, if Fortune smiles upon me. For my part, Miss Gordon appears to be the embodiment of Fortune and, if I am successful with her, I, too, shall be wealthy enough to partake of the pleasures of pasteboards on green baize tables."

"Hmph!" snorted his lordship. "Confessions of a Cad. You ought to write your memoirs, they would make a perfect penny dreadful."

"Hmmm! I never thought of that. I say, Andrew, it is a smashing idea! I am sure I should receive a deal more for the threat of publication than the publishing itself. I shall have to take your suggestion under sober consideration."

"Don't you dare! Ivo, if you press me, I shall take steps to put you where you belong!" exclaimed Andrew, with ire.

Ivo laughed disdainfully. "And precisely where may that be, my lord?"

"In a spunging house, you idiot! Newgate eventually, for you owe me more than you can ever repay."

"And that is a fact!" stated Ivo, unperturbed. "Andrew, if you cherish the slightest hope of my settling the score, you will be well advised to abet me in my designs upon the fair Miss Gordon."

"You are incorrigible! Very well, I warn you once again, stay away from the Gordons or you shall have me to deal with."

Ivo frowned. "Indeed, you do make it difficult for a fellow. It is not what *you* do, but the manner in which circumstances get all tangled when you are about. I never have experienced such a setback as I did at Patterdale. I shall have to watch my step in the future when you are about."

"Whatever the cause, mark me well. I shall always be about. In fact, until you are resolved to forgo Miss Gordon, I intend not to let you out of my sight."

"Heavens! A fate worse than death—but there is a good side to it when one gives it a bit of thought. For example, I have every intention of settling my score below and rushing off to London. You see, I have got to gather up some of my acquaintances in higher circles in order to make a better impression on the Gordons than I have. By the time they arrive in the City, I shall have gained such entrée as even they will envy. I shall be able to introduce them to the very *nicest* circles. It should work to take their minds off the Patterdale debacle. Therefore, you may as well order up your carriage and drive me down, my friend."

"The devil you say. I have but a two-seater, and I have got Symonds to think of."

"You are made of money. Send the dear chap home, post chaise—or you will not be able to keep your eye on me. I would not suggest this, except for the fact that

135

mine host will leave me very little of this forty pounds, the token of your generosity—unless, of course, you are willing to part with another hundred or two to see me to the City in the style I am forever trying to achieve."

Andrew glared at him. He did not reply for a while as he sat and thought.

Finally he spoke. "I should be delighted to refuse your charming suggestion but for a number of things. Symonds is under the impression that I am nursing a tendre for Miss Gordon and is full of that sage advice I can do without. I cannot contemplate a return to London, listening to his blather. Then, too, it would permit me to keep you in sight, something less than a positive pleasure to me but a distinct necessity, for the cad that you are. And, lastly, it would be ever so much cheaper for me in the long run. I am not in a mood to underwrite your escapades unless I know precisely what they are going to be."

"Excellent! When do we leave?"

Andrew got up and replied: "Early in the morning. I shall see Symonds off this afternoon. Be you ready at ten on the morrow—and be prepared to take your turn at the reins. By heaven, you shall do a little work for your fare to London!"

12

It was a very long drive, if such it could be called.
As neither gentleman wished to dawdle in the various
cities and towns they passed through: Manchester,
Derby, Leicester, Northampton, Luton, they spent each
day on the roads, making as good a time as the weather
and the conditions of the roads allowed. By the time
they pulled into Luton, late on the afternoon of the fifth
day of their travels, both of them were as jaded as their
horses and not in a mood to say another word to each
other.

At the beginning, as they were quite fresh, there had
been much to talk about, but showers and crowded lodgings over the next few days took their toll.

Andrew, finally, commanded Ivo to draw up along
the side of the road and come to a halt.

"Dammitall!" he cried. "Must we be forever harping on the frailties and attractions of the Sex? Is there nothing else in that feeble excuse you call a mind to speak on?"

"Now, what is eating at you? It is a topic of conversation that is nothing unusual between gentlemen, nor is it at all exceptional. But if your taste runs in another direction, I pray you will suggest a topic, more to your liking—but I draw the line at a disquisition concerning the burning of air, which I consider as sheer a bit of nonsense as can be conceived."

"No, you have got it all wrong! The thinking is that whatever does burn, does so only in the presence of air—that it is one of the components of the air we breathe, which incidentally, as the late M. Lavoisier was beginning to demonstrate, is that which supports our living. Now, you see that this points to the fact that—"

"Andrew, will you shut up! I do not care a farthing what you do with your air. Leave mine alone! If you will not fill it with tempting descriptions of lovelies you have known—a short discourse, I am sure—and you will not allow me to regale you with my own charming memoirs of the same, then I suggest we pursue our journey in silence and with all speed."

"You have never said better. It is agreed."

So it was that upon reaching the George in Luton, neither Andrew nor Ivo had a word to say to each other; but, as soon as the horses were put up, each retired to his own chamber, supped in solitude and went to bed.

They were both up the next morning and out upon the roads, the early sun making merely a shining button through the thick blanket of cloud that threatened a dismal day.

138

It was Andrew's turn at the reins and he was, as usual, letting the horses find their own pace. He had peremptorily refused to change horses at the various stops and so the hacks must be pampered or they would have collapsed from exhaustion. To Ivo, this was non-sense and a sheer waste of time. There was naught that was precious about his lordship's nags and he told him so. Andrew had not appreciated his friend's criticism and had invited him to hire his own rig. The Captain managed to restore a semblance of cordiality, calling heavily upon his inexhaustible charm, but a definite strain remained which, added to all the other strains, made the final demise of their conversation not long coming.

If Lord Linford had taken the road which led directly south to London, they might well have arrived in the City, completely speechless; but Andrew followed a turning that was marked for Hemel Hempstead instead of St. Albans.

"My lord, may I point out that you have made the wrong turn?" inquired Ivo in acid-drenched tones.

"That, my friend, depends upon one's point of view. If one is determined to get to London, then, yes, I have made the wrong turn. On the other hand, if one is determined to go to London by way of Slough, I have made the proper turning. As I say, it all depends upon one's point of view."

"But why Slough? It is hardly on a direct line from here."

"I decided that I have some business in Slough. I do not expect it will take more than a day to accomplish. I am sure you will manage to amuse yourself in my absence. There are bound to be barmaids in any of the local taverns, and they are as much of a lady as you seem able to aspire to."

"You are going out of your way to be insulting, my lord. I aspire to the hand of a lady who is unexceptional, even by your criterion; Miss Gordon. I demand an apology!"

"Very well, I apologize, though I count your aspiration as an insult to the lady."

The Captain smiled; "Ah, that is better. We are now back to the beginning, I think. But I still should like to know what sudden business brings you to Slough when I have got business of my own in London. I have much to do before the Gordons return."

"I have spent the last fortnight in conversation of the dullest sort. First there was Symonds. Although I have a modicum of respect for Symonds' powers of cogitation, he is a cleric and his philosophy gets in the way of any normal conversation. Now there is you, my friend, and if you can think an inch beyond your appetites and your ambitions for yourself, I have not heard or seen the proof. I want to engage a mind that has powers beyond my own. I might then be able to learn something—and have an interesting coze into the bargain."

"So, I take it that there is one of your scientific cronies residing in Slough, is that it?"

"That is it. I have a wish to speak to the Astronomer Royal, Sir William Herschel. I had been in correspondence with him for Cavendish, and as we are so close by, I see no reason why I may not stop by his observatory for a chat. I am considering giving up pneumatics for astronomy. Sir William is doing wonders in the field and I should like to have a hand in it."

"You may count me out of it. I cannot think of anything more dull."

"I never planned for you to come along with me. I

140

recollect how well you absorbed the lectures in Natural Philosophy at the University."

"As well as any of the others," said Ivo, with a laugh. "I have not lost anything by it. I have found my diversions in a more charming field and am content to continue. What have you to show for your honors degree?"

"It purely amazes me that we call each other friend," replied Andrew. "We cannot talk together for five minutes without boring each other to distraction."

"You amuse me, Andrew."

"And you amuse me, but painfully so, Ivo."

"To assuage the pain, my friend, I shall leave you in Hemel Hempstead. I ought to be able to find a connection for London there. There must be a stage—but of course it need not be a stage. I shall hire me a post chaise and enter the City in a manner fitted to a bosom beau of the Viscount Linford—especially as it will be his money which will pay the shot."

"Ah yes, now that will be money well spent that deprives me of your company," retorted Andrew with a chuckle. "When we get to Hemel Hempstead, I shall wait until you have found your transportation."

"Awfully good of you, old man; you have been a regular brick despite everything. Actually, it hurt me to set you down before the ladies but all's fair in love and war, you know."

"Yes, the tears in your eyes were quite touching. I remarked them at the time," replied Andrew, drily. "Now, let us see if we cannot get a little more energy out of these beasts of mine. They have been loafing all morning."

"Ach, Lord Linford, it is so goot of you to come to speak vith Vilhelm. He vill be so pleased. You are Mr. Cavendish's young gemtleman. *Ja*, I know you from the Society in London. Please to be seated. Vilhelm vill be vith us soon. Last night, the viewing, it was not so goot, so to bed ve vent early, *ja.*"

Andrew was happy to have Miss Herschel recognize him. She was assistant to Sir William and had made a name for herself in scientific circles by her own efforts in astronomy. In fact, she had contributed a number of papers to the Royal Society which was more than he himself had been able to accomplish.

They sat down and she inquired: "So, you are going somevhere?"

"As a matter of fact, Miss Herschel, I am on my way back to London. I have been up to the Lake Country on a repairing lease—"

She smiled and her eyes opened wide. "Ah, the life in London, it is, how you say, fast." She shook her head at him. "Better you devote yourself to the pneumatic chemistry, my lord. Vilhelm says Mr. Cavendish had a brilliant mind, so there is much you must have learned from him. Ach, but you are such a good-looking man, it vould be a shame to spend all of your time in that man's library. *Ja*, I have been to it and it is no place for such a handsome gentleman to be forever. Ach, but vhat am I thinking of! It is in the evening that the young folk make merry, *ja?* It is not like in astronomy. The best nights, when you are at dancing and parties, ve are at the telescopes, peering up into the night skies. It is not a life for a young one. You know John, my nephew? now he is following in his poppa's footsteps. *Ja*, he has given up the law and is making his own great glass, vith Vilhelm's assistance. I do not know that this is a good thing—ach, but it is in the blood, I think. Give a Herschel a glass and a sky and he is happy."

She laughed heartily. "See, there is myself. I am as

142

bad as the both of them. Ach, but I do not think Lady Herschel, my sister-in-law, vill allow it. She has been goot for Vilhelm. I think she vill be good for John. *Aber* you, my lord, you have not to worry. You are not an astronomer. You have a lady, *ja?*"

Andrew's composure was thoroughly shattered. He had come to have a learned discussion of the savant's latest discoveries and was not at all prepared to enter upon a conversation dealing with his personal life. It was an invasion of his privacy and he would have resented it had it come from an English colleague; but as Miss Herschel was so obviously a foreigner and no fly-brain, he was forced to make allowances. Nonetheless, he was unable to mask his confusion and his cheeks took on a pinkish hue.

"Oh, I–I s–say!" was all he managed by way of response.

Miss Herschel laughed gaily. "Oh, you English! You are so quickly to be embarrassed—but I am glad for you. It is not goot to be all the time vith such a one as Cavendish. He is gone and you are young and should enjoy life. *Ja,* I am glad you have a lady."

In the interest of scientific accuracy, Andrew thought to disabuse Miss Herschel of her mistaken conclusion, but just then, in walked Sir William.

"Ach, Vilhelm, vhy have you been so long? This is Lord Linford and he has a lady."

"*Ja, ja,* Caroline, I remember his lordship vell. He vas Cavendish's man. Bright, I should like for John to talk with him. Ach, that *junge,* first, it is the law and that is goot. In England the lawyers make much money, *ja? Ja,* you English spend as much time in the courts as you do in bed." He paused to laugh heartily and Miss Herschel joined him.

Andrew wore a patient smile and his cheeks reddened again.

"But he is a Herschel," Sir William went on as he sat down, "and so it is the heavens for him. Now, he is making a glass. *Such* a glass! And I am to help him, but do you think he vill listen to me? Sometimes! I, who have made a forty-feet glass vith vich I have seen so much, to me he listens—sometimes! Ach, but he knows vhat he is about, that one! I think he vill do great things greater than his father, *ja*. So vhere is Mrs. Herschel, Caroline? She should be vith us entertaining our guest, no?"

"Vilhelm! You forget yourself! It is Lady Herschel you are speaking of!" admonished Miss Herschel.

Sir William laughed, good-naturedly. "You must forgive me, Lord Linford. The honor is so new to me. Imagine! A music-maker from Hanover to become—now, how did His Highness put it? Ach, yes! A knight of the realm! Me! Villiam Herschel! My father would have liked it, to have seen how high his son has risen."

Full of apology, Miss Herschel turned to Andrew and explained: "My lord, Vilhelm vill never be as English as you. I pray you vill forgive him, if he has not the—the reticence of a proper Englisher."

"Oh, I assure you, I do not mind at all. Quite refreshing, you know. But I had hoped to speak with Sir William about—"

"So you have a lady, Lord Linford?" broke in Sir William.

Since Andrew had not yet fully recovered from Miss Herschel's inquiries on that topic, he was caught with his mouth open, without a word to say that he could think of.

"Ach, you are bashful. It is nothing, Lord Linford. I only vish that my John, for one minute would put aside his telescope and talk to me. But do not worry. It vill come, the time vill come when I shall go out of my mind vith his talk about vimmen, *ja*."

"I do not think that Lord Linford is comfortable vith me in the room, Vilhelm. I go to see about tea, *ja*? My lord, you vill drink tea vith us?"

"Why—ah, of course, but you need not put yourself to the trouble, Miss Herschel—"

"La! No trouble at all, it is. I go now."

When she had left the room, Sir William turned upon Andrew and declared: "Vith all the observations I am making at night, and sleeping and making calculations during the day, I have no time to talk or think of anything but the sun and the stars. Now you have come to me, a fine example of a handsome Englishman, and I would talk of things, other things. So how is this lady of yours? She is beautiful, no?"

Before he had a chance to ponder the question, Andrew's tongue answered for him: "Yes! Er—that is, I do not think so. I mean to say, as there is no young lady, there is no proper answer to your inquiry, Sir William."

The astronomer's face fell. "No young lady? But Caroline said it was so. Villiam, she said, his lordship has a lady. She said it, yes?"

"Oh, that is quite so, but that is not to say that Miss Herschel quite understood me, you see."

The astronomer leaned back. "No, I do not see, your lordship. I cannot believe that such a fine, upstanding Englishman, with so much in the head—" he tapped his temple with a finger as he spoke— "should not have a lady to interest him—more than one, I am villing to vager."

Andrew was at a loss how to continue. Sir William seemed intent upon talking gossip with him rather than his scientific work, and Andrew's breeding was at war with his sense of the fitness of things. To continue in this vein was highly improper, for this was the very first time he was enjoying an opportunity to speak with the eminent man. At the meetings of the Royal Society, the exchanges he had with him had been of such a perfunctory nature, he had never been sure Sir William would recognize him again. To his utter consternation, Sir William was dealing with him as though they were old acquaintances and long-fast friends, and he was being asked to divulge to him what he would have hesitated to even suggest to Ivo.

But a quick re-examination of the matter showed him that he truly had naught to lose by humoring Sir William. In fact, he might be pleased and proud that the Royal Astronomer was taking an intimate interest in him. This was more than Mr. Cavendish had ever shown him.

"I would not say that I had no interest in a female, Sir William. There is a person whom I have met recently who struck me as being something above the others of her sex."

"Goot! Goot! I vas sure there had to be someone. Tell me about her."

"Hmm. Well—ah, she is rather beautiful...." he paused, not knowing exactly what he would say next.

"Of course, she is beautiful! To me you do not have to say so. But what is she like? Is she young? Is she vealthy? She is a noble lady, of course, *ja?*"

"Oh, she is quite young. Some years my junior, I am sure. And not wealthy, that is to say, whatever she may be heir to would never be a consideration to me."

"Goot! That is very goot. I vas not so fortunate that I could look vhere I pleased. His Majesty pays me two hundred a year. It is better than I make as a musician, but it is not enough for all this."

He waved his hand about. "But then I am lucky. Lady Herschel brings to me a fortune and gives to me a fine son. John, he is an English boy and I am very proud of him.

"So, this girl—this lady, she is not vealthy, but you love her. Vhy does she not marry you?"

"Why, I have not asked her; besides, I have just met her—and what is more, I never said that I was in love with the lady!"

"Then vhy do you get so hot under the collar? I do not *accuse* you of being in love with her—yet, I think there is something there or you would not have mentioned this lady to me. After all, who am I? Almost a perfect stranger to you."

Andrew could not agree more, but by this time, he was so deeply enmeshed in the conversation, he could see no way of getting out of it.

It struck him as rather ridiculous, his present circumstances, and he laughed.

"My dear Sir William, you did persist, you know, and I was but making conversation when I mentioned the lady."

"No, no, my boy, it is not so simple. This lady is somebody to you, or you vould not have brought her to my notice. You could have said: No, there is no one, and this I vould not have believed. Or you could have said there are many but none to your taste, and this I vould have believed. But you did not say so, either one. You said: there vas *a* lady, so this lady has got to be a special person to you, no?"

"You would condemn me out of my own mouth, despite my protest?"

"Condemn? Is this a nice word to use for such a tender business? Condemn, my lord?"

"A poor choice of language, I admit. What I mean to say is that—well, no matter what I do say, you insist upon drawing your own conclusions and I tell you that they do not march with mine own."

"Sometimes, it is that ve do not truly know vhat is in our minds. I think, my friend, that it is the case vith you, *ja*. This lady, she is beautiful to you, but she is not vealthy. She stands out in your mind, but you are not interested in her. Do you see how strange that sounds? It is not logical, my son. Even in love there is logic, and' ve are scientists. Ergo, you should re-examine your feelings vith regard to this young lady."

"Oh, I do assure you, Sir William, it would be a sheer waste of my time to do so. The young lady will have none of me. I have managed to cut a very poor figure in her eyes."

"This I find hard to believe. I do not see that there is anything to take exception to about you, my lord. You do not give her a chance, I think."

"Speaking of logic, it is not you I would impress in that way, but the young lady—and with her I have failed completely. To tell the truth, I have managed to act the perfect ass with her and she will never see me again."

"She has said this to you?"

"No, but I can assume that that must be her attitude towards me."

"My boy, in matters of the heart, never assume anything at all. No matter vhat you may think, you must be brave. You must put every little hypothesis you can imagine to the test. Until she has said no to you, there is work for you to do. Vhy do you sit around talking to an old man like me vhen there is this young lady you love, who is waiting for you to come to her?"

"Oh, I say, you do not expect me to reply to that, do you?"

"No, of course, I do not, but, my lord, it is something you should be thinking about at your time of life."

"Oh, I am *thinking* about it, but I do not see that it is any business of yours, Sir William, if you will pardon me for saying so."

"But, of course, it is my business. Ve are friends, *ja?* Then your happiness is my concern, *ja?*"

"Friends? Intimate friends? I say, you have seen so very little of me, and this is the first time we have sat down and talked together."

"What more is necessary? I have seen you and we have talked and I like you. Ah, but if it is not the same with you, then we are not friends and I beg your pardon, my lord, for presuming."

"No, no, not at all, Sir William! I am honored, deeply honored—and, dash it all, I do like you, so that I am truly pleased that you like me."

"Goot! Now that ve have settled it ve are friends, vhat about this nice young lady?"

"Oh, for goodness sake, but you are persistent! What about this nice young lady?"

"I should like very much to meet her."

Andrew brought a hand up to the back of his head and scratched absent-mindedly as he said: "I fear that may take a bit of doing. I am not sure she will even speak to me."

"You must try—for the sake of our friendship," said Sir William, with a gleam in his eye.

"I should very much like to, you know, but I fear that an invitation from me will not be received very well."

"Be brave, *mon enfant,* as the French say. If the lady is as *you* say, and *you* have this feeling of affection for her, she cannot be such a monster."

"Of course, she is no such thing, but there is a problem there: A friend of mine, a longtime chum, who has expressed an interest—"

"Goot! Goot! That means vhen she chooses you, you are the one she vants above the others—"

"Oh, but you do not understand. He is not above hunting out a fortune, you see."

"But, my lord, did you not say she vas not so vealthy?"

"He is a pauper in gentleman's clothing, Sir William."

"Then you must not let him vin her. It is simple!"

"At the moment, I understand there is little fear of that, for he, too, has managed to get himself into bad odor with her."

Sir William looked confused and he had to pass a hand across his brow to clear his thinking.

"My dear Lord Linford, I am beginning to think that the affairs of people are more complicated than are the stars in their courses. If this lady is vorth your trouble, then you must take the trouble. If she is not, you must put her out of your mind—but that is for you to decide. As for me, I have many calculations to make and the time has fled. You must come again soon. I like to speak vith you and, perhaps, the next time, I can introduce my son, John, to you. We must speak of your vork and of mine, too. I should like to hear what you are doing to further the studies of Cavendish."

Andrew arose and took his departure, marveling at the little he had learned of astronomy in all the time he had spent with England's leading scientist in that field.

13

As Lady Gordon came out of Mrs. Bell's Millinery Establishment at 22 Upper King Street, she wore a strained expression on her face. Her daughter, who was accompanying her on this, the first shopping expedition since their return to London, was saying: "Thank heaven for Mrs. Bell! I do not know what we should have done without her. Can you imagine how much fashion has changed in the little while we were away? From what she has said, it would appear that one must be put to the expense of completely renewing one's wardrobe each year."

"Yes, times are changing, my dear. I think it was all due to that fellow, Bonaparte. It is all this Empire Style that they are importing from France—not that we do not have our own, but one has to admit the French do it up something better than we. They have a better appreciation of the female figure, I am thinking. But, oh dear, Covent Garden has changed so since I was a little girl. It is grown most unsavory and I am thinking seriously of taking my custom elsewhere. I said as much to Mrs. Bell, and she will be well advised to heed me."

"Yes, Mama, but here is our carriage. I shall feel happier to be gone from this place. I quite agree. Covent Garden is not a place for ladies to visit."

They mounted up into the carriage and were driven away.

As they sat back upon the soft squabs, Ancilla remarked: "It has been all of a week since we have returned from the Lakes and we have not heard a word from anyone."

"Whatever do you mean, child? We most certainly have! Our friends have been calling upon us and we have been visiting them in the old way. It is just as though we were never away."

"Oh, I do not mean that, Mama. I was referring to our acquaintances at Bowness. You remember—the two gentlemen."

"Oh, those two. Yes, I remember them quite well, and the one I can do quite well without if I never see him again, and the other, if I recall, was not in your style—a rather moody sort, not given to graciousness. A poor specimen of a viscount, I must say. Ah yes, that was very unfortunate indeed. You might have had your chance with him if he had showed the least interest in you."

"Truly, Mama, there was not all that bad in Captain Wildish. He is just something of a romp and not to be taken too seriously. As for Lord Linford, I never had the slightest interest in him, so how you can speak of my having any chance with him, I surely do not know.

He could be the last man on earth, viscount or not, and I could not care less."

"Nonetheless, my child, you might have had a chance with him had you not sided with Wildish. That was not very nice of you and I do not blame his lordship for taking exception to you."

"I told you that it was a misunderstanding—"

"And I counseled you to straighten the matter out with him, but what does a mother know of these matters? Now, we shall never see his lordship again—"

"And that, Mama, will be soon enough. If I had suspected you would have gone off in a tirade about him, I should never had brought Lord Linford into our conversation."

"Ancilla, viscounts do not grow on trees! One just does not go about and pick them off a bough as though they were some ripe fruit. How many of your friends have a close acquaintanceship with a viscount, I should like to know?"

Ancilla smiled. "Two, I know, have as close a one as I have."

"Now you are being facetious and I do not appreciate it! But, so long as you have seen fit to bring up Diana and Caroline, for all you know the viscount may be parked on their doorstep this very moment."

"If that is so, I pity them."

"Oh, there is no sense in speaking with you! What if his lordship should happen to pay us a call? What then, Miss Particular?"

"I am sure I should deal with the Viscount with cordiality and the respect due his station; but, as he is at the Lakes, I see no point in discussing such an unlikely prospect. I should much rather prefer another topic, Mama."

"Yes, I dare say—and there is *one* that has roused

153

my dissatisfaction. It is the house. I have never in my life seen such a pigsty! Whatever do we have servants for! We have not been away for a fortnight and I do not recognize my own home!"

Ancilla chuckled. "Oh dear, are you on that tack again? It is nothing so bad. Obviously the servants have not been as attentive to their duties in our absence as one could hope, but it is no more than one could expect—"

"Oh, you are just like your father, bless the man! When he was about, he would say the very same thing. Can you not see how an unkempt residence must reflect upon us?"

"Of course it must, but all has been put in order once again and we can be proud to invite the Prince Regent himself and not be ashamed."

"Yes, but if it had been left up to you, my dear, I am sure His Highness would have scowled fretfully at the mess."

"As *I* have no intention of asking Prinny to call, I am not particularly worried over the business. The place is well enough dusted and ordered so that one would never suspect that we have been away from it."

"But we are paying good money in wages that it should not be necessary to—"

"Oh, Mama, what can you expect of servants? I fear you will just have to put up with it, for I can assure you, we have got as fine a set of them as can be found. They are all the same. When the cat's away, the mice will play."

"And that is another thing, now that you remind me. I do think that there is a mouse in the house. Do you think it would be wise to purchase a cat?"

"Why yes, it might be pleasant to have a puss to sit by the fire."

"Ah, but there is the care of her. She cannot long subsist upon one mouse. We shall have to feed her, of course."

"Of course," agreed Ancilla, patiently. Then to quickly change the subject, she said: "I have a wish to visit Somerset House. Perhaps we can stop off there before we return home."

"Somerset House? Whatever for? Whom do we know at Somerset House?"

"It is not a person I wish to see. I believe I can find out about something that has been a bother to me."

"But they are mostly government offices there, my dear. We have nothing to do with Government."

"The chambers and library of the Royal Society are located in the building and I desire to inquire concerning some works of recent date."

Lady Gordon stared at her daughter in dismay. "But that is for scholars and suchlike, my dear. I am sure there is nothing there to interest a female. They talk about things that are quite beyond one and I often wonder why anyone would make such a to-do about it. Our friend, the Viscount, is one of them I believe and—" She gave a little gasp and began to nod her head. "Why that is a most excellent suggestion! One never knows whom one might meet with at the Royal Society!"

"*That* is not my reason for wishing to go there, Mama, so do not allow your hopes for me to become expectations. It is my curiosity I wish to satisfy and not my interest."

"As you wish, my dear. I shall speak to the coachman," replied her ladyship, smiling sweetly.

Lady Gordon would have preferred to await her daughter in the comfort of the carriage, but to her mind, the Royal Society was an establishment for males ex-

clusively. She was, therefore, put to the trouble of accompanying Ancilla into Somerset House and resign-
ing herself to a thoroughly boring interlude. She hoped
her instincts were to be relied upon, that Lord Linford
might be on the premises or some other gentleman-
savant of high rank. She was not sure that she would
have liked it if it were to get out that her daughter was
showing signs of becoming a blue-stocking—unless, of
course, that was the sort of female that appealed to
those gentlemen, eminent all of them, who enjoyed
membership in the Royal Society.

The Royal Society Librarian, an elderly, soft-spoken
gentleman gave every sign of delightful surprise that
Ancilla should express an interest in the *Transactions*
of the establishment, and he went quickly to work to
provide her with those volumes containing papers of
the late Honorable Henry Cavendish. He was regretful
to the depth of his soul that he could not furnish anything representative of any works by Viscount Linford,
but assured Ancilla that some part of Mr. Cavendish's
work undoubtedly included an effort or two of Lord
Linford's.

Overall, the illumination in the dark-paneled room
was not great, but there were a number of tables, with
chairs about them, that each had its own lamp. Some
of the tables were occupied by other gentlemen, a number of whom, it surprised Ancilla to notice, were very
poorly attired. Their clothes were rumpled as though
they had been slept in and upon their foreheads, as
though they were badges of literacy, perched spectacles
that were constantly being pushed up and down their
noses as the readers required them or put them out of
their way.

Lady Gordon and Ancilla were led to a table where
volumes of the *Transactions* were displayed. Ancilla

found it difficult to picture Andrew as being one of the lot. For all his awkwardness, he was of a cleaner cut and gave no sign of long hours poring over the works of natural philosophy that lined the shelves.

The two ladies sat themselves down and Ancilla drew one of the volumes to her. Lady Gordon looked about the chamber and remarked: "This is not a very cheery place, is it?"

At once the room was filled with the sibilance of "Shhhh!" arising from every other table, and the sounds were accompanied by stares of annoyance on every side. Lady Gordon smiled to all in turn, apologetically, and subsided.

Ancilla bit her lip and, with a tight little smile gave her attention to the book before her.

In order to gain some idea of what she was about to delve into, she opened to the title page and read *"Philosophical Transactions,* Vol. 74, for the year A.D. 1784."

It was not at all illuminating, so she turned to the page that the kindly old librarian had marked with a bit of pasteboard.

Her eyes found difficulty, as she scanned the page, in lighting upon anything that made sense for more than a phrase or two. She tried very hard to concentrate and read the following: "Now, it must be observed, that as all animal and vegetable substances contain fixed air, and yield it by burning, distillation, or putrefaction, nothing can be concluded from experiments in which air is phlogisticated by them."

If it had not been for the terms "fixed air" and "phlogisticated," Ancilla was sure that she could have made some sense of the business; but try as she might, re-reading the sentence again, and yet again, shed no more light on its meaning to her than the first. Slowly, she closed the book and looked at her mother.

"Did you learn what you wished, child?"

"I—I am not sure. It is quite beyond me, I think, and I marvel that anyone can make head or tail of it."

"Then you do not intend to take up the study of pneumatics, I pray."

Ancilla smiled: "No, Mama, you may rest easily on that score. It was never my intention. I was merely curious to see what this would reveal about Lord Linford's interests. All it has told me is that, as he is a recognized authority in the field, his comprehension is something to marvel at."

"How nice of you to say so, my dear. I do believe those are the first kind words you have had for his lordship."

"Oh, I am sure that his lordship has no need of kind words on his work from me!" she exclaimed—a little too loudly.

"Shhhh!" resounded from all sides.

Lady Gordon arose. "If you are done, we ought to leave. This is not a very good place to hold a conversation. I do not know how these people can stand it, sitting about and never a word to say to a body."

With that, Ancilla arose and the Librarian came quickly over to replace the volume of *Philosophical Transactions,* inquiring if it had served her purpose. She nodded and thanked him, and she and her mother left the chamber.

While her mother went on about the queer fish who inhabited the Royal Society library, Ancilla listened with but one ear. As they drove along, she was finding it necessary to devote her thoughts to Lord Linford and his strange taste in studies. Although the little that she had read in Mr. Cavendish's paper had been incomprehensible, the on dit had it that the late Honorable Linford had made major contributions to natural philosophy, or science as it was being referred to more and more frequently these days. That Andrew should be recognized by the very same body of great thinkers was a circumstance that was in violent opposition to her own view of the gentleman.

Off Bowness, in Windermere rather than upon its surface, he had seemed like the greatest fool in creation. At the Assembly, by comparison with the Captain, he had appeared clumsy and in no way fascinating. Then the biggest disappointment of all was the aborted trip to Airey Force. She had wanted to view the falls, but more, she had thought it would have provided an opportunity to discover what went on in Andrew's mind. For once, in her estimation, Andrew stood out before Wildish. It was obvious from the Captain's manner, that he found nothing attractive in a visit to a scenic spot. For that very reason she had been looking forward to sharing it with Andrew, if that were possible. At least, Airey Force might have provided the common ground for her to become truly acquainted with Andrew as neither the Lake nor the Assembly had permitted.

But the misunderstanding had arisen and, as far as she could determine, Andrew had retreated so far that there was no prospect of her ever seeing him again. It piqued her annoyance with him. Had he broken off for some good reason, there was nothing more left to be said, but it had not happened that way. He had gone off under the impression that *she* had taken her stand against his wishes when, actually, she had only been trying to retrieve the situation so that the excursion could be put off for another, more propitious day.

If he was so intelligent as to understand the nonsense of the late Mr. Cavendish, why could he not have seen what she had been trying to do? No, instead, he had gone off in a great sulk and there was an end to it! He had never had one thought as to how she might have felt about the business! He had assumed with his great mind that which was completely untrue and she was left with the problem, nigh insurmountable of correcting his poor impression of her.

Even as her mother prattled on—she was back on the servant problem, now—Ancilla congratulated herself on being so unaffected by the Viscount. What a misfortune to fall in love with a man like that! Well, she had no fear of anything of the sort occurring and, therefore, could devote herself to solving the problem without fear of entanglement.

But she was disappointed to discover that there was no easy way to the crux of the situation. To correct Andrew's impression of her, it was necessary that they meet. Obviously, he was not about to arrange it, so it remained for her to do so. But that was not easily accomplished. She could not pay a call upon him, bachelor that he was; no, not even in her mother's company, for how must that look? As though her mother and she had "plans" for the gentleman and that impression was even worse than the one he already had of her.

No, there had to be some other way. Perhaps they might meet by chance at some mutual acquaintance's house, at a dinner party or a rout. No, there was little chance of that, considering Andrew was not a dancer, nor given to dining about. She was not sure that she saw him in any different light than her opinion of the late Mr. Cavenish, the recluse. Is that how it was with these gentlemen of science? The representatives of the field she had remarked in the library tended to reinforce that picture of them rather than anything else. Oh, but Andrew was too attractive a man and much too young to dedicate himself to such an unlovely and unfulfilled existence. If that were the road he was bent upon, then it must be her duty to rescue him from so dull a fate.

The conclusion added nothing to the resolution of the problem but it did augment her determination to meet with Andrew again. Then she recalled that promise of Captain Wildish to call upon them in London. Now, *there* might be the opportunity she required. Two more unlikely friends could never be found, but there was this connection between them, and the possibility to use the one to meet with the other was not to be overlooked, especially as it was the only ruse her imagination could devise.

It only remained for Captain Wildish to make his promised call.

She turned to her mother who was demanding: "Ancilla, why do you not heed me? You just sit there and nod at me like some village idiot!"

"Oh, I beg your pardon, Mama, I was at woolgathering. But I was just thinking that we ought to have a dinner for our friends."

Lady Gordon nodded approvingly. "Yes, I think we should. We have been at home now for more than a week and it is only fitting."

"We can invite the Colenvilles and the Darcys—Oh, but that is already too many ladies and no gentlemen."

"If you mean eligible gentlemen, that is quite true, my dear, but we shall not have any trouble on that score. The Shellfords have got a son, a very nice young gentleman—and, of course, the Taylors have two sons, both a credit to their family. Yes, and I can think of a host of others that—"

"Oh, but that is *too* many, and what is more, all the sons of your acquaintances are rather dull. We need someone to give life to the affair, preferably a gentleman of charm and grace and wit, you know."

Lady Gordon eyed her daughter, a shrewd expression on her countenance. "And pray, just whom do you have in mind?"

"I think it would be ever so much more delightful if Captain Wildish had returned to London. I dare say he would manage to add more than a bit of spice to the proceedings."

"Hah! I thought as much!" exclaimed Lady Gordon, triumphantly. "Ancilla, if you will recall my last conversation with that young man, it quite wrote him out of our society until I had had a chance to consider his character. At the time, I had no intention of doing so. His behavior during Lord Linford's outing and subsequent conversations I have had with my very close friends have done naught to bring me to reconsider my impression of him. I think a word to the wise is sufficient and as you are wise, you will see that I have said my last word on the subject of Captain Wildish."

"You can at least tell me what has been said about the gentleman. Surely, I am of an age to be able to form a valid opinion," rejoined Ancilla.

"It is not precisely what they *said*, my dear. It was rather the manner in which they said it. It is quite obvious that he has not much reputation. Do you know that he has, and more than once, paid court to Cits?"

"Oh, Mama, what has that to say to a man's character? Times have changed, you know. Everyday, there is gossip about this lord wedding that lady—and she is a lady merely for having wed the lord. I mean to say, there are females, these days, of humble breeding, their fathers merchants of substance, marrying well above their station. If a Lord may condescend to a Cit, surely Captain Wildish may do so as well and with more grace."

"I think it is shocking! How can you possibly be interested in a fellow who forgets what is owed to his station in life?"

"There you go again! It is always the same! I may not say a word about a gentleman but I am nursing a *tendre* for him! Truly, Mama, you have got to remember that I am no child of twelve and never so easily smitten as that."

"Then why, in heaven's name, do you bring up Wildish's name at this pass?"

"For the very reason I stated. He would make good company at our party. That is not to say that I shall invite him to pay me court."

"But what of the other young ladies who will be exposed to his wiles?"

"Oh, let their mamas worry about that! Why do *you* have to?"

"Because I am the hostess, my dear, and am in a sense sponsoring all the people whom I invite to dine under my roof. When you are your own hostess, it is one of the considerations that you must take into account with every guest list you prepare. Mark my words, it is of prime importance, for you can lose your reputation if you are not careful."

"Mama, we are speaking of Captain Wildish, not some rakehell with rattles for brains! If there is nothing that can be *said* against him, I see no call for ostracizing him because some biddy has smirked and raised her eyebrows at the mention of his name."

"My dear Ancilla, there are some things that no lady will give tongue to. You know that as well as I. Now that will be quite enough upon the subject of Captain Wildish. In any case, even if he was returned to London, I can scarcely believe he would have the stomach to face us after that awful business at Patterdale."

14

But Lady Gordon was quite out in her thinking. When they arrived at their house in Queen Anne Street, they found the subject of their last remarks, patiently cooling his heels against a lamppost before their front door.

As he helped the ladies descend from their carriage, smiling brightly and filling the air with compliments upon how well they were looking, Lady Gordon answered him, smile for smile, but she made no move to enter the house.

Ancilla, also had a smile upon her lips, but there was a little tightness about it as she said: "My dear Captain Wildish, I pray that you can spare us a little of your time. Do come and visit with us and tell us how you have been getting on."

Thus outflanked by her daughter, her ladyship had no recourse but to second the invitation, even though it was with a marked lack of enthusiasm.

The little party of three entered the house and soon they were seated comfortably in the reception hall. That was as far as Lady Gordon would allow, retaining her hat upon her head as she sat, primly upright, conveying the strong impression that this visit was to be a short one.

Neither Ancilla nor the Captain were incommoded by her ladyship's lack of hospitality as they continued to chatter away at a great pace.

Ancilla inquired as to what he was engaged in, now, that he was returned to the city, and he was happy to inform her that his social obligations were quite filling his days. The season was coming to an end, people were leaving London or preparing to leave and he had his work cut out for him to pay his calls before they quite disappeared from the London scene for the remainder of the year.

"Ah, that is too bad," said Ancilla. "Then it would be pointless in us to invite you to a little diversion we are planning."

The Captain's ears perked up. "Oh, not at all, my dear Miss Gordon, not at all! Any invitation from the Gordons must take precedence over all the rest! I do assure you, you have but to ask, and I shall be there, filled with delight and eagerness."

"Oh, I am so glad. Mama, just think of it! Captain Wildish is so taken with us he would put us before the world. We can hardly refuse to ask him after such a declaration."

A slight line appeared across the Captain's brow as he looked quickly from mother to daughter. He did not give Lady Gordon a chance to respond but said, quickly:

"Ah, my dear Lady Gordon, it does not make me happy to remind you of my distressing behavior that day at the Lakes, but I must if I am to regain your respect. I would have you know, my lady, that since that day, I have been on needles and pins until I could speak with you again. That is why I have not dared to call upon you until now. I had to be sure that I understood precisely wherein I had caused you pain. In fact, it was just the other day I was discussing this very point to my relation, the Countess de La Warr. My word upon it, her ladyship quite agreed with you that I had given cause for affront. But, as she has an affection for me and knows me to be unexceptional in my demeanor, she offered to invite you ladies over to her town house, just off Park Lane, if it would help to restore me to your good graces."

At that point, a bright smile still illuminating his features, he sent a look of appeal towards Ancilla.

"Well!" exclaimed Lady Gordon, patting at her hair escaping from beneath her hat. "Lady de La Warr? Ancilla, I am sure you have heard mention of the de La Warrs. Captain Wildish, I pray you will not run off yet a bit. I shall just step down to the kitchen and see to having some tea served. You do drink tea?"

"Delighted, my lady, delighted, I am sure."

As soon as she was gone, he said: "My dear Miss Gordon, I am so pleased that you were willing to take my part with your mother. You cannot know how many miserable nights I spent, trying to find a way to erasing the bad impression I had made with you."

"I am sure you did, Captain. But, pray tell me, did you return with Lord Linford?"

"No, I am sorry to say. We saw fit to part company in the neighborhood of Maidenhead. You may find this difficult to credit, but he insisted upon paying a call on the stargazer in Slough. You may have heard some mention of Dr. Herschel, the King's astronomer."

"How very impressive! Sir William Herschel's elevation to knighthood was gazetted some months ago. It was in the Court Calendar. I say, do you think that Andrew will be accorded such recognition?"

"Oh, then you *do* know about Herschel. My dear, you surprise me! Not many females would have; in fact, *I* only came to know about him through Andrew. *Andrew?* I say, since when have *you* become so friendly with his lordship?"

"It was at his insistence. Why do you look so surprised?"

Captain Wildish smiled. "It sounds so—so fast for the old boy. I do believe he has stolen a march on me! My dear Ancilla, I pray that you will grant me equal privilege."

"If you wish, Ivo."

"Indeed, my dear, I am abashed that Andrew should have moved so quickly. I'd not have thought it possible."

"I took the occasion this afternoon to stop by the Royal Society, and they very graciously permitted me to peruse some of Mr. Cavendish's papers. I say, do you know anything about the matters he treated in his work?"

"Except that it is called pneumatics, not a word. I doubt that I could understand any of it. Andrew has referred to his studies, but beyond the fact that it was about gases, I learned nothing more."

"Are you not ashamed to admit it?"

"Not a bit! I never was one to waste my time on anything to strain the mental faculties to no profit. That is the difference between Andrew and myself. At school, he would pore over his notes late into the night. *I* would have none of that. As you can see, it has not done him the least good whereas I am now a man of the world with excellent connections, connections as good as his own, despite the fact he is a viscount and I am but a mere Captain in the Volunteers."

"I was wondering about that, Ivo. I have never seen you in uniform. Had you been to France in the late war?"

"Er—no. As a matter of fact, I was prepared to give my life in the defense of my country, you see. Until England comes under attack, one might say my rank is, er—honorary."

"How interesting. But to get back to the invitation, you will come?"

"How can you ask? But of course, I shall come!"

Ancilla smiled. "And Andrew, do you think that he will come if we were to invite him?"

"Now, why should you do a thing like that? The fellow is a crashing bore who will detract rather than add anything to the festivities."

"That may be so, but I imagine that he will think we are snubbing him if we do not."

"I do not see why. He was most ungracious at Patterdale as I recall. Has he made any attempt to get in touch with you?"

"No. Is he back in town?"

"I have not been around to his quarters to call so I cannot say—but you can understand that he has no interest in your direction if he has not sent you at the least a missive."

"Oh, that is quite all right, Ivo. It is not that I expect that he will come; it is just that, once he learns that *you* have been invited, he will feel we have slighted him. I should not like it."

"If you like, I shall inform him."

"No, I think it better that we send him an invitation. As you are his friend, you might prevail upon him to attend."

"I say, Ancilla, are you setting your cap for him? I assure you he is no more interesting than what you have already seen. He cannot dance, he is forever having moods. He will be a positive damper at any party, to say nothing of his prosing on about his studies. The man is a chronic student. He has neither taste nor breeding for all his rank."

"That is not truly friendly of you to say so," remarked Ancilla.

"There are times when more serious matters must transcend friendship, my dear, and this is one of them."

"How so, Ivo?"

"Ah, I would not have your plans disrupted by a presence that was inimical to them. In short, much as I love Andrew, I cannot recommend him as any sort of guest for a young lady."

"How thrilling that you should be so concerned, Ivo."

He smiled broadly, with a hint of relief. "Your appreciation of my concern for you is more than rewarding, my dear Ancilla."

She smiled back at him. "Then you will prevail upon him to accept, for that must please me no end. You must remember that I do not boast of such high connections as you, my dear Ivo. Lord Linford is, therefore, the most eminent gentleman in my acquaintance. His presence at our affair must add to our prestige. I am sure that is something you comprehend quite well, Ivo."

He nodded, his smile having lost some of its brilliance. "Of course, Ancilla. In fact, it confirms me in my impression that we might treat very well together."

"I am sure of it, Ivo," she said, very sweetly.

"Er—when might you be planning to send out the invitations?"

"Not for a week or so. The idea of the party is quite fresh with us at the moment."

He brightened considerably. "Then, of course, I shall do my best with Andrew—but I cannot *promise* he will come."

"I quite understand."

Lady Gordon returned at that moment and said, with a judicial air: "My dear Captain Wildish, I am more than willing to believe that the little impasse at Patterdale was all due to a misunderstanding and it will be our pleasure to send you an invitation to our forthcoming affair. Now, I should like to have the Countess de La Warr come, too. Unfortunately, I cannot claim an acquaintanceship with the lady. If I were to have delivered to you an invitation for her ladyship, would you be kind enough to present it to her with all due deference?"

"My dear Lady Gordon, it would be the pleasure of my life to oblige you, and I thank you very much for including me in your plans. I am sure I shall have a most delightful time."

"I am so pleased. I shall be looking forward to an introduction to her ladyship."

"Of course, you must realize, my lady, that I can but make the presentation to her ladyship. She is so much in demand these days, it is quite possible that her calendar is quite filled already."

At this Lady Gordon's face fell, and he rushed on to say: "But you are not to worry. I would not have you disappointed for anything. I shall do all that is in my power to convince the Countess to condescend. Believe me, I shall!"

"Oh, I shall be heartbroken if she cannot, Captain."

"Of course, I understand. Rely upon it, the Countess will be at your party, my lady."

"Thank you. I feel so much better for your word upon it."

Captain Wildish was still smiling as he left the Gordon residence, but it lasted only until he turned the corner onto Harley Street. There his features sagged and his brow furrowed as he came to a halt and looked up and down the street.

He was about to hail a cab when he bethought himself to feel for his wallet. To his consternation, it felt no thicker than it had some hours ago when he had been forced to walk the distance to the Gordons. Then fatigue had got the best of him and he had decided to loiter about the door until he had either recovered himself or they had returned from the shopping trip as the servants had informed him they might.

Now, he was faced with a similar predicament. He had all that distance home to traverse and he could not afford the hire of a cab. But there was also the necessity of determining if Andrew had returned home, for he had to see the Viscount. He had not much left to subsist on. As the funds which Andrew had loaned to him began to dwindle away, he had tried his luck at Watier's and turned as green as the cloth laid out upon the gaming table to see how quickly his financial situation had gone from bad to worse.

It was imperative that Andrew be back in London and his purse full, and it was imperative that he have a talk with his friend before the Gordon invitation reached the Viscount. Ivo was growing rather fatigued, living upon his uppers and, mainly, the generosity of friends of both sexes, especially that of Lord Linford. He could not be sure any of it would continue and he had to take precautions against that day when people started to say no to his most charming supplications.

Unfortunately, Andrew's lodgings were not on a line of travel with his own, so that if the Viscount was still away, he must needs walk almost twice the distance. Besides which, the soles of his boots were wearing thin and there was not a bootmaker in London who would make the slightest repair for him on tick. His past performance on his accounts was too well known.

To say that his case was desperate was to say truly. He had great plans for himself but each of them called for some money if only to insure that he made a fitting appearance before the world. So far he had managed quite well but the strain was beginning to tell. Andrew had *got* to be home!

Andrew greeted Ivo as the latter came into the Viscount's dressing room: "Ah, speak of the devil, my friend, and see who shows! The Reverend Mr. Symonds was just discussing your baleful influence upon myself. So nice that you are in time to join the discussion."

"My dear Mr. Symonds," said Ivo, grinning, "if I have any influence at all upon your patron, it is only for his betterment, I do assure you."

"My dear Captain, we were discussing the state of his lordship's soul. Yours, sir, is beyond speaking."

"Ah, Symonds, how unchristian of you! Indeed, I shall have to pray for you."

"Captain, *I* pray that the mockery of all things fine I suspect you indulge in will leave my lord unaffected— but alas, I must give the devil his due. I fear I make no headway with my Lord Linford."

At this point, Andrew's valet was helping him into his coat. Ivo gave a start and whipped out his eyeglass to make a detailed inspection of the garment.

"I say! Where did you get that coat, Andrew? Now, do not tell me! I can recognize a master tailor's work at forty yards distance. Let me see! Ah yes, you have had that coat from Stultz."

"No, my dear fellow, it is from Weston. I do not think that Stultz is quite up to him. How do you like it?"

"Then all I can say is that Weston is changing his style. It is an excellent fit—but how do you come to it? You have never cared a farthing for what was on your back."

"I have decided to change all that. Weston assured me that I have got a perfect figure for the styles, and I thought I should be wise to take advantage of the fact."

Captain Wildish began a slow promenade round the Viscount, who turned this way and that, to assist him to a better view.

"I must say, Andrew, when you go to do a thing, you manage it quite well. It is a suit I should be proud to wear myself."

"A greater compliment than *that* I could not hope for. Thank you, Ivo."

Said Mr. Symonds: "Captain Wildish, you ought to be ashamed of yourself for turning my lord's thoughts to the vanities of the world. It is not to be expected, however, that you will do anything to dissuade him from this folly."

"Perhaps if I knew precisely what this folly is, I might have a thing to say."

"It will hardly be edifying to hear," retorted Mr. Symonds.

"I should think it would depend upon the listener, dear sir. Andrew, how can you stand to have the fellow about?"

"You see so often in the papers cartoons depicting

the subject with his good conscience personified by a figure in white, and his bad, by a black devil. That is exactly how I feel at this moment. Mr. Symonds, my good conscience, pray introduce yourself to Captain Wildish, in whom you will find all that is evil in me."

"My lord, I do not appreciate your levity upon this so serious matter. As I do not feel I shall accomplish anything further with you, I beg leave to withdraw."

"Go in peace and do not worry about me so much," replied his lordship.

"But, Symonds, you may not withdraw!" exclaimed Ivo. "Would you leave the field to the very devil himself?"

"Fie upon you, Captain Wildish. I shall pray that you will be forgiven your blasphemous words."

"Leave the poor fellow alone, Ivo. He is a good man, something you will never come to understand, I fear." Mr. Symonds departed.

"If you had but a drop of the milk of human kindness in you, my lord," said Ivo, "you would take pity upon me and offer me something to fortify myself. It was a perishing long walk I have had and I am perishing with thirst."

"You know where it is. Help yourself and permit me to finish with my toilet."

The two gentlemen repaired to his lordship's spacious library—drawing room, drew up two chairs by the window overlooking the street and sat themselves down.

"I suppose it is money again," remarked Andrew, staring out the window.

"You seem to imply that that is the only reason I ever call upon you," said Ivo, truculently.

"I would not say the only reason, rather the most likely reason. How much do you need?"

"If you are bound to take such a high-nosed attitude with me, make it a twenty," he retorted.

Andrew laughed. "Truly, it amazes me how quickly you can spend the stuff. I but gave you forty less than a fortnight ago. It was at Windermere if you will recall."

"But that was some time ago—and Windermere is not London."

"Nevertheless, you returned home with me—at least as far as Maidenhead—and I footed all the expenses. If I did not know you so well, I should suspect you of having left most of it at this new hell, Crockford's."

"I say, haven't you come up in the world! How come you to know the first thing about gambling?"

"Never you mind! Was it Crockford's?"

"No, it was not Crockford's. If I am going to lose my money, I shall do it at the height of fashion. I lost most of it at Watier's."

Andrew sat back and regarded his friend with flinty eyes. "I am not made of money, you know."

Ivo was suddenly very uncomfortable. He squirmed a bit in his chair and smiled sourly. "Really, Andrew, is it not rather late in the day for you to refuse me my pittances?"

"Good God, man, have you no thought for the future? At some very great cost to myself, I appear to have defeated your designs upon Miss Gordon. I begin to wonder how much your friendship is worth to me."

"Oh, I say, Andrew, you are coming down rather heavy, you know. I mean to say that little misunderstanding at Patterdale was as much your fault as it was mine. Besides, what is this great cost you mention?"

"If you must know, I found Miss Gordon a most interesting person and I should have liked to have got to know her better."

"Well, my friend, if that is what you wished, you certainly went about it from the wrong end, I must say. Why, there is nothing to it! I have managed to restore myself in the Gordons' esteem, and it was not at all difficult."

Andrew nodded. "I was afraid you would manage it, you charming blackguard."

"Some of us are blessed and some of us are not," said Ivo, cheekily.

Andrew sighed. "Since it is obvious you have been with them since their return to London, I should like to know how they fare."

"Very well, and I thank you in their names for inquiring, my lord. Now that you have mentioned the Gordons, I am beginning to wonder if *they* would refuse me a small loan," said Ivo, cagily.

"You would not dare to ask it of Lady Gordon!" thundered Andrew.

"I might—if you refused me. I should *have* to, I think."

"Ivo, I do not know precisely upon what terms you have managed to establish yourself with them, but this, I assure you, I shall take it upon myself to pay a call, the point of which will be to inform them of the viper they are entertaining. No matter what they might think of me, the facts and figures I shall present must cause them some concern in your direction."

"Oh, I say, Andrew, there was never a need for you to go to such lengths! Of course, I was just jesting. What sort of an odd fish do you take me for?"

"The strangest, my old chum!"

Ivo got up and strode dramatically to the door. "It

is obvious to me that you wish to withdraw your notice of me, my lord. I shall not trouble you further."

"I doubt that very much," retorted Andrew, drily.

Ivo put a hand on the doorknob, opened the door slightly, then closed it and came back to stand in front of his friend.

"We cannot part like this, Andrew."

"I did not think we should, Ivo."

"You think I am bluffing."

"I do."

Captain Wildish let out a laugh and resumed his seat. "Aye, I cannot pull the wool over your eyes, my friend. I dare say that is why I value your company so much."

"That was never the problem. The question is why do *I* put up with you?"

"All right, Andrew, let us put jesting aside and get down to business. How much do you wish to be restored to the good graces of the Gordons?"

"To tell the truth, very much; but I—"

"I can grant your wish. In fact, I shall do it. As a favor to my nearest and dearest friend, I shall patch up things between you to the extent that they will extend an invitation to you. In fact, I think I can manage that it will be to one of their functions—but you must let me handle the business. It will not be easy and I shall have to take special pains, for you did yourself so much harm in their eyes. That, I do not have to tell you."

"Are you serious! I have always known that you can get your way with the Sex against the greatest odds, but that was for yourself. You can do it for me?"

"As you are my friend, you may consider it done! My word on it!" said Ivo, very firmly.

Andrew sighed. "I have never known you to go back

on your word, Ivo." He reached for his wallet and counted out a number of bills which he handed over to the Captain.

Ivo accepted them calmly and without counting them filled his wallet. "Of course, you understand this is a loan, Andrew."

"I understand, sir, a great deal more than you give me credit for. Had I half your presence, I should think seriously of entering the political sphere."

"Had I a sponsor, I might give the matter serious consideration. It would take a deal of money, you know, for expenses."

"Yes, my dear Captain, and to set your mind at rest, you may rest assured you have not found him in me!"

Ivo laughed and stood up. "I did not think so. Now you rest easily and have a little patience. The invitation is as good as on its way to you. Oh dear, I have another call to make, so I had best take my leave. Adieu, my friend."

"I should be very disappointed, if I attended the Gordons' party and found you there."

"Then I regret to say that you will be disappointed, sir, for I do not intend to miss it. Whatever my intentions towards Miss Gordon are, I leave it to you to guess. Good-bye!"

"Whom did you say?" asked the Countess de La Warr, an expression of annoyance on her patrician features.

"It is a Captain Wildish, madam," replied her butler, very stiffly. "The gentleman did not proffer a card."

"Oh yes, the darling Captain, Hutchins," returned her ladyship with a laugh. "The poor dear cannot afford such an extravagance as a *carte de visite,* and he can be somewhat of a nuisance; but you can climb down off your high horse, Hutchins. If you had been with me long enough, you would know the Captain. Actually, I am not in a very good humor to entertain him, but you may show him in, nonetheless. He *is* a relative, you know, and one must not put on too many airs with one's own relations. I wish he were connected on the Earl's side, though."

"Very good, madam."

Although Ivo was smiling broadly as he came into the Countess's sitting room, it was a lop-sided smile, expressing a silent regret.

"So, Ivo, you have finally decided to pay me a visit. How long has it been—not that I am particularly interested?"

"Ah, my lady. I am devastated—but you must know it was not by choice but by circumstance that I have been kept from devoting myself to you."

"I am sure it was, the circumstances being that you needed nothing of me for a while. I am grateful to circumstance."

"My lady, you are witty as ever. Perhaps it is all for the best that the interludes between our meetings are rather long. It gives us a chance to appreciate one another more, don't you think?"

"I know it is no strain at all, my dear Ivo, not to see your smiling face for years on end. Perhaps you are right. Pray that the next time we meet will be some ten years from now if not later."

Ivo laughed heartily and sat himself down. "Now, you know you do not mean a word of it, for if you did, I should be thoroughly devastated."

"I understood that you were already. I should think that now you would be destroyed. But, seriously, why do you come to bother me at all? I know that you are my relation, but you are aware that I had no choice in the matter. Truly, there is no need for you to try to take further advantage of the connection."

Ivo's smile finally faded. "I pray you are not serious, Countess."

"Ivo, of all my relations, you are the only one for whom I appear to be answerable to society. The on dit is forever concerned with your goings on, and each distasteful episode is presented to me as some choice tidbit. I am getting tired of the business, considering how little regard we have for each other—"

"Oh, my lady, do not say that! I have all the regard in the world for you!" declared Ivo.

"All right, let me put it another way. I have not the least regard for *you,* and I should be ever so much happier if you did not come to bother me. I have not the least doubt but that the day your friend, Linford, closes his pockets to you, you will be discovered on my doorstep with your hand out."

"You know about Linford and me?"

"Is there a soul that does not? Ivo, you have managed to get yourself such a reputation for rake and spendthrift that it is something to marvel at, I am ashamed to admit to his lordship, you and I share a drop or two of the same blood."

"Heaven forbid that I should come between the Earl and you, my lady."

"You need not worry. You never could—but I wish to God you would change your ways and settle down. For everyone's sake, go marry yourself an heiress!"

Ivo sat still for a moment's thought. Then, his smile flashing as broadly as ever, he exclaimed: "My dear Countess, by a most remarkable coincidence, that is precisely what I am determined to do. In fact, that is why I have come to you."

"No, no, Ivo, I have too much liking for my friends to introduce *you* to their daughters. Find your own heiress."

There was a hint of triumph in Ivo's voice as he replied: "Ah, but indeed, my lady, it is precisely what I have done. I have found me an heiress. Despite all rumors, I have been intent upon a particular young lady. If I did not feel that I was upon the verge of a successful conclusion, I should never have inconvenienced you with my visit."

Her ladyship frowned. "I am very happy for you, and if it is my blessing you seek, you have it. I suppose that I shall have to make preparation to appear at the nuptials?"

"Oh, I should truly hope so, but there is a bit of business that must come before it, you see. It is not a business that is cut-and-tried. Having found the young lady, I must press my suit with her."

"Good heavens, Ivo, will you speak directly to the point? Are congratulations in order or are they not?"

"Not quite, my lady. You must consider that I have a reputation to mend. I am on excellent terms with the lady and her mother. I come to them with the highest connections, my relation to you of course, madam—and that last I would prove to them incontrovertibly with the evidence of their own eyes."

"I am not witless, you know. You are preparing to beg me to have them over for tea, no doubt."

"Far be it from me to try to put anything over you, my lady—but actually, the situation is a little different. Lady Gordon—the mother of the young lady—is about to give a dinner party and I would have you come to it. Lady Gordon is understandably anxious to meet with my relations, and she is terribly impressed with the Countess de La Warr. You can see how much that would mean to me—and to my undertaking."

"Do you have any idea of how thoroughly my calendar is filled? Ivo, it is enough I have given you these few moments I can barely spare from my correspondence. Now you would have me attend an affair of a woman I do not know, never met, and have not the least desire to become acquainted with? No, it is out of the question!"

"My lady, I beg you to reconsider. Think how important this business must be to me. Think of how important this business must be to the de La Warrs."

"The de La Warrs? What has it to do with them, may I ask?"

"I blush to say so, but there is my reputation to consider. You have just been making complaint of it. I am sure that your connections cannot be too pleased to know that they are related, even so distantly, to a source of such demeaning gossip. Now, I would change my ways—I am trying desperately to do so—"

"What, out of the goodness of your heart?"

"No, my lady," he retorted, grinning, "out of the emptiness of my pocketbook."

She laughed. "That has ever been the one quality I liked in you, Ivo. You are unabashedly frank about your intentions."

"It is little enough, you must admit, and never enough to support my continuing intrusion upon you, my lady."

"For a moment, I was beginning to think that you had lost your touch; but I see now what it was you were about. And it is very clever of you I must say. Of course, it begins to sound like a bit of extortion—I pay a call upon Lady Gordon in exchange for your absence from these premises. The point you make is that married, you would not be the continuing subject of gossip. Have I read you right?"

"I assure you, my lady, you will find the Gordons, mother and daughter, quite charming and you will have a pleasant time—but I would not ask all that of you. Merely allow me to inform Lady Gordon that you will accept her invitation. She would never dare to send one else."

"It is a hard bargain you drive, you blackguard, and I shall expect to see you a proper and fitting husband once you are wed. If I find your lady reasonably attractive in manner, I may condescend to bring her into my circle. We shall see. You may inform Lady Gordon, I shall be pleased to attend her function."

"My lady, you have made me the happiest man in London. I have no doubt but that Miss Gordon will be very much impressed to see you under the Gordon roof. Of course, it would speak volumes for my connection if the Earl was pleased to accompany you."

"Ivo, you *can* push yourself too far, by heaven! The bargain was for the Countess and not the Earl! Be satisfied that you have got that much, for I am not sure but that his lordship would frown upon this entire business if he ever got wind of it."

Ivo quickly raised a hand in denial. "No, no, my lady. I am more than satisfied to have you accept the Gordons' invitation. I should have been honored to have the benefit of his lordship's approval, but it is obvious your presence in Queen Anne Street will speak for the both of you in my behalf."

"Now that we have got that settled, and you have thoroughly ruined my afternoon, you may as well join me for tea and tell me how you came to meet this young lady heiress...."

184

15

Lady Gordon was not one given to extravagance without good reason. This evening she considered more than sufficient reason for an expenditure that allowed no pains to be spared to make the party her greatest achievement since the passing of her husband.

Never before had the house on Queen Anne Street entertained such an illustrious assortment of dignitaries and the Countess de La Warr proved to be the key which opened the door to a circle of society in which she had never moved about before.

Once she had received the Countess's acceptance, she went busily to work spreading the news amongst her friends, and then proceeded to invite the Grand Dames of Almack's along with Lord Liverpool, the Prime Minister. Although the latter returned a gentle refusal, Lady Jersey and Lady Cowper did accept. And these acceptances, when bruited about, encouraged her to send out to other lesser lights of society and the arts so that by the time of the affair, her guest list was an imposing one.

Ancilla was somewhat dumbfounded to understand how they, the Gordons, could have so suddenly achieved an importance in the social world when they had done nothing to gain anyone's attention.

"My child," explained her ladyship, "it is quite simple, actually. We have Captain Wildish to thank for it. He promised us the Countess de La Warr and that was all that was needed, you see. That she should honor our domicile was sufficient sign to the world that the Gordons had come up in the world. I never truly believed the Captain, I must admit; but his connection with the Countess must speak well of him."

Ancilla had nothing to say to this, but it was, after all, her suggestion to hold the party, and her only purpose had been to see Lord Linford again. It was dizzying to see how elaborate an affair had resulted from her simple and private desire. She was feeling disappointed, despite all the excitement attendant on the preparations for this grand affair, because Andrew must, with his usual diffidence, be lost in it. She was pleased that he had sent notice of his acceptance of the invitation. So much she had accomplished, but she could have wished he had come to call at least once before the event. He had not and it was obvious that the party would offer her no opportunity to speak with him very much, if at all.

But Captain Wildish did come to call. Once the Countess's acceptance was in Lady Gordon's hand, her manner to the Captain improved greatly and she consulted with him at every opportunity as to the decorations and the details of the dinner that was to be served. She even went so far as to discuss the musical selections for the evening and listened intently to his advice. Ancilla would have been happy to forgo these conversations, but her mother insisted that she be present. It was not that Ancilla was uninterested in the planning. On the contrary, for it was to be a gala occasion and a rare one; but the Captain had assumed a proprietary air about him concerning herself and she did not feel comfortable in his presence any longer. Although he made no move to speak to her alone, she had the distinct impression that he was biding his time.

There was a change in the wind from a different quarter, too. Both Diana and Caroline were very enthusiastic about the Gordons' party and found many reasons to be present in the Gordons' house each day. Ancilla marveled at how both ladies had warmed to the Captain once they had learned that his eminent relation was about to bless the affair with her presence. No more for him were their noses in the air, no more for him was there the retort tinged with contempt. Ancilla wished she could hold up the mirror of memory for them so they could see how they had been towards the Captain when at the Lakes.

For that matter, she was finding that she herself was being haunted by that very same mirror with regard to Andrew. Now that time had lent a different perspective to all that had occurred, she was finding that her view of Andrew was not at all clear. True, she recalled his awkwardness, but she recalled his gentleness as well. His lack of self-assurance was not necessarily unattractive. When compared to the cocksureness of Wildish, it was in fact, a deal less fatiguing to contend with.

And he was inclined to be moody—but was he truly? There had been that misunderstanding between them at Patterdale, something that at best ought to have been of the most insignificance; yet it had loomed up out of all proportion and, in effect, brought to an end their interest in each other.

Yes, she was sure that there had been something of the sort between them, or why should she now feel disappointed that an opportunity to speak with him might be denied her in the crush of the forthcoming party? Oh, but it was hardly worth one's breath to make an excuse for him! Only an imbecile would have got his wind up over the nonsense!

But Andrew, if he was anything at all, was not an imbecile. A young nobleman who could talk freely with the scholars of the nation had to be a deal more than an imbecile. Could she sit in easy conversation with the King's Astronomer? For that matter, would Captain Wildish be capable of presenting himself before the Royal Society and those august thinkers not laugh at him?

Somewhere things had gone awry between Andrew and herself, and she was beginning to think her own lack of patience with him was the cause. She understood that Captain Wildish was bound to be not a little envious of a chum who was wealthy, of a high rank, and an acknowledged intellect. That was enough to explain his ambiguous attitude to Andrew. If she had but taken that into account, she would have realized that Andrew was being continually put out of countenance by his friend. She was sure that she did not like Captain Wildish very much. The greater her dislike grew, the more in sympathy with Andrew she found herself. She wanted very much to talk to Andrew.

* * *

Andrew had arrived! Ancilla, from her place at the other end of the dining room where people were gathered, busily chatting before sitting down to dinner, saw him enter, look about him shortly and then go over to join an older gentleman. She herself was engaged in a conversation with a very important personage and so was not free to do more than observe him.

"...So it comes as a great surprise to me, Miss Gordon, that a young lady as pretty as you and from a fine family should never have sought a voucher. Indeed, I shall take the matter up immediately with Lady Jersey— Now where has she gone off to?"

"Thank you very much, your ladyship. It was ever a wish of mine to enter Almack's and I shall be grateful for the opportunity."

Lady Cowper nodded. "Yes, my dear, it is a positive wonder what you have been able to accomplish. I mean to say, we all of us *knew* Wildish to be a faint connection to Lady de La Warr, but that *she* should go to such a length to recognize it verges on the incredible. I am not about to say much for Ivo. We shall just have to assume that marriage will change his ways. Everyone knows him for a charming, light-pockets of a scapegrace and the last person alive we should want to see within the portals of Almack's. The forthcoming nuptials will remedy the affliction of his pockets and we can but hope that he will settle down, losing none of his charm in the process."

Ancilla stared at Lady Cowper. "By any chance, your ladyship, are you referring to Captain Wildish and *myself?*" she asked, a bit dazed.

Lady Cowper laughed. "Now there is no denying it, child. If you wish to keep it a secret, you will have to do better than you have done—although there are very few secrets that do not reveal themselves to me. In any case, my dear, I wish you and Ivo to be very happy—and that is wishing you a great lot, for I cannot say that Ivo's wife will have it so very easy."

Ancilla had recovered herself sufficiently to inquire, "May I ask from whom you have had this bit of joyous news?"

Lady Cowper's eyes sparkled as she put a finger up to her cheek and looked thoughtful.

Her cheeks dimpled charmingly as she declared: "It would be quite naughty of me if I told you—but then I am *always* quite naughty. My dear, I have had, if not the word, the implication from none other than Katherine de La Warr herself. What am I to think when she gives the wink to me and says: 'Emily, my dear, if it should turn out to be in the nature of an engagement party, I should not be at all surprised.'"

Ancilla could think of no better reply to do than to smile blandly.

Lady Cowper caught sight of Lady Jersey and excused herself, and before Ancilla had a chance to catch her breath, Diana and Caroline were upon her, breathless with the news that had quite floored herself.

In the rush of their questions and their accusations for keeping it from them, Ancilla floundered and blushed which only added a coy note of untruthfulness to her denials. In the end, she had to go to great lengths to placate her friends and to beg them to withhold their opinions until the matter could be made clear. This they did not find particularly satisfying and would have been at her again but that dinner was announced and the company began to take their seats.

Lady Gordon had studied the seating arrangements with the greatest concentration. She feared to make a blunder by placing high-ranking guests too close to those of appreciably lower station. When it turned out that Captain Wildish's card remained to be placed alongside of Ancilla's, she concluded it was most fitting and that is how Ancilla, who had never been consulted in the matter, found herself at table next to the Captain. It did not add to her happiness in the occasion.

As the platters were being loaded onto the table, an especially long and heavy monstrosity hired for the occasion, Captain Wildish smiled brilliantly at the young lady on his left and remarked: "Ancilla, I pray you have not met with the Countess de La Warr as yet, for I would reserve the pleasure of presenting you to her ladyship myself."

Coolly, she replied: "You are very kind, Captain, but as I was with my mother receiving our guests, of course, we have met.

"But I have a word to say to you, sir—" she attempted to remark.

"Were you not amused by our friend Linford, showing up late as he did? For a moment I thought he had gained some sense and would not come, but he does not learn easily."

"My dear Wildish, you are referring to one of our honorable guests, all of whom were invited with the very best intentions. If you insist upon proceeding in that derogatory tone, you will regret it. What, in heaven's name, did you tell Lady de La Warr?"

"Oh, is that what has put you out of sorts with me, my dear? I swear to you, I said nothing to her that you need be in the least ashamed of."

"Then how comes it that Lady Cowper, whom I have met for the very first time this evening, is filled to overflowing with best wishes for me on this great occasion?"

"You find that exceptional? I am sure that everyone

wishes your mother and yourself every success on the occasion of this affair."

"Captain, *that* is not what I am referring to!"

"I say, Ancilla, when you are angry you are even more beautiful than I can recall, but you will have people staring at us—"

For the benefit of any audience, Ancilla smiled at him and replied: "There is something very strange going on, sir, and I begin to wonder to what extent your fine Italian hand is involved in it."

"I swear I have not the vaguest idea of what you are implying."

"It is Andrew. Why was he late? Why has he not said a word to me? What is wrong?"

"Andrew? Ancilla, he is but one guest and without doubt the least of them. Although he is sadly in need of a keeper, I am not he. I suggest you take your inquiries to Symonds, if you recall that little— Oh, Lord but that is hot!" he cried leaping up from the table.

It was as though it had a life of its own, the bowl filled with soup placed before Ancilla, for it had quickly tilted itself onto the Captain's lap.

"Oh, my dear Captain, how awful for you!" exclaimed Ancilla, arising and stepping back to avoid being splashed by the spray from Captain Wildish's desperate attempts to wipe away the scald from his midriff.

"How did it happen?" he demanded, from a mixture of embarrassment and pain.

"A bit of clumsiness, I fear. You had best retire and have one of the maids help you to dry off."

"Yes, I had better, hadn't I? Ladies, gentlemen, a thousand apologies for my clumsiness! Please! Do not let it disturb you," he said as he backed out of the dining

192

room, a napkin hiding the stain, his smile lacking something of its usual brilliance.

The meal was resumed and Ancilla felt as though she had accomplished something she had, for a very long time, been hoping to do.

A fair proportion of the guests had other functions to attend that evening and so had to take their leave once the dinner was at an end. This eased the crush and, as the dining table was now dismantled and placed in the lumber room, the dining room and the drawing room, with the connecting doors slid wide open, together made up a fair-sized ballroom.

Ancilla had hoped that she had seen the last of the Captain, for she was furious with him. Only he could have given so outrageous a hint to his relation, and she could not help wondering if Andrew had heard the spurious news and what he thought of it.

Was she never to get the chance to speak with him? His coming late might have been unavoidable, his being seated with the three Countesses by her mother was understandable—but she wished she had been informed—his remaining with the gentlemen after dinner for the usual drinking and smoking was unexceptional; but, now that the meal was at an end and everyone was gathering about for the dancing, where the devil was he hiding? Why did he not come to her and request a dance?

Amongst those who had departed before the dancing were the Countesses Jersey and Cowper. The two great ladies took with them most of the air of formality which had attended the dinner and there was a general feeling of ease now that they were gone. Lady Gordon had not thought that, after so heavy a meal, there would be all that many who wished to dance and so she had made no formal provision. The ladies and gentlemen were left to choose their partners as they pleased, without the assistance of dance cards. It was a little daring for the time but her ladyship did not think it would be remarked upon.

The older folk who remained were content to sit about and chat, drawing up their chairs about Countess de La Warr, to bask in her magnificence, as it were. The younger folk gathered in groups and gossiped while some few of them took advantage of the small orchestra and danced.

Ancilla thought that this would be a most opportune time for her to seek out Andrew and hold the long-wished-for conversation with him; but he was not to be found. Instead, Captain Wildish made his appearance in a new set of clothes. He had returned to his lodgings and changed.

He came right up to Ancilla and said: "I am just in time, Ancilla, and in the greatest luck, for you are not dancing. May I have this dance?"

There was no reason she could think of to refuse and so she joined him on the floor.

When it was over she still could not get a glimpse of Andrew, and she felt a little strange. Captain Wildish was staying quite close to her and she found this irritating. He seemed to be intent upon being her company for the evening, and considering the rumors that were flying, she strongly suspected his purpose. It was becoming obvious to her that no one else was about to ask for her as long as her supposed fiancé was at her side, looking for all the world as though he belonged there. She decided to have the matter out with the Captain.

She turned on him and, with the sweetest smile, she

said: "My dear Captain, I am beginning to find your company oppressive."

He smiled back at her as though he had received a compliment and was about to reply when the import of her remark struck him. A bit of color drained from his cheek.

"My dear Ancilla, how can I have offended you? I swear I do not understand why you should find my presence distasteful."

"The oddest things have been happening at this party, and *I* am not satisfied that you have been on the square, my dear Captain."

Ivo looked about him with care and laughed. "The last time you made a similar remark, I was deluged with soup. I was just making certain there was not a bowl of the stuff in my vicinity."

Ancilla blushed. "I admit it was dreadful of me to have tipped it over on you, but you were being insufferable and so I cannot sincerely apologize to you."

"Stab me if I know what I said to cause you to take such a reprehensible action. I assure you, my dear, I'd sooner tear my tongue out than say anything to cause you the least discomfort."

"Oh, you talk a fine game, Captain, but it seems to me that you have done something or said something to Andrew. If not, why has he been avoiding me this evening? Do you realize the party is almost over and I have not had one word even of simple greeting from him?"

"I do protest, Ancilla. I am not the one to whom you should address such an accusation. Look yonder! There is the simpleton now! Go to him and demand your explanations. When you have done, I pray you will join me. I shall be with the Countess. She has expressed a wish to speak with you."

He turned on his heel and left her without smiling.

Ancilla hesitated. She was uncertain of what she ought to do. It seemed to her that the Viscount knew she was there but that he was sedulously keeping his eyes away from her.

When Andrew took a step that was bound to lead him away from her, she made up her mind. Walking quickly over to him, she said, "Lord Linford!"

He stopped, turned himself about, took a deep breath as he looked at her; then he bowed and smiled, saying: "Indeed, Miss Gordon, what a pleasure to see you again."

"I pray that it is not an unexpected pleasure, my lord. I have this strange feeling that you were at pains to avoid me all the evening."

"Oh yes, that. I had no wish to intrude, you see, and now I think that I will depart. It was a delightful party and I thank you—and Lady Gordon for having invited me."

"Intrude? Andrew, what has come over you? How can you intrude when you are our invited guest? And that is another thing I would discuss with you. It is rather exceptional, you know, not to pay your respects to your hostess and the daughter of the house."

"Oh, I paid my respects to her ladyship, your mother," he said, looking very uncomfortable. "I er—dare say I should have got around to you before I departed."

"Thank you very much for your belated condescension, my lord. You need not have bothered if that is how you feel about me."

"I say!" he exclaimed, looking very earnest. "Miss Gordon, I do not feel at all that way about you. The thing of it is that I am sure I owe you some sort of an apology for my less than cordial behavior at Patterdale—but thought it might not count for anything with you at this late stage."

"I should think that between friends an apology, if one were required, must be offered—but I do not think so much as an apology is at all necessary. Rather, the circumstances you have reference to require a clarification."

"I do not see that they could be any clearer. You showed your favor to Wildish and I went up to the box and sulked. Now, when I would make an apology for such childishness on my part, I realize it is too late for anything. Ivo has quite taken the field, as it were."

"And what, may I ask, is this field you speak of?"

He stared at her and seemed to be thinking. "Are you being coy or do you truly not know?" he asked.

"I am not being coy, and I suspect I know very well what you mean; but I wish to be sure that we both know what we mean. You completely misunderstood my action in Patterdale, and I do not want that to happen again. Andrew, I am trying to be friendly! Do you reject me?"

"Heavens, no, Ancilla! Were we truly friends, I should be as pleased as Punch. But there is Ivo. What must he say to it?"

"Anything he wishes, but it will not count with me. He is your friend and I leave him to you. He has nothing to say that I care to hear—and never had."

"But you did side with him at Patterdale, did you not?"

"No, I did not! It was perfectly obvious to me that the excursion would not fare well with the weather so threatening and Ivo being a perfect monster about it.

I was going to suggest that it be put off for another day for those of us who wished to see the falls. I should have been one of those; but you never waited to hear me out and went off in a dudgeon."

"Oh, I say!" he murmured, looking very much confused. "I did it to a turn, didn't I?"

Then he frowned. His manner grew cold and he said: "Yes, Miss Gordon, I should like very much to be friends with you, but I do not think we are at all suited. I am not much at playing games, you see. I understand what it is you are saying, but I cannot bring myself to credit it. There is all the other that speaks against it."

It was Ancilla's turn to frown and in puzzlement. "What other?" she demanded.

He sighed, looked about for a bit and then returned his gaze to her. "The only reason that I am here is that Ivo arranged it. I had heard about the party from him and he offered to procure me an invitation. He did, ergo I am here."

Hard anger stirred within Ancilla's breast and, for a moment, she was unable to respond.

"My lord," she said finally, "I am beginning to think I am wasting my time with you. I am beginning to think that Ivo is just the sort of friend you deserve. By your leave, my lord, you are a simpleton and badly in need of a keeper. The fact of the matter happens to be that it was *I* who suggested this affair to my lady mother on particular purpose to see you again. I wished to make clear to you that you had no reason to believe that I would sacrifice your interest for Ivo's—ever! But it is all become pointless, has it not? I thought I should gain some understanding of you if I dipped into the late Mr. Cavendish's works at the Royal Society, but I found them incomprehensible as, at this very moment, I find *you*, sir!"

With that she turned on her heel and walked away from him. She went off into the other room where Captain Wildish, apparently waiting for her to appear, took one look at her angry face, smiled, took hold of her arm and led her over to where the Countess de La Warr was holding court.

16

Andrew's dressing room was cluttered with port-manteaus, some partially filled, others still empty, and he was discussing with his valet the advisability of taking his new clothing with him.

"There is something to be said for properly fitted clothing. These things of mine from Weston, why I hardly knew I had them on."

"That, your lordship, is only because you have an excellent figure. It is what I have been telling you ever since I was honored to be taken into your service. When you hear of someone complaining of how tightly he has been fitted, it is not, I assure you, my lord, the fault of his tailor necessarily. I mean to say I have served gentlemen whose figures were simply impossible to clothe in any decent style. Some had to be corseted until they turned purple from lack of breathing whereas others suffered a distinct lack of flesh and recourse was had to stuffing them with straw until they could have taken their place in the cornfield to scare the crows. Truly, my lord, you are blessed with a most excellent figure and you should take advantage of every opportunity to show it off."

"Rubbish! To what end? I am off to Scotland, as far north as I can find. I shall send you off with an excellent reference and half my wardrobe. I shall have little need of Weston's latest silks and broadcloths amidst the sheep and kilted savages. Wool is what I shall be needing and I daresay I can buy what I need when I get there."

His valet looked quite glum as he shrugged his shoulders and pulled out into the center of the floor another portmanteau.

A footman came to the door and informed his lordship that Captain Wildish was below.

Andrew made a face and looked about him at the shambles packing had made of the dressing room. To himself, he muttered: "I do not know which is worse, having to look at this or spend half an hour basking in the light of my dear friend's beaming countenance."

Another glance about him and he had made up his mind. It was not that Ivo was the greater attraction but that Andrew was quite curious to know how the Gordons' party had ended. He followed his footman out and descended to the drawing room.

To his surprise, Ivo was wearing a frown and there was not the hint of a smile on his lips.

"Bless my soul! You look as though you have lost your last friend!" exclaimed Andrew.

Ivo laughed bitterly. "If I may no longer count upon

you, then indeed I have. Damn your soul, Andrew, you have done me up again! What did you say to her?"

"To her? To Miss Gordon? Stab me if I said much of anything to her. In fact, it was quite the other way about. The lady lit into me for being an ass and in need of a keeper. Before I could make any sort of amends for whatever she was complaining about in me, she went off and I saw her go with you up to your Countess."

"If you had been a friend, a true friend, you would never have let it happen. Damn your soul, I have been read out of the family!"

"I do not understand. For what reason? I never thought that her ladyship doted upon you, but she did tolerate you. Whatever occurred?"

Ivo waved his hand about. "No more until I have had a chance to restore my wits about me. I have been pacing the floor all night. I have not had a wink of sleep. Andrew, what is to become of me? I had a chance to gain me an heiress for wife and you have taken her from me. Without the Countess to support my pretensions, I shall never find another like her. You have got to do something!"

"Old chap, I think you are in need of a drink to restore more than your soul. Come and sit down. Help yourself to the brandy and, while you are at it, you may pour me a finger or two. You know where it is kept."

The Captain did as he was bid and brought the two glasses back with him to where they were sitting. They each raised their glass to each other and took a sip.

"Ah, I needed that!" sighed Ivo.

"I suspect that I *shall* be needing it. Now I wish you would relate the whole of it to me. You have thrown out bits and pieces and I have not the shadow of an idea of what you are talking about."

"Wait a bit. What was it you said but a few moments back? Ancilla had words with you?"

"Yes, she did and I never got the chance—"

"Then, you are not the one she has chosen?" asked the Captain, plainly puzzled.

"Do you think I should be packing my bags for Scotland if she had—and what is this business of her choosing anyone? I thought she had set her sights on you! Before she had done with me, I thought to have understood that it was not so; but as she went right to you afterwards, I was assured I had been mistaken in my thinking. In fact, I am not sure what I am thinking anymore where she is concerned. Something about being a friend to me but I needed a keeper—the sort of thing *you* are always saying to me. Truly, Ivo, you ought to show me a little respect."

"I thought I knew a female pretty well but this Miss Gordon has quite put me out of countenance on that score. If you are not he and I am not he, who the devil *is* he?"

"Who?"

"This other chap she has set her sights on, you ass!"

There was a pained look in Andrew's eye. "My friend, you are beside yourself. This is the first I have heard that Miss Gordon is interested in anyone—in that way. But, I say, if she did not plight her troth with you last night, then we are both up against it, aren't we?"

"Yes, blast! It is just like it was at Bowness. You put me in bad with Lady Gordon and Ancilla and you have managed to do it again—and, Andrew, neither time has it done you the least bit of good. Why must you be a dog in the manger?"

"I do assure you I did nothing at the party to harm you in her eyes. Come to think of it, anything bad that was said about you was said by the lady, not by me."

"Precisely what did she say about me?"

"It is hard to recall because as you will understand I do not give a damn what she says about you now. But, as near as I can recall, it was something to the effect that you were just the sort of friend I deserved— and then it was she commended me to the care of a keeper. Now, it does not *sound* so bad, but there was a deal of passion in her tones when she said it. Oh, and a curious thing she added. I thought it was rather touching and I could have wished she had stayed long enough to explain it further."

"What was that?"

"Can you believe that this young lady actually made application to the Royal Society to investigate Cavendish's works so that she might gain some understanding of me? Touching, but futile of course. She did not understand a word of it. I should jolly well like to explain it all to her. It would be rather fun, don't you think?"

Captain Wildish was shaking his head as he gazed at his friend. There was sheer disbelief in his eyes. "You let her go after that? You imbecile! You ass! After she said all that, you let her go before the Countess who was expecting to be introduced to my future wife? You call yourself friend!!?"

"Why the deuce are you so agitated?" asked Andrew.

"Because you allowed me to go up the garden path like the very simpleton that *you* are! I had informed her ladyship that I was about to pop the question to Ancilla! Now do you understand the barrel of pickles I found myself immersed in when Ancilla said, as mildly as you please, to her ladyship her prospects for the future were not all that exciting. I tell you I could have dropped through the floor! There was I standing right beside her, the Countess, relying upon my representations, thinking that she had come to welcome Ancilla into the family.

"As if that were not bad enough, the dear girl then turned to me and remarked: 'You know, Ivo, you ought to settle down. If you would like, I should be pleased to introduce you to any number of fine young ladies who might find you attractive.'"

Andrew was beginning to chuckle.

"Oh, you heartless monster!" cried Ivo. "But wait! She was not done with me. She went on to say, as though, she had made a slip: 'I beg your pardon, your ladyship, but that was impertinent of me, I am sure, for you could find Ivo a magnificent wife with hardly any trouble at all.' Impudence! Insolence! I cannot understand what I ever saw in that female—but, it was you that turned and twisted her so that she must make a fool of me! You did it before and now you have done it again! I cannot face the Countess de La Warr ever again. Oh, the odious look she conferred upon me! Andrew, you have got to do something or I am lost!"

Andrew shrugged but still he smiled. "So there we have it. Miss Gordon has no taste for either of us. She left me in a fury and vented it upon you. I am glad I got out when I did for she'd have done me to a turn, too."

"No, no, you have got it all wrong. The reason she was so angry with me was that, somehow, I had come between the two of *you*, you see. I admit I was trying to set you down in her eyes. I do not know why I tried so hard, for you can do yourself all the damage and without help from anyone. Oh, but you are a fool—or is it that you have no liking for Ancilla?"

"What has that to say to anything? It is what Ancilla thinks of me that is all that counts—and she made herself quite clear upon that score, it seems to me."

"Bah! You have the wit of a babe when it comes to females. I tell you, you are out in your thinking and, if you have the slightest interest in Ancilla, you must go to her before it is too late."

"What is this? From you, Ivo, it sounds like just another one of your tricks. I am not about to make a fool of myself. I agree with you that in the past I have done little else."

Ivo stared at Andrew and his frustration made him hot. He took out his handkerchief and mopped at his chin even as he said: "Andrew, it is not out of the kindness of my heart that I urge you to go to Ancilla. It is just that I have got to have a ready supply of funds if I am to get married and ease the burden of myself on your pursestrings. I believe that if I get you out of your shell and on your way to happiness, I shall stand a chance of borrowing enough from you to allow me to proceed with my next prospect."

"What a fine thing is true friendship!" declared Andrew, cynically amused.

"It is the fact that we *are* friends that permits me to be open with you, my friend. After all, you will recall that I told you before we began I should make every attempt to gain Miss Gordon for myself. Now that my goose is thoroughly cooked with the lady, I must move on to easier game. It hurts my pride to think that you cut me out with her, and you did it, if I understand what has occurred, without any effort on your part."

"Why do you not take up the law, Ivo? With no grounds at all, you make a most excellent case."

"Oh, blast your hide! Why do I waste my breath on you! If you are not going to shell out the ready, I am wasting my time here."

"This performance of yours amused me no end. I think forty pounds is worth the price of admission."

"Could you possibly make that eighty, old man? This is London, you know, and the new darling, I have reason to suspect, will prove a deal more expensive than Miss Gordon."

"Hmmmm! And may I inquire the name of the lady you are planning to pursue?"

"Oh, I do not mind. She is Lady Diana, daughter of the Earl of Clandon. They are the Colevilles, you know, a family even the de La Warrs may not look down upon. I am thinking I shall be able to kill two birds with one stone in that direction. The Countess is bound to raise her estimation of me if I can bring such a prize into the family."

"I say, Ivo, do you never think of being in love with the lady you would choose to be your wife?"

"I have no time to waste upon such inconsequentialities. But I dare say you, my lord, can afford it. How do you feel about the eighty?"

"As long as you are so determined, it is possible you might be successful in the chase, and that would be a relief to me. Here is your eighty and I wish you luck."

Ivo smiled and blew out his breath, his handkerchief busy with his chin once again. "I say, this is beginning to take a lot out of me, Andrew. You are become quite hard-nosed about everything. I am not looking forward to the next time I have to come to you for the ready."

"Neither am I. In any case, you will have your work cut out for you. I shall be in the north of Scotland and I have not made up my mind exactly where."

"Ah, then I had best put this money to good use and quickly. I should hate to have to scour Scotland to find you. Never cared for the place to begin with."

"That is most encouraging to hear. As long as you remain unwed, I may never return."

"Oh, but I say, you are not going into exile without a word to Ancilla, are you?"

"I should much prefer it, but I think that courtesy demands I take leave of the Gordons, don't you?"

"I do not care what excuse serves you so long as you call there. If I should prove to have been correct in my thinking, the merging of her wealth with yours should make it ever so much easier for me to receive my pittances from you—if I should have need of them again."

Andrew groaned. "If I had any thought that you might be correct, the prospect of having to support my best man for the rest of my life could make me forgo any part of marriage."

Ivo laughed. "My conscience is clear. I have done well by you even if you do not think it. I shall be able to come to you for financial assistance with an easy grace. If you do not profit by all I have said, it is on your head, not mine."

17

It was the afternoon of the second day after the party and Lady Gordon and her daughter were seated in the small drawing room, looking pale and drawn. One might have concluded that they were suffering from the effect of all the tidying up and rearranging of the household that had been done the day before, but it was not so. Each had her own thoughts and it was these that were plunging the both of them into depths of blue despair—but not for the same reasons.

"Oh!" wailed Lady Gordon, "it was going to be such a fine party! It was going to be such an elegant affair! Why, had it gone off properly, we should this very moment be receiving invitations from the most select people—but there has been nothing! Just a few cards from our friends. Ancilla, what did you do!? What did you say!? All was going well until, suddenly—and I tell you I had not an inkling that anything was wrong until that very moment. Lord Linford departed with a most unhappy look as he said his good-byes to me—did he even have the decency to say good-bye to you? And not minutes after, the Countess de La Warr, whom I thought to become a most excellent friend to us, swept out with but a bare nod, followed by that dashing Captain Wildish—and bless my stars if, for once, the gentleman was not all smiles! Ancilla, you were there! What ever occurred?"

"Oh, Mama, must we go into it? It is over and done with and I, for one, am glad. They both of them were either too much or not enough. I shall be happy if I never see either gentleman again!"

"Whatever are you saying, child? Neither of them? Do you mean to say the both of them were prepared to ask for your hand and I did not know it?"

"Mama, you do take on so about every little thing! No, it was not like that at all. The Viscount, as is usual with him, was utterly graceless to me, and the Captain, as is usual with him, took far too much upon himself. It was as simple as that!"

"Simple? I do not find the business simple at all! Here, I go to the trouble of preparing a most excellent dinner for the best people in the world. I was sure that my daughter, my backward daughter, was about to come into her own and I should be called upon to give her my blessing in the absence of her late father. But not a bit of it! Oh, the disappointment! The embarrassment before all my friends! My daughter is still unpromised and never like to be!"

"Well, I declare!" exclaimed Ancilla. "You never mentioned a word of this to me! For heaven's sake,

Mama, did you even hint at any of it to Captain Wildish?"

"Of course I did not. I did not have to. It was all too obvious. That is, it was all too obvious to all but my very own daughter. Ancilla, how can you be so unfeeling? I can hardly *believe* that you *are* my very own daughter!"

"Oh, Mama, there are times when I do not know what to say to you! Captain Wildish and myself? Never! He could be the last man on earth and I would not have him!"

"And, of course, you are bound to say the same for Lord Linford, I suppose. You must have said as much to the gentleman—although why you should have, I truly do not know. *He* never counted for much with you—or me! Still, my love, one does not insult one's guests and turn a festive occasion into one of disappointment and contempt. I do not think I shall be able to hold up my head, henceforth. I shall be a lady disregarded by all of society, saddled with the burden of a daughter who is resolved to be an eternal spinster."

Ancilla smiled slightly. "I hardly think so. True, we may not rely upon the Countess de La Warr to notice us, but is is possible that Lady Cowper was sufficiently impressed to have a good word to say. But it was all Ivo's fault—and Andrew's, too. Ivo took too much upon himself and Andrew—Oh, I do not know what to think about Andrew! I think we are fated never to give sufficient ear to each other to ever understand what it is that is wrong between us. I do not know why I turned away from him, but I was so exasperated with him. Here, I had gone to all this trouble just to gain an opportunity to speak with him and he had the nerve to inform me that it was all due to Ivo's intercession that he had received his invitation from us. Can he be so obtuse that he cannot see what is going on before his very own eyes?"

Lady Gordon's eyes opened wide as she looked at her daughter. "What is this? I am your mother and you never said one word about it to me! Were we at cross purposes? Ancilla, will you kindly inform me as to how many gentlemen you have got dangling after you?"

"As of this moment, Mama, I should say not a one. Perhaps we ought to go back to the Lake Country and start all over."

"Now you are being facetious! I wish you would take everything more seriously than you do. Just think of it! Here, we had two birds in the hand and we have lost the both of them—"

"Mama, I could wish you would not put it that way! I was not out to snare anyone. I only wished to have an opportunity for some conversation with Lord Linford. I did not think that there was any other way to accomplish it after Patterdale, and something had to be said. I could not leave him to think that I had been against him."

"Oh, what is the use of talking! You have been marvelously unskillful if that was your purpose. Once I had been made aware of the Captain's connections—you know he is not the sort whom one can believe at the start—I was sure that he would have made an unexceptional husband for you. As far as the Viscount is concerned, considering his exalted rank, it was too much to expect—and when he turned out to be a proper imbecile, there was nothing to desire—"

"Andrew is not an imbecile! He has a very fine mind—and he is not unhandsome in appearance, either. You must admit that he compared quite favorably with the Captain, sartorially, at the party. I had never seen him dressed so nicely before."

At that point, Lady Diana was announced and she came into them with news that seemed to have an exhilarating effect. In response to their invitation to sit with them, she demurred, giving as an excuse that she had so many things to attend to. She wanted them to know that the Countess de La Warr had invited her to attend the Opera with her ladyship, and Captain Wildish would be one of the party. Then, with hasty farewells, she swirled out of the room and was gone.

As soon as the front door was heard to close behind her, Ancilla burst into hearty laughter.

"Oh, that Ivo!" she exclaimed while her mother regarded her with a questioning look.

"Really, my dear, I do not see this as a laughing matter at all!" said Lady Gordon with indignation. "It means that you have certainly lost the Captain's regard and the Countess's as well. Now where does that leave you? You ought to be green with jealousy, I should think, for the opportunity that you have let slip into Diana's hands."

"She is more than welcome to the fortuneseeker. I never wanted any part of him—oh dear, is there more?" This in response to the announcement that another caller had arrived. It was the Viscount Linford.

Said Ancilla: "My, is not this become one busy afternoon! Er—Mama, would you object to leaving his lordship and myself alone together?"

"You know that it would be highly improper—"

"Mama, if there is one thing good that can be said for his lordship, it is that he is proper to a fault! Besides, the gentleman seems never to be able to speak freely with me and I am curious as to what he has to say. If you are by, we shall never learn a blessed thing from him. He will be a stick."

Lady Gordon stared at her daughter. "My love," she

said, as she arose, "you never tell me anything, do you? Very well, have it your way. Give his lordship my kind regards—and I shall never forgive you if you do not relate the whole of the conversation to me."

Ancilla sat placidly, as placidly as she could manage, intently observing Andrew as he came into the room. She was immediately aware of an air of uncertainty about him and it roused a feeling of anxiety in her, something she had not expected.

"I am pleased to see you, Ancilla," he said, heavily. "How is her ladyship?" he asked looking about the small room.

"My lady mother is very well, thank you, and has asked me to proffer her kind regards, Andrew. I am sure she will be joining us in a little while. Please be seated, Andrew."

"Thank you," he replied and sat himself down, looking quite ill-at-ease.

"Andrew, I wish to—"

"Ancilla, at the party—"

They both stopped to allow the other to continue, but then neither did.

"You were about to say, Andrew?"

"Oh, but I was interrupting you, Ancilla."

"No, do you go on with what you wish to say, Andrew."

"Ah—I was about to say—ah—I am off to Scotland," he ended in a rush.

"To Scotland? Whatever for?" demanded Ancilla.

"Oh, I do not know. I just thought I should like to see Scotland is all."

"I see. *We* might be for the Lakes again."

"The Lakes? Whatever for? You have but returned," he pointed out.

"The party was a dismal failure, and my lady mother feels that she has failed as a hostess. You see she had a purpose in mind and it did not work out."

"Oh, I say, I thought the party was delightful—"

"But you never stayed to the end, so you do not know how it turned out."

"Oh, you mean the business with Wildish and his countess? I heard all about it from him, but I should not let it discourage me."

"Oh, I am not in the least discouraged. It is my lady mother who is suffering. You see, she had it in her mind to see me engaged at the party."

"Oh, I say, not to Wildish, I pray."

Ancilla nodded, never taking her eyes from his face. "The very same. I fear I quite scotched her plans when I spoke with the Countess."

"Oh, but Wildish is no bargain! Not for you—and though he is my friend, I should not hesitate to say it to his face. He knows it, too!"

"I am pleased to see that we are in agreement about the Captain, but alas, my poor mother believes it was my last chance to be wed. Can it be true, Andrew?"

It was very forward of her to take this tack with him and she feared lest she had gone too far. But she was relieved to see that there was no shock in his eye. He merely appeared to think about what she had said.

He thrust out his lower lip in thoughtful fashion and slowly shook his head. "No, I fear I must contradict her ladyship, Ancilla. I have no doubt but that you are bound to find a gentleman with whom you can be happy."

"And so you are going off to Scotland, is it?" she remarked.

"Huh?" he said, startled by the sudden return to a past topic. He stared at her and bit his lip.

She smiled at him, trying to control her racing pulse.

"Come to think of it, I am not all that certain I should like Scotland very much. I imagine it could be quite lonely up there, don't you?" he said.

"I could *well* imagine that."

"Yes, perhaps I do not truly wish to go to Scotland."

"Where do you wish to go?"

There was a calculating look in his eye and a little smile on his lips as he looked at her before replying. "Ah, what do you think of the Lake Country?"

"I think well of the Lake Country. In fact, there is a spot I am longing to see. If you should decide to go there, perhaps we could go together. We never did get to Airey Force, you know."

"No, we never did manage, did we?" he said, and lapsed into silence.

She waited as long as she could for him to say more, but he remained silent.

"Well?" she said.

"Well?" he replied, looking confused.

"Are you going up to the Lakes with me or are you not, Andrew?" she demanded, more vehemently than she had intended.

"Why—why I should like that very much, er—but your mother would have to come along, would she not, as chaperone?"

"Not necessarily. It could be arranged that we could go by ourselves."

He frowned. "I should think we would have to be married then."

Oh! thought Ancilla, has he feathers for brains? Can I make it any clearer?

He said: "Er—by any chance, Ancilla, would you be thinking of marrying me?"

Out of all patience, she exclaimed: "How can anyone

who is so brilliant be so stupid! My lord, you are sadly in need of a keeper!"

"So everyone tells me," he said, getting up out of his chair and coming over to her.

Standing before her, his features in a very sober cast, he went on: "However, as long as no one offers for the post, what am I to do?"

"Engage someone! It is that simple!"

"Consider yourself engaged then, my dear!" He reached down for her and experienced no difficulty in gathering her up into his arms.

Lady Gordon thought that enough time had elapsed for her daughter to have had sufficient conversation with his lordship to have covered any number of topics.

As she came into the chamber, she sensed that something important had occurred. Both her daughter and his lordship were regarding each other in a very interesting manner.

Her heart began to beat excitedly and she had to press a hand to her bosom as she looked an inquiry at her daughter.

"Mama, Andrew has had a wish to go to Scotland," said Ancilla.

Lady Gordon looked disappointed. "I am so sorry to hear it, my lord."

"But I have brought him to change his mind."

Lady Gordon beamed. "That was very good of you, child."

"Instead, he has decided on the Lakes, Mama."

Once again, her ladyship's face fell. "Oh, not really, my lord. You have but returned from there."

"Yes, it is a shame, Mama, but then I have not yet visited Airey Force, so I have agreed to go with his lordship."

"Oh dear, then we shall have all that packing to do over again. Perhaps his lordship would rather go to Bath. It is not half so far, and I fear I am not up to so long a journey in so short a time."

"Never you mind, Mama. You can remain behind. I suspect that neither Andrew nor myself would care to have you along this once."

"Child, you do not know what you are saying! My lord, surely you are not proposing—"

"No, my lady, I am not proposing," interrupted Andrew. "I already have, and your lovely daughter has accepted me. I pray, therefore, you will have no objection if we wish to be without your company on our honeymoon?"

Lady Gordon had not the slightest objection to that at all!

Let COVENTRY Give You
A Little Old-Fashioned Romance

CURRENT CREST BESTSELLERS

☐ **THE MASK OF THE ENCHANTRESS**   24418 $3.25
by Victoria Holt
Suewellyn knew she wanted to possess the Mateland family castle,
but having been illegitimate and cloistered as a young woman, only
a perilous deception could possibly make her dream come true.

☐ **THE HIDDEN TARGET**   24443 $3.50
by Helen MacInnes
A beautiful young woman on a European tour meets a handsome
American army major. All is not simple romance however when she
finds that her tour leaders are active terrorists and her young army
major is the chief of NATO's antiterrorist section.

☐ **BORN WITH THE CENTURY**   24295 $3.50
by William Kinsolving
A gripping chronicle of a man who creates an empire for his family,
and how they engineer its destruction.

☐ **SINS OF THE FATHERS**   24417 $3.95
by Susan Howatch
The tale of a family divided from generation to generation by great
wealth and the consequences of a terrible secret.

☐ **THE NINJA**   24367 $3.50
by Eric Van Lustbader
They were merciless assassins, skilled in the ways of love and the
deadliest of martial arts. An exotic thriller spanning postwar Japan
and present-day New York.

GREAT ADVENTURES IN READING

ROMANCE From Fawcett Books